THE WHITE VIXEN

By

David J. Tindell

David J. Tindell

To Susan.

My muse, my inspiration, my wife.

David J. Tindell

"Be brave, my heart. Plant your feet and square your
shoulders to the enemy. Meet him among the man-killing
spears. Hold your ground. In victory, do not brag; in defeat,
do not weep."

Archilochus

PROLOGUE

Tokyo, 1961

"Round Eyes! Round Eyes!"

Jo Ann tried to ignore the taunts. She turned her head neither right nor left as she walked, but always faced straight ahead, as her father had taught her. Yet she also remained alert, as taught by her martial arts instructors. Her brown eyes flicked here and there, taking in her surroundings, missing nothing. Her stride purposeful, she kept her shoulders back. What she did not realize was that this made things even worse for her, but she was only eleven years old and had much to learn.

Today, the words weren't nearly as bad, or as plentiful, as they sometimes were. Today she could walk relatively unmolested. She walked alone, of course. Most of the other girls in her class at the embassy school were Americans, and they stuck together. As for Japanese girls from the neighborhood, there were some she thought of as friends, and sometimes she visited them at their houses or apartments. Very rarely would they would visit her home. When that happened, they laughed and played as girls do, but they would not walk with her. To be seen with her in such a public way might invite some of the ridicule to be heaped on them.

Jo Ann was beginning to understand why the other children acted the way they did. For one thing, she was taller than every other Asian girl her age, taller even than some of the boys. She took after her father, who was taller than most of the other Western men she knew. Like most Asian women, her mother was short, although that was a relative term, her father had told her. Here, *Umma* was of average height, but among Westerners, like the women at *Apba*'s embassy, she was short.

Jo Ann looked different, too, from the Japanese girls she knew. Her complexion wasn't quite the same as theirs, and hints of copper ran through her black hair. And of course there were her eyes. Not as round as Western eyes, but certainly much more so than those of the other children. The eyes were the first things the other kids picked up on.

"Round Eyes! Hey, Round Eyes, how's the weather up there?" Laughter followed the remark, from the group of boys that started following her. One or two trotted in front of her, then turned to face her in a belligerent pose. Though she walked past them without acknowledgement, they were getting more persistent, and she was still some blocks from her destination. Her heart beat so loudly she thought it possible the boys would hear it.

"Hey, Round Eyes, what kind of silly outfit is that?" She didn't see who had shouted that question. Then a boy stepped directly in front of her. His arms akimbo, a smirk on his face, he said, "I asked you a question, Round Eyes. What is that silly outfit called?"

Other boys hemmed her in on either side, forcing Jo Ann to stop. She recognized the boy from her neighborhood. He didn't go to school at the embassy, as she did, but Jo had heard of him from other girls. He was two or three years older than her and renowned as a bully.

Older he might be, but she was almost as tall as he was. She realized this probably aggravated the boy all the more. She tried to control her breathing, as her instructor always advised. "This is what I wear to *keiko*," she said politely, even though these boys didn't deserve to be treated with politeness.

"Is that some sort of dress?" he demanded.

"It is called a *hakama*," she said of the navy-blue, wide-pleated skirt, which extended to her ankles.

"And that?" He pointed to her plain white belt.

"It is an *obi*. And this is my *keiko-gi*," she said, touching her white cotton jacket. "This is what I wear to *naginata* class." Thinking about her class gave her a much-needed shot of pride. She stood straight and lifted her chin slightly, looking straight into the boy's eyes. Her right hand gripped her wooden naginata staff. It was only a children's training staff; the *ebu*, made of stout oak, was five feet long instead of the standard six to eight, and the *habu* blade was two foot-long strips of bamboo tied together. When she got older, Jo would be allowed to use a full-sized *shiai* naginata, with a steel blade up to three feet in length.

Jo Ann had studied naginata since her family moved back to Tokyo from Seoul two years earlier. She picked up the art quickly, and once a week participated in keiko with a

3

dozen other girls. At eleven, Jo was the youngest student in the class, but she was progressing faster than her instructor had expected. Jo was not surprised, since she had spent four years studying *tae kwon do* in Seoul and now held a brown belt. Her father encouraged her study of martial arts, and had procured a private tae kwon do instructor for her here in Tokyo, as formal classes in the Korean art were unknown. Naginata, however, had been taught in Japan for centuries; the wives of *samurai* warriors developed the art as a means of self-defense for women and girls.

"Well, I think it is a silly outfit," the bully said. He poked her in the chest. "Just what I'd expect from a round-eyes."

"Please let me pass," she said. "I have done nothing to offend you."

"Oh, you haven't? You don't talk to any of us. You walk through the neighborhood with your nose held high. But what else can we expect from a round-eyed *yariman*?" Jo Ann didn't know what that word meant, although she'd heard it whispered once or twice among older girls. She was pretty sure it was an insult.

"I am not a yariman," she said. "Now please let me pass."

"Yariman *ama!*" The boy flung the words at her. His companions fell silent, shocked. Jo Ann knew the meaning of that last word. One of the American boys in her class had told her it meant "bitch", and the way he laughed convinced Jo that it was a derogatory. Used in combination with yariman, the bully surely intended it for a truly filthy purpose.

That was enough. She refused to stand there and be insulted any longer. Her mother had always taught her to be properly deferential, like a good Korean—or Japanese— woman, but her father said that American women were not always deferential; polite and respectful, yes, but also proud, and able to stand on their own. "You will let me pass, and you will do it now," she said, calmly but forcefully.

The bully laughed. "Or what, round-eyed yariman? Will you hit me with your little stick?"

"Yes," Jo Ann said. She moved into a sideways fighting stance, with the tip of her naginata blade pointed right at the bully. But instead of striking with that end, she quickly reversed the staff and performed a perfect strike into the bully's solar plexus with the butt-end of the naginata, punctuating the strike with a loud *kiap* spirit yell. The bully let out a woof and collapsed like a sack of potatoes. Before his comrades could react, Jo struck the boy to her left on his knee, eliciting a howl of pain. Turning with expert footwork that would have made her instructor proud, she lashed out at the two boys behind her. One went down after a crack to his shin; the other was reaching down for a rock when the bamboo blade cracked him on the wrist. He shrieked.

The remaining boy, on Jo's right, faced her, trembling, and Jo saw the front of his pants darken. Then he yelled and took off at a run.

The lead bully struggled to get to his feet, and he coughed out a curse at her. Jo swung the naginata around and brought the blade within a few inches of the boy's face. His eyes opened wide. She poked slightly with the staff, and he fell back onto his seat with a yelp, even though the blade had not made contact.

"I will now pass," Jo said.

She tried to stifle her sobs that night, pressing her face against her pillow. Why did they hate her so? Even the few girls she'd befriended here seemed to be uncomfortable around her. And boys? Most ignored her. They seemed to be afraid of her, and yet she had noticed them looking at her. The demure outfits her mother dressed her in could not quite hide the developing curves of her body and her budding breasts. She wanted to talk to the boys, but they wanted little to do with her. Even the American boys snubbed her.

A hand touched her shoulder, and she heard a soft voice speak in Korean. "Why are you crying, little one?"

"Oh, Umma!" She sat up and fell into her mother's arms. The tears flowed freely. Earlier, when she first told her mother about the encounter with the bullies, she held the tears in. She felt such shame, yet she couldn't quite understand why. She had acquitted herself well in the fight, and indeed was proud of her abilities. But she couldn't help feeling it had been wrong, so wrong, and she said so.

"Now, now, little one," her mother said soothingly, stroking Jo's hair. "Why are you so upset?"

"The boys, they...they don't like me," she said, also in Korean. "Nobody likes me!"

Her mother kissed the top of her head. "You are different, little one. Sometimes people don't understand something that is different."

"Why am I different, Umma? Because you are Korean and Apba is American?"

"That is partly true, Jo Ann. But it is more than that. Your heritage runs much deeper. Your father will explain it to you."

"Is Apba home?"

"Yes, and he will speak with you shortly. He has wonderful news for you. He just shared it with me."

Suddenly the bullies were forgotten. "What news, Umma?"

Her mother smiled. "He will tell you, little one. But first, about today. You must not feel ashamed. You are different from the other boys and girls, so this may happen again. You must be like the white fox."

"The white fox, Umma?"

Her mother smiled, and her eyes took on a far-away look, which they always did when she told Jo Ann stories of her childhood in Korea. "There is a legend," she said. "It is about a white fox who is a hundred years old. He has nine tails, and can do many wondrous things. The most wondrous thing he can do is transform himself into any other animal. This is how he protects himself, and how he helps others. You must be like the white fox, little one," she said, stroking Jo's hair again. "You have the ability to do wondrous things. Later you will learn how to use these abilities to protect yourself, and help others. You will be a female fox, though. A vixen."

Somehow that made Jo Ann feel much better, and she sighed, drying her tears with the sleeve of her pajamas. "Thank you, Umma."

Umma kissed her again. There was a tapping on the bedroom door. "Your father is here now."

Jo Ann looked up expectantly, and burst into a smile as her father walked into the room. Oh, how she worshiped him! He was so tall, so regal in his suit and tie. His face was lordly and yet kind, with its pencil-thin mustache and thinning hair on top. His gray eyes were soft now, although sometimes Jo had seen them turn steely as he talked to people about very serious things.

Joseph Geary sat down on the bed in the spot his wife had just vacated. "How is our little warrior this evening, Kim?" he asked his wife in his deep voice, speaking in English.

"She is fine, my husband," her mother said in her adopted language. "I will leave you two alone now." With a slight bow, Kim Nam-soon Geary left the room.

"Your mother told me what happened today," Joseph said. He touched her cheek. "I'm sorry for what happened, but I'm proud of the way you handled it."

"Thank you, Daddy," Jo Ann said in English, deferring her eyes and nodding in a slight bow. Then she looked up. "Mama said you would tell me about my heritage."

He smiled. "Yes. Well, one's heritage is a special thing, Jo Ann. It says much about who you are, and what you can be."

"I know that you are American, and Mama is Korean."

"Yes. Your mother's family is very important in Korea. She is descended from great warriors, in the Silla Dynasty. You remember reading about them in your classes in Seoul, don't you?"

"Yes, Daddy. The Silla united Korea a thousand years ago. Their warriors were the *Hwa rang dan*, even better than the samurai of Japan."

"Well, I'm sure our Japanese friends here would disagree with that," he said with a modest chuckle. "But the Silla were indeed mighty warriors, and they developed the martial art of *tang soo do*, the forerunner of tae kwon do, which you are learning so well. As for your American side, my ancestors have always served our people, going all the way back to the Revolution."

Jo Ann's eyes were wide. "So your people were mighty warriors, too, Daddy?"

Joseph smiled. "You might say that," he said. "The Gearys fought for our freedom, all the way back then and through the years to this day."

"You were a warrior in the war, weren't you, Daddy?" She was learning about the war in her history classes. It had been a terrible thing. The Japanese she knew said nothing about it, but some of the buildings she saw in Tokyo still bore its scars.

Joseph looked away, and his eyes grew distant. "Yes," he said. "Someday I will tell you the stories, Jo Ann. In those days the Japanese were our enemy. But today they are our friends."

"Those Japanese boys today are not my friends," she said angrily. "They wanted to hurt me."

He took her by the shoulders. "Maybe so," he said, "but they learned their lesson today. I doubt if they'll bother you again."

Jo Ann hesitated. "Daddy, they called me a name today. A Japanese name. I am sorry, but I do not know its meaning." Although she was fluent in the Korean and English she had learned as a toddler, she was still struggling with Japanese. "What does 'yariman' mean?"

Her father frowned. "It is a very bad name, I'm afraid," he said solemnly. He sighed. "I will tell you now what the word means, but we will discuss it at another time, because it will lead to a whole other subject. The closest English word for it is 'slut'."

The way her father said the word convinced Jo that it was truly bad, and she decided she would look it up in the school dictionary, or perhaps the one her father kept in his study here at home. But that was for another time. She looked up at him proudly. "I want to be a warrior, Daddy. Like the Hwa rang dan. Like the Gearys. I will be a great warrior, even though I am a girl."

Joseph smiled at her again. "I believe you will be, Jo. You have some real gifts. You have a gift for languages, and the martial arts, too. I think you have many other gifts we are just beginning to see." He paused. "How would you like to go to a place where you can really develop those gifts?"

Her eyes were wide. "Yes, Daddy! Where?"

He smiled, and touched her hair again. "I just found out today, my little warrior. Soon we will be moving to America."

***

Rio Negro Province, Argentina

THE WHITE VIXEN

"There is nothing to be done, then?"

The short, gray-haired man with the brushy mustache shook his head. "He has a day or so, perhaps only hours." He glanced at the stocky, plain-faced man in the other chair. "You may want to alert the others. He might wish to see them one last time."

The stocky man shook his head, looking down at the schnapps in his glass. "No, he wouldn't recognize them anyway." He threw back the schnapps with one swallow. Putting the glass on a side table, he rose from the stuffed chair and walked to the large fireplace. Dominating the dark oak mantle was a bronze sculpture of a bull, its wicked-looking horns set to gore whoever might dare to get close. Flanking the bull were a few framed black and white photos. As was his wont, the stocky man gazed at the sculpture. A small brass plate on the wooden base bore the words *Der Stier*. The Bull.

It had been a gift from his wife on their tenth wedding anniversary, a tribute, she said during a particularly rapturous moment, not just to his husky, broad-shouldered physique, but to his sexual prowess. She had borne him ten children, and he fathered several more over the years, and every one of his many women—he never used the term "lovers", or anything with any connotation of emotional attachment—praised him for his size and vigor. Thus he chose the code name Taurus when he began planning this particular endeavor. From the standpoint of astrology, he wasn't really a Taurus; his sign was Gemini, having been born a few weeks too early to be under the Sign of the Bull. He didn't care. Unlike some of his colleagues, he paid no attention to astrology. Taurus was chosen for other reasons.

The doctor was little more than a quack, he knew, yet the Bull trusted his diagnosis in this case. The doctor had proven useful before, with his experiments and so forth, but Taurus tolerated him then only because his work kept certain associates happy and occupied. Taurus was a man of politics, not of science, but even he knew enough of the latter to doubt the dubious value of the doctor's research. Yet several important men, including the man dying in the next room, valued the doctor enough that they insisted he be included in the Relocation. Now, he had come to examine the man in the next room; not at the behest of Taurus, who did not trust him or anyone else, but at the urging of certain others among the *Kameraden*, who evidently still did. Taurus could have refused, but decided it would do no harm to let the quack have a look.

"He is, after all, seventy-two years old now," the doctor said. "His age, combined with his various ailments...well, quite frankly, I am surprised he has lived this long."

"He is a survivor," the Bull said, still gazing at one of the photos on the mantle. "He survived the trenches and the gas in the first war. Prison. The bombing. The shooting in the bunker."

"It is most fortunate that you intervened when you did, that night," the doctor said.

"It was my duty," Taurus said, remembering that terrible night, with the earth above them shaking from the artillery shells, women sobbing uncontrollably, some men disappearing as they made their own desperate escapes. Only sixteen years ago, yet it seemed much longer sometimes.

Duty. Coming into the bedroom, seeing the woman lying on the bed amidst her own blood, and seeing the man in a nearby chair, hand shaking as he turned the Luger toward his own mouth. Duty had made him grab the pistol and pry it from the trembling fingers before they could pull the trigger. Duty had made him take the man with him and a few most-trusted companions a few hours later, through the secret tunnels, into the dark of night lit up by explosions. He suppressed a shudder as he recalled one particularly vicious artillery barrage, so fierce it separated him and his companion from the others. He kept going, though. Duty kept him by the man's side for the next harrowing days, hiding by day, moving by night, always concealing the man's identity, somehow getting them to the coast, where the submarine, thank the gods, was waiting as planned.

Yes, duty required him to bring the man across the ocean, enduring the brutal undersea journey, the terror of the depth charges in not one but three different attacks, the destroyer captains up on the surface having no clue as to whom they were really trying to kill. It was good that they had not known, or their entire fleet would have come to pursue them to the ends of the earth.

And what was his duty now? To the man in the other room, to his vision? A vision that, despite the Bull's work behind the scenes, had led to disaster. They had fled a nation in ruins, crushed under the heels of the invading Bolsheviks. And today, what was left? A third of their country still enslaved by the enemy from the east, the other two-thirds...well, it might as well be. The invaders from the west called the shots there, and they were only slightly more civilized than the Slavs. Both sides, facing each other, armed to the teeth, ready for only a spark to ignite a conflagration that would be the final act, the *Gotterdämmerung* that would wipe his precious country off the face of the earth.

13

It could not be allowed to happen. Taurus looked again at the photo on the mantle. It showed a group of soldiers—Taurus was not among them, for he had not been a soldier then, and in fact few photographs of him even existed—sitting at a café in Paris, twenty years ago now. He knew none of their names, but from the moment he first saw the photo, he was profoundly moved by its significance. Four young men, wearing their nation's uniform, holding wineglasses to the camera in a toast to their conquest, while a pretty but sullen French waitress stood next to them. To the Bull, the picture represented his beloved nation at the zenith of its power, and power was something the man understood very well. He'd once had it, and so had his country, but he had let loose one or two strings at the wrong time, and it all came tumbling down.

Almost all of it. A small bit of it remained, here in this new land on the other side of the world. Enough of it, perhaps, to rectify the mistakes of the past, to lead his people into the glorious future that was their destiny. He took a deep breath, and with one last look at the long-ago soldiers, he turned back to the doctor.

"Thank you, Josef," Taurus said. "It is late, and I'm sure you are tired."

The doctor stood up, recognizing the dismissal. "Indeed I am. Good evening to you, *Herr Reichsleiter*." With a short bow, the quack left the room.

In the next room, the old man lay on the bed, his breathing shallow. The once jet-black hair was pure white now, and a few strands of it drooped down across the sallow forehead. The famous mustache was likewise white, hard to distinguish from the pale skin.

THE WHITE VIXEN

The Bull stood next to the bed, watching the old man. "So it has come to this," he said. "Thirty-five years together, through the back-room maneuverings, the clashes in the streets, the marches and rallies. You were the voice, I was the brain. You were the inspiration, I was the one who did the dirty work of politics. You were the symbol, but I was the Party." The old man's eyes flickered, then focused on him. "You stood up with me at my wedding, and three years later I repaid you by having your niece liquidated as she was about to tell the police of your sordid affair. Without me, Geli would have brought you down, brought us down, but I acted then, and you became chancellor, and together we nearly captured the world."

He sighed. Not for the first time, he regretted entering that room in the bunker. "Well, it is not too late after all," he said. "The Kameraden, those who still worship you, will not hear your voice again, will not be privy to your final testament, will not carry one last image of you into the years ahead, when we have so much work to do and cannot be distracted by dreams of past glories. They must look to me now, and only to me."

The old man's head lay on two pillows. The Bull gently pulled the bottom one away, and as his head lowered, the old man's eyes grew wide. The mouth opened also, the famous mouth that had once uttered words that moved a nation and frightened the world, and a bit of drool ran down into the pillow from one corner.

The old man was fully awake now, and lucid. He turned toward the stocky man standing at his bedside. The rheumy eyes blinked, then re-focused with that strange combination of charm and danger. "Martin?" The voice was but a rasp now, its old power long gone.

15

"Rest now, *mein Führer*," Taurus said as he lowered the pillow onto the old man's face.

CHAPTER ONE

Fonglan Island, China

November 1981

No one paid any attention to the woman as she shuffled along the dirt path that was no more a street than the collection of shacks on the nearby waterfront could be termed a village. Yet it was a village, home to a few dozen fishermen and their families. The men were weather-beaten but plucky as they plied the nearby waters in their junks to scrape out a living. Their women were equally hard working as they struggled to raise their few children in some semblance of a home. By comparison, the People's Liberation Army base was huge and luxuriant. Helicopters buzzed overhead constantly, back and forth to the mainland some twenty kilometers away, or out over the sea to keep watch on the English and Americans who sortied their gray ships out from Hong Kong. The villagers had heard of that

17

wondrous place, tales of fabulous riches and food beyond belief, and while the men knew how close it actually was from a physical sense, they also knew that in a practical sense it might as well be on the moon.

Carrying a basket in one hand and a steel cooking pot in the other, the woman shuffled along, her head down, hair covered by a shawl, a heavy cloth coat protecting her against the biting November wind that never ceased its scouring of the island. Shapeless gray trousers covered her legs and her feet were shod with sandals. In one coat pocket she carried her identity papers, and in the other a well-worn copy of Chairman Mao's Little Red Book. The cover of the cooking pot couldn't prevent the spicy aroma of the fish and rice from escaping, and the cloth over the basket was likewise helpless against the fresh-baked bread.

She approached the gate with caution. The base was ringed with a chain-link fence topped with razor wire, and this was one of three entrances. The gate was barely large enough to accommodate a vehicle, and the road leading to it from the village was not the main road. Vehicles almost always used the main gate farther east. Soldiers still guarded this one around the clock, though, and she saw two of them inside the wooden guard shack.

Dutifully, she stopped when she got within two meters of the shack, and one of the guards came out, his automatic rifle held loosely at port arms. She catalogued the weapon automatically as a Type 56, the Chinese copy of the venerable Soviet-made Kalashnikov AK-47. "Who are you?" he barked.

"I bring food, as instructed by Sergeant Lu," she said, eyes lowered.

The guard stepped closer, then tilted her head up by the chin, none too gently. "I don't know you," he said. "What happened to the old woman?"

Keeping her eyes averted, she said, "Madame Zhi is ill tonight. I am her niece. My papers are in my pocket."

The guard released her chin and used the barrel of his weapon to pull the cloth away from the bread. "Smells good," he said. "You come give me some later, eh?"

"There may be none left," she said.

"Then make sure you save something, eh?" The guard laughed. "Go on, you know where it is?"

"Yes, sir," she said, "I do. Thank you." Wasting no time, she shuffled past him. The other guard was holding the gate open for her. He eyed her hungrily as she went by.

Jo Ann Geary allowed herself to exhale deeply when she was safely inside, but she never let up her pace. Raising her head slightly, she took in her surroundings. The layout was familiar, thanks to the reconnaissance photos she'd carefully studied. There was a concrete landing pad about three hundred meters away, and a helicopter was coming in for a landing. She recognized it as an SA 321H Super Frelon, manufactured in France by Aerospatiale, and used by the PLA primarily for personnel transport. Two soldiers ran to a side door of the chopper, heads low to avoid the slowing rotors. Three officers emerged from the Super Frelon; at this distance Jo couldn't recognize faces or insignia, but the deference shown by the troops told her much. She knew she didn't have much time.

Her destination was the stockade, a brick building in the midst of six smaller buildings, about two hundred meters from the gate. Two more soldiers, looking decidedly more alert than those at the gate, flanked the doorway. "Papers!"

She carefully set down her basket and pot and produced her identity booklet. The guard tilted her face up to compare it with the photograph in the book, then issued a grunt. His partner looked inside the basket and the pot, then nodded to the other. "Okay," the first one said.

Inside, she passed a bored corporal sitting at a desk and clacking away on an ancient typewriter, continued down a hallway and stopped at a closed door. She had memorized the simple routine always used by her "aunt", and rapped twice on the wooden door. "Come in," a voice said in response.

A man sat behind a desk inside the small office. He wore the same baggy PLA uniform as the other soldiers, but Jo saw the sergeant's insignia. She'd seen his photo during the briefing, and through a cloud of cigarette haze she recognized the face: Sergeant Lu. "I bring food, as requested, honorable sir," she said, eyes lowered. She'd only needed a quick glance to take in everything.

The sergeant grunted, then rose from his creaking chair and come around the desk toward her. "Where is Madame Zhi?"

Jo gave her standard answer. Lu was not very much taller than her, and she knew he was in his late thirties. Non-coms in the Chinese Army were not nearly as professional as those in the Western services, one reason why the PLA was not very highly regarded as a fighting force. What they lacked in efficiency, though, they more than made up for with numbers. And brutality, when necessary. She took note of the pistol holstered on his right hip.

Lu tilted her chin upward. "I haven't seen you before," he said.

"I just arrived for a visit to my aunt and uncle," she said. It was an effort to keep her eyes averted and shoulders hunched. She named a village on the mainland, hoping Lu wasn't that familiar with it. The briefing hadn't told her much about him.

"Ah. Well, you come with me."

She followed him down a short hallway to a barred metal door. An armed guard stood a little straighter as Lu approached, then unlocked the door in response to the sergeant's order. Lu and Jo Ann entered the cellblock.

Just as her briefing had anticipated, the block was small, about ten meters long. Four cells lined the wall to her right. The first was empty. The next contained a Chinese man wearing an unmarked PLA uniform. He looked to be about eighteen years old and quickly averted his eyes from Lu as they passed. An older Chinese man in civilian clothes was in the next cell, lying on a blanket on the stark cement floor, staring at the ceiling.

They stopped in front of the final cell. "Dinner time!" Lu announced.

The man inside was sitting in a corner, head between his knees, but when he looked up, Jo immediately recognized the face, despite its bruises and cuts. One eye was almost swollen shut. Two fingers of his left hand were tied together with a piece of rag, doubtless a makeshift splint applied by the prisoner. He was wearing a gray shirt and pants, nondescript and baggy, and his feet were bare and bruised.

He was Brian Jamison, a colonel in the British Royal Air Force, and one of the most valuable operatives of MI-6, the

U.K.'s foreign intelligence service, and he was a dead man unless Jo could get him out of here. She estimated she had only an hour to accomplish that task. Maybe less, depending on how quickly the men from the helicopter arrived.

Lu unclipped a ring of keys from his belt and used one to unlock the cell door. Jo made a careful mental note of the key's position on the ring. Fourth from the end, around five o'clock. The sergeant swung the door open and gestured for Jo to take the food inside.

This was the most critical phase of the entire operation. If Jamison did not recognize her signal, valuable time would be lost later when she came back for him. Worse, if he had already been compromised, she might be moments from being captured herself. She had been carefully briefed on the interrogation methods used by the Chinese and had no desire to experience them first hand. By the look of Jamison, he was only in the early rounds of what would be a long fight that he would inevitably lose. Lu had only gotten the show started here. The men from the helicopter would be taking the agent back to the mainland for the main event.

She got to the middle of the cell and stopped when Lu barked, "No farther!" Gently, she set the pot and the basket on the floor. Jamison was staring at her with his good eye. Carefully, Jo extended her tongue, flicked it off her upper lip first, then her bottom, then twice more off the top.

"Thank you," Jamison said in a croaking voice. Jo suppressed a smile of relief. He had gotten the message. Each flick of her tongue had sent a different signal. *I am here to help you. Be ready to move. Twenty minutes maximum.*

She bowed to the prisoner and then shuffled backward out of the cell. Jamison made no move for the food. Jo noticed that Lu's hand was on the butt of his sidearm. With his left hand, he closed the cell door firmly. Only after it locked did Jamison reach out for the basket and cook pot.

"Eat well," Lu said in Chinese. "You're going on a trip tonight." Jamison made no reply, although Jo knew he was fluent in the language, as was she.

"Come with me," Lu said, taking her by the arm and hustling her back toward the cellblock entrance.

"I must go tend to my aunt," Jo said, forcing her voice up an octave to show fear.

"Later."

The guard quickly let them through the door, but not so quickly that Jo couldn't catch the position of the key on his ring. First one on the right. Good, that would save a second or two. Still gripping her upper arm, Lu moved her down the hallway and toward another room. He opened the door and pushed her inside.

Her many years of instruction allowed her to think and react instinctively. *Know your environment.* A bare bulb hanging overhead illuminated the room. It was a storeroom of some sort. Along the wall to her right, shelves held a few piles of papers and files, some books, cleaning supplies. To her left, a mop and broom leaned against the wall, next to a sink. Ahead of her was a rickety cot, canvas supported by metal legs. A rumpled blanket lay on top of it. She heard the door shut behind her, and the lock clicked. *Program for engagement.* Anticipating Lu's movements, Jo planned her own. She concentrated on bringing her breathing under control, reaching deep within herself for her *kokoro*, her indomitable spirit, knowing that the next few minutes would determine whether she lived or died.

"Undress and lie down," Lu ordered.

23

"Please, honorable sir, I beg you not to hurt me." Her back was still toward the sergeant, so he could not see her slip the dart from the hem of her left sleeve. She slipped effortlessly into a state of *kiai*, a relaxed but intense focus upon her life force, her *ki*.

"Do as you are told," he said. She could hear the slap of leather; he was unbuckling his belt. Keeping the dart concealed in her right hand, she began unbuttoning her coat. Behind her, she heard the clump of the belt being dropped on the floor.

Pulling off her coat, she turned to face Lu. This time she stood up straight, and noted the glint in his eyes as he saw that she was nearly as tall as him. Instead of averting her own eyes, she stared directly into his, bringing her inner spirit into a state of *aiki*. The words of one of her past masters came back, quoting an early Japanese *jujitsu* master: "Aiki is the art of defeating your opponent with a single glance." She saw uncertainty, and perhaps a touch of fear, enter Lu's eyes.

Still, he was arrogant. "I am going to enjoy this," he said huskily, reaching for Jo's scarf. He had no idea she was already feeling *haragei*, an intuitive sense focused on her abdomen, the center of all movement. She had entered a state of *mushin,* a sense of mind/no mind, allowing her to react and move almost literally without thought.

"I doubt it," Jo said as Lu's right hand grasped the edge of her scarf. She reached up with her left hand, covering Lu's and pinning it down onto her head. With her right, still protecting the dart, she pushed up into his right elbow, thumb finding the nerve and squeezing, pushing up as she moved her body fluidly underneath Lu's arm, stepping behind him and then bringing his arm up into a gooseneck

24

hold. Lu gasped in pain and surprise, from the pain in his arm and then in his neck as Jo released his elbow long enough to drive the dart into the right side of his throat. Her entire movement took less than one and a half seconds. The drug carried by the dart began flowing through the sergeant's neck, reaching the carotid artery in moments. Lu tried to yell, but the rapid closure of his windpipe only allowed a near-silent rasp. Two seconds later, the drug reached his brain and his eyes rolled backward.

Jo caught him as he collapsed and moved him quickly to the cot, laying the unconscious body out carefully. It took her only two minutes to strip off the uniform and shoes. Probably too small for Jamison, but they'll have to do. She turned the sergeant onto his left side, facing the wall, and covered him with the blanket.

She removed Lu's pistol and key ring from the gun belt and hid the belt and shoes in a nearby bucket, stuffing the uniform on top of them. Putting her coat back on, she tucked the gun into the waistband of her trousers at the small of her back. The keys went into a coat pocket. She checked her right sleeve; the second dart was still in place. Grabbing the mop, she went quickly to the doorway, surveyed the room one last time, and switched off the light.

She had just shut the door behind her when the corporal from the front desk came down the hall. "Where is Sergeant Lu?"

Back in her servant's posture, Jo Ann bowed to the soldier, no more than a boy himself. "The sergeant is...resting," she said.

"Ah, so," the man said.

"He asked me to clean the empty cell before I leave."

"Very well," the private said, with a last knowing glance at the closed door of the storeroom. Then he turned and walked back to his desk.

Letting out her breath carefully, Jo shuffled down the hall and found the cellblock entrance quickly. The guard didn't come to attention this time, but she noticed his grip tighten ever so slightly on his rifle. Jo would have to time this carefully. She bowed to the guard. "Honorable sir, Sergeant Lu ordered me to clean the empty cell."

The guard was older than the corporal, and smarter. He took out his keys, but then leaned over slightly and looked in the bucket. Jo had shoved the uniform down as far as she could, but it wasn't a very deep bucket, and the guard's eyes widened as he realized there certainly was no water inside. He dropped the key ring and took a quick step back, bringing his rifle around as he moved.

Jo was just a bit quicker. The dart from her right sleeve was out and moving fast, but instead of embedding itself in the guard's neck it merely grazed the skin. The guard yelped at the bite of the dart, but he was experienced enough to keep moving backward, allowing room to bring his rifle to bear.

The broom handle became Jo's best weapon now, and in one swift motion she used it, knowing that split seconds counted now. Her first target was the guard's right arm, the one holding the rifle, and her hard strike was right on the money, impacting on the area containing the nerve. Her survival, and Jamison's, now depended on her not allowing the guard to fire a shot, even as a reflex action. The nerve strike worked; the guard cried out, but his hand suddenly became useless, the fingers unable to find the trigger.

The gun was falling to the floor as Jo struck again, whipping the end of the broom handle around with her body in a 360-degree turn, then thrusting the blunt end of the handle deeply into the guard's abdomen. The air whooshed out of him with a guttural gasp as he bent over nearly double. Now she brought the broom up with both hands, cracking the wood solidly into his chin and snapping his head back, where it thudded against the cement wall with a crack that sounded like the world's biggest eggshell being broken open. He slumped to the floor, unconscious, bleeding from the nose and mouth.

She hadn't intended to kill him, and indeed he might survive with at least a concussion and perhaps a skull fracture, but he was out. Jo pulled out the sergeant's sidearm and reached for the guard's keys, but another movement from down the hall caught her eye and she brought the gun up quickly.

It was the corporal from the front desk, drawn by the commotion. "What is this?"

"Don't move," she said. The pistol was pointed directly at his face, and even ten feet away the business end of the weapon must've looked very large to him. "Cooperate and you live. Make one sound and you die."

Panting, the soldier nodded a yes. "Over here," Jo said, motioning with the pistol. The corporal obediently stood next to the downed guard. Jo had already taken the rifle; the guard had no sidearm. She tossed the key ring to the private. "Open the cellblock door," she said. Stepping back, she gestured again with the gun just to add a little incentive. "No, the one on the other end," she said as the corporal fumbled with the keys. "Be quick about it."

The soldier found the right key and unlocked the door. "You first," Jo said. Keeping the pistol trained on him, she tucked the rifle under her other arm and picked up the bucket.

The Chinese prisoners looked at them wide-eyed as they entered the cellblock. A stern look from Jo convinced them to keep quiet, but she knew they'd have to be bound and gagged before they left. That would take up more valuable time, but it couldn't be helped.

They reached the end of the block. Jamison was ready, standing near the door. "Good show," he said in English.

Jo tossed him the sergeant's keys and told him which one to use. Reaching through the bars, Jamison struggled a bit but managed to unlock his cell door. "There's a uniform in the bucket," she said in English. "Probably a bit small but it'll have to do."

Twenty agonizingly long seconds later, Jamison was pulling down Lu's coat, barely reaching his waist. The shoes were way too small. "I'd prefer not to go barefoot," he said. He looked at the corporal. "You have some big dogs, there, son," he said in Chinese. "Off with them."

Sitting on the floor of Jamison's cell, the private pulled off his shoes and handed them over. "Stockings, too." The plain gray socks went on easily, but Jamison had a hard time fitting the shoes. "I can put up with a little foot discomfort," he said finally.

"We don't have much time," Jo said in English. "I saw a helicopter coming in with some officers."

"Probably from their Central Investigative Department," Jamison said. That was one possibility, Jo Ann knew, but they might also be from the PLA's Second Department, which handled military intelligence. Jamison took the sergeant's sidearm from Jo and put it in the holster. "Or perhaps from the Central Security Regiment," he added.

"The 8341 Unit?" Jo asked. She'd been told that particularly notorious branch, which had served as Mao Tse-tung's personal security service and thus as China's secret police, had been disbanded following Mao's death five years ago.

"Still around, yes," Jamison said, hefting the guard's rifle. "Nasty blokes. Let's get moving."

"We have to secure the prisoners," she said.

"Right. I'll take care of this fellow." The MI-6 agent began stripping his prisoner's tunic apart. Jo took the sergeant's keys and went to the next cell.

The older of the two Chinese prisoners looked at her strangely as she unlocked the door and entered. Jo realized she should've kept the pistol, but she couldn't waste time to get it now. "Take your shirt off," she ordered. The man dutifully complied, and in seconds Jo had used the filthy garment to bind the prisoner's hands behind his head and also as a blindfold and gag, a nifty technique she'd learned from an intelligence officer who'd defected from North Vietnam.

She was worried about the younger prisoner, who'd appeared fairly excitable. She found him holding onto the bars of his cell door. As soon as she came into view, he began jabbering. "Who are you? What did you do to the sergeant?"

"Stay back," she said, inserting the key in the door's lock.

The boy's voice got higher. "I did nothing wrong! The other man, he told me what he wanted—"

From next to her, Jo Ann heard a metallic click and the prisoner stopped in mid-sentence. "That's good, son, now do as the lady says." Jamison had the sergeant's pistol out and carefully targeted.

It took only moments for Jo to bind and gag the boy. "Thanks," she said. "I owe you one."

"We'll down a few in Hong Kong tonight," he said. "Assuming, of course, that we can get out of here."

"There's a boat waiting," she said. "Two klicks past the village on the coast. I have transport waiting in the village." Madame Zhi, her cover now blown, would be evacuated with them. She'd managed to borrow one of the village's few vehicles, a dilapidated truck, in exchange for three cartons of American cigarettes. If their luck held, now that darkness was approaching, they could get past the base perimeter, down the road to the village and then hop aboard for the two-kilometer ride to the rendezvous point. The extraction team would meet them there with a Zodiac boat.

"There are two guards outside the building," Jo said. "Can you imitate the sergeant's voice?"

"I'll try," he said. "Lord knows I've heard it often enough the past few days."

"Good. When I go past them, I'll get their attention. Then you order them to avert their eyes somehow."

"That will be hard for them to do," he said, and even from his battered face the smile looked appreciative. Men.

Jo went out first. The guards stiffened automatically as they heard the door open, then relaxed as they recognized her. Back into her peasant shuffle, Jo went down the two wooden steps and scuttled off, stopping ten feet from the guards. She turned and smiled at them. "Hello, boys," she said in perfect Mandarin. "Are you as big as your sergeant?"

One guard laughed. "Bigger," he said.

"Private!" Jamison barked from the doorway. "I heard that!" The guards shot to ramrod straight attention. "One hundred push-ups! Both of you!"

Like automatons, the guards set their rifles on the ground and assumed the universal push-up position. The guard who'd spoken started quickly, followed by his comrade a second later. "Count them off!" Jamison said.

"One, two, three, four..."

Without saying another word, Jamison strode past them to Jo Ann. They began walking toward the same gate Jo had used only a short time before, although it seemed like hours to her.

"Very clever," she whispered to the agent.

"By the time they finish we'll be far enough away so they won't recognize me," Jamison said. "How many guards at the gate?"

"Two."

"Our dog and pony show won't work there."

"We'll have to be more direct. I'll take the pistol." Jamison handed her the sidearm and she tucked it inside her sleeve.

Dusk was upon them, and the base's usual high level of activity was slacking off. A half-dozen or so soldiers passed Jo Ann and the British agent, but none came within ten yards. They had another hundred meters to go to the gate, and Jo began praying that no other soldiers would choose to use it right now. She knew that most of them were probably in the mess hall for dinner, but give them another half hour and some might be off duty and ready to head to town. The officers from the helicopter were probably dining with the base commander right now, but they'd soon finish and head over to the lockup. Jo estimated they had thirty minutes, tops, before an alarm was raised. They'd be cutting it close.

CHAPTER TWO

Fonglan Island, China

November 1981

Two lights at the top of the fence served to illuminate the gate, but at this hour the lights were ineffectual, and the fact that they were designed to shine on the area outside the fence, rather than inside, helped them. They would be right on top of the guards before they'd have to move.

Jamison kept the rifle at a stiff port arms and his head down, Lu's cap pulled low, and he hunched a bit to disguise his height. Jo took the lead as they approached the gate. One of the guards, standing outside the shack and smoking a cigarette, saw them and automatically moved to the gate, tossing the cigarette aside. Everything was quiet, so he had no reason to be suspicious of anyone coming out.

Jo shuffled past the guard. "Thank you, sir."

The guard turned away from the gate as she kept moving. "Hey, you got any food left?"

There was no way they'd bluff their way past the checkpoint. Jamison had the barrel of the rifle stuck in the side of the guard's head as his last word was still hanging in the air. Turning and drawing her weapon in one movement, Jo aimed directly at the guard still inside the shack. "Hands behind your head!"

Firing either weapon right now would bring the base to full alert within seconds. Jo was counting on the element of surprise, catching these two toward the end of their duty shift; tired, hungry, bored, slow to react. It worked. Instead of dropping down below the level of the open window and hitting the alarm, the guard in the shack did as he was told. Jo quickly ran the few steps to the shack and forced the guard onto the floor.

Jamison followed with the other guard prodded ahead. Jo was using a telephone cord to tie the second guard's wrists behind his back, and then she gagged him with his snot-encrusted handkerchief.

"Truss this fellow up, too," Jamison said. "I'll take care of the alarm."

Jamison was panting when they started out down the road, walking quickly but resisting the urge to run. Jo could tell his reserves, depleted by the confinement and beatings, were fading fast. "Hang on," she said. "A half klick to the village. The truck should be waiting for us." He nodded, too tired even to speak.

"I have two men waiting with the truck, plus a native woman we have to extract," she said. "Two more men at the boat."

"We're...slightly outnumbered, then," he gasped.

"If we can make the boat, we'll be in international waters in five minutes. Help will be waiting for us." So much depended now on how long it would take for an alarm to be raised over the escape, and how efficiently the Chinese responded. In their planning, the allied force had allowed for at least ten minutes of safety after making it through the gates. Jo thought it had been about five already and there was the truck.

A siren started wailing behind them. They wouldn't get that extra five minutes now. "Run!" she shouted, pulling out the pistol.

In the twilight she saw two figures near the truck. One jumped into the cab and started the engine. There was a grinding, a cough, and then it thrummed to life. Another figure stood near the back of the truck, a submachine gun held ready.

A hundred meters from the truck, Jo shouted the password in Chinese: "Pelican rising!" The man with the submachine gun, a Republic of China Marine Corps sergeant, shouted back: "Nest is waiting!" He waved them forward.

Jo and the MI-6 agent leaped into the bed of the truck. They had barely hit the hard metal bed when the driver jammed the accelerator, throwing them backward as the vehicle lurched ahead, rear wheels spitting gravel. The truck's tailgate had disappeared long ago, and Jo scrambled to find a grip on something to keep from sliding out. Hands grabbed her by the shoulders, pulling her roughly, until she managed to find a wooden slat and steady herself. Her left shoulder throbbed where she'd landed on it. Sitting up, she fought the swaying motion of the truck. It was old, probably a Soviet-made model dating back thirty years, but it was solidly built with wooden slats extending the side walls an extra three feet up, giving them precious cover. She saw Jamison crouching near the tailgate, his rifle at the ready.

"Any pursuit?" Jo yelled over the roar of the engine.

"Not yet," he said. He looked back at her. "Who are they?"

For the first time, Jo looked at the two other figures crouching on the bed of the truck, their backs to the cab. One was Madame Zhi, the other a boy of about sixteen. "Who is the boy?" Jo asked Zhi in Mandarin.

"My nephew," she said. "He is my only relation in the village. They will execute him because of me. I had to bring him."

The boy was trembling, clearly frightened nearly out of his mind. "All right," Jo said. To Jamison, she yelled, "They're friends."

The Taiwanese marines were in the cab, and one of them shouted back through the glass-free rear window: "One more kilometer!" The driver fought the wheel, trying to avoid the chuckholes, sometimes succeeding. In the back, Jo had the pistol out but was desperately hanging on as the truck rocked and jolted.

"Helos taking off from the base!" Jamison yelled. Risking a look, Jo clambered up one side of the box to peek over the edge of the wooden wall. Off in the distance, she saw one— no, two sets of lights rise up into the dusk. These wouldn't be the Super Frelon, which was unarmed, but smaller and faster H-5's. Her briefing had told her there would be half a dozen or so on the base at any given time, with perhaps three or four ready for quick deployment. The Chinese-made version of the Soviet Mi-4 all-purpose light helicopter, code-named "Hound" by NATO, the helo could serve as a troop carrier or light attack vehicle. It was no match for British or American gunships, but wouldn't have much trouble with an old pickup truck.

Their only advantage now was that the Chinese didn't know exactly where they were. The helicopters would have to deploy in a quick search pattern. Sure enough, Jo saw them split up, one heading away from them, toward the north, and the other turning toward the village. Once that pilot gained a little altitude, he would spot the truck and be after them. Jo figured they had half a minute or so before that would happen. Maybe enough time to get to the boat, maybe not. She hoped the other two commandos were ready.

Jamison had the Type 56 ready. Jo hoped they wouldn't have to rely on it against the Hound. "You said two men at the boat?" he yelled, his eyes never leaving the nearer helicopter as it scuttled toward the village, climbing to about three hundred feet.

"Yes," Jo answered, crouching next to him. "Both SBS."

"Good," Jamison said, doubtless giving thanks that the troopers were Special Boat Squadron commandos, members of the Royal Marines' elite Special Forces unit. It had been a tough go just to get this operation off the ground at all, given that the British commander in Hong Kong received only two days' notice. Was it only three days ago she was on the beach in Singapore, enjoying a much-deserved leave? Jo forced those much more pleasant thoughts aside and kept her eye on the Hound. It was turning toward them.

"The bugger's spotted us," Jamison growled, bringing the rifle up. "How much longer to the boat?"

"Any second now."

"Hope those lads are prepared," he said, tracking the incoming chopper. "Joe Chinaman up there'll make short work of us if they're not."

The truck was starting to slow as it rounded a curve. The shoreline here was rocky and barren, but the road led down to a small cove that was occasionally used by fishermen for relief from squalls. The Hound was closing on them, and Jo saw something winking from its port side pylon. "Incoming!" she shouted. To their terrified passengers, she yelled in Mandarin, "Get down!"

The Chinese helicopter was perhaps half a kilometer behind them when it started firing. Jo couldn't hear the sound of its gun over the roar of the truck engine, but she saw the dirt of the road tattooed as the shells traced their path, getting closer, closer. Jamison held his fire; the Type 56 would be useless unless the chopper got within a hundred meters or so, and by then...

The truck lurched violently to the right as the chopper's gunner stitched the road right up to where they'd been an instant before. Jamison squeezed off a burst just before the truck sideswiped a boulder on its left. There was a screech of torn metal, screams from the Chinese woman and her nephew, and the wooden half-wall above Jo shattered to splinters. Covering her head, she caught a glimpse of the helicopter roaring overhead and peeling off to its right, preparing to come around for another run. The truck shuddered to a stop.

"Everybody out!" One of the Taiwanese marines was leaning over the buckled sidewall of the truck, grabbing at Madame Zhi. Jo looked back and saw that the other marine was slumped over the steering wheel.

Jamison was firing at the chopper, and Jo thought she saw blinks of ricochets on its metal side as the agent found his target. Jo helped Madame Zhi over the side, then her nephew. "Here he comes!" Jamison shouted over the chattering of his weapon.

Jo knew her only chance was to get out and find cover in the rocks. Where were the SBS men? Had they taken the boat back out to sea, or been captured already? If they were gone, Jo's little party was finished. "Come on, Brian!" she yelled at the MI-6 man.

"Get under cover!" he shouted back at her. "Bastards aren't taking me again!" He took aim and squeezed off another burst as the Hound began its run, coming in at treetop level. Its gun started winking and this time Jo could hear its harsh clattering. She levered herself over the top of the truck bed's wall and onto the ground. The marine and the civilians were huddled behind a large rock, and the marine had his MP-5 submachine gun out and aimed at the incoming helo, but held his fire, conserving his valuable nine-millimeter ammunition until the target got much closer.

The Hound jinked from side to side to avoid the fire from the ground, throwing its own aim off a bit. The chopper was perhaps two hundred meters off. Jo thanked God that it was lightly armed, with no air-to-surface rockets. But still, when it got closer, its heavier machine gun would overwhelm them. She scrambled behind the rocks, looking down at the cove where the British commandos should've been waiting.

Bullets were slamming into the truck and off the boulder, forcing the Taiwanese to pull back and hunker down. Jamison was still firing from inside the box, using its pitiful cover. With the light weapons they had, she doubted they'd be able to bring down the chopper.

Twenty meters away toward the cove, Jo saw a solitary figure rise up and bring a weapon to bear. Faster than her eye could follow, a rocket leaped out of the man's launcher. A Stinger missile. Jo barely had time to turn her head and follow its flight before it slammed into the Hound and exploded. She dove to the ground and covered her head. The helicopter seemed to bellow like a prehistoric beast as it broke apart and crashed, hurling pieces of itself in all directions. Jo felt something thump into the rock just above her head. She opened her eyes enough to see a bloody hand lying on the ground two feet away. She swallowed and looked away.

Seconds later, she heard no more sounds of anything falling; instead, she heard the crackling of the fire consuming what was left of the helicopter, the crying of Madame Zhi, and the sound of boots scrambling over rocks, coming toward them. She struggled to her feet, keeping the pistol ready.

"Anybody hurt?" The British-accented English came from a man dressed entirely in black as he ran across the rocky ground toward them, his Uzi submachine gun at the ready. It was Colour Sergeant Powers, one of the two SBS commandos she'd left behind only what, twelve hours ago? They'd put her and the Taiwanese marines ashore just before dawn, then returned to their ship. Thankfully, they were able to keep the rendezvous for extraction; there'd been the possibility that harassment from Chinese naval units might delay them. Jo was never so glad to hear a voice in her life, but she knew they weren't safe yet.

"Check the men in the truck," she said. "We have two civilians. I'll take care of them."

"I'm all right," Jamison shouted. Jo turned and saw him, half falling out of the bed of the truck. Blood was seeping through a cut in one sleeve of Sergeant Lu's ill-fitting green PLA tunic.

"Have you been hit, sir?" Powers said, running to the agent.

"Just a crease, I believe. Check the bloke at the wheel."

The marine who had made it out of the truck was already at the open driver's door. Jo saw the grimace on the man's grimy face and knew the other marine was dead. "Here, now, let me give you a hand," Powers said gently. The British sailor and Taiwanese marine, men who had grown up half a world apart, then united for a brief time on this mission, began to work together wordlessly in a task dreaded by soldiers throughout history. Somewhere, a mother would want to grieve over her son's body, and his comrades would risk their own lives to make sure she would get that chance.

Madame Zhi and her nephew had recovered themselves enough to be able to walk. Jo began helping them over the rocks toward the cove. The other SBS commando came up to help them. "Glad to see you, Captain Geary," he said, addressing Jo by her U.S. Air Force rank.

"Not as glad as I am to see you, Lieutenant Smythe," she answered. "We have three passengers to take back with us."

"Colonel Jamison?"

"He's all right, but he'll need medical attention on the ship."

"He'll get it. Come along then, folks."

"Lieutenant," Jo said, "the Chinese put two Hounds in the air. If the one you shot down managed to get off a radio report of the pursuit, his partner will be here soon. Any more Stingers?"

"'Fraid not, Captain. It'll have to be small arms till we're out at sea."

"I'll use your radio and see if we can get some help."

"Capital idea. Okay, folks, nice and easy now," the lieutenant said to the Chinese as he helped them down to the black Zodiac boat, bobbing at the shoreline.

The boat was designed to hold a squad of fully-loaded commandos, so Jo had no doubt about its ability to handle her party of eight, including the body of the dead marine. Even though Jamison technically outranked her, she was in overall command of the mission. She had a lot to do and a short time in which to do it.

"Powers, let's get everyone aboard on the double!" she shouted to the SBS sergeant, who was helping Jamison down the stone-strewn slope to the shoreline. The Taiwanese marine, kneeling near his comrade's body, crouched at the top of the slope, waiting for Powers to return. The marine was a professional, though, and instead of watching the Englishmen, he kept his eyes turned inland, his weapon at the ready.

"Lieutenant, prepare to shove off the moment everyone's on board," she ordered.

"Aye, ma'am. Radio's in the box."

Scuttling to the middle of the boat, Jo flipped open the waterproof box and turned on the radio transceiver, pulling the antenna upward with one hand as she worked the

42

controls with the other. Finding the approved frequency, she held one earphone to her left ear and keyed the mike. "Dog Pound, this is Golden Retriever. Do you copy?"

A British voice crackled in her headphone. *"Golden Retriever, this is Dog Pound, we copy you five by five. What is your situation?"*

"Retriever has the prize, plus two souls. We have one KIA. The rooster is awake. I repeat, the rooster is awake."

"I copy, rooster is awake, we will have a chicken hawk at the ready, sent from Coop Two."

"Our ETA is approx one-five minutes. Retriever out."

Three kilometers out to sea, the Royal Navy destroyer HMS *Cambridge* was waiting for them, and its radio operator was now alerting the frigate HMS *Cumberland*, some ten klicks further out, to put its helicopter in the air to support the extraction. *Cumberland*'s Lynx Mk7 helo could reach them in minutes. *Cambridge* normally carried a similar helicopter, but the quick deployment for this mission had caught it in the middle of extensive repairs. Fortunately for Jo's team, *Cumberland* was in the area and its helo was fully operational. That additional distance would mean they'd be without air cover for an extra few minutes, though. She had to hope the other Chinese Hound would give them that time, but she had a feeling it wouldn't.

"All aboard, Cap'n," Smythe said as he scrambled past her to the stern. "Everything okay back at the pound?"

"Help is on the way," she said.

"Right, then." Smythe pulled the crank on the Zodiac's small but powerful outboard motor, and it purred to life. "Shove off!" Powers pushed the boat off the rocks and leaped over the bow as Smythe's outboard bit into the water and began pulling them out to sea. "Hang on!" Smythe shifted the motor into forward, pushed the tiller hard to the right and twisted the throttle to full open. The boat swung sharply to port and headed out to sea, waves crashing into them as they challenged the cold surf.

Jo knew that the boat's top speed might be twenty-five knots, perhaps thirty, but that was with a light load over calm seas. Now they'd be lucky to get twenty knots; struggling with the math, she estimated at least five minutes' travel time to *Cambridge*. What was the top speed of the Lynx? Something around 180 knots; if the helo's pilot had a decent fix on their position, he might be able to give them cover just before they reached the ship. So for a minute or two, they'd be on their own.

Where was that second Hound?

"What have they got in the air?" Smythe had to shout the question at her, even though he was only three feet away.

"One other H-5, like the one you brought down," she yelled back. "They might be able to scramble one or two more."

"Anything from the mainland?"

"Don't know." The nearest PLA Air Force base was about thirty klicks away. Jo knew from her hastily prepared briefing that the base was a mid-sized field that had a full squadron of F-6 fighter jets. She wasn't worried too much about those; by the time the elephantine PLA bureaucracy figured things out and launched the fast movers, they'd be safely aboard *Cambridge* and in international waters to boot. No local Chinese general would risk an attack on a British warship on the high seas unless he received direct orders from Beijing.

There was one other possibility, though—and it depended on whether any PLA Navy units were in the area, and if the base C.O. could cut through the red tape quickly enough to get a ship vectored their way. She was more worried about the remaining Hound.

For good reason. "Incoming!" Powers screamed.

The second Hound had found them, no doubt helped by the funeral pyre of its companion. Now it was coming for them, still half a mile away but closing, only a hundred feet above the waves. The helicopter's machine gun started to wink.

"Evasive action, Lieutenant!" Jo yelled. Smythe yanked the tiller, and the Zodiac yawed to starboard, breaching a wave and spraying everyone aboard. The Hound kept tracking them, and Smythe cut to port, but not too sharply, not wanting to risk the boat getting swamped. Sitting near the bow, Powers opened up with his Uzi, joined shortly by the marine with his heavier MP-5 and then Jamison with his Type 56. The Chinese weapon loosed a short burst before running out of ammunition. The MI-6 agent tossed the useless gun into the ocean. Jo picked up Smythe's Uzi and tried to aim, almost an impossible task considering the Zodiac's violent turns and the heaving of the swells, combined with the Hound's maneuvering. She knew they'd have to be extremely lucky to bring effective fire on their target. The Hound's gunner, though, would have a much easier task.

"The ship!" The Taiwanese marine's yell tore everyone's attention away from the pursuing helicopter, if only long enough to see *Cambridge*'s murky outline on the horizon. So close. Jo turned back and fired another volley at the Chinese chopper.

The Hound veered off suddenly, and Jo wondered for a moment if she'd managed to score a hit. The thought was barely formed when she heard a ferocious ripping sound from overhead. Arrows of light flashed toward the Chinese chopper. Tracer bullets!

An instant later, the British Lynx swept past them, its Rolls Royce turbine engines screaming. The Chinese pilot had no stomach for this kind of fight, and the Hound turned back to the island, heading off at top speed, chased by yells of triumph and relief from the boat. "Cheeky bugger wanted no part of our lads up there!" Smythe shouted, laughing. "Could've put a missile up that Chinaman's arse anytime he wanted."

She knew the Lynx pilot had to be under orders not to bring him down unless challenged. The British were willing to do just about anything to get their valuable agent back, but a full-scale military incident was probably a bit much for them.

The Chinese, though, thought otherwise. A minute after the Hound's departure, the Zodiac was within a few hundred meters of *Cambridge* when the orbiting Lynx turned quickly to the northwest. Jo followed it with anxious eyes, and then saw the dark shape of the oncoming ship against the graying horizon. There was a flash from the ship. "Incoming!"

The shell landed fifty meters ahead of them, sending a geyser high into the gloom. Smythe jerked the tiller, nearly pitching the exhausted Jamison overboard but for the grasping hands of the Taiwanese marine and Powers. Jo lost sight of the Lynx as it closed on the Chinese gunboat and fired a stream of tracers across its bow.

"What kind of ship?" Jo yelled at Smythe, whose smile of confidence had disappeared.

"Probably a *Swatow*-class gunboat," he said. "Forty knots, top speed. Six machine guns, no torpedoes."

"That was no machine gun round!"

"Right. They must've mounted some sort of heavy mortar on board. They'll be very lucky to get us, but they could raise bloody hell for *Cambridge*."

The Chinese gunboat ignored the Lynx's warning and kept coming on an intercept course. Were they in international waters? Jo knew the Chinese frequently claimed much more than the standard two-mile limit. That would be something for the diplomats to sort out, if it came to that. She had greater concerns now, though, as the sleek gray lines of the British destroyer crept ever closer.

"I'm gonna make a run for the ship!" Smythe yelled as he straightened the tiller and twisted the wide-open throttle, trying to urge every last bit of horsepower from the overworked little outboard. "She's making about three knots! I'll try to get around her stern, get some cover!"

They were close enough now to see men running on *Cambridge*'s deck. Some looked to be readying a boat to be dropped. The ship was steaming roughly north-northeast, putting the Chinese gunboat about fifteen degrees off its port bow. Jo saw the four-and-a-half-inch gun of the destroyer's forward battery swing to port, coming to bear on the gunboat.

The Chinese gunners sent a volley of machine gun fire toward the Lynx, which veered violently to its left to avoid being hit. Another shell leaped from the Swatow's mortar, crashing into the sea only thirty meters from the Zodiac. The

Chinese gunner was deft, putting his shell in between the Zodiac its mother ship. Smythe instinctively turned the boat to starboard. Cambridge's forward battery opened fire with a violent crack, and Jo saw a geyser of flame and water erupt only twenty meters from the gunboat's port bow, an astonishing display of gunnery.

The destroyer's marksmanship had the desired effect. The Swatow ceased fire on the prowling Lynx and slowed. The British were probably sending warnings to its skipper by radio, punctuating the message with the gunfire. A semaphore light blinked from the destroyer's deck. "Bring us around to starboard!" Powers yelled from the bow of the Zodiac.

Only a hundred meters away from the protective shield of the ship, Smythe turned the Zodiac slightly to starboard, swinging it around well to the stern of the destroyer. Jo's last glimpse of the frustrated Chinese gunboat revealed it turning away to the west. Its skipper would have a lot of explaining to do, but probably not so much as if he had decided to engage a British warship in what surely would've been a short fight. For the first time in what seemed like days, Jo felt herself starting to relax.

Smythe expertly maneuvered the Zodiac toward *Cambridge*'s starboard rear quarter where a pair of rope ladders had been hung down from the deck. A sailor yelled something, and then another device came down, swaying next to the ladders. Jo saw it was a breech's buoy, a rope-and-wood chair.

The destroyer's skipper had ordered his engines to all stop, but the momentum of the ship was still carrying her forward at a couple knots' speed. Smythe had no trouble matching that as he brought the game little Zodiac boat alongside at the ladders. Powers grabbed hold of the breech's buoy. "You're up first, m'lady," he said gallantly to Madame Zhi, who gripped his hand and allowed herself to be hoisted into the seat and strapped in. Powers gave a signal to the sailors on the deck above and they hauled the Chinese woman quickly upward.

"Let's get the lad off next," Smythe said behind Jo, who had forgotten for a moment that she was still in command.

"Of course," she said, turning to the SBS commando. "Well done, lieutenant. You brought us home."

A smile creased his face, splitting the dark camouflage paint. "Wouldn't do to have the Yanks upset at us for losing one of their best, now, would it?"

"No, I suppose not." She was about to say more, but a torrent of shrill Mandarin came from the side of the boat.

Madame Zhi's nephew had panicked, struggling with Powers as the sergeant tried to get him into the chair. A British marine—Jo thought it looked like an officer—was coming down the near ladder to lend a hand. Jo crabbed forward in the boat. "It's all right!" she yelled to the youngster. "You'll be fine!"

"No! No!" The boy kicked out at Powers, who avoided the first blow but not the second, taking it on his left shoulder. He fell back down into the Zodiac with a grunt. The boy was halfway onto the small platform of the chair, eyes wild, and Jo reached for him as he tried to slide out of the chair back into the boat. Jo grabbed a wrist as the boy came out, but the swaying of the lift brought him a bit too far forward, and he bounced off the hard rubber bow of the Zodiac and flipped into the sea, pulling Jo after him.

The shock of the cold water numbed her, even though she'd been drenched with spray during their wild ride from the island. It was pitch black, and Jo fought against panic as she tried to gain some measure of control and stop her descent. She felt the boy's flailing arms crash into her, and then one clamped around her neck, followed by the other. She gagged, forcing out some of the precious air she'd been able to inhale before going in.

Jo's underwater training came back to her, and she quickly pried one arm loose by pinching the ulnar nerve at the elbow. But the training was so long ago, and she was so tired and it was so cold...The boy thrashed with his suddenly useless arm but locked the other even tighter around Jo's neck. She felt her lungs about to burst, and then came a sharp blow on her head that made everything even blacker than before.

CHAPTER THREE

Estancia Valhalla, Argentina

November 1981

They seemed nearly without end. *La pampas*, the natives called them, the prairies stretching so many kilometers to the west, to the foothills of the distant and invisible Andes. The man gazing upon them now, from the veranda outside his office, knew them by that name, but also by another, seemingly less elegant name: *die Steppen*. His father's name for the vastness, and the son knew that name, but also the native name, because in truth he was a man of two cultures, and many days, like today, he felt them pulling him this way, then that.

For perhaps the thousandth time, he wondered if it was it like this when his father and fellow countrymen first pushed eastward from occupied Poland, forty years ago, into Russia. As they looked upon it from their airplanes, their tank turrets, their troop trucks, were they awed by the vastness, by the challenge before them? No. They would have gone forward with apprehension, certainly, but tempered with the iron discipline of their race and profession, the confidence bred by years of triumph, and the admonition of their superiors that only inferior peoples stood between them and a victory unmatched in their nation's history.

He looked down at the cognac swirling in his glass. Ah, but if they had only succeeded, he wouldn't be here now. Where would he be? Perhaps in that very place now, enjoying the new *Lebensraum* bought with blood by his father's generation, the living space seized from the subhuman Slavs and their Jewish masters. An industrialist, with factories belching smoke around the clock and churning out ever more tanks and planes and ships, or maybe consumer goods for the people whose sacrifices had made it all possible. Yes, they would be driving his Volkswagens along mighty *Autobahnen* stretching from the Urals to the Pyrenees.

Or maybe he would be a landowner, with thousands of hectares under his dominion, breeding horses and cattle, and people would give him the title of *Freiherr*, even if such appellations were archaic in modern times. He liked the sound of it, though. Baron Wilhelm von Baumann. It had a ring to it, as the Americans would say, especially when he added the formal *von*.

Yet he also liked the sound of *el jefe*, the chief, the title used by many of his native employees when they spoke to him. When he gazed out over the lands his father had amassed, and which would someday be his own—were his already, in all but name—he felt a fierce sense of pride. The call of the pampas was strong, and even now he felt his heart race from the memory of his powerful horse beneath him as they thundered across the prairie, the hot bloodlust that gripped him when he watched the *señoritas* dance the *chacarera*, even the pleasant tug of lethargy when he saw someone taking an afternoon siesta or talking about putting something off till *mañana*.

His mixed heritage could be a blessing or a curse, and sometimes he wavered between the extremes by the day, even by the hour. More often, he felt it was a curse. He knew, for instance, that if his father's cause had been victorious, he never would've been able to take his wife back to his homeland. Although Anna Baumann's heritage was primarily German, like many of her countrymen, it was not purely Aryan. She would have been considered below his station, and her Spanish blood might have caused her to be considered little better than a common Gypsy.

And with a shudder, he remembered what had happened to those people.

No. While he appreciated the charms of his mother's heritage, the benefits of living in the country in which he had been born, he had always identified more with his father. Like most of his expatriate countrymen, Dieter had sought a wife with strong German roots, and almost without exception the children, especially the males, were raised in their fathers' culture. A culture that had produced a warrior class so proud, so mighty, that their nation had come close to capturing the world.

But they had failed. No, that wasn't quite true, he thought, remembering his reading, and the stories told by his father and his Kameraden, of heroism on the battlefield undone by political bunglers back home, fools who had snatched defeat from the jaws of victory even as the soldiers could see the onion-shaped domes of the enemy's capital. Bunglers...idiots...some of the milder words he'd heard from the Kameraden about those dark days. And yet, weren't some of those same men among the very group who had made those disastrous decisions? Willy knew from his reading that must be so, yet it had never been spoken of. Not for the first time, he wondered about that, about where the truth really lay.

In any event, he was here, on a warm November day, so many thousands of kilometers from where he sometimes felt should be: in the land of his father's birth, on the continent that should be his now, his and his generation's. Instead they had this one. A beautiful and bountiful land, to be sure, but with no history, no tradition. A land where Stone Age savages had built a semblance of civilization, but one so weak it would be swept away by a few hundred Spaniards on horseback. And what kind of legacy had those *conquistadores* built? Tinpot dictators who plundered the land and then hid from the people behind toy armies that wouldn't have lasted five minutes in the field against the *Wehrmacht*.

The glass door creaked open behind him, and he heard the tapping of his father's cane, the shuffling of the slippered feet upon the wood. He turned to face the old man. "Hello, Father," he said with genuine respect. Germany's defeat had not been caused by men like Dieter Baumann, who shed his blood on the steppes of Russia and then came to this foreign land to work tirelessly for the Fatherland.

"*Ach*, but it is a beautiful day," his father said in his native German. He knew Spanish, of course, even spoke fluently it with a cultivated Buenos Aires accent, but within the family, and the Kameraden, it was always German. How many times during his childhood had Willy been scolded for lapsing into the language of their adopted country? He'd heard *"Sprechen sie Deutsch!"* too many times to count. "What are you drinking so early in the day?" the old man said now.

"Cognac," Willy answered. "Would you like some?"

"French goat-piss," Dieter Baumann spat. "I suppose you left the schnapps inside?"

In spite of himself, the son grinned. "I'm afraid so," he said. His hand moved to a nearby button. "I can have Ernesto bring you a glass."

The old man waved it off. "Thank you, no." He adjusted the threadbare smoking jacket around his bony shoulders and shuffled forward to the railing next to his son. "Yes, a beautiful day," he said again, hooking his cane on the railing and leaning forward, supported by his hands.

"It will be warm again," Willy said, looking outward with his father.

"After all these years, I'm still not used to it," Dieter gruffed. "Summer in the wintertime. Raising a glass and saying *'Fröhliche Weihnachten!'* during a heat wave." He shook his head, one lock of gray hair coming loose and dropping across his furrowed forehead. Dieter absent-mindedly brushed it back into place with a liver-spotted hand.

How much time does he have left, Willy wondered for the first time today. He was seventy-four now, elderly, and yet still among the youngest of the Bund's surviving founders. How many of the old men were left now? Dieter knew, certainly. Frail though his body might be, his mind was still as sharp as ever, something that couldn't be said for many of the Kameraden. Enough of them were still around and sharp enough to be firmly in charge of the Bund, Willy had to remind himself, with a touch of envy. Well, his generation's time was coming, hopefully soon.

Dieter coughed once, then again. He pulled a brilliantly-white handkerchief from the left sleeve of the smoking jacket and wiped his lips with it. "How are you feeling?" his son asked.

"Like any old man, some days fine, some days like *scheiss*," Dieter croaked. He coughed again, then barked out a laugh. "If your mother were still here, though, I could muster up enough good days to enjoy myself a bit."

Willy Baumann looked at his father in surprise. He had never heard him speak of his late wife with such lustiness. And yet, who could blame him? Anna Baumann may have been ten years in the grave by now, but her memory was still clear in the mind of her son, and undoubtedly even more so in that of her husband. She had been a beautiful woman indeed, a cultivated daughter of Argentine high society who nevertheless was called *"meine Feuerballerin"*, my fireball, by Dieter on the few occasions Willy had been witness to real intimacy between husband and wife. He could imagine what had gone on behind closed doors, though, having known a few native *fräuleins* himself.

"So, what is happening?" Dieter asked.

Willy knew that he meant the family business, and not the business they engaged in openly. The cattle, the cement works and power plants, the newspapers and radio stations, all purchased and built up over the years, the companies that made Baumann a name of influence in Argentine politics and high finance, were tended to quite efficiently by Willy now that Dieter was in retirement. So efficiently, in fact, that the family was now one of the richest in the country. No, his father was asking about the family's real business.

"Alles ist in ordnung," he answered. All is in order, a phrase that was particularly pleasing to any German's ear, no less his father's. "I spoke with Heinz by telephone an hour ago. He will be meeting with the General tomorrow to discuss the South Georgia question." The General was Roberto Viola, the current head of the junta that ruled Argentina. Heinz Nagel, a close friend of Willy's, was the Bund's chief operative in Buenos Aires and its main contact with the junta.

"What does Heinz think?"

"He believes the general will be agreeable to our timetable," Willy said carefully. In truth, Heinz was certain that Viola would do exactly as he was told, but as always, Willy wanted to be cautious. They had not gotten this far by being reckless.

Dieter nodded, and Willy could almost hear the gears turning inside. His father had been in this country more than forty years now, and knew its people better than any of the other German expatriates ever would. After all, he'd had the ear of Juan Perón himself, and were it not for his father's tireless dedication to the cause, Project CAPRICORN never would have happened. And now, after all the years, all the work, all the danger and intrigue, they were so close...

"Make sure to inform the Reichsleiter as soon as you have confirmation from Heinz," Dieter said firmly.

"Of course," Willy said, automatically glancing around to see if any servants were present. Only among select members of the Bund was the word "Reichsleiter" even uttered; it appeared nowhere on any correspondence, could be found in no file. The Reichsleiter's real name was even more of a secret. Dieter knew it, of course, and so did Willy, but beyond the two of them, how many knew the true identity of their leader? Twenty? Thirty? Certainly not many more. It was the Bund's most coveted secret. If the man's existence were revealed, the Jews would go mad for revenge. Everyone remembered what had happened to Eichmann.

Even mentioning the man's title was risky, but Dieter felt secure enough here, on his own estate, with only his son within earshot. Dieter had taught his son early to be very careful in trusting anyone. The Bund's success, indeed its very survival, depended on its true nature being kept secret from the outside world. Even their Argentine hosts had no real idea, although some of the higher-placed and smarter ones undoubtedly suspected. If any did, though, they wisely kept quiet. The Bund had been active on this continent for nearly four decades, and its reach was long.

"Assuming the general is as agreeable as Heinz believes he will be," Dieter said, "when will we move on South Georgia?"

"March," Willy answered at once. Anticipating his father's next question, he said, "The Malvinas in April."

"And the *Englandern*?"

"They have one ship still in these waters, HMS *Endurance,* a destroyer. Their Admiralty is in the process of reducing their fleet and our contact in London predicts the ship will be recalled early in the New Year."

"The fools," Dieter said. "The South Georgia occupation will come after that?"

"We will set our date and move then, whether or not the ship is still on station," Willy said confidently. "The very same ship was on station when we took South Thule in 1976, and the English did nothing."

"They will do something when the Malvinas fall," Dieter said, once again using the Argentine name for the islands the English knew as the Falklands.

"Let us hope so," Willy said. "Sometime around late May, we think." It was ironic, really. If they waited to seize the islands in late May, just before the onset of the brutal South Atlantic winter, the operation would be a tactical success but a strategic failure. The Argentines were almost fanatically focused on regaining control of the islands they'd lost to the English over a century before, but they weren't stupid. Capturing the islands just before winter would keep the Royal Navy out of the fight for months, and by then the doves in the British government would have taken over. They would push for a negotiated settlement of the issue. Somehow, the junta had to be persuaded to move early enough to make sure the English would have enough time to send their fleet. That would take some delicate maneuvering on the part of the Bund, but Heinz was confident it could be done. Willy trusted his friend's instincts, but there was a contingency plan in case the junta decided to wait.

The old man grunted. "Six months from now," he said. "I hope I will live to see it."

Surprising himself, Willy reached out and touched his father's arm. "You will," he said, emotion making his voice a bit husky.

Dieter nodded, his lips a thin smile. "You are a good son, Willy. So good that I don't have to ask you if everything is going well at Pilcaniyeu."

"We are ahead of schedule there, Father," Willy said with a touch of pride. The Bund had entrusted the Baumanns with this most vital part of the project, thanks to the family's experience in the energy industry, not to mention Dieter's influence within the upper hierarchy and his political contacts back in what was left of the Fatherland. It was said the Reichsleiter himself had anointed the elder Baumann with this responsibility some fifteen years ago.

Dieter nodded again. "When the Union Jack is lowered over the Malvinas, their hag of a prime minister will assemble her fleet and send it south," he said.

"She will have to," Willy said, "or her government will fall. Then her successor will do it anyway."

"She'll do it," Dieter said confidently. "She will want to show she has *die Hoden* of a man." That brought a laugh from his son, knowing from his own reading that Margaret Thatcher's opponents already suspected she might somehow have had testicles surgically attached.

"When their fleet arrives, we shall be ready, Father, that I can promise you."

Dieter Baumann looked at his son, and his gray eyes were as hard and cold as Willy had ever seen them. "We had better be," he said. "Seven million Germans gave their lives in the last war. We must ensure they did not die in vain."

The shrilling of the telephone interrupted the moment. The two men looked out at the land in silence for a minute, until Ernesto cleared his throat behind them. "Pardon me, Herr *Oberst*," he said in fluent German, using Willy's military rank of colonel. "There is an urgent telephone call for you from Buenos Aires."

"Thank you," Willy said. He walked quickly past the Argentine butler into the office. Five minutes later, he returned to his father's side.

"What is it?" the old man asked. He squinted at his son. "What has happened?"

"That was Heinz," Willy said. "General Viola has suffered a heart attack."

Dieter slammed his cane on the wooden deck. "Scheiss!"

•

CHAPTER FOUR

Lamma Island, Hong Kong
November 1981

"You know, I'd be happy to take you to a nicer place."

Jo Ann smiled across the table at her escort. "This is fine," she said. "I've been told the food here is excellent."

"Perhaps, but the atmosphere is somewhat...rustic." Major Ian Masters was possessed of a fine wit, as Jo had already discovered. "The Royal Navy is rather parsimonious, but I can certainly afford something a bit more, shall we say, upscale?"

"Nonsense," Jo said. "Besides, it's my treat. You did say I could buy you dinner, remember?"

"Indeed," he said. "Well, all right, then. At least the view is nice."

Like most Chinese restaurants in Hong Kong, the Han Lok Yuen was Spartan when it came to its accommodations.

The inside dining room had a few tables but little else; out here, on the veranda, there were twice as many tables, and even though they were equipped as sparely as those inside—four plain chairs, white tablecloth, simple settings—the view of this part of Lamma Island and the inner islands was spectacular, especially on this warm evening. The sun was about an hour away from dipping below the hills of Lantau Island to the west. To the northeast was Hong Kong Island, with the lights of Aberdeen beginning to flicker on; the larger city of Hong Kong was hidden from them, on the other side of Victoria Peak, but its lights, and those of Kowloon just across the bay to the north, would provide a sensuous glow on the northern horizon if they stayed past sunset.

The other tables were filling up quickly. Waiters scurried to and fro, speaking English to most of the customers, Chinese to each other. Jo had been right to suggest they arrive early. Their boat had deposited them at the Yung Shue Wan dock, leaving them with a nice fifteen-minute walk to the restaurant. "When we go back, we'll take a different path," she said.

"We will?"

"I was told the walk to the Sok Kwo Wan dock is very scenic. It's also a bit longer. About an hour."

Masters raised an eyebrow. "If you insist," he said, but he was smiling.

A waiter appeared at their table and Jo ordered in Chinese: lettuce cups with minced quail, then roasted squab served with fried rice on the side and a pot of strong tea. "I'll have what the lady is having," Masters said in English. The boy nodded and rushed away. "I'm sure I'll enjoy it, whatever it is," he said with a wry grin.

63

"Ian, you said you've been in Hong Kong several times. You don't always eat aboard your ship, do you?"

"No, but it's not that often a lady offers to buy me dinner ashore," he said as he spread his cloth napkin on his lap.

"It's probably not very often you save a lady's life," she said with a smile, suppressing the shudder she felt at the memory of being pulled down, down, into the dark and cold water. She hadn't seen him dive in from his perch on the rope ladder, hadn't felt his hand grasp her hair and keep her from sinking, long enough for another marine—Sergeant Powers, she'd been told—to pry the arms of Madame Zhi's nephew from around her shoulders. Masters hauled her to the surface, unconscious by then, while Powers followed with the luckless nephew. Other marines and sailors got her aboard *Cambridge* and a medical corpsman quickly revived her. A half-hour later, she awakened in the ship's sick bay, and was told the story of her rescue.

"I just happened to be in the right place at the right time," he said with false modesty. In the past week, Jo had heard plenty of stories about this particular Royal Marines officer. Which ones were true, well, that she'd have to find out.

Their first course was served. The lettuce with quail was excellent, and the main course arrived in due time. "Now, there's no real delicate way to eat squab," she said.

"And so the indelicate way prevails?"

"Yes, just dig in," she said, and demonstrated by picking up the bird and taking a bite. The succulent juices started running down her chin, and she quickly lapped at it with her napkin. Ian followed suit, leaning forward quickly to keep a squirt of juice from reaching his sport jacket. "Nicely done, Major," she said.

"Rather like a Cornish game hen," he said. "Tastier, though. Quite delicious, in fact."

They weren't able to talk much as they finished the squab, washing it down with tea. But there was plenty of laughter as they negotiated the birds and managed to finish them off without spotting their clothing. Their waiter appeared within seconds after they completed the main course. "Dessert, please?"

Jo had an idea, and ordered in Chinese again. "What is it this time?" Ian asked.

"A surprise," she said as the waiter bowed and hustled toward the kitchen with their plates and the remains of the squab.

Ian leaned forward on the table and fixed his lustrous blue eyes on Jo. "This entire evening has been a very pleasant surprise," he said.

She leaned forward on her elbows also, bringing her face within a foot or so of his. "It has?"

"Yes," he said. "I didn't quite know what to expect when I accepted your invitation." His voice lowered a tone, and his face came another inch toward hers. "Americans are fairly unpredictable, you see."

"Oh, really? But do I seem like a typical American to you?" Subconsciously, she had lowered her voice and leaned forward, too.

"Indeed not," he said. The table wasn't really that wide, and if they both leaned forward a little bit more, their lips would touch...

"Dessert!"

The waiter was back, with two bowls of vanilla ice cream, topped with chocolate syrup, a dab of whipped cream and a cherry. Jo and Ian sat back in their chairs as the waiter set the bowls in front of them. Jo was disappointed that their moment had been lost, but felt fairly sure they'd have another chance.

"Well, what's this, now?" Ian said, mock sternness in his voice.

"Don't tell me you don't have ice cream sundaes where you come from," Jo teased. She dipped into her sundae with a spoon and took a succulent bite.

"Of course," he said. He shoveled in a large spoonful. "Oh, my", he said, barely able to get the words out. Another spoonful followed. He looked at her, eyes twinkling, and winked.

The hike to Sok Kwo Wan dock was as scenic as had been promised. The sunset was spectacular, silhouetting Lantau Island to their west, across the West Lamma Channel. Their ferry ride back to Hong Kong would be longer, but it was a pleasant evening and seas were light.

Jo Ann's hand found Ian's as they negotiated the twisting path through the rocks and trees. She feigned stumbling and grabbed hold of him, and he didn't let go. "Good thing we're not trying this in full darkness," he said. The path was not lighted, and the moon wouldn't be up for another couple hours.

"Normally I'm fairly agile," she said. "That one got me, though."

"Well, we'll do our best to keep from a repetition." He squeezed her hand.

She'd learned a little bit more about him over dinner. He was from Cornwall, in the extreme southwest of England, middle-class family, his father a World War II Army officer who'd survived the beaches of Normandy. Ian went off to join the Royal Marines at eighteen, made officer within two years, and by twenty-five had worked his way into Special Boat Squadron. He was thirty-three now, just two years older than Jo.

"You've never married?" she asked.

"Came close once or twice," he said. "Ultimately, neither of them wanted a husband who'd rarely be around. They wanted home and hearth, children, all that."

"Not a bad life," she said.

"True, but not what I was looking for at the time. Perhaps later." She could certainly understand why a woman would want to marry him. Not particularly tall, maybe about six feet, but strikingly good-looking, resembling an actor she'd seen recently, a British actor in a movie...what was it?

They passed another couple sitting on a bench, watching the sunset. Ian nodded to the man, a Caucasian, while his Asian companion pointed out something to the west. An airliner, lights flashing, was coming in to land at Hong Kong Airport, on the other side of Lantau Island.

"He's an officer aboard *Cumberland*," Ian told Jo when they'd passed out of earshot of the couple. "We've worked together once or twice."

David J. Tindell

A few minutes later, they came to another bench, this one unoccupied. "Do we have some time for a break?" he asked.

Jo checked her wristwatch. The ferry was due an hour from now, and they were about halfway there, so she figured they could spare about fifteen minutes. "Yes," she said, leading him to the bench.

"You're quite the one for precision, aren't you?" he asked after they'd sat down. The evening was beginning to get a bit chilly, and she sat closely against him; his arm found its way around her shoulders.

"I have to be, in my line of work," she said.

"Ah, yes, now what is it, commando, secret agent?"

She looked up at him, and the dying sunlight twinkled in his eyes. "Maybe a little bit of both," she said. "I'm sure you've already had a look at my jacket." Her USAF personnel file had surely found its way to Ian's commanding officer, who put together the rescue mission.

"Well, I am the ranking Royal Marine aboard," he said. "Let's see...a rather interesting childhood and adolescence, going hither and yon with your parents, then college at Stanford, graduate school at your Air Force Academy. When did you join the military, exactly?"

"I was an Air Force ROTC cadet at Stanford," she said. "I went on active duty as a second lieutenant after graduation. Got my master's in international relations at Colorado Springs."

"International relations. Based on the course of our evening so far, you know your stuff." Jo gave him a playful elbow in the ribs. "Ow," he said, feigning pain. "I must be more careful, since I read you are also somewhat of a martial arts expert."

She laughed. "I've studied tae kwon do for several years. That's a Korean martial art, and when we lived in Japan I also studied naginata. Since then I've picked up some things from other arts—a little judo, *kung fu*."

"Really? Kung fu, as in the movies?"

"Kung fu as in the ancient Chinese martial art, developed by the Shaolin monks," she said. "But during my college days I did study it under Bruce Lee in Oakland."

"*The* Bruce Lee?"

"Yes," she said, remembering the incredibly-fit, incredibly-intense yet kind and patient man who had instructed her at his *jeet kune do* academy for nearly a year. Like anyone who visited Hong Kong, Masters must have seen Lee's picture on magazine covers at every newsstand; even now, eight years after his death, Lee was an icon in his native city. "It was quite an experience."

"I'm sure it was."

They watched the sunset for a few minutes. It was brilliant this evening, and even though Jo had seen many memorable ones in the States, somehow seeing one in the Orient made it all the more exotic. She sighed.

"Penny for your thoughts?" Masters asked.

"Oh, I was just thinking about my mother. She always likes the sunsets, but only if they're here, in the East. She never really enjoyed them in America."

"Your family, they emigrated to the States?"

"No," she said. "My father is an American, my mother is Korean."

"Well, that explains your looks," he said. He turned to her, and she looked up at him. "I've never really met anyone like you, Jo Ann Geary. I'd like to get to know you better."

"I think that's entirely possible," she answered, and their lips met.

CHAPTER FIVE

Hong Kong
November 1981

Sunlight was just starting to seep underneath the drawn curtains of the bedroom. The bedside clock radio glowed 5:53, and Jo Ann, fully awake now, slipped silently out of bed. After using the bathroom, she found her panties on the bedroom floor and stepped into them.

Ian stirred and turned over, facing the still-warm spot where she'd lain, but he didn't awaken. Smiling, Jo went into the living room of the hotel suite, carefully closing the bedroom door behind her.

She went to a window and drew the curtains back just enough to see the cityscape beyond the glass. The great city was waking up, many of its millions already hard at work in the streets below. A few blocks away, the Union Jack fluttered over the Government Building. Jo thought sixteen years ahead, when the red banner of the People's Republic would replace it. How would the city change then? Well, she would have to come back and find out.

For now, this was the last morning of her first visit to Hong Kong; her flight to Tokyo departed at noon, and she had packing and last-minute shopping to do. To business, then.

Wearing only the white panties, she sat cross-legged on the carpeted floor and assumed the lotus position. It was time to begin her daily *dan ki gong* meditation. She half-closed her eyes and started clearing her mind of unimportant details: the faint noises of the city from outside, the dim shadows of the furniture, the whisper of the air conditioning. Soon, even important things would be set aside as she focused ever more deeply on bringing in energy, the force she had come to know as ki, , from around her and merging it with her inner ki.

She visualized the ki, imagining it to be an amorphous cloud of white light above her head. Inhaling through her nose, she drew the energy into her lungs, pushing it downward with the muscles of her chest and abdomen, into her *dan jeon*, the central point of her body just below the navel. As the ki traveled further downward into her groin, an image from last night intruded: Ian's tongue, gently teasing her there, and then his hardness inside her. Allowing herself a slight smile, she banished the memory, pleasant as it was.

Still inhaling slowly, she felt the ki continue its journey, upward now along her spine, along the back of her neck—she felt the tingling—and over the top of her head. She held her breath for twenty seconds, then exhaled through her slightly parted lips and felt the ki move down the front of her face, into her nose, and then out. Taking another deep breath through the nose, she continued.

After about ten minutes, she held her breath for a full sixty seconds and exhaled for the final time of the exercise. Opening her eyes fully, she returned her breathing to normal and began moving into a series of yoga stretches. As always, she felt invigorated by the dan ki gong. Her instructor had told her that mastering it would give her greater control over stress and contribute greatly to her body's physical and mental wellness. It had to be true, since she couldn't remember the last time she'd been ill.

Midway through her yoga routine, she sensed, rather than heard, the bedroom door opening behind her. She knew it was Ian, and so she didn't automatically go into self-defense mode, but she did pay closer attention to that part of the room she couldn't see, the sounds coming from there, even the smells: a whiff of musky air from the bedroom mixing with the faintly stale air of the living room. She attuned her hearing and caught Ian's breathing, the scratch of his fingernails three times through his chest hair, the slight movement of his feet as he shifted his weight from one to the other, the even slighter sound of his shoulder coming into contact with the doorway as he leaned against it.

"Good morning," she said without turning. She was finishing the first part of the routine, a series of three poses: the child's pose, on her knees with haunches resting on her heels, arms stretching forward and palms on the floor, head bowed between her upper arms; the cobra, stretching forward with legs fully extended and then pushing her upper body upward until she was supported on her fully extended arms; and the downward-facing dog, with hands and feet flat on the floor and bending over sharply at the waist, her body forming a perfect inverted V.

From the doorway, Ian had a nice view of her posterior. "Good morning back," he said. "This is yoga?"

"Yes," Jo said, as she moved into the second half of her routine. She assumed the mountain pose, standing straight up with arms at her side. Jo told Ian the Sanskrit name, then its English equivalent, and proceeded to the next pose. "The chair pose." She squatted slightly as if sitting in an invisible chair. "The extended triangle." Stretching her legs out, she reached down to the floor with her right hand, bending at the waist, while reaching high with her left. "The warrior pose." Left leg bent at the knee nearly at a right angle, left foot pointing left, right leg stretched out, trunk facing forward, arms held straight out over the legs, head facing left. "The tree pose." Controlling her breathing, she reached both hands high overhead and brought her right foot off the floor, tucking it under her hip with the knee extending outward at a forty-five-degree angle from the left leg. She repeated the routine, this time switching sides for the last three poses.

Twice more from each side, and she was done. She drew in a deep cleansing breath, let it out slowly, and felt the ki move through her body, extending to her limbs. A slight sheen of perspiration glossed her skin. With Ian still behind her, she decided to try something. She hadn't done it for years, but maybe...Reaching straight upward, she bent herself backward at the waist, reaching over and behind her, further and further, fighting the gravity, until her fingertips touched the carpet, then her palms, and she was looking at Ian upside down, her body forming an inverted U. "Good God," he said. "I am very seriously impressed."

"That's good," she said with a gasp, "because now I need your help to get out of this."

Laughing, he came to her, holding her under her shoulders and helping her to get upright again. He was wearing only boxer shorts, and as he pulled her to him she felt how aroused he was. They kissed. He wanted more, but she gently pushed him away. "Ian, I'm sorry, but I really have to start getting ready."

"Rubbish. You said your flight's at noon. That gives us, what, five and a half hours?" He was grinning. "I outrank you, you know. I could issue an order for compliance."

"That presents some interesting possibilities," she said. "Maybe next time we're in uniform." She turned and walked toward the bedroom and the adjoining bath with its shower. Halfway there, she slipped her panties off and tossed them backward over her shoulder. She heard the very slight sound of the cloth striking flesh as Ian caught them in mid-air, and she sensed his approach, dialing down her instinctive response just in time. He swept her neatly off her feet and carried her to the bed.

***

"That leaning-back thing you did in there..."

She laughed. "Okay, but hold onto my hips," she said. "Don't break the rhythm."

It was a bit more difficult this time, with her legs tucked under her hips and Ian deep inside her, and the two of them rocking together besides, but she leaned back, supporting herself with her arms, and arched her back. To her surprise, this produced an extremely pleasant sensation, which Ian accentuated with deeper thrusts. She felt her orgasm building quickly, much more quickly than the night before, and before she could help herself she began moaning, then he shouted and heaved upward just as she reached her own zenith. She actually felt his essence erupt inside her, and they held the delicious pose for a few seconds before he slowly lowered his buttocks back onto the damp sheets, his powerful hands still clamped on her hips, and he released them as she leaned forward and lay forward on top of him. Their panting gradually slowed.

"You really must go?" he said at last.

"Yes," she said reluctantly, and the finality of it began to take on real meaning to her. Two weeks since the mission, one week since their first dinner together, and now they had just made love for the, what, fourth time? Fifth? Ian had gotten forty-eight hours' liberty, they'd spend that first night together and that was the first time, the next morning the second, and then last night after one final day together exploring Hong Kong. "I was lucky to get my leave extended, actually."

"I rather think I'm the lucky one," he said, kissing her. She met his tongue with hers, and inside her, she felt the stirrings of desire again, but deeper this time, and that voice she'd dreaded hearing: *Be careful. Remember the pain.* She pushed the voice aside and surrendered to the desire.

Three hours later, they were at the airport. Her flight would be on time, and she looked forward to the comfort of the commercial jet. In Tokyo she'd catch an Air Force cargo plane to Hawaii, another to Los Angeles, and yet another for the final leg to Hurlburt Field, Florida. The free passage on the military birds would almost make up for the Spartan conditions she'd have to tolerate. That would make the jet lag even more difficult, to say the least. Well, she'd done it before.

"I said, 'A penny for your thoughts?'"

She turned to Ian. "Sorry. Just thinking about the time changes and so forth."

They were walking down the broad aisle of the terminal toward her departure gate. She had one bag slung over her shoulder, with Ian pulling her suitcase. Back at the hotel, she'd fretted somewhat over her outfit, finally choosing the same black pin-striped pants-suit she'd worn on the flight to Singapore, only this time she wore a white tee shirt underneath. A single Chinese ideogram, which could roughly be translated as "strength", was printed in red on the chest.

Ian laughed. "You know, you're really quite remarkable."

"How do you mean?" she asked.

"Well, a few hours ago you were practicing the most elaborate yoga poses I've ever seen, with exquisite discipline. Then, of course, in bed you are, shall we say—"

"A bit less rigid?" she filled in with a grin.

"I wouldn't really call it that, because it implies you're rigid otherwise. No, I meant you're not quite like you are at other times. Like now, for instance, or earlier, when we were shopping."

They arrived at the gateway and she led them to some empty seats. "And how am I now?"

He looked away from her, gathering his thoughts, then back at her. "There's something about you," he said, looking at her intensely. "I've never been around a woman like you. And damn few men, for that matter. The Americans call it charisma. Yet you don't flaunt it, like so many do."

She sighed. She felt flattered, yet at the same time embarrassed, just a bit. "The Japanese call it *shibumi*," she said after a moment. "You could translate it to mean a sort of restrained elegance."

"And I presume this is from your martial arts training?"

She nodded. "It's the martial way, the way of the warrior," she said. "Most study the martial arts to learn how to fight, or to show off. It's much more than that. It's a way of life."

She looked back at him, and his eyes were still intense. He was trying desperately to understand her, she knew, because he cared for her so much. And how did she feel about him? She'd been in love before, and over the past couple days she'd felt the stirring deep inside her heart that heralded its coming, but she'd pushed it back with a determination that surprised her. She would not allow it back, because if it came, the inevitable pain would follow. The voice came again from within: *Remember Jimmy? Remember Franklin? It will happen again!*

But now Jo Ann felt the warmth stirring around inside her again. She reached over and touched Ian's hand. "My art of tae kwon do has five basic tenets," she said. "Courtesy, integrity, perseverance, self-control, and indomitable spirit. The tenets provide me with guidelines, with means of focusing my ki, and things like shibumi sort of naturally follow."

"They're quite effective, believe me," he said. He leaned over and kissed her. For a moment, their lips parted and his tongue sought hers, and she responded. Then she pulled away. "Something wrong?"

Eyes moist, she turned away. "I'm sorry, Ian," she said. "I'm just...just not sure where we are going." Or where she wanted it to go. Did she want to go there again? Take the risk?

His hand gripped hers. "Neither am I, but I'd certainly like to see it go somewhere. Wouldn't you?"

She blinked away a tear, surprising herself. "I don't know," she said. Why did she put herself in this position? Things had been going so well; she had her work, and her training, and her studies, and someday she would achieve her ultimate goal, a steady posting so she could get a house of her own, some cozy little rural place, with a couple of cats, and a garden. She could see the living room right now, could see Ian sitting in it, snuggling with her as they watched TV, or read together, or just talking, their lives joined....

No. She reached deep down inside, summoning her strength, and pushed the emotions away. Her discipline had kept her going, gotten her through Stanford and the Academy, through the endless hours of training, through the peril of her missions, all the way up through Fonglan Island. Discipline had kept her alive, yes—but life was more than just staying alive, wasn't it?

Discipline had also gotten her past Jimmy, and then Franklin. But they weren't over, not really; the memories were still in there, the joy and the love, then the searing pain of betrayal. She dealt with them only by ignoring them. But any time a new man came along, the memories started rustling back in their dark corner, trying to get out. She had to keep the new man from getting too close, or they'd come out and hurt her again.

She looked back at Ian. He could understand discipline, certainly. He was a warrior, too, although a Westerner, and thus different. He saved her life...and then fell in love with her. Could he ever understand why she couldn't, wouldn't allow herself to love him?

Reaching up, she touched his cheek. "Ian, I really can't explain how I feel. But I do care about you. A great deal. You must believe that."

He took her hand and kissed it. "That makes me feel better," he said. "Thought I was losing you there."

She glanced at a clock on the wall, and saw that her flight would be called in about twenty minutes. "When will you be returning to England?" she asked.

"We sail day after tomorrow," he said. "Heading east, calling in Tahiti, then Chile and around the Cape and over to the Falklands. The Admiralty apparently are a bit concerned about the Argentines. A couple days there, then likely home. A long haul, but I should be in London in about ten weeks."

"Perhaps we can see each other then," she said, surprising herself.

He smiled. "I'd like that. I'd like that a great deal, in fact." That grin, so dashing...

"*Wuthering Heights*," she said.

"What?"

"The movie," she said. "I finally remembered. You reminded me of someone, an actor in a movie. I saw it in college, in a film appreciation class. Laurence Olivier in *Wuthering Heights*."

"Oh, my," he said. "What a coincidence. I had been thinking that you resembled an actress. France Nuyen, French and Vietnamese, I believe. She played an alien warrior queen on an episode of *Star Trek.*" He laughed. "I had no idea we were so famous."

She smiled back, and this time when the stirrings came, she didn't move to stop them.

CHAPTER SIX

Buenos Aires, Argentina

December 1981

"The president will be with you in a moment, sir," the attractive secretary announced, putting her telephone back in its cradle.

"Thank you," Wilhelm Baumann said, but she was already back at her typewriter, staring at a steno pad through horn-rimmed glasses. Willy looked over at the door to the inner office, and at the stern-looking, sidearmed *suboficial* of the *Gendarmaria Nacional* standing at parade rest next to it. Besides himself, the secretary and the sergeant, there were no other people in this office, which occupied a surprisingly small section of *La Casa de Gobiermo*, the Government House, known since 1873 as *Casa Rosada,* the Pink House. Willy had never been inside the massive building, but had occasionally viewed it from Plaza de Mayo across the street, pondering its rather odd mix of styles, the result of decades of modifications by Swedish, French and Italian architects. A few times he'd been part of crowds who filled the plaza to hear a speech by the president from the building's large balcony. Dieter told him of hearing Juan Perón, and his charismatic wife Evita, speak more than once from that very stage. The current president had not yet chosen to address his people that way, although he spoke to them on nationwide television and radio shortly after assuming power. Even though he had an appointment, Willy made sure to check the flagpole on his way in; yes, the presidential banner flew underneath the Argentine colors, signaling that the president was in.

In some respects, Willy Baumann should have felt insulted. His request for an audience with General Leopoldo Fortunato Galtieri should have resulted in a personal invitation to meet him at his estate, perhaps even for a private dinner. Instead, there was this rather brusque summons to this office, in the mid-afternoon of what had turned out to be a hot December day. Another indication of how much—or how little—importance Galtieri attached to this meeting; even the lowliest Argentine bureaucrat typically would have left his office by now, especially during summer, when his unreliable air conditioner would be taxed beyond its capacity to provide tolerable working conditions indoors.

The German inside Willy Baumann forced him to shake his head at the thought. Dieter Baumann had worked from dawn to past dusk for years, and even today spent two to three hours a day on official Bund business, if his health permitted. His son had naturally grown into the same habit. The Americans would call him a workaholic, but the Baumann men were only doing what their fellow Germans had done for centuries. When there was work to be done, you did it, and there was always work to be done.

But being forced to meet Galtieri here was not a good sign. The general was definitely sending a message: the junta's relationship with the Bund was about to change. Well, that was most likely true. There had been days when the president of Argentina would present himself to the *Bundesführer* at the German's estate, and come literally with hat in hand. Perón himself had done it with the Reichsleiter back in the forties; rumor had it Perón even offered the Reichsleiter the pleasure of Evita's company for an evening, an offer that may or may not have been accepted, depending on who was telling the story. Knowing the Reichsleiter's legendary capacity for women, Willy tended to believe it. While this president, or his successor, would eventually be reminded of who was really running this country, Willy hoped things would be a bit more businesslike this time.

As he waited for his summons, Willy reviewed what he knew about Galtieri. In his fifty-sixth year, a 1949 graduate of the School of the Americas, Galtieri was in command of the Argentine Army's II Corps upon the junta's takeover in 1976. He was known as one of the more ruthless members of the high command, and had been personally in charge of one of the government's most notorious detention centers during the "Dirty War" in the late seventies. As part of the junta's campaign to eliminate dissent in the country, thousands of Argentines were arrested and imprisoned, most of them tortured, many executed, many others simply made to disappear. Willy had read one particularly chilling account of a female prisoner and her visit with Galtieri: "He asked me, 'Do you know who I am? Do you know that I have absolute power over you? If I say you live, you live. If I say you die, you die. As it happens, you have the same Christian name as my daughter, and so you live.'"

While Willy was not afraid of Galtieri, or any Argentine alive, he knew this man was not one to be trifled with. This president not only had command of the entire armed forces, but the Gendarmaria, and while that body was not nearly as formidable as Germany's *Schutzstaffel*, the dreaded SS, it could still cause no end of trouble for the Bund. So, things would have to be handled rather delicately, but firmly. Willy was grateful that Dieter had asked him to handle the meeting. The leadership of the Bund was well aware of the challenges that lay ahead, especially now that the more reliable, and recovering, Viola was out of power.

The door to Galtieri's office swung open, and the Gendarmaria sergeant snapped to attention. A man wearing the uniform of an Argentine Army infantry captain stepped out into the secretary's office, and Willy rose to his feet, automatically straightening his suit with an unobtrusive tug of the jacket.

"*Señor* Baumann," the captain said with a tinge of distaste, "*el presidente* will see you now."

"Thank you, Capitan," Willy said, nodding. He nodded also to the secretary and flashed a smile. "And to you, señorita." The captain stepped aside as Willy strode confidently into the presence of the second most powerful man on the continent.

Galtieri's office was spacious but not ostentatious. The walls were adorned with paintings from Argentine history. Willy recognized one of them, showing Manuel Belgrano at the signing of the country's Declaration of Independence in 1816. The only portrait was one of Julio Roca, the general who quashed the Indians for good in 1879 and later served twelve years as president. Roca's victory had opened the pampas for settlement by European immigrants, mostly

85

Italians and Spaniards, and not a few Germans. Galtieri, like most of his countrymen, had the blood of many nationalities flowing through his veins.

The furnishings were sparse. A sitting area to the left contained two stuffed chairs, two sofas and a coffee table. Straight ahead was a fireplace, obviously a relic of an earlier time, topped by an empty mantle. Above it hung the Roca portrait. And to the right was the desk of the president.

Galtieri stood as Willy entered the office. The general was in full Army uniform, the left breast of the jacket sagging with medals and ribbons. Willy guessed it had just been removed from the slightly swinging hanger on the nearby coat tree. Galtieri himself had a leonine head crowned by full white hair, his face tanned and lined. He was about six feet tall, close to Willy's own height. Galtieri was standing ramrod straight, but not comically so; a military man, comfortable in command. His opinion of Galtieri moved up a notch.

The captain announced him simply as "Señor Wilhelm Baumann". Willy took three steps to Galtieri's desk and came to attention, although not as rigidly as if he'd been in uniform, and bowed slightly. "*Mi* presidente, it is an honor and a privilege to be received by you," Willy said in perfect Spanish Lunfardo, the dialect common in Buenos Aires.

Galtieri did not offer his hand, but merely nodded and motioned to one of the two chairs facing his desk. "Please be seated, señor," he said in a baritone voice that was obviously accustomed to command.

Willy had been carefully prepared for this interview. His father, along with two other senior Bund members, had impressed upon him the need to show courtesy and respect, no matter what Galtieri's attitude. Forty years of dealing with

Argentine leaders, military and civilian, provided plenty of experience to draw upon. "He is accustomed to ordering people around," Dieter said. "They all are. Once they sit behind that desk they are quite full of themselves. They are convinced they will succeed where others have failed, that they will bend this country to their own will. They will fail, of course, and eventually be ousted, and we will still be here. A part of him will know this, and he will fear that knowledge. You can use that, but carefully."

"What can I do for you, Señor Baumann?" Galtieri asked, sitting back in his chair. In his right hand he gripped a fountain pen, twirling it casually.

Willy offered his most respectful smile. "Mi presidente, I have come to pay my respects to you on behalf of my father, Dieter, and the entire membership of the Siegfried Bund. I bring to you our sincere congratulations upon your accession to the presidency, and our desire to work closely with you to help build a greater Argentina for all of us."

Galtieri smiled. "You Germans. You are, as the Americans say, full of shit."

Willy blinked, but didn't lose his smile. "I beg your pardon, sir?"

The pen kept twirling. "So you come here representing the Siegfried Bund," the general said. "Dieter Baumann saw fit to send his boy to meet with me, did he?"

Willy's smile narrowed. "My father sends his regrets that he cannot attend personally. He is not in the best of health."

"So I have heard," Galtieri said. "Perhaps if my good friend General Viola were in this chair, Dieter might have been healthy enough. But there are others who might have come, from the Old Guard. Perhaps even your Reichsleiter. But then, he does not travel much, does he?"

He had to be careful. Galtieri may have known all there is to know about the Reichsleiter, but chances were all he knew was what his predecessors knew, which was very little. "I am afraid I do not know—"

"Come, come, señor, let's not play games. I know all about your beloved leader. We have quite a dossier on him, you know. Did you think such an influential man could live in our country for over thirty years and we would not have a dossier?"

Willy fought to keep his composure. Surely, Galtieri was bluffing. He was being courted heavily by the Americans, who had fawned over him during his visit to the United States several months earlier. One of them had even referred to Galtieri as "the Patton of Argentina", a comparison almost as ludicrous as if he'd been associated with Rommel. No, if Galtieri really knew as much about the Reichsleiter as he claimed, he would have tipped off the Americans as a means of gaining their favor even more. And of course the Americans would have immediately told their great friends the Jews, who would have acted by now. And they hadn't. Thus, it was bluff and bluster. Willy decided not to call it, for now. Instead, he said, "Mi presidente, I came here today to pay my respects and to reiterate our Bund's support for your government. It appears that I have not properly communicated that to you, and for that I'm sorry."

Galtieri leaned forward, elbows on his desk. "Señor, I want you to take a message back to your father for me. I presume he will pass it along to the Reichsleiter."

Willy did not break eye contact with the older man. Galtieri's gaze drilled into him, but Willy summoned up his

German discipline and held his own. "What message would you like me to convey, sir?"

"Just this: I am in this chair to restore Argentina's honor, its pride. I intend to rule this country for a long time, señor, and before I am done this nation will stand in its proper place in this hemisphere. And I will let no one, no group, and certainly no Siegfried Bund, stand in my way."

"Mi presidente, let me once again state that we in the Bund wish only to work together with your government—" Galtieri sighed and leaned backward in his chair, tapping the pen impatiently. Willy continued smoothly. "Our goal is yours: a strong, prosperous and independent Argentina. This is of course our country, too."

"I have another appointment, señor. Please be so kind as to convey my message."

Willy stood up, as did his host. Galtieri again did not offer a hand. Willy clicked his heels and bowed again. "Thank you for your time, sir."

"Before you leave, Señor Baumann, could you answer a question for me?"

"I will do my best, sir."

"If I were to nationalize your installation at Pilcaniyeu, what would the Bund's reaction be?"

That one gave Willy pause. Pilcaniyeu had to remain under Bund control at all costs. The success of CAPRICORN depended on it. Everything depended on it. Letting the facility fall into the hands of Galtieri and his henchmen would be a disaster. "The facility is private property, as you well know, mi presidente, a status that has been guaranteed by your predecessors for more than a decade now."

"My predecessors are not here, señor. I am."

"Are you telling me you are considering such a thing, sir?"

Galtieri's eyes narrowed. "I am the president, señor. I have many things I must consider for the sake of my country. My soldiers are already providing security there."

Willy's reply was immediate. "For which the Bund is generously compensating the government." He decided it was time to gamble, to see if the Bund's status among the Argentine ruling class was truly as high as he'd been told. If not, all was probably lost anyway. He offered a thin smile. "Mi presidente, I trust that once you examine all the, shall we say, rather unique facts surrounding this particular issue, you will decide that maintaining the status quo is in the best interests of your government."

Galtieri leaned forward menacingly on his desk. "Is that a threat, señor?"

Willy's smile never wavered, although his heart was racing. "I will convey your message to the leadership of the Bund, as you requested, sir. May I ask that you also convey a message from us to your fellow junta members?"

"And that is?"

"Pilcaniyeu is not to be touched. If it is, there will be serious consequences. Consequences of the most extreme nature. Good day, sir." Willy turned on his heel and strode to the door of the office. The infantry captain, who had been standing next to the door all during the interview, stiffened at his approach. Willy saw the captain's eyes glance toward his master. Willy knew he'd reach for the doorknob or for his sidearm, depending on what gesture he'd receive from

Galtieri. Willy paused at the doorway, staring at the captain...who reached for the doorknob.

Five minutes later, Willy was on the street outside the building, breathing in the hot, somewhat acrid air of Buenos Aires, sucking it in deeply. After a moment, he walked down the block, past the military guards, and crossed the street to where Heinz was leaning on the parked Mercedes. Heinz did not greet him, but simply opened the door to the driver's side and got in. Willy entered on the passenger side. The engine was running, with its blessed air conditioning, and Heinz quickly turned on the radio, tuning it to a special frequency that was in fact designed to produce a background of white noise to foil any listening devices that might have been planted inside or trained on them from outside.

"How did it go?" Heinz asked.

"Not good," Willy replied. He reached for the portable telephone and punched in a number as Heinz pulled the powerful car out into traffic. Willy heard a male voice on the other end of the line say a single word: "*Ja?*"

"This is Oberst Baumann," Willy replied. "Authentication Friedrich seven-three-nine. Initiate Condition Yellow."

"*Verstehen,*" the voice said. Understood. The line went dead.

***

The clock down the hall chimed two a.m. as Leopoldo Galtieri lurched from his bed to the adjoining bathroom. He had been asleep maybe two hours, and his bladder roused him again. Too much champagne at dinner, although fortunately not enough to prevent him from enjoying the pleasures of his mistress later on. The raven-haired Carlotta, only twenty-two, and what a tigress she was! He had thought of eventually getting someone younger, but he would never stoop to what Perón had done, bedding young teenagers until he was bewitched by the siren Evita. Carlotta would do for the time being. She was gone now, no longer allowed to spend the night. He was the president, and some sense of propriety had to be maintained.

As he washed his hands, he chuckled at the fresh memory of that young pup Baumann, in his office hours before. Threatening the president of Argentina! Who did these Germans think they were, anyhow? They might have been able to intimidate Viola, but Viola was not in the Pink House now, was he?

Scratching his hairy chest, Galtieri flicked off the bathroom light and walked back into the bedroom. If his senses hadn't been dulled by champagne and sex and then sleep, he might've noticed something different in the room, some slight change. He climbed back onto his four-poster bed, drank in the smell of Carlotta's perfume and the musk of their recent coupling, and rolled onto his side, pulling the covers back up over him. The great man's head hit the pillow and he was almost asleep when something prompted him to shift his head. That's when he felt it underneath the pillow, something hard, something that hadn't been there before.

He reached over to the night stand and switched on the light, then flipped the pillow aside. The light glinted off the blade of the dagger. The polished blade was a good eight inches long, and the wooden handle bore the German eagle clutching a swastika in its talons. With shaking hands,

Galtieri turned the dagger over. On the opposite side of the blade, the words *Alles für Deutschland* sent a message that got through loud and clear.

CHAPTER SEVEN

Estancia Valhalla, Argentina

December 1981

It was nearly ten at night when Willy arrived back at the estancia. He'd put in three hours at the Bund's offices in Buenos Aires after leaving the Pink House, most of that time on the telephone to Pilcaniyeu and selected other important locations. While he doubted Galtieri had the nerve to move against them this early in the game, one could never be sure, and so precautions had to be taken. By six o'clock, he'd managed to convince himself that Condition Yellow was being implemented as quickly and efficiently as possible. He and Heinz had dinner at a nearby restaurant favored by the city's large German population, finishing around seven-thirty, early by Argentine standards. Then the two old friends had parted, driving their own cars, Willy to his estancia, Heinz to another location in the city, to take care of one other matter.

Willy was surprised to find his father still up. He'd called Dieter, of course, to report on the meeting with the president. Now he found the old man sitting in the library, nursing a glass of schnapps and accompanied by another older man, whom Willy instantly recognized, and a younger man whom he did not. The two men rose as Willy entered the room.

"Ah, son, welcome back," Dieter said. "We have some overnight guests, old friends of mine who arrived this afternoon."

"Good evening, Herr Baumann," the older man said, extending a hand.

Without thinking, Willy came to attention, clicked his heels, and bowed. "Herr Oberst, it is a great honor to meet you." Almost reverently, he offered his hand. The man, who was in his mid-sixties, smiled self-consciously, but his handshake was firm.

"I am pleased you recognize me, Herr Baumann."

All his fatigue and tension forgotten, Willy was almost giddy. It was an effort to remain dignified. "What young German boy has not read of your exploits, Herr Oberst? Hans-Ulrich Rudel, the greatest fighter pilot who ever lived!" That last just came out, but it was true. Rudel flew *Luftwaffe* fighters, always the Junkers-87 *Panzerjäger*, against the Russians in the last war, and no pilot in any air force had flown more courageously, or more effectively. The statistics flashed through Willy's mind: nine enemy aircraft shot down, over 150 antiaircraft and artillery positions destroyed, more than 500 tanks, more than 700 trucks, four armored trains. Rudel had even sunk two Soviet warships single-handedly, the battleship *October Revolution* and the cruiser *Marat*. Shot down himself thirty-two times, he had once escaped on foot from more than forty kilometers behind enemy lines, swimming a frozen river along the way, chased by Russian soldiers anxious to claim the 100,000-ruble reward Stalin had placed on the German's head. Rudel was the only German soldier ever awarded the Knight's Cross with Golden Oakleaves, Swords and Diamonds.

"You are too kind, Herr Baumann," Rudel said with a shy grin, but Willy could tell he enjoyed being recognized. The old ace stepped somewhat awkwardly back to his chair and sat down; Willy recalled that he had once been wounded in the right leg, and now had a partial prosthesis.

Dieter coughed. "Wilhelm, allow me to also introduce Herr Johann Biederbeck, from Munich."

The younger man stood, clicked his heels and bowed slightly, then offered his hand. "A pleasure, Herr Baumann," he said with a smile.

"The pleasure is mine, Herr Biederbeck," Willy replied. "What brings you to Argentina?"

"Some business, some pleasure," Biederbeck replied casually. The Bavarian accent was noticeable.

Dieter coughed. "Willy, it's getting late, and we'll all be retiring soon, but there are a few trifling matters I need to discuss yet with our guests."

As always, his father's suggestion was elegantly phrased, but the meaning was clear: time for you to leave us. "Of course, Father," he said. He bowed slightly to the guests. "Gentlemen, I will see you at breakfast."

Dieter waited until the door was shut before speaking. "He's a good boy."

"I see much of his father in him," Rudel said with a smile. "He reminds me of a certain young officer I knew on the Russian Front. You must be proud, Dieter."

"Indeed I am." The elder Baumann pushed himself to his feet. "May I freshen your schnapps, gentlemen?"

Rudel declined, but the man introduced as Biederbeck accepted. His real name, known to these two men but to nobody else in Argentina, was Johann Becker, and he was a colonel in the ASBw, the *Amt für Sicherheit der Bundeswehr*, Office for Security of the German Armed Forces, the intelligence arm of the West German military. He was the number two officer in the ASBw's Munich district headquarters. What his commander back in Bavaria did not know was that he was also the Siegfried Bund's top agent in the southern part of the Federal Republic. Becker was traveling in Argentina with the Biederbeck passport he used, on rare occasions, to travel behind the Iron Curtain.

"How much does your boy know, Dieter?" Becker asked after sipping his refreshed drink.

Dieter settled into his soft chair with an audible grunt. "Not everything," he said. "CAPRICORN, of course, but nothing about VALKYRIE."

"Do you intend to tell him?" Rudel asked.

"Not for now. The Reichsleiter has ordered that VALKYRIE remain classified Most Secret. Only the Cabinet members know about it."

"That is good," Becker said. "Secrecy is of the utmost importance, for both projects."

"CAPRICORN must work for the other to succeed," Rudel said.

"True enough," Dieter said. "CAPRICORN's success will be VALKYRIE's trigger."

The three men were silent for a moment, engrossed in their own thoughts, considering the possibilities. Rudel was the first to speak again. "Are your pilots properly trained, Dieter? Are you sure they can deliver the weapon?"

Dieter nodded confidently. "If the engineers can complete the weapon on time at Pilcaniyeu, we have more than enough pilots to ensure success." He gestured at his desk. "I have their service jackets, Hans. You are welcome to examine them tomorrow." Rudel nodded.

"I have no doubts about our pilots," Becker said. "Most of them attended OSLw." *Offizierschule der Luftwaffe* was the West German air force academy in Fürstenfeldbruck. "But about the mission itself: one weapon will be sufficient? Will it have enough yield?"

"We hope to have two, although only one will go on the mission," Dieter said. "The expected yield will be close to one hundred kilotons."

Becker nodded. "Yes, I would think that will be sufficient," he said, "depending on how closely packed the English fleet will be."

"My experts tell me that an air burst over the center of their formation will be more than adequate," Dieter said. He sipped his drink, clearly relishing the thought. "Will you be ready to move then, Johann?"

Becker seemed to be examining his own drink carefully. "Yes," he finally said. "Things are well underway."

"Will you have enough men to control the situation in Bonn?" Rudel asked. "East Berlin, too?"

"Yes," Becker said. "The key will be the capture of the American and Soviet tactical nuclear arsenals in the opening hours of the operation. If we seize their weapons, we seize the day."

"We seize our country back," Rudel said.

"My one concern," Dieter said, "is that the Bolsheviks will think it will herald the rise of the Party again. They will go insane if it appears that is happening. Your few small weapons won't stop them. They will sacrifice thousands of troops to prevent another invasion of their country." Inwardly, he shuddered at the memory of the how savagely the Russians had fought him forty years ago. So many good young German boys had gone east, and so few had returned.

"I agree with Dieter," Rudel said. "I did not fly for the Nazis. I flew for Germany." Dieter raised an eyebrow. Rudel had been a member of the Party during the war, and in the first version of his biography he'd supported Party policies. Before it could be published in Germany and America, it had been re-edited to remove Party references. But Dieter would give the old ace the benefit of the doubt.

"We will make it abundantly clear that National Socialism has no part in the drama," Becker said. "Brezhnev is old and sick. Andropov is maneuvering to be his successor. They have no strong, decisive leadership. By the time they decide what to do, we will have consolidated our gains and present them with a united, nuclear-armed nation. A nation that renounces National Socialism." He looked at Dieter. "You must make sure the Reichsleiter does not interfere, my friend."

"The Reichsleiter will never leave Argentina," Dieter said. "I am more concerned about what the Bolsheviks will do. VALKYRIE may very well topple Brezhnev."

"Perhaps, but Andropov is no fool. He will not move against us if he doesn't perceive us to be a threat to him, and he will still have his buffer states. Poland, Czechoslovakia..."

"We won't be a threat to him right away," Rudel said. "But what about later?"

Becker smiled at the old ace. "Later is later, Herr Oberst. Five years from now, ten years, who knows?"

Rudel wasn't completely reassured. "What about the French? They will not necessarily follow any instructions from the British or Americans to hold back."

Becker waved a hand dismissively. "We are not concerned about the French. They will not move against us without the British and Americans alongside them. They will posture and complain, as they always do, but we will ignore them. There will be time enough to deal with the French later."

"You must not align yourselves with the West," Dieter said. "If the Russians believe you are in league with the NATO countries, they will strike you. It is imperative for you to remain independent from the two blocs."

"We understand that, old friend," Becker said. "Like you, I have no love of the Bolsheviks. Eventually they will fall on their own sword. It is inevitable. Already, the Americans are putting pressure on them to match their military buildup. They cannot hope to match the Americans, but they will try, and they will fail, and then they will fall, leaving one nation as the true master of Europe."

Rudel and Dieter both nodded their understanding. Dieter raised his glass. "Well, gentlemen, one last toast before we retire. To CAPRICORN."

"To VALKYRIE," Becker said, raising his.

"To the Fatherland, once again united and strong," Rudel said.

They drank.

***

Ernesto had his feather duster in hand as he entered the study the next morning, stopping short as he saw the man behind the desk. "I beg your pardon, Herr Oberst," the butler said, bowing slightly.

Hans-Ulrich Rudel closed the file in front of him and stood up. "Not at all, Ernesto," the old pilot said with a friendly smile. "I was just finishing up here. Herr Baumann is going to take us on a tour of the estancia. I won't keep you from your duties."

"Thank you, Herr Oberst," Ernesto said. He stepped aside as Rudel limped past him through the doorway and down the hall. Ernesto liked the legendary ace; unlike many of the Germans, especially the older ones, there was no hint of arrogance behind his dignity.

Ernesto went to a side window, which had a view of the driveway that led from the garages behind the main building around to the veranda. A Mercedes SL convertible, with young Wilhelm at the wheel, motored slowly toward the house, raising only a hint of dust from the well-maintained gravel road.

The butler walked back through the hallways to the library, one of his favorite rooms in the mansion. Hundreds of volumes in German, English, Spanish and French crowded the bookshelves. There were several dark leather chairs and couches, with a poker table near one end of the room and a billiard table at the other. The main window looked out through the wide veranda to the front of the building. Dieter Baumann and his two guests were climbing aboard the Mercedes, and in a moment Wilhelm drove them toward the gated entrance to the estancia's main complex.

Trying to control his anxiety, Ernesto walked back through the house to the study. Keeping the door open, he took one more look around and then, satisfied he was alone, went to the desk. Going around behind, he nudged the leather chair aside and began flicking the feather duster over the dark teak surface of the desk. The file Rudel had been examining lay in the center of the desk. It was closed.

His vantage point gave him a clear view of the doorway and part of the hallway, and he could also clearly see through the French doors to his left that the side veranda was empty. No one could disturb him without announcing their presence by heels clicking on the hardwood floor of the hallway. Still flicking the duster with his left hand, he opened the file with his right. The first page, bearing the crest of Baumann Enterprises as its letterhead, contained a list of six names. Alternating his gaze between the page and the doorway, Ernesto committed the names to memory, then quickly riffled the remaining pages. Photographs, service records, letters of commendation. Ernesto knew a military service jacket when he saw one. The names were the important things. Giving the front page one last glance, he closed the file and resumed his dusting, moving on to the credenza behind the desk.

Five minutes later, he left the study and went to his own quarters at the rear of the house, a small bedroom and a sitting room with a view of the rear grounds of the estate. Closing his door and locking it, he retrieved a blank piece of paper from his small desk and jotted down the six names. They were all German surnames, although none he recognized in particular. That was all right. Someone else would know who they were, and perhaps what significance they carried. Folding the paper into quarters, he slipped it into the inside pocket of his jacket.

CHAPTER EIGHT

Eglin Air Force Base, Florida
December 1981

"Another difficult decision," Jo Ann Geary said, frowning.

"Those captain's bars tend to weigh you down with responsibility," her companion in the line said. "But making tough calls is why Uncle Sam is paying us the big bucks."

"Yeah, sure," Jo said. She made up her mind. "Apple, please," she said to the white-aproned private behind the counter. "No ice cream."

"Certainly, ma'am," the E-2 said, sliding the slice of apple pie onto Jo's plate. "Fresh baked, ma'am, taste just like your mama's, I'll bet."

Jo smiled at the young man's drawl. Arkansas, probably. Well, her own mother had never done very well with traditional American baking, but this boy's mom had probably filled him with pie and a lot more before sending him off to Air Force basic training, and by the look of him that had happened not too long ago. "Thanks, airman."

Stepping aside, she let Kate take a look at the dessert offerings.

"Lemon meringue, hot damn. I'll take that good-sized piece there, Mr. Dowling." The young man happily served up the slice. Kate was a regular visitor to the dessert section, so she knew every worker by name. Yet those visits didn't seem to add up to any extra inches on her thighs or midriff. Jo sighed with envy. The women found two empty chairs at a nearby table.

As usual, Kate dug right in, taking a big bite out of her ham and cheese sandwich. Jo used her knife and fork almost like a surgeon, picking at her chicken breast before cutting off a small piece. "Eat up, girl," Kate said after chasing her first bite with a swig of milk. "We got a lot of work to do yet today."

Jo smiled as she ate. In a profession that seemed designed to foster intense friendships and then yank them apart on the whim of some nameless Pentagon bureaucrat, she had found it made good policy to avoid getting particularly close to anyone. Kate Simmons was the one exception she'd made to that rule over the years, and Kate's effervescent personality had a lot to do with that. You couldn't help liking Kate, and Jo supposed they made an odd pair: the slender Oriental woman with the exotic looks, and the tall, solidly-built black woman with the loud laugh and merry eyes. Nobody would call Kate a beauty, and yet she'd had her share of boyfriends. And a few girlfriends, too, Jo knew, but she didn't let that bother her. Kate sure didn't seem to mind.

Perhaps Jo liked Kate so much—and the feeling was surely mutual—because of the way they'd met. Nearly seven years ago, Jo reflected now, the air-conditioned comfort of the officer's mess clashing with her memory of the cold rain on that spring morning in 1975 when an even one hundred women, apprehensive and a little bit scared, disembarked the olive-drab Army buses at Fort Bragg, North Carolina. Jo slipped in the mud and dropped her duffel bag, only to find herself hauled upright by a powerful hand. Kate's other hand held Jo's duffel, her own bag was slung on her back, and she was laughing. "You be careful, girl," Kate said then. "You drop in the mud here, you be liable to splash me, and I ain't aimin' to get down and dirty till I have to." Jo's inauspicious introduction to the Diana Brigade had led to the start of her most enduring friendship.

She thought of that now as Kate chatted away about the training schedule that lay ahead of them in the afternoon, what they should do this weekend in town, and isn't that new Lieutenant Kittoe a real stud muffin? The three months at Bragg, a good deal of that time spent in the surrounding countryside, had shaped their lives like no other experience possibly could. One hundred women began the training, designed to see if women could withstand the same rigorous Special Forces training as men, and the sixty-three who survived the ordeal formed a unique bond. To this day, when Jo saw the Diana Brigade ribbon bar on the uniform of another woman soldier, sailor, airman or marine, she immediately recognized the face, put it with a name, called up a shared memory, and felt the strength of the bond. Sometimes the women would only be able to share a special nod and a smile, but usually they found time to exchange greetings, talk a bit about old times and new, maybe plan to have dinner together. Jo would always try to find time to spend with a fellow Huntress.

She and Kate had gone off to different postings after Diana, but the vagaries of military life had brought them together twice since then, most recently here, at Eglin, in the 6th Special Operations Training Squadron, 1st Special Operations Wing, 9th Air Force. Jo had arrived on the base nearly a year ago, just days behind Kate. The women quickly renewed their friendship and had worked together closely since then. Their duties consisted primarily of training new Special Ops troopers, not an easy task since most of them were men and women's liberation, despite the results of projects like Diana, was still finding the going pretty hard in this man's Air Force. But a good portion of their duty was learning new things themselves, retraining on skills already learned, and the occasional tasking for special assignment. Jo had gone overseas three times since arriving at Hurlburt. Kate had returned from an assignment in Kenya just a week ago.

Jo enjoyed the military life, but it was slow going sometimes. She was in her tenth year of active duty and still only a captain; some of the male officers she'd known, younger than her and with fewer years, had already made major. Kate had three fewer years in the service and was a grade below Jo, at first lieutenant. Jo felt Kate deserved more, but her friend's sometimes too-cavalier attitude might have held her back as much as her gender. And yet, Kate seemed to have fun wherever she went, and often kidded Jo as being too serious. Jo had heard the scuttlebutt among some male officers, too; Kate was considered a good time on a date, while Jo got her share of offers but few follow-up invitations. With a few exceptions, Ian Masters being the most recent, she thought with a smile.

Ian. His last letter had reached her a week ago, posted two weeks earlier from Tahiti. He certainly missed her, and she fought to keep herself from blushing now as she recalled some of his steamier paragraphs. She made a mental note to write another letter to him that evening.

The women finished their lunch and began the walk across the base from the mess hall to their unit headquarters building at Hurlburt Field. They could have taken a jeep but Jo preferred to walk, and the Florida weather was good today, mid-seventies, very nice for two days before Christmas. Kate, as usual, carped about the walk but went along with the idea. They were halfway to the unit when a blue jeep with a sergeant at the wheel pulled alongside them. The man snapped off a salute. "Captain Geary?"

Jo and Kate returned the salute. "Yes, Sergeant?" Jo asked.

"Just went looking for you at Officer's Mess, ma'am. Colonel Reese wants to see you right away. Be happy to give you a lift."

Jo knew that the offer of a ride wasn't just a friendly suggestion. When the colonel wanted to see someone, he wanted him, or her, in his office yesterday. "Thanks, sergeant," Jo said. "Kate, I'll see you later." She climbed aboard.

"Betcha this means we won't be going to the Beach this weekend," Kate said over the roar of the engine. Jo waved goodbye as the sergeant wheeled the jeep around and headed back down the road. A summons to the colonel's office could mean a lot of things, but for Jo it likely meant her planned weekend with Kate down at Fort Walton Beach would be canceled. They intended to drive there Friday afternoon, returning Sunday evening. Well, there would be other weekends for golf and a night or two on the town.

Maybe she was being deployed. There had been scuttlebutt on the base about a move against Iran; many of the airmen had been in on the disastrous Operation Eagle Claw, the failed attempt to rescue the hostages in Tehran, nearly two years ago now. But somehow Jo doubted this had anything to do with Iran. She kept a close eye on political developments and figured something was about to happen in El Salvador or Nicaragua. Good thing she had been brushing up on her Spanish.

The office of Lieutenant Colonel Brian Reese, the squadron's commanding officer, was in one corner of the wing's headquarters building on the eastern perimeter of Hurlburt. Jo was shown in by Reese's aide, a female tech sergeant. She came to attention and saluted. "Captain Geary reporting as ordered, sir," Jo said.

Looking up from the papers on his desk, Reese rose to his feet and returned the salute. "At ease, Jo Ann," he said. "Have a chair." That in itself was a bit unusual. Reese was a good C.O., but in the year she'd worked for him, he went strictly by the book and tended to be a bit formal. Maybe a little more than he should, sometimes, but she knew that Reese had a legacy pushing him: his father had flown thirty missions in P-51 Mustangs escorting B-25s for the Air Corps over Germany, and before that his grandfather went aloft over France in spindly Spad biplanes for the Lafayette Escadrille in World War I. Reese himself flew Phantoms over North Vietnam, and between them the Reese men had accounted for seventeen enemy pilots going down.

Reese was around forty, with specks of gray clouding his close-cropped dark hair. He picked up a paper from the file on his desk. "I have received a rather interesting letter from a member of Congress," Reese said.

That couldn't be good. "Which one, sir?"

"Lacey Chamberlain, Representative from Maryland. Heard of her?"

Jo's spirits sagged. "Yes, sir. She's...not been too terribly friendly to the military."

Reese smiled. "Your discretion is admirable, Jo Ann. The congresswoman has been pretty outspoken on the subject since her days in college. She was one of the anti-war movement's leaders, if I recall." He glanced at the letter again. "She's chair of a pretty important committee in the House and is going to conduct hearings right after the holidays about women in the military, and she wants you to testify."

That was a surprise. "About what, sir?"

"Evidently, as much as she dislikes the military, she does like military women, and she believes they're not being promoted quickly enough, by comparison to their male peers. You've made a bit of a name for yourself in the Special Ops community with the Fonglan Island mission, not to mention your earlier missions. She found out about Fonglan, and apparently wonders why you're still a captain after ten years' service and a pretty impressive record."

Jo's head whirled a little bit, and she forced herself to focus. "First of all, sir, that op was classified Top Secret, and as important as this lady is in Congress, I don't know how she could've been brought into the loop on it, even after the fact."

"She wasn't, at least officially, I'm pretty sure about that," Reese said, "but leaks do get out of the Pentagon now and then. Something we have to live with. And your second point?"

"Sir, if I go before a committee of Congress, then whatever cover I might have for future missions is blown. Even if Fonglan Island isn't brought up, which I'm sure it would be, if she wants to showcase my record as an example of a female officer who hasn't been—" Jo stopped herself. "Sorry, sir. I didn't mean to imply—"

"That's all right, Jo Ann. For the record, after I reviewed your report on that operation, I put you in for a commendation. Also for promotion to major. They haven't come through yet, but I'm pretty sure both of them will."

Jo blinked in surprise. "Thank you, sir."

"No thanks necessary. I recognize good work and a good officer when I see them. Now, about this thing with Chamberlain. I could ask my superiors here and in Washington to lean on her to have you removed from the witness list for this hearing, but I think it would be better for you to make that case yourself. The hearing is set to begin January eleventh. I'm sending you up to D.C. next week, to meet with some people at the Pentagon about some routine matters concerning your unit, and then to sit down with the congresswoman, privately. You can convince her that having you testify would be a bad idea all the way around."

Jo was thinking of a photo she'd seen in a recent Newsweek article about Chamberlain, showing the congresswoman sharing a table at a fundraiser with a prominent actress who'd made a name for herself with her open support of the Viet Cong during the war. That name, among the military, wasn't very complimentary. Jo would have to be very careful during this private sit-down. "I understand, sir. When do I leave?"

"Next Monday morning. Congress isn't in session till after New Year's, but you'll be meeting with Chamberlain at her district office in St. Charles on Tuesday. Your Pentagon appointments are Wednesday, and you'll take an evening flight out of Andrews back here."

"Very well, sir."

"I'll have your orders cut this afternoon. I understand you're off-duty this weekend?"

"Yes, sir. Lieutenant Simmons and I were planning on going down to the Beach for a couple days."

"Well, I see no reason why that shouldn't happen. You're on duty Christmas Day, but it should be pretty quiet. A good day for you to hit the base library to get some background on Congresswoman Chamberlain. Pick up your orders for the D.C. trip here tomorrow morning." He set the letter aside and stood up. "That'll be all, Captain."

Jo stood, came to attention, and saluted. "Thank you, sir."

Reese returned the salute crisply. "Oh, by the way, don't your parents live near D.C.? You'll have the rest of Monday to visit."

"Yes, sir."

CHAPTER NINE

Buenos Aires

Christmas Eve 1981

"Merry Christmas, my love," the woman said. She placed the brightly-wrapped box on the table in front of her husband.

"What have we here?" Antonio Gasparini said in mock surprise. "Theresa, I hope you did not spend too much money." He was not convincing in his tone, and the beautiful dark-haired woman laughed. Gasparini untied the bow, gently placed the ribbon aside, and lifted the cover. His eyes went wide when he saw the book. Reverently, he reached inside and lifted it up, turning its leather cover toward the candlelight. "*Santa Maria*," he whispered.

Theresa's eyes filled with tears. "You are happy?"

Antonio's hands almost shook as he opened the book. "It is in Italian!" he said. He looked up at her, his eyes shining.

"I have not seen a Bible in Italian since I left...I left..." His lower lip began to tremble.

She reached across the small table and covered one of his hands with hers. "I know, my love. Since Livorno." Antonio Gasparini had left his native Tuscany nearly twenty years ago, at the age of ten. After his parents were killed in an auto accident, leaving four *bambinos*, relatives in Livorno were able to take in three, but Antonio, the oldest, came here to Argentina, to live with his Uncle Humberto. In the La Boca barrio, with its heavily Italian population, Antonio grew to manhood, not too far from this very house. At eighteen he met Theresa, a daughter of immigrants from Naples. They had two children now.

Antonio placed the Bible delicately on the table. "Thank you, my love. I am afraid that my gift to you does not measure up."

"Oh, nonsense, husband," she said, reaching to the chair next to her. The briefcase was beautiful, hand-crafted by a man in the village near Antonio's post. "If I am to be taken seriously as a student, the professors must see me with something besides a common backpack to carry my books." She would have preferred jewelry, of course—she was a woman, after all—but men were men. Antonio was a fine one, devoted to her and the children. She had watched him tenderly tuck them into their beds a half-hour before. What more could a wife ask? Well, perhaps to have a husband who was around more than once a month.

"Your studies, they go well?"

"Yes," she said proudly. "In a year, you will have a wife with a degree in economics, from the University of Buenos Aires. Then I will get a job, and soon after that we will be able to afford to move."

Antonio's eyes glazed over a bit. "Yes, perhaps to Recoleta," he mused. Many residents of working-class barrios, like La Boca, dreamed of living one day in the fashionable Recoleta, with its upper-class homes and beautiful parks. He and Theresa occasionally took a Sunday afternoon drive to its Plaza Francia, strolling through the craft fair, the largest in the city.

"Eduardo wants to live there and be a *pasaperro*," she said with a laugh. She remembered how the children had marveled at the professional dog-walkers, who sometimes had as many as a dozen canines at the ends of their leashes.

"Well, we shall see," Antonio said. "My tour is up in six months. Then I should be posted somewhere much closer."

Theresa's eyes softened. "Oh, I hope so, my husband. Pilcaniyeu is so far away..."

"Too far," he agreed. Once a month, he was allowed a weekend leave to visit his family. Fortunately, he was almost always able to hitch a ride on an Air Force transport, so the thousand-kilometer journey went fairly quickly. The ride back, though, was always long. "*Coronel* Reinke likes me, I think, which is unusual. They're almost all Germans, you know, at least among the officers."

"As you've said before, Antonio," she said. There was a definite social pecking order in Argentina, and the Italians, despite being more numerous, tended to be under the Germans. "But you are a good officer. Reinke knows that."

"I hope so," he said. He paused, thinking, then said, "I have not told you, but now I will: there is a good chance I am to be promoted, perhaps as soon as next month."

"Promoted! To *mayor*?"

"Yes," he said with a grin. "Major Schaaf is being transferred to a combat unit. I am next in line."

Theresa was excited now. "A promotion! To major, and second-in-command?"

"Hopefully," he said, trying to curb his own excitement. He'd intended to hold off telling Theresa until it was official. No point in getting her worked up over something that might not happen. But, well, it was Christmas...

"My husband, second in command of the security force at such an important place. Perhaps then, commander one day?" In her excitement, she had forgotten about the distance. Of course, if Antonio were given command, they would have to move...

He shook his head. "I think not, my dear. The Germans are in firm control of the facility. They would never have an Italian in charge of security. A legacy of the war, I'm afraid."

"No matter," she said. "You will be an important man. Even more important than now," she added quickly. Her face was a bit flushed. Was it the wine they had at dinner? She stood up and took his hand. "Come, my husband. The children are asleep now. Come to our bedroom and make love to me."

He looked at her, and marveled that her body had ripened into robust womanhood, not too much different than when they had married, despite the two children she had carried. "A request like that, how can I refuse?"

CHAPTER TEN

Estancia Valhalla, Argentina

Christmas Day 1981

Dusk was settling over the estancia. Willy Baumann sat on his deck, enjoying the warm weather, his cognac, and the aftereffect of the sumptuous Christmas dinner he'd eaten just an hour before. A few hundred meters away, his *gauchos* were playing a raucous game of *pato*, a combination of basketball and rugby played on horseback. Wearing helmets and kneepads, the competing teams vied for a large leather ball with six handles, passing it among each other until they could throw it through their opponent's goal, a large hoop. Willy had played the game many times and enjoyed it, but was glad he was far away now. The gauchos were still celebrating *Felice Navidad* and some were a little the worse for wear already.

The estancia was spread over thousands of hectares, supporting hundreds of head of cattle and horses, employing some three hundred people, including a general manager who reported directly to Willy. It was a minor part of his overall responsibilities, but his favorite, doubtless due to his Argentine blood. The other businesses were run by competent managers and occupied a fair amount of his time, but since the advent of CAPRICORN three years earlier, the Bund had required more and more of his attention. Right now, on the table next to his chair, sat a stack of monthly reports from the Bund's various *gauleiters*, the regional commandants. There were twenty-four of them, one for each of the twenty-three provinces, plus the federal district that encompassed Buenos Aires. They all were directly responsible to the *Bundesobergruppenführer*, the Bund general, a position held by Dieter Baumann since 1974. Number three in the Bund hierarchy behind the Reichsleiter and the Bundesführer, Dieter was in charge of the Bund's day-to-day operations and its special projects. In the past three years his duties had largely been administered by his executive officer, Oberst Wilhelm Baumann.

It was more than a full-time job, and not for the first time Willy wished it wasn't his. He glanced at the reports, which had come to the estancia by messenger the day before. They could wait. His eyes returned to the broad vistas stretching to the west.

"No paperwork today, eh, Willy?"

That drew a short laugh. "Not today, Heinz. Come, sit, have a drink with me."

Heinz Nagel folded his lanky frame into the chair next to Willy's. He was about two inches taller than Willy, and three months younger. They had been friends since kindergarten; Heinz's father, Günther Nagel, operated the neighboring estancia, and was a prominent Bund member in his own right. "That was an excellent dinner," Heinz said, stifling a burp. "Please give my compliments to the chef."

"You can tell him yourself, when you ask for his daughter's hand," Willy said with mock seriousness.

Heinz laughed. "I have no intention of marrying Sophia," he said, "and you know that." The estancia's chef, Luigi, had been brought over from Italy ten years before, after Dieter enjoyed a fabulous meal at a struggling *ristorante* in Genoa. Willy's father, in need of a chef back home, convinced the owner and chief cook of the establishment to accept his generous offer of a buyout, bring his family to Argentina and go to work on Dieter's estancia. Luigi brought his wife and ten-year-old daughter, Sophia, who had now grown to voluptuous womanhood, something Heinz had not been hesitant to appreciate.

Both men were still single, and as they neared thirty— coming up next year, in fact—they were starting to feel a little pressure from their fathers to find women, settle down and start producing grandchildren. For Heinz, always the more carefree of the two, it was easy to laugh that off and continue indulging his bachelor whims. For Willy, consumed ever more by the work of running the Baumann business empire, not to mention his growing obligations with the Bund, romance had never really intruded into his life. There were women, of course, both here and abroad; some of them made their intentions quite clear and were willing to do virtually anything to become the next mistress of the estancia. A very few of them caused a spark inside him, but nothing had yet happened to fan that into a flame.

The latest spark had been ignited by his dinner companion for the day, something Heinz was well aware of. "Sophia is a playmate of mine," he said now. "But your

Giselle, now, she is a real woman. You should marry her, you know."

Willy took a sip from his glass as he contemplated the virtues of Giselle Carmaño. There were many. The daughter of Roberto and Barbara Carmaño, a family of mixed Spanish and German blood, Giselle was twenty-five, bright, educated, and stunningly attractive. Her father's estancia, Santa Barbara, was some fifty kilometers to the south and was almost as large and prosperous as Valhalla. Even better, from the perspective of a possible son-in-law who might be interested in such things, Señor Carmaño also owned one of the largest import/export firms in Buenos Aires. But unlike many young Argentine men of means, Willy had never been interested in a woman as a means to facilitate a business merger. He had known Giselle since childhood, and had been involved with her for about two years now, since her return from an extended stay in Spain, where she completed her education at the Complutense University of Madrid. She stimulated him physically, to be sure, but more importantly she stimulated him intellectually.

"Yes, I should," Willy said, "but you know why I haven't yet."

"So her father is not a member of the Bund," Heinz said. "You won't be marrying her father."

"I'd be marrying her family," Willy corrected, "you know that as well as I do. We have to be careful about who knows of our work, Heinz, especially now." With CAPRICORN near completion, marriage to Giselle was out of the question for at least a year. If everything went according to plan in the upcoming year, perhaps by next Christmas, he could ask Giselle's father for her hand.

But there were so many ifs.

If the work at Pilcaniyeu proceeded on schedule; if Galtieri didn't interfere; if the South Georgia operation went forward on time; if the English reacted as they predicted; if the Americans stayed out of it; if CAPRICORN remained a secret...

A lot of ifs. Too many. Something was bound to go wrong. Well, that's why they had contingency plans, including one that was meant to deal with a government takeover of the Pilcaniyeu facility. Willy had put that particular plan on alert status two weeks earlier, after his meeting with Galtieri, but, fortunately, the president had not made good on his veiled threat to move against the Bund in that direction. Heinz had done his part well.

"You are thinking of things perhaps way too serious for the occasion, my friend," Heinz said.

Willy had to chuckle at that. "Perhaps," he said. "But we have important days ahead, Heinz. Very important days." Heinz was of necessity aware of most of CAPRICORN's scope. Like Willy, he had been carefully groomed for his position; his father had been head of the Bund's security arm for nearly thirty years. Over the objections of some of the Bund's more cautious members, *Brigadeführer* Nagel insisted that his operation use the name *Sicherheitsdienst*. What made these members nervous was the fact that this was the same name used by the security wing of the Nazi Party's notorious SS. Heinz had once revealed to Willy over a bottle of schnapps that Günther insisted on using the name for that very reason. Knowing Günther's wartime background, Willy had not been surprised. Still, he rarely referred to the group by its initials, SD, and neither did Heinz.

In a way, the very existence of the Bund SD was a perfect illustration of what Willy often thought of as the conflicting, evolving state of the Bund. Its founding fathers, the Kameraden, meant for the Bund to serve a certain purpose, and it had achieved success, thanks in large part to the iron discipline of those men. They brought that with them from the Fatherland, and also many of its institutions and traditions. Thus, a man like Günther Nagel could take the title of Brigadeführer, the *Waffen-SS* equivalent of brigadier general. Other arms of the Bund, however, if they utilized military ranking at all, stayed away from those used by the SS. Dieter Baumann, for instance, had the ceremonial rank of *Generalmajor*, equal in rank to Brigadeführer. Willy himself had risen to the rank of colonel in the Argentine Army before resigning from the service, and was still referred to by that rank. Heinz made captain before getting out.

By the mid-fifties the Bund had largely achieved what it had set out to do, and then, according to what Dieter told him, came a period of reflection and indecision. Some of the Kameraden were content to retire and enjoy the lives they had built as landowners and businessmen. Others wanted more; they wanted not just to enjoy Argentina, but to run it. Finally, the Reichsleiter himself stepped in and made the decision: the Bund would move forward, and Willy often wondered if the seeds of CAPRICORN had been sown around an argumentative conference table on some estancia in 1956.

But what about tomorrow? By the time Willy was his father's age, it would be the twenty-first century, and a third generation of Bund members would be getting ready to take command, just as Willy's generation was doing now. What would it be then?

Well, a lot of that could very well be determined in the next year. In fact, whether or not the Bund survived into the 1990s, much less a decade later, would likely hinge on what happened in the next twelve months.

"Have you given any thought to what will happen when those important days are done?" Heinz said now, breaking Willy out of his reverie. "Let us assume, for the sake of argument, that CAPRICORN succeeds. One year from now, Willy, what will we be planning for 1983, and the years after that?"

Willy grinned at his friend. "We will be good Germans, Heinz, and do what our superiors tell us to do."

Heinz smiled, and nodded. "Good Germans, yes. But of course we aren't Germans, Willy. Never have been. We're Argentines. We were born here. We are not our fathers."

"What are you saying, Heinz?" Willy was surprised; he had rarely heard his friend reveal thoughts of a political nature. Heinz had a razor-sharp intelligence underneath his devil-may-care exterior, and Willy had never for a moment doubted his fealty to the Bund. But like his father, Heinz devoted his professional energies toward what was perhaps the most apolitical organ of the Bund. Others would make the decisions, and the SD would make sure they were carried out with the greatest efficiency.

"Well, I have been thinking of what will happen after CAPRICORN. Haven't you?"

"Some," Willy admitted. In truth, his thoughts had strayed in that direction more than once lately.

"So, a year from now, Willy, we are toasting a successful 1982. The Argentine flag is flying over the Malvinas, the English have retreated to their islands in disgrace, the

Brazilians and the Chileans are afraid of us, even the mighty Americans are cowed by our daring and our strength. What then?"

"We go on from there," Willy said, not liking where this was going, but intrigued nonetheless.

"Yes, but where? What do you suppose the Reichsleiter has planned, Willy?"

"You know as well as I do, Heinz, I'm not privy to the thinking of the Reichsleiter or the Cabinet. Not even my father tells me about those meetings." Dieter Baumann filled one of the few seats on the committee that actually ran the Bund. How much influence the Reichsleiter held over it was a matter of speculation. Sometimes Willy thought that it was not very much, that the Reichsleiter, respected as he was by the other Kameraden, was not much more than a figurehead these days. Other times, he wasn't so sure.

"The men of the Cabinet are old, Willy. Our fathers will not see the next century. We will."

"I'm not sure where you are going with this, Heinz."

His friend stared back at Willy with his cobalt-blue eyes. "The next century will be ours, Willy, ours and our childrens'. If CAPRICORN is successful, that can be a springboard to the new century for us. It is up to us to determine how our children will toast us, let us say, on Christmas of 2031. Will they be fat and lazy on their estancias, and say we were the men who humiliated the English, and avenged our fathers, and then went back to making money and raising horses, or will they say something else?"

"Such as..."

Heinz grinned, but it was a different one than his usual one. This one had less gemütlichkeit and more steel behind it, and his eyes were shining now. "Perhaps, on that day fifty years from now, my friend, my son will raise a glass with yours, and they will say, 'To our fathers, who challenged the world and won for us a continent!'"

In spite of the evening's warmth, Willy felt a chill.

CHAPTER ELEVEN

Virginia

December 1981

Jo was adjusting her uniform Tuesday morning when her father appeared in the bedroom doorway. "Heading out pretty soon?" he asked.

"My appointment with the congresswoman's not till three," Jo said. "I thought I'd head over to the Pentagon this morning, look up some old friends. I might not have time tomorrow." She checked her watch: six-fifty. Her driver, arranged by the Air Force, wouldn't arrive for another half-hour. As usual, she was early. Just like her father; Joseph was already well into his workday routine, rising at five, twenty minutes on the stationary bike down in the basement with the morning news on the TV, two newspapers devoured along with his breakfast, out the door by seven. It hadn't changed in years.

"I have to leave in about fifteen minutes, but could you stop by the den when you're done here? Just need a minute."

"Sure, Daddy."

Joseph Geary's study was like something out of the fifties, with crowded bookshelves lining three walls and a solid oak desk topped with a blotter and a telephone. At least it wasn't a rotary phone anymore, she noticed. The room was solid, old-school, just like her father. He was putting some files into his well-worn briefcase when he looked up as Jo entered. A wide grin broke out below the graying mustache. "My, you look sharp," he said.

She tried to put aside her thought that he looked a lot older than the last time she'd seen him, six months earlier. Well, he was past sixty now, and he had a high-stress job. Being Deputy Director of Operations for the CIA wasn't an easy posting. "Thank you. What's up?"

"I have a reception to attend in Georgetown tonight, so I won't be home till late, and I have to leave early tomorrow morning. I wanted to catch you while I could, before your meeting with the congresswoman today." He snapped the briefcase shut and came around to the front of the desk. Jo sat casually on the corner, as she had so many times in the past, no matter what home her father's desk happened to be in, and there'd been a few.

"JoJo, this is pretty close-hold, but our friends in the Hoover Building have been keeping an eye on Congresswoman Chamberlain. To be precise, it's her chief of staff they're interested in."

Jo's research had mentioned little about the young man who ran Chamberlain's office. Ethan Blaine was in his late twenties, graduate of the U. of Maryland, and the son of a wealthy Chamberlain supporter. "The FBI doesn't get involved unless it's pretty serious, Daddy. Why are they looking at Blaine?"

"I got this from a friend at the Bureau as a heads-up, because the fallout might impact one or two of our areas of concern. Blaine is known as a ladies' man, so that's one thing right there you should watch out for." This brought a smile from Jo, but her father stayed serious. "The important thing, though, is that he's been seeing a woman the FBI suspects of being an Argentine agent."

"I'm not sure how I fit into that picture, Daddy. I won't be spending much time around him."

Her father looked away briefly, as if he was making a decision, then looked back at her. "I'm told Blaine's girlfriend is rather new to the game. This is her first overseas assignment, and Blaine is apparently her target. He's not suspected of giving her any classified material yet, but we would prefer he not get any further involved with her."

"Why doesn't the FBI just tell him about her?"

"They don't want to take the chance she'll find out her cover is blown. She works out of the Argentine Embassy and met Blaine at an official function a few weeks ago. The Bureau was hoping to steer her toward another man, who is working with them. They felt they might be able to turn her, but not if she keeps seeing Blaine." He hesitated again, then said, "I didn't want to involve you in this, JoJo, but when we heard about Chamberlain's plans to hold these hearings, we thought we might have an opening. All we want you to do is ask Blaine out to dinner tonight, and meet him at a certain restaurant in Georgetown. The Argentine woman will be there. We think when she sees you with Blaine, she'll react by breaking things off with him. That will allow the FBI to bring their man back into the picture."

Jo considered it. There really didn't seem to be any downside, and it wasn't as if she had never done undercover work. A simple dinner, allow herself to be seen by a certain woman, and that would be it. What could go wrong? "All right, Daddy. I'll see what I can do."

He smiled. "That's my girl." From his inside jacket pocket he produced a card. "Here's the number and address of the restaurant. On the back is another number. If there's any trouble, call that number. The code phrase is 'purple sundown'. That will get an FBI tactical team on the scene within two minutes. But that shouldn't be necessary." From another pocket came a photograph of an attractive blonde. "Here she is: Carmen Suarez. Tall, and I'm told she favors short skirts and pumps."

"Okay," she said. Something in his briefcase buzzed.

"That's my driver, calling my pager," he said. "Give me a hug, honey."

She embraced him gladly, smelling his so-familiar musky cologne, feeling the warmth of his affection. "I had such a good time last night, Daddy. Thank you."

"Yeah, it was great." Her mother had cooked a wonderful dinner, and after the meal they looked through old photo albums as a fire crackled in the hearth. Even though she hadn't grown up in this house, Jo felt at home here. She would be sorry to leave.

**

The table she'd reserved gave her a view of the entrance. Her dinner companion didn't seem to mind, as his focus was entirely on JoAnn. "Have you been here before?" he asked.

"No, but I've heard good things about the food," she said, forcing herself to smile. Being here with this man was a real test of her professionalism, not to mention her acting ability. This was her first dinner date with a man since her time with Ian in Hong Kong, and the difference between the two men couldn't have been more apparent.

It wasn't that Ethan Blaine wasn't attractive. He was; tall, well-groomed with wavy dark brown hair, striking green eyes, and sharply dressed. But Jo had seen those eyes on her the moment she walked into Chamberlain's district office. Blaine was standing at a filing cabinet, pulling a thick file out of a drawer, but that all ended when Jo stepped into the rather small reception area of the office. She was in her Air Force Class-A uniform, which she had never considered to be sexy, yet Blaine evidently thought so. She could almost feel his eyes roving over her. Fortunately, she was on time for her appointment and she'd only had to endure a couple minutes of small talk with Blaine before the secretary ushered her into Chamberlain's inner office.

It hadn't taken any persuasion at all to convince him to join her for dinner. He was waiting when she and Chamberlain came out from their meeting, and he offered to show her out. They shook hands and he held hers a little longer than professional courtesy dictated. When he asked if she was going to be in town for a while before going back to her base, she said yes, and her dinner invitation was quickly accepted.

He'd offered to pick her up, but she declined, saying she'd meet him here. The Air Force driver had dropped her off a block away, and Blaine was waiting for her at the bar. They shared a drink until their table was ready. Jo hadn't seen Suarez anywhere, and now was beginning to think the

Argentine spy would be a no-show. Well, she'd just have to endure the dinner and call it a night. Things didn't always go according to plan.

Blaine had his own plan, though, but she had to give him credit, he was smooth. Lots of eye contact, always a smile, and occasionally he'd reach across the table to touch her hand. She allowed the contact, thinking that it was usually the woman who did that, to show she was interested in the man. Now he was probing a little too much, asking her about her Air Force work. She had to assume that he didn't know the full extent of it, but it was better to steer away from it entirely.

"I thought the meeting with the congresswoman went well," Jo said, dodging his question about what type of training she was doing down in Florida. In truth, she wasn't sure how it had gone. Chamberlain was businesslike, cordial, but clearly she didn't like the military and had every intention of following through with her hearings when Congress convened in the New Year. Explaining that her work was often of a sensitive nature, Jo asked to be removed from the witness list. Chamberlain said she'd consider it, and Jo didn't leave feeling very hopeful. But maybe Blaine had heard something different.

"You made a good impression on her," Blaine said, sipping at his glass of merlot. "Normally, military people have the opposite effect. You must've said something right in there."

"Some of my work for the Air Force is classified," Jo said, telling him as much as he needed to know. "I think I was able to impress upon her that there are plenty of other female officers who could talk a lot more freely about their experiences."

"Good experiences, and bad ones?"

"It's like any other job in that respect, Ethan," she said, sipping her Chablis. "Women have a ways to go in the military, but things are a lot better now than they were fifteen or twenty years ago, or so I'm told."

"What about combat arms?" he asked. "Doesn't the fact that women aren't assigned to front-line units limit their chances of promotion?"

Jo had to smile at that. She'd already seen a lot more combat in her career than most men did, but it wasn't the kind that would show up in the newspapers. "Women have been in combat in all of our nation's wars," she said. "The Air Force and Navy already have women pilots."

"But not in fighter wings," Blaine said. "Can women handle that kind of stress?" He said it with a sly grin, sipping his wine, but his eyes were intense.

"You'd be surprised what kind of stress women can handle," Jo said, meeting his gaze. He blinked first, then sat back.

"Enough about that," he said. "You look great out of uniform."

"I take that to mean you like my choice of civilian attire," she said. For this particular dinner date she'd gone with a low-cut off-white blouse, showing off what cleavage she had, and a tight skirt that showed more leg than her uniform had offered him earlier. Stiletto heels not only brought her height closer to his but accented her legs, something she knew he'd appreciated when he followed her back to the table.

"Very much," he said. She knew that look, having seen it from men before. But she hadn't seen it from Ian. Was he thinking of her, now, on his ship thousands of miles away? She stifled a sigh.

"Well, shall we order?" She picked up her menu.

They'd just finished the main course when she saw the woman. Not quite as glamorous as the photo made her out to be, but it was definitely her, turning heads as she walked toward the bar. Her hair was shorter than in the photo, though, and her outfit wasn't as daring as her father had described, but it was close: she wore a black pantsuit, her jacket covering a revealing red blouse, and the pumps matched the blouse color. Taking a seat at the bar, she glanced around once, then quickly back to zero in on the table Jo shared with Blaine.

"There's a woman at the bar staring at us," Jo said.

"What?" Blaine turned to look, then did the briefest of double-takes. "Oh. Just someone I know," he said.

"A friend?"

"Yeah." He turned his attention back to Jo, but she could tell he was on edge. "Say, what do you think about getting a nightcap somewhere? I know a place a couple blocks from here, and they have a jazz combo tonight."

"Well, I don't know, Ethan, I have an early flight back to my base tomorrow."

"Just one drink. It's still early."

Jo considered her options. The bait was dangling in front of Suarez, but she hadn't taken it quite yet. "Can we walk there?"

"Sure." He beckoned at the waiter.

***

They hadn't been at their tiny table in the jazz club five minutes when Jo said, "Your friend just walked in."

She could see the briefest hint of panic in Blaine's face, but he recovered quickly. "It's a free country," he said. "What would you like to drink?"

Her glass of wine at dinner had taken up half of her personal limit. Anything more than two, she knew from past experience, would shave precious split-seconds off her reaction time, if something came up that required a reaction. "A gin and tonic," she said.

Within a few minutes, a well-built young man joined Suarez at the bar. It was evident that they were acquainted. She laughed at something he said, but to Jo it looked forced, and Suarez had been glancing their way every minute or so. She was on her second drink already, and that was on top of the one she'd had at the restaurant bar.

Jo decided to let this game play out a little longer. Two couples were on the small dance floor as the band got into a Wynton Marsalis number. "You like to dance?" Jo asked.

She led him to the floor and held him close as they started moving together. He relaxed, moving his right hand down her back to her hip, then slowly over the cheek of her derriere. Jo turned them slightly, and a glance told her Suarez had seen the hand.

Back at their table, Blaine had evidently forgotten about Suarez completely. He was focused entirely on Jo. "So, you're heading back to your base tomorrow?" he asked.

"Yes," she said, "'fraid so." Over his shoulder, she saw Suarez finish off a drink and stare at her. Jo gave her a bit of a smile. Next to Suarez, the man touched her on the arm and nodded toward the door. She shrugged him off and got up from the bar stool. Jo saw her start walking their way. It was showtime.

Blaine was making his pitch. "Look, Jo, I don't want to seem forward, but I really enjoy being with you. My place is only a few minutes away—"

"Let me guess, Ethan, she's your long-lost cousin from Japan, right?" Suarez said, slurring a couple of the words. Jo sat back in her chair making sure her hands were free. The well-built man was right behind Suarez, his face a bit flushed. Jo knew this could go either way.

Blaine's eyes went wide, but he recovered quickly, turning to face her. "Carmen! I didn't see you come in."

"Obviously. You've been pretty focused on your cousin here." She only had a slight accent, Jo noticed, and that struck her as odd. An Argentine national speaking English was certainly not unusual, but one without a real accent was. Something wasn't quite right here.

"JoAnn isn't my cousin," Blaine said. "She was a guest of the congresswoman today at the office, and I offered to buy her dinner before she leaves town." He looked back at Jo with a tight smile, but she could see he was getting more agitated.

"Just dinner? I'll bet I know what you want for dessert."

Blaine stood up. He was taller than Suarez, but a good six inches shorter than the man behind her, whose high-and-tight haircut had military stamped all over it. "Carmen, you've had a little bit too much to drink," Blaine said. "Why don't you have G.I. Joe here take you home? I'll give you a call tomorrow."

"Watch your mouth, wise guy," the man said, moving forward a couple inches. Jo moved slightly to her right, clearing her legs from the table. She carefully scanned both Suarez and the soldier. No sign of weapons, but you never knew what might be in a pocket.

Blaine looked the soldier right in the eye. Jo could see his body language change slightly, and not in a good way. He was about to get confrontational. That would not be a wise move. "Ethan, perhaps we should leave," she said. "We don't want any trouble." She stood up carefully, taking a short step away from the table, bringing her closer to Suarez and the soldier. She steadied her breathing, allowing her senses to expand and focus on the man and woman who had now become potential threats.

She could see Suarez starting to soften a bit, but the soldier chose that moment to ratchet things up. "Yeah, buddy, why don't you take her home? Chinese take-out's pretty tasty."

"Tommy, don't—"

Blaine ignored Suarez and took a step toward the larger man. "You better watch your mouth, wise guy."

Jo saw the punch coming even if Blaine didn't. She grabbed his arm and pulled him back toward the table, but Tommy's fist still managed to clip him across the face. Blaine crashed backwards into the table. Out of the corner of her eye, Jo saw the bartender pick up a telephone.

Tommy was moving in to pound Blaine, but Jo stomped down on his left foot with the heel of her stiletto. The heel broke but Tommy yelled in pain, hopping backward. Suarez now came at Jo with a yell, throwing a wild right cross. Jo easily blocked the punch and controlled Suarez' arm, bringing it around easily into a chicken-wing hold behind her back. "Calm down, missy," she said into Suarez' ear, "your joints are very fragile back here."

"Fuck you!" Suarez screamed.

"Wrong answer," Jo said, applying a bit more pressure. Suarez gasped as the pain shot from her wrist down to the elbow and then up to the shoulder. Jo saw Tommy starting toward her and she maneuvered the helpless Suarez in between them. "Back off, soldier, or I'll break her arm."

The door to the bar opened and two policemen rushed in. Jo breathed a sigh of relief. A bar brawl wasn't exactly how she had wanted to spend her evening.

***

Jo was waiting up for her father when he arrived just after ten. She'd changed into pajamas covered by an old bathrobe that her mother had kept since Jo's high school days, always waiting for her in the closet of the guest bedroom.

"Is your mother asleep?" Joseph asked as he hung his overcoat up in the hall closet.

"Yes, just a few minutes ago. I thought you'd want to hear what happened."

"Already did," he said. Joseph tossed his suit jacket on a side chair, loosened his tie and sank into his favorite recliner. "Got a call from my Bureau contact during the reception. I'd let him know where to reach me."

"The tac team wasn't needed, thankfully."

"That's what I understand," her father said. "I'm told you handled the situation very nicely. Not that I ever doubted that you could," he added with a smile.

"The police arrested Suarez and the soldier," Jo said. "Probably just disorderly conduct, they'll get fined and walk." She hesitated. "One thing bothered me, Daddy. Suarez spoke without much of an accent, and I can hardly believe the Argentines would post an operative here who has such trouble keeping her cool. What's going on?"

"You're very observant, and you're correct to be suspicious," he said. He sighed, then leaned forward, elbows on his knees. "My friend told me that Suarez is of Argentine descent, but she's a native-born American. She's also a lieutenant j.g. in the Navy, posted at the Pentagon. The FBI and Naval Intelligence have suspected her of being the source of a security leak, probably the one that landed you on Chamberlain's witness list."

Jo felt her temper rising. "I have to ask you, Daddy: did you know she wasn't an Argentine agent?"

"Not until tonight. What I told you this morning was what I was told the day before."

"Then why the deception?"

He sat back, his brow furrowed. "I don't know for sure, but I suspect it's because of your involvement, and the fact you're my daughter. The Bureau and the Navy saw a chance to expose Suarez, and keep you off that witness list. Telling me there were foreign interests at play was probably designed to make it more attractive to me as far as getting you involved."

"But, that doesn't make any sense," Jo said. "As if you would refuse to help them out in a purely domestic intelligence case. As if I would refuse."

"That's the way things work in this town sometimes," her father said. "My friend has always been reliable before. I'll have to have a chat with him about this. In any event, the Bureau is interviewing Suarez right now. Her friend will walk, he isn't part of the security problem."

"So, what will happen now?"

"Suarez will tell them what she knows, I'm pretty confident about that. Their interrogators are quite good. I would imagine that Mr. Blaine will be getting a visit from some agents tomorrow."

"Will they arrest him?" In spite of everything, she wasn't sure she wanted Blaine to go to prison. Getting some information during pillow talk and passing it along to his boss wasn't necessarily ethical, but she doubted it was illegal, especially if he hadn't known the information was classified.

"It will depend on what Suarez tells them, probably," her father said. "If she told him the intel was classified, if he pressed her for it, and then knowingly turned it over to his boss, that won't be good for him. But we can be pretty sure the good congresswoman will be getting a visit from the Department of Justice, probably quite soon."

"What do you think will happen with that?"

He sighed. "Politics is everything in this town, JoJo. Chamberlain and the administration have been at odds on a lot of things, not all of them related to military affairs. I'm pretty sure they'll lean on her pretty hard over this. Blaine might be allowed to quietly resign, but you can be sure Chamberlain will be much less of a thorn in the administration's side for the foreseeable future. I would say the chances of you being called to testify next week are now virtually nil."

Jo considered that. It would be welcomed news, if it turned out to be true, but the political angle left her feeling somewhat...dirty. That was a little naïve, she knew, and her father confirmed it, as if he could read her mind. "JoJo, I wouldn't feel sorry for Chamberlain, or Blaine, for that matter. She's been playing hardball politics all her career. When you play that game, you're going to get brushed back every now and then."

She offered a bit of a smile. "I know, Daddy. It's just, well, in my line of work, the difference between the good guys and the bad guys is usually pretty easy to tell."

"Welcome to Washington, honey."

CHAPTER TWELVE

Rio Negro Province, Argentina

New Year's Eve 1981

The voices were old, but their gusto managed to overwhelm the scratchy old recording, following the music coming from the ancient gramophone in the corner of the dining room. For the thirty-sixth time, the New Year's Eve meeting of the Siegfried Bund Cabinet concluded its dinner with a singing of the *"Horst Wessel Lied"*. Once again, Dieter Baumann heard the nostalgic old sound of the SA chorus and band, and once again he sang along:

Die Fahne hoch, die Reihen fest geschlossen

S.A. marschiert mit ruhig festem Schritt

Kam'raden die Rotfront und Reaktion erschossen

Marschier'n im Geist in unsern Reihen mit.

"Flag high, ranks closed, the SA marches with silent solid steps. Comrades shot by the red front and reaction

141

march in spirit with us in our ranks." The second verse always brought a lump to Baumann's throat, as he remembered the old days, the exciting times in Dusseldorf some fifty years ago now, when he'd been a young man wearing the brown shirt, fired with the spirit of his Leader and his vision of a new, vibrant, strong Germany:

Die Strasse frei den browned Battalionen

Die Strasse frei dem Sturmabteilungsmann.

Es schau'n aufs Hakenkreuz voll Hoffnung schon Millionen

Der Tag fuer Freiheit und fuer Brot bricht an.

"The street free for the brown battalions, the street free for the Storm Troopers. Millions, full of hope, look up at the Swastika; the day breaks for freedom and for bread."

They sang the last two verses, some with tears running down their faces, some unable to continue as they choked with emotion. The man at the head of table sang loudest, and when the last verse was sung and the long-lost horns blared the final fanfare, the right arms of the men around the table shot out automatically in the familiar old salute, not to be done again until next year at this same time and place.

The Bull waited a few moments for his comrades to compose themselves, then raised his glass. "My friends, let us offer a toast to the New Year," he said in German, the only language spoken in these meetings.

"*Prosit!*" Ten glasses went to ten pairs of lips, vintage liebfraumilch wine was sipped, or tossed back, depending on the degree of thirst. The butler re-filled those glasses that had been emptied.

"To the success of CAPRICORN, and to VALKYRIE," Günther Nagel said. The others joined him in the toast, and then they sat down again. The Bund SD leader, gray and thin but with sharp blue eyes that belied his seventy-four years, looked across the table at Dieter Baumann. The dinner had been splendid—*krautersteak* for some, *hasenpfeffer* for those with lesser appetites—and it was time for business. "Tell me, Dieter, how goes CAPRICORN?"

The Bundesobergruppenführer returned Nagel's stare. The fact that Taurus had allowed Nagel to begin the conversation was not lost on Baumann. It bespoke the close ties between them. Baumann and Nagel had been neighbors for thirty-one years, but they were not close friends. Nagel really wasn't close to anyone, inside the Bund or out. The nature of his work, Baumann thought. "Quite well," he replied, and then turned his attention to the head of the table. "Herr Reichsleiter, we are on schedule. Pilcaniyeu shall be able to deliver a workable device no later than the middle of March."

The Bull nodded in satisfaction. To his right sat Ernst Gehlen, the current Bundesführer. Elected to the post by this group of men, the Cabinet, in 1976, his five-year term would expire in a few hours. None too soon, as far as Baumann was concerned. Gehlen suffered a slight stroke in '79 and had been ineffective in the post since then. The new Bundesführer, Reinhard Schacht, was on the Reichsleiter's left. It was largely a ceremonial job, anyway. The man at the head of the table had ruled the Bund since its formation in 1946, shortly after his arrival in Argentina, and he would rule it until his death, which might be many years in coming; for a man of eighty-one, Taurus remained remarkably healthy.

It was too bad about Gehlen, really. In the fifties he had been quite useful, especially since his cousin was in charge of the West German intelligence service in those difficult days. From that relationship, VALKYRIE had been born. Schacht would be an efficient administrator, while the Bull continued to make the important decisions. In the months to come, those decisions would be important ones, indeed.

"It is crucial that the details of VALKYRIE remain most secret," Taurus said now. "It has come to my attention that certain younger members of our organization are getting somewhat, shall we say, restless."

"How so, Herr Reichsleiter?" Schacht asked.

The flat-faced features of the Bull turned toward the incoming Bundesführer. "Perhaps we should ask our security director." He looked down the table at Nagel. "Günther?"

"There has been some talk among some of our mid-level officers," the SD director answered smoothly. "They are anxious to see CAPRICORN succeed. They are fired by their Argentine blood, in many cases, but that same blood limits their vision, and that is good." He looked back at Baumann. "Dieter's son is doing a fine job. From everything I can discern his priorities are in proper order."

Baumann offered a thin smile to his neighbor. "They are," he said. He turned to the Bull. "Herr Reichsleiter, the young men of the Bund are restless, that is so. But their energies are concentrated on CAPRICORN. They know nothing of VALKYRIE. That is not their concern, but ours. Trust me when I say that we need not worry about them. Your decision to have the execution of CAPRICORN entrusted to them was a wise one." Actually, Baumann wondered whether or not this was really true, but he did know that the Cabinet had its hands full with VALKYRIE.

Why not let the youngsters run with CAPRICORN? He kept a close eye on Willy, and knew that things were going well.

In the past decade, most of the day-to-day operations of the Bund had been turned over to the next generation, the sons of the founders who had escaped the Fatherland in the last dark days of the Reich, or in its chaotic aftermath. Willy had done a particularly fine job, and Dieter was proud of him. Heinz Nagel was virtually running the SD now, but Dieter had no doubt that Günther was aware of everything that his boy was doing, and would step in immediately if need be. The elder Nagel was nothing if not efficient. Ruthlessly so, as many Bund opponents found out in the early years, and again during the Dirty War. The junta had presented the Bund with a marvelous opportunity then, and Nagel did not hesitate to use it, making sure key Argentines who were enemies of the Bund managed to disappear.

The Bull stared at Baumann for another few uncomfortable seconds, then nodded. "Very well," he said. "You will keep us informed, Dieter?"

"Of course, Herr Reichsleiter." Baumann tried hard not to swallow noticeably. Even after all these years, Taurus could still make him uncomfortable. Well, not for very much longer, he hoped.

The Bull turned his attention to another man. "Franz, could you please give us the latest about our friends in Washington and Moscow?"

Franz Müller, the Bund foreign minister, nodded gratefully. Müller was a fussy little man who bore an uncanny, and perhaps unfortunate, resemblance to the late Heinrich Himmler, director of the SS during the Reich years. His title of *Bundesaussenminister* was a bit ostentatious; Müller did not treat directly with foreign governments, of

145

course, but his responsibility was to keep the Cabinet informed about the goings-on in various capitals. Using his cover as the head of one of Argentina's largest banking conglomerates, Müller traveled widely in the Americas and Europe, even occasionally behind the Iron Curtain. Baumann did not particularly like Müller; he was married, but it was known that he preferred young men, something Baumann could not approve of. But he grudgingly admitted that Müller was good at his job. The light from the overhead chandelier glanced off his round spectacles as the Aussenminister cleared his throat.

"Herr Reichsleiter, gentlemen, I can report to you that our work is going well in the capital cities of our enemies. The new administration in Washington hates the Bolsheviks almost as much as we do. Ronald Reagan will not shed any tears to see the Russians ejected from Central Europe."

"Reagan will not idly stand by when his own troops are ejected," Baumann said, unable to contain himself. "The English and the French will not feel very good about it, either."

Müller gave him a patronizing glance. "The whole point of the plan is to present the occupying powers with a *fait accompli*, is it not? Will the NATO generals order their troops to fire on their brother Germans?"

"They will once they realize the German troops are trying to seize certain weapons," Nagel said. "The Russians, of course, won't hesitate to fire on anyone."

"I would not worry about the English," Schacht said. "Once CAPRICORN succeeds, they will have so much internal turmoil to deal with, they won't be able to pay much attention to what is happening on the Continent. As to the French..." He waved a hand dismissively, bringing nods from most of the other men. Without their English and American friends to back them up, the French would cave in, as they had since Napoleon's day.

"Brezhnev is old and weak," Gehlen said, without a trace of irony. "There will be an upheaval in his government when VALKYRIE succeeds."

"That is true, Herr Bundesführer," Muller said with proper deference. "Andropov will succeed him, but his hands will be tied politically when he finally has consolidated his position. By then our propaganda campaign will have begun telling the world about the new, united and peace-loving Germany."

"Andropov will not want to begin his rule with the Third World War," Schacht said. He was a pragmatist, but tended to be a bit overconfident, Baumann knew. Schacht had been one of the last to leave the Fatherland in the final days of the Reich, barely escaping the Russian ring of steel before it closed around Berlin. He'd kept his faith in the Führer a bit too long.

"My latest communications from our operatives in the respective governments all report progress on schedule," Muller said. "My friends, VALKYRIE will succeed, barring any unforeseen circumstances."

"The success of CAPRICORN is critical, of course," Nagel said. "VALKYRIE is doomed unless CAPRICORN works. My son Heinz tells me that young Baumann is doing quite well in the plan's execution." His eyes twinkled as he looked across the table at his neighbor.

"CAPRICORN is proceeding as planned, gentlemen," Dieter Baumann said, looking first at Nagel, then at the rest of the men around the table. "You have my word. We will not fail."

"Good," the Bull said. "Failure is not an option."

CHAPTER THIRTEEN

HMS Cambridge, *Southwest Atlantic*

January 1982

Cambridge had been away from home for a long time and still had a long trip ahead of her. The east-bound crossing of the vast Pacific from Hong Kong was hard duty for her sailors and Royal Marines, though it had been tempered by pleasant stops at some of the islands of Fiji and Tahiti. Like virtually every European male making his first visit, Ian fought to maintain his self-discipline upon encountering the world-class beauty of Polynesian women. Unlike many, if not most, of his predecessors and contemporaries, he succeeded, but it had been touch and go. Memories of Jo Ann kept him on the straight and narrow, and he was one of the few men aboard who was glad when the ship set sail for South America.

Their next port of call was Valparaiso, Chile, where Ian and his best friend, Lieutenant Steven Hodge, sampled the local pubs and the colorful plaza of the seaport. A platoon of

Chilean Naval Infantry came aboard, led by a swarthy veteran, *Capitan* Ernesto Arroyo, and the officers of the two Marine contingents began planning their next mission, a joint exercise to seize the uninhabited, British-claimed Carpenter's Island on the Atlantic side of Tierra del Fuego, the archipelago at the southern tip of the continent. For the SBS men, it would be the last in a series of training exercises on this long voyage; they'd already worked with their counterparts in Sri Lanka, Malaysia and Australia. The mission in Hong Kong, which most definitely had not been a mere exercise, had been a welcome addition to their schedule.

With her crew of 409 swelled not just by the SBS platoon but now by the Chileans, *Cambridge* transited the Strait of Magellan, beheld its scenic wonders, and was joined by the Chilean frigate *San Miguel*, from their Punta Arenas base. All the talk in Valparaiso had been about the Falklands, and whether Argentina's new president, Galtieri, would move on them. Ian was pretty sure they were talking about that back in London as well, which was why *Cambridge* was way down here, rather than taking the much shorter route for home via the Panama Canal and the Caribbean.

A meeting with *Cambridge's* skipper, Alec Stone, just after leaving Valparaiso confirmed it. The ship was being sent to Argentine waters to show the flag, provide any assistance HMS *Endurance* might require, and demonstrate British capabilities with the Carpenter's Island exercise. Adding the Chileans was a ploy to increase political pressure on the Argentines, Stone suspected; the two nations had never been on very friendly terms, and their dispute over the Patagonia region went back to the early days of the century. If the Argentines decided to challenge Britain over the

Falklands, they had to be kept guessing about their western flank.

"Admiralty is concerned," Stone told Ian. "I am to have the ship on war-time footing as we enter Argentine waters. *San Miguel* will be several hours ahead of us. I doubt very much if the Argentines would attack her, but I'm not so sure about their intentions toward us. Your landing on Carpenter's might prove to be more exciting than anticipated, Major."

"We'll be ready, sir."

***

The first sign of trouble came in a radio call from *San Miguel*. Ian was up at 0400, still feeling sluggish from the dinner he'd shared with several Chilean Marine officers ashore in Punta Arenas the night before. At 0430, freshly showered and shaved, his intercom barked with a message: "Major Masters, report to the bridge."

It took him five minutes to finish dressing and get topside, where Captain Stone was waiting with a flimsy in hand and a furrowed brow. "A message from *San Miguel*," he said, handing the flimsy to Ian. It was a typed English translation of the radio call:

0810 ZULU

STONE, COMMANDING, HMS CAMBRIDGE

MESSAGE FOLLOWS:

BE ADVISED, WE HAVE RADAR INTERCEPT OF TWO UNIDENTIFIED AIRCRAFT, BELIEVED HELO, PASSING

5 KM SOUTH OF OUR POSITION, COURSE 093, SPEED 110 KT,

ALTITUDE 3000 M.

MARTINEZ, COMMANDING, SAN MIGUEL

Ian handed the message to Captain Arroyo, who had just arrived, looking more swarthy than usual in his freshly-applied camo paint. "Let's take a look at the chart, shall we, gentlemen?" Stone suggested, and led the way to the nearby navigation area. Stone's navigator, Lieutenant Carruthers, was on duty, and had the proper charts displayed on his table. The executive officer, Lieutenant Commander Fields, was with him. Stone had evidently spoken to them already. "Lieutenant, what was *San Miguel*'s position a half-hour ago?"

The navigator looked at a flimsy, then used his pencil to mark a spot on the map. "She would be right about here, sir, on station as called for in the outline for the exercise, I believe." The point of the pencil was about forty kilometers east-northeast of Carpenter's.

"And you've plotted the path of those bogeys they spotted?" Stone asked.

"Yes, sir. Presuming a straight course, the flight would probably have originated here, on the mainland." Using a straight-edge, he drew a line from the Argentine coast directly to Carpenter's Island. "The nearest landfall would be Carpenter's, sir."

Arroyo pointed at the spot on the mainland where Carruthers' line began. "The *Argentinos* have a naval base there, at Rio Gallegos," he said.

"The message said two aircraft, probably helicopters," Ian said. "Ernesto, what kind of troop-carrying helos do they have?"

Arroyo looked off into the distance as he searched his memory. "They have some French-made helicopters, but I believe these would be from their complement of Soviet-made aircraft. Perhaps the Mi-14. We have some as well."

Fields already had a reference book in hand and was flipping through the pages. "Here, sir," he said, showing a page to Stone. "The Mil Mi-14, NATO code name 'Haze'. Used mainly for coastal submarine patrol, but also for transport."

Stone took the book from his XO, examined the page with a grunt and handed it to Ian. "Maximum speed 124 knots," he read aloud. "So they were going close to full bore when *San Miguel* spotted them. Range, 1135 kilometers."

"A round-trip would be well within their range," Fields said.

"If modified for troop transport, they could each carry two dozen men," Arroyo said. That drew a hard glance from Stone.

"Do you have the time, Mr. Fields?" the captain asked.

The XO checked his watch. "Almost 0500, sir."

"So we can assume, gentlemen, that these helos were headed for Carpenter's, and if *San Miguel* spotted them nearly an hour ago, they've already landed and had ample time to off-load any troops." He glanced out a porthole on the starboard side of the cabin. "Dawn in another half-hour or so, perhaps. Not ideal light for a helo landing on an unmarked island, but evidently enough."

"If they remain on the island, those helos could be a threat to the ship," Fields said. "Their ASW birds can be armed with torpedoes as well as depth charges."

Stone considered that, then turned to Ian. "Major, it appears likely our recent conversation will be pertinent after all."

Ian took a deep breath. "Request permission to carry out the exercise as planned, Captain."

Stone had shown himself to be a very capable commander during this voyage, earning the respect of the marines, which was not easily given. But would he sail toward the sound of guns? "I'm not inclined to send your men into harm's way needlessly, Major."

"Carpenter's Island is British territory, sir," Ian said firmly. "Shall we have another Southern Thule episode? I think not, sir. Not when we're this close."

Stone looked at the Chilean. "Captain Arroyo, I'm even more hesitant to involve troops from a third party in what could be the opening rounds of a conflict between two other nations."

Arroyo came to attention. "Mi capitan, I formally request permission to accompany your men ashore, as planned, even under these circumstances. We will stand with our British comrades, sir."

Stone nodded. "Noted. But, gentlemen, I must inform Admiralty that circumstances on the island may have drastically changed. I have strict orders not to engage the Argentines unless clearly in defense of the ship."

"If the Argentines are ashore on Carpenter's, sir," Fields said, "one could interpret that as an aggressive act all by itself."

"Indeed. But as they haven't fired on this vessel—yet—I must cable London for instructions." He turned back to Ian and Arroyo. "Gentlemen, have your men ready to disembark as planned. I'm off to the radio room."

***

Lieutenant Colonel Gerhard Schmidt barked a few more orders at his hard-working men as he walked through their defensive position. His demeanor didn't indicate it, but he was pleased with their progress so far. Only three hours ago they'd landed here, and they had already turned the old whaling station into a fortified defensive position. He paused and gazed out to sea, toward the west. It was overcast this morning, but he thought he could see a speck on the horizon. The English ship? It had to be.

"*Hauptmann* Winkler!"

His adjutant, following close behind as always, answered immediately. "*Jawohl*, Herr *Oberstleutnant!*"

"I believe our friends are about to arrive. If you please, tell *Kapitänleutnant* Speth he may conduct his reconnaissance mission now."

"Jawohl, Herr Oberstleutnant." Winkler trotted off in the direction of the hidden helicopters. Schmidt was glad he had insisted that the helos remain on the island, rather than returning to base immediately after their landing. Now he could use them to recon the enemy, and if push came to shove, their torpedoes would prove quite useful.

He breathed in deeply, sucking in the salt air. *Mein Gott,* but it felt good to be in the field again, even on such a Godforsaken rock as this island, with a real enemy out there, trained men who would test his mettle. No more chasing common bandits or fanatical insurrectionists through the mountains and rain forests. Schmidt hadn't slept more than four hours in the last twenty-four, but he felt refreshed. He checked his wristwatch. It was nearly 0800. Surely the English would be making their attempt to land soon, assuming they still planned to assault the island.

Schmidt's unit was officially known as Company A, 2nd Battalion, 7th Parachute Regiment, 3rd Infantry Division, of *Ejército Argentino,* the Argentine Army. Within the regiment, which was probably the smallest in the entire army, were two separate battalions; the regiment, due to its ethnic makeup, was allowed to use German unit names and ranks that harked back to the Wehrmacht days. Each of the *Abteilungen* had three companies. In the old German *Heer*, a regiment would've included at least two thousand troops; in this modern, Argentine version, the regiment's numbers were half that. What made the regiment unique was its roster. Every one of the men was of German extraction, and many of the officers, like Schmidt, had served in the Wehrmacht during the last war.

That service had proven fortunate again, when his unit was ordered to Patagonia for training. Even though his orders always came through the official chain of command, Schmidt knew that orders for the Werewolves were cut at the headquarters of the Siegfried Bund. For this particular mission, he had no doubt at all where the mission was initiated. The phone call he'd received last night, upon reporting to the naval base at Rio Gallegos, hadn't been from just any Argentine, but from Dieter Baumann himself. Schmidt immediately recognized the aged but still vibrant voice of his former commander.

"The English have sent a ship into our waters. We believe they intend to land marines on the Island of the Penguins, along with some Chilean commandos. They call the island Carpenter's. That island is ours, Gerhard. You must take it and hold it at all costs until relieved."

"Jawohl, Herr Oberst," Schmidt replied, using Baumann's old Heer rank.

"We stood together against the Bolsheviks, Gerhard. You fought bravely for me then. I know you will stand with me now."

Emotionally, Schmidt had answered, *"Sieg heil!"* Hail victory!

Schmidt had been unable to sleep on the noisy helicopter ride to the island. His thoughts went back to the events that had brought him here. He'd seen much in his fifty-eight years, and more than once he'd thought he'd be lucky to see forty. A seventeen-year-old professor's son when he left Heidelberg to join the Heer in 1940, he saw a lot of action in the last war as an infantryman who rose to the rank of *Hauptfeldwebel*, or Chief Sergeant, and was decorated with the Iron Cross 2nd Class for valor in Russia. He'd saved three wounded comrades from being overrun by a Soviet squad backed by a tank, shooting all four infantrymen and disabling the tank with a well-aimed grenade. He was reminded of one of those wounded men now, as he stopped to assist two young troopers in preparing their machine gun position. One of them looked just like Gustav, one of the young soldiers he'd saved back in '43.

"What is your name, son?" Schmidt asked.

"*Obergefreiter* Heinrich Rehberg, Herr Oberstleutnant," the young man said proudly, snapping to attention.

"Did you, by chance, have a relative in the Wehrmacht, during the last war?" Schmidt asked.

"Yes, Herr Oberstleutnant. My uncle, Gustav Fröhlich, was an infantryman on the Russian front."

Schmidt felt himself choking up. He'd saved Gustav, only to have them both captured a month later. Schmidt watched him die at the hands of the brutal Russian guards in '46. Impulsively, the lieutenant colonel reached over and patted the young soldier on the shoulder. "I knew your uncle," he said, trying not to let too much emotion into his voice. "He was a good man. He would be proud of you. Carry on, Corporal."

Eyes wide, the young man stiffened, saluted and said, "Jawohl, Herr Oberstleutnant."

Schmidt hurried away, eager to complete his inspection. Such men as this, how could he be any more proud of them? What a legacy they carried! A proud nation had sent its sons to fight the Bolsheviks, only to be betrayed by the "Golden Pheasants" back in Berlin, those poppycock Party hacks who had dared to wear the uniform. At least they hadn't been regular Heer officers, but they wore the black and red of the SS and lorded it over everyone, even the Wehrmacht generals and admirals who were real warriors. Why, even the Führer's valet had been named a colonel in the SS. Such men had brought his nation down.

Well, it would not happen again. Today, he wore the uniform of his adopted country, and once more he faced an enemy who would take from them what was rightfully theirs. Today, they would not fail.

He looked out to sea again. The speck had grown a bit larger. Hauptmann Winkler ran to his side, just as Schmidt heard the sound of a helicopter engine spinning up. "Herr Oberstleutnant, the helicopter is about to take off for recon."

"Very good," Schmidt said. "Is the flagpole ready?"

"Yes, Herr Oberstleutnant."

"It's time to make our statement." He glanced at Winkler. "Klaus, there is a young corporal about fifteen meters back there, at a machine gun emplacement. His name is Rehberg. Tell him that I would like him to have the honor of running up the colors."

Winkler snapped off a salute. "Jawohl!"

Schmidt took out his binoculars and scanned the sea to the east. Yes, it was an English ship, all right, flying their naval ensign with pride. Now Schmidt would see how much pride they really had.

***

"Bloody hell," Stone said, his binoculars failing to hide his angry scowl. "They've launched a helicopter. I believe they've also raised the Argentine flag." He handed the field glasses to Ian. The SBS commando was fully kitted out in his standard Royal Marines uniform with the Number 8 Dress Temperate Disruptive Pattern Material, the distinctively British camouflage print. The only uniform markings

159

distinguishing him from any other Marine officer in the field were his parachute wings on his left breast and Swimmer-Canoeist badge bordered by laurel wreaths on his right shoulder. A British flag patch was on his left upper arm. Underneath his camo jacket he wore a high zip-neck shirt patterned after those worn by the Norwegian Army. A Royal Marines green beret topped his ensemble. Behind them, the marines were being mustered by Hodge, Ian's second in command.

Ian focused the lenses until he could clearly see the blue-white-blue Argentine banner flapping in the wind. "Indeed they have, sir. What do you intend to do about the chopper?"

"I certainly don't intend to let it fire a torpedo at me, Major," Stone said. To the ensign next to him, he said, "Mr. O'Toole, send word immediately to Mr. Fields to launch our Lynx."

"Aye, aye, sir," the ensign replied, and raced off to the bridge.

"Will you fire on the Argentine?" Ian asked.

"Only if he appears to be readying a torpedo for launch," Stone said firmly. "I can't very well take evasive action while I'm lowering your lads' boats. I may be a sitting duck, but I can also send out a bee to sting him."

From the aft end of the ship came the roar of the ship's helicopter's engine, and Ian turned in time to see the Lynx lift off and head east, toward the Argentine, which was gaining altitude and turning off to the northwest. "Perhaps he means only to get a good look at us, sir," Ian offered, handing the binoculars back to the skipper.

"Perhaps." After another long look at the island, then at the enemy helicopter—Ian had to start thinking of it in that way, he knew—Stone said, "Prepare to disembark your troops, Mr. Masters."

"Aye, aye, sir," Ian said, snapping off a salute.

The orders from London had been fairly straightforward. Reconnaissance in force approved. Chilean participation is approved via Santiago. Do not fire unless fired upon. Captain's discretion regarding any opposing force on Carpenter's. The last part was typical politics, Ian thought. Admiralty was giving Stone—and by extension Ian, his man on the island—fairly wide latitude in dealing with any Argentine presence on the British island. If push came to shove, Stone was authorized to shove back. But Ian was sure the orders to Stone had been approved by 10 Downing Street, and the politicians were leaving themselves a loophole. Very nifty, Ian thought; if this went a bollocks, the captain would get the blame, and some would be handed his way, as well.

Well, he would do what had to be done. He thought of Jo, and the mission in Hong Kong. That was hairy enough, but this, now, this was the real deal. He'd never been too concerned about the Chinese firing on them, but now, just a few miles away, men with loaded guns were waiting for him, and might very well try hard to kill him. He hoped he would be up to the challenge. He had to trust his training, and trust his men.

Now, some three hundred meters off shore, riding the choppy waves in one of the two ship's launches carrying his men to the island, Ian's binoculars helped him see that the Argentines had done a good job of deploying their forces.

The beach, such that it was, stretched barely fifty meters between two outcroppings of rock. A few penguins waddled here and there. Scrubby trees and a scattering of rocks dotted the landscape for about five hundred meters inland, ending at a hardscrabble hill that supported half a dozen ramshackle metal buildings, the remains of a long-ago whaling station. The Argentine troops had fortified the hill, giving his opposite number a commanding field of fire on the beach. There were some machine-gun emplacements, to be sure, and they probably had some light mortars as well. If they opened up on his men as they came ashore, Ian's mission would be a very short one. He would be going in out-gunned as it was.

Stone had decided to call the Argentines' bluff and send his men ashore. He assured Ian the ship's guns would open fire on the enemy position the moment Ian came under attack on the beach, if it happened. Ian could only pray that wouldn't be necessary. If he could get his men safely ashore, they could find enough cover and engage the Argentines, and perhaps flank them on one or both sides of the hill, provided the terrain allowed it.

Ian heard a crunching sound from underneath the boat's keel, and the coxswain in the bow of the launch waved for his helmsman to come about. "You've got about three feet of water, Mr. Masters!"

"All right, lads, out we go!" Ian ordered, and he levered himself overboard.

CHAPTER FOURTEEN

Island of the Penguins, Southwest Atlantic

January 1982

Schmidt watched the English and Chilean commandos scramble out of their boats and head for the beach on the double. Visibility was excellent, and he could easily have decimated the enemy's ranks with a mortar barrage. But his orders had been specific: he was not to engage the English unless they fired first. He suspected the enemy commander had received the same orders from his superiors.

That would make for an interesting situation. He couldn't fire on the Englishmen to stop their landing on what was now an Argentine island, yet he couldn't very well allow them to walk up to his breastworks and ask to join him for lunch.

"Spread the word," he said to Winkler, "everyone is to hold their fire."

"Jawohl, Herr Oberstleutnant," Winkler replied, and repeated the order to the nearest positions, adding that they should spread it through the ranks.

He raised his binoculars to the sea again. The English helicopter was engaged in a playful dance with the Haze, which was under strict orders not to fire on the destroyer unless given a direct command by Schmidt. "We have a tactical challenge, Klaus," Schmidt said to his adjutant. "We have been ordered to hold this island, yet we must hold our fire, and so, it appears, must the enemy. What do you make of it?"

"One of us will have to leave the island in the other's hands, eventually," Winkler said.

"Very true," Schmidt said. "I would say that they have roughly the same number of men ashore now as we have in our position. We have two helicopters, they have one. But they have a ship that is capable of bringing down our choppers and shelling us into submission. Yes, an interesting tactical problem, wouldn't you say?"

"Y-yes, sir," Winkler answered hesitantly. Schmidt glanced at him. The young man was clearly nervous. Well, he should be; he had not yet seen the elephant, as the saying goes. Schmidt had seen his many years ago, in Belgium and France and then on the steppes of Russia, in situations far more desperate than this, against a very tough enemy that surely was far more savage than these English dandies and Chilean fishermen would ever be.

He trained his glasses on the scrambling enemy troops. One of them clearly appeared to be in charge. How would he react?

Ian was grateful the Argentine commander hadn't chosen to open fire on his men the moment they left the boats, when they were the most vulnerable. But the enemy would know that an attack like that would surely bring a response from *Cambridge*, and the destroyer's 4.5-inch gun could fire a shell every two or three seconds, more than enough to decimate the Argentine position.

He deployed his men as quickly as possible, sending Arroyo and his Chileans to the left, holding the center himself and tasking Hodge with half the SBS commandos to the right flank, which looked to be a bit rougher ground than the left. If the Argentines opened up on him, Ian hoped he could quickly flank the enemy position on both sides and employ a withering crossfire. He could always call for supporting fire from the ship, but he knew Stone would have to deal with the enemy helicopter first to avoid a torpedo attack from the air.

Colour Sergeant Powers huddled behind a rock next to Ian's. "Well, we're here, sir," Powers said with a wry grin. "When does the welcoming committee come down to greet us?"

Ian peered over his rock at the Argentine position. "I don't know, Sergeant. We may very well have to crash the party ourselves." He grabbed his walkie-talkie. "Hodge, are you in position?"

The speaker crackled with Hodge's tinny voice. "Just about, sir. Another hundred meters or so. No response from the enemy yet, but I'd say they've spotted us, sir."

"Make sure you have plenty of cover in case of mortar attack."

"Aye, aye, sir."

Ian clicked the send/receive button, then said, "Arroyo, this is Masters, report."

"We are in position, mi Mayor," the Chilean marine announced with a confident voice. "The Argentinos are dug in, about 250 meters from us. We have good cover for an assault."

"Understood. Hold where you are, report any movement and stand by."

"Si, mi Mayor."

Schmidt made a decision. "Klaus, is *Oberleutnant zur See* Brunner ready with the second helo?"

"On your command, Herr Oberstleutnant."

"Very well." He checked his wristwatch. "Hand me the radio, please." He took the German-made two-way device from his adjutant, clicked a button, and said, "Oberleutnant Brunner, this is Schmidt."

Brunner replied immediately. "Jawohl, Herr Oberstleutnant."

"Alois, I am going down to meet with the English commander. In exactly five minutes, I want you to lift off and get into position to the south of the destroyer. Speth is to the north. The English have their helicopter shadowing him. Should we come under fire here, I want you to put a torpedo into that ship."

There was a brief hesitation, then Brunner said, "Jawohl, Herr Oberstleutnant."

"A question, Alois?"

Another brief moment. These younger officers, they didn't quite have the discipline of Wehrmacht veterans. Not yet. "Herr Oberstleutnant, I could attack the Englishman's gun mount to prevent him from firing on the island."

"Negative, Herr Oberleutnant," Schmidt said firmly. "His missiles would bring you down before you could do any damage. You will follow your orders. Am I clear?"

This time there was no hesitation. "Jawohl, Herr Oberstleutnant! I am spooling up my engines now."

"Very good. Once you are airborne, you will tell Kapitänleutnant Speth that he is to engage the English helicopter if we are fired upon here. That will give you a clear line of fire on the destroyer."

"Jawohl, Herr Oberstleutnant!"

"Five minutes from right now, Alois. Schmidt out." He put the radio back into its pouch on his web belt, then reached into a back pocket for his handkerchief.

"Blimey, the bugger's coming out with a white flag," Powers said incredulously, just as Ian's radio crackled to life with reports from Hodge and Arroyo, reporting movement from the center of the Argentine position.

"All units, hold your fire!" Ian nearly shouted into the radio. He looked at Powers. "Sergeant, I'm going out there to see what he has to say. You're in command of the center if it goes bollocks on me."

"Aye, aye, sir," Powers said. "Good luck, Major."

Lazily waving the handkerchief on the end of a meter-long stick, Schmidt picked his way carefully over the rough ground. His heart was racing, but he felt exhilaration, not fear. Whoever this Englishman was, he couldn't possibly be as rough a customer as the Russians had been, and Schmidt had taken the worst of what they'd thrown at him, at the front and in the camp, and come out alive. That would be the case here, too. He knew that a number of rifles were being trained on him and he was only a fraction of a kilogram's pressure against a trigger away from entering the next world. Well, that was fine. The Englishman was in the same boat, so to speak.

Ian carefully walked out to meet the Argentine. He could see the man was armed only with a pistol, and that was holstered. Ian kept his own assault rifle dangling at his side by its shoulder strap, where it could easily be brought to bear. The Argentine was fifty meters away now, and didn't appear Latino at all. Ian realized he had never met an Argentine, and assumed they'd be of Spanish extraction, like Arroyo and his men. This one was definitely of northern European stock.

The Argentine officer stopped when he was twenty-five meters from Ian, who took the hint and came to a halt himself. The man was smiling.

"Good morning," he said in English, with a distinctive German accent.

"Good morning to you, sir," Ian replied. "I am Major Ian Masters, 42 Commando, Her Majesty's Royal Marines. And you, sir?"

The Argentine clicked his heels and offered a slight bow. "Lieutenant Colonel Gerhard Schmidt, 2nd Battalion, 7th Parachute Regiment, of the Argentine Army. Major, I must request that you and your men depart this island immediately."

"On the contrary, sir, it is I who must request the same of you and your men. You are trespassing on sovereign British territory."

From behind Schmidt, Ian heard the sound of a helicopter engine, and the second Haze lifted into view. He tensed. "Don't be alarmed, Major," Schmidt said. "My helicopter is merely going to take up station to protect us from shelling by your ship. He will not fire unless we are fired upon first."

Ian fought to maintain his composure. Once Stone saw the second Haze in the air, the rules of the game might very well change. "I must repeat my request, sir, that you recall your helicopters and disembark this island. My government have been informed of your action, and have ordered me to reclaim this territory for Her Majesty." That was not entirely true. Ian wasn't sure if Stone had informed London about the Argentine landing, or if London had told the captain what to do about it, if anything. A little bluffing wouldn't hurt, though. Probably.

Schmidt looked to his left, and then his right. "I see no English settlers here, Major. No buildings, except those old shacks left by the whalers many years ago, and they were Norwegians, if I'm correct. You are very far from home. What would your Queen possibly want with this rock? Is she that fond of penguins?"

"That is for the diplomats to debate, sir," Ian said. The Argentine was playing with him, stalling to let his helicopters get into position. Very soon now, Stone's hand might be forced. "I can guarantee your safety if you recall your helicopters now. If they make threatening moves against the ship, all bets are off."

Schmidt was more serious now. "My government ordered me to seize and hold this island, sir. I intend to follow my orders. If your government disputes our action, they can take it up with mine." He smiled again, and gestured with his free hand. "There is no need for bloodshed here, Major. Surely you can see that you are out-manned and out-gunned. A battle here would be senseless, would it not? Take your men back to your ship and go home. Your wives and children want you back alive, I am sure."

"Sir, are you refusing my request to disembark?"

Some three hundred meters away, *Corporeo* Rodrigo Hernandez of the Chilean Navy Infantry was lying prone behind a scruffy tree, trying to stay comfortable. Easier said than done, but he had to keep that Argentine rifleman in view, about a hundred meters in front of him. The enemy soldier was in a foxhole at the far right flank of their position. The twenty-two-year-old corporal shifted himself again, trying to adjust a little bit and still keep his modified M16 assault rifle trained on the Argentine's position.

He heard the squawk of the penguin and turned his head just in time to see the bird eyeing him from only a foot or so away. It was a big one, a female, he assumed, because he could see a nest partially obscured by some rocks. Hernandez had a thing about birds. As a child, he'd been clipped by a seagull while on his father's fishing boat, and then he'd seen that American movie, *The Birds*, and it had terrified him.

"Go away!" he hissed at the creature. *"Vamos!"* The bird squawked again, but refused to move. *"Mierda,"* he swore, trying to think of a way to get rid of the damned thing.

It is sometimes the small things upon which history turns. Hernandez found a pebble with his left hand, keeping his right around the trigger guard of his weapon. He meant only to scare the bird, but his left hand wasn't his better one, and he was cramped and cold besides, and his aim was off. The pebble hit the penguin squarely on the chest, and the bird retaliated. Its beak dug deep into the Chilean's thigh, grabbing the flesh through the fabric of his camo pants. Hernandez cried out in pain, and his right hand reflexively pulled the trigger of his rifle.

Ian heard the sharp crack of the rifle and his body was moving within an instant of recognizing the sound. He dove to his right, rolled behind a scruffy bush and brought his rifle up. Schmidt was gone—no, there he was, scuttling behind some low rocks. Ian aimed and squeezed off a round, saw it ricochet off one of the rocks, and then a pile of small stones next to the bush exploded, followed within a second by the distinctive whipsaw snap of a high-powered rifle.

Any thoughts of getting Schmidt were banished by the need to find cover and survive. The Argentine marksman wouldn't need much more time to zero him in. Sure enough, another round tore through the leaves of the bush, not half a meter above his head. Hugging the ground, Ian frantically searched his surroundings for something that might provide better cover.

His radio crackled to life. "Major, this is Powers, we've got the sniper targeted." The sergeant's voice was loud but calm, almost cheery. "On count of three, break for that boulder ten meters to your right. One, two, three!"

Ian didn't hesitate. He sprang to his feet and dashed for the boulder as automatic weapons fire erupted from the British positions behind him and on the right flank. The ten meters were the longest he'd ever encountered, and he expected to feel the impact of a sniper round at each step. But none came, and he made it safely, crouching down and breathing heavily. Rounds were now flying overhead as both sides opened up.

He grabbed for his radio. "Hodge! Report!"

"Someone from the left flank fired off a round, sir," Hodge yelled back, with the sound of gunfire in the background. "Don't know which side. I've got their C.O. targeted. Should we take him out?"

Ian thought fast. Had Schmidt double-crossed him? That seemed unlikely; the Argentine would have known that any shot at Ian would have immediately brought return fire at him. Something was wrong here. "Negative, negative!" he shouted into the radio. "Keep them pinned down but don't fire on him."

"Aye, aye, sir," Hodge replied, almost regretfully.

Ian clicked his radio. "Arroyo, this is Masters, report!"

"We are taking fire, mi Mayor. The Argentinos have not moved out of their position."

"Who fired the first shot?"

"I do not know, mi Mayor. I believe it came from our position. I will try to find out. I did not authorize it, though."

Is he lying? Although Ian hadn't known the Chilean that long, he'd sensed he could trust the man. But what if Arroyo

172

had received secret orders to instigate some sort of incident between the British and Argentines? A naval war over the Dependencies could allow Chile to make a move elsewhere, perhaps Tierra del Fuego. Ian's mind whirled with the possibilities, but he didn't have time to think them through. "Hold your position, Arroyo," he ordered.

"Si, mi Mayor."

Think, man, think, Ian's mind raged. Find cover. Get back to Powers. Get this under control somehow, before it really gets bollocksed up.

CHAPTER FIFTEEN

Island of the Penguins, Southwest Atlantic

January 1982

The second Argentine Haze had just taken up its position to the south and east of the English destroyer when an urgent radio call came in. "Oberleutnant Brunner, this is Winkler, we are taking enemy fire. Repeat, we are taking enemy fire. Proceed with your attack on the ship."

The lieutenant felt a cold ball form in his gut. "Hauptmann Winkler, this is Brunner, where is the Herr Oberstleutnant?"

"He is trying to get back to our position. I have taken temporary command of the situation. Follow your orders, Herr Oberleutnant!"

"Jawohl, Herr Hauptmann!" Brunner looked at his copilot, Leutnant zur See Karl Friedrich. They had grown up together in central Argentina outside Cordoba, went through school and basic training together, and had been reunited in this helicopter squadron just a few months ago. Now they were going to war together. "Karl, prepare the torpedoes," Brunner said, more calmly than he felt.

"Jawohl, Herr Oberleutnant." Friedrich's hands trembled just a bit as he began setting the controls for the weapons. The helo carried two Set-40 Soviet-made torpedoes. Brunner swung the helicopter around and began to set up his attack run. He would have to come in from the east, setting up a broadside shot on the Englishman, and he'd have to make it a good shot, because these older torpedoes would hit only what they were aimed at. Once they were launched, they'd go straight and true, but that was it.

Cambridge's radar operator had to shout to make himself heard over the growler, above the increasing volume of voices on the bridge. "Captain! Target Baker is turning away!"

Captain Stone's instinct told him what was happening. "Sound general quarters!" he ordered, and immediately swung his field glasses toward the second Haze. As klaxons blared, he watched the Argentine helo swing around to the south, then east, but he was continuing his turn, now starting to come back in a westerly heading. "Mr. Fields, you have the conn, I'm going to CIC," Stone announced.

He was down the ladder in record time, soon enough to hear the radarman shout, "Target Baker is turning again, altitude decreasing! Range, two kilometers!"

"Mr. Fields, order the Lynx to engage Target Able," Stone ordered. "Gunnery officer, target the Sea Wolf battery and the Goalkeeper on Baker, and be quick about it, please."

"Captain, message from the beach," the radio officer said, "Major Masters reports he is taking fire."

"Acknowledge and tell him to hold his position," Stone ordered. He kept his eye on the radar screen. The blip representing Baker was making its move. "The bastard's coming in for a run," he said. "Helmsman, prepare for evasive action! Engine room, I want flank speed at my command!" A talker immediately relayed the captain's commands over the growler.

"Aye, aye, sir!"

"Alois, their missile battery is coming to bear!" Friedrich shouted.

"I see it," Brunner said, trying to keep his voice calm. The intercom carried their voices easily despite the roar of the helicopter's engine. "Prepare number one torpedo." He would launch his first weapon at the Englishman and then break off to evade what would surely be a missile launch. The second torpedo could be saved for a second run, if they survived.

"Torpedo ready! Five seconds to launch point!"

"Easy now, Karl," Brunner told his friend. "Remember our training." He was only twenty meters above sea level now. Hopefully that would make it difficult for the English missiles to lock on. But it also meant he would have less maneuvering room.

The destroyer was steering straight south and hardly moving, the better to stay aligned with the landing beach. Brunner guessed that the English captain would order flank speed and steer to port when the torpedo was in the water, coming about to offer as slight a target profile as possible. So, he was aiming for a spot forward of amidships. He wanted to launch the weapon at about five hundred meters. Another second or two...

"Launch point!" Friedrich shouted.

"Fire one!"

Friedrich mashed a button on his panel. The helicopter lurched upward. "Torpedo away!"

"Hang on!" Brunner pulled the cyclic to port and increased his speed, hoping he could show his tail to the English missiles, giving them a smaller target. If they were heat-seekers, though, that might not be enough.

"Torpedo in the water!" several voices yelled.

"Gunnery officer, fire on Baker!" Stone shouted. "Evasive action! Flank speed, full reverse! Helm, left full rudder!" A missile leaped from the Sea Wolf battery, trailing flame and smoke, followed quickly by another. Men stumbled and struggled to find handholds as the ship lurched to its right and surged backward, and Stone could feel the throbbing of the engines through the deck plates. Going full reverse was a desperate gamble, but from a standing start he knew he couldn't outrun the torpedo. He would have to outsmart the Argentine pilot somehow.

The hard turn to port, combined with the reverse thrust of the engines, was slowly swinging the bow of the ship to starboard. Stone could see the wake of the torpedo now, heading toward the front of the ship. He wiped sweat off his brow and grabbed the armrests of his chair. "Brace for impact!"

"Missile in the air! Two missiles!" Friedrich screamed.

Brunner juked the Haze violently. He had no defensive weapons against SAMs, no chaff, nothing. It was just his skill and luck now. He fought the cyclic and pushed the chopper for all it was worth.

The Sea Wolfs were coming so very fast now, and he barely had time to see them on the cabin's small radar screen. The lead missile was almost on him, but he pulled the cyclic back with all his strength. The helicopter clawed into the air, standing almost vertical, and the stall alarms buzzed as the missile rushed past them, nearly clipping their rotor. Brunner didn't have time to congratulate himself because the second Sea Wolf slammed into the Haze's tail rotor and exploded.

A cheer went up from the forward missile battery as their second shot hit the Argentine chopper. Then the sailors saw the deadly white wake of the incoming torpedo, only a hundred meters off the port bow and coming fast. Suddenly the water around the torpedo was churning with something else.

A kilometer away, Target Alpha was showing no inclination to fight. That was really starting to irritate *Cambridge*'s Lynx pilot, Lieutenant Harry Carson. The Argie helo driver was a good one, though; Carson hadn't been able to score more than a couple hits with the Lynx's machine guns as the Haze danced with him. He was about to order his copilot, Sub-lieutenant Peter McNally, to prepare to fire a Sea Skua missile when his third crewmember, Warrant Officer Robert Fischer, yelled that Baker was commencing a torpedo attack run. Loosing one last machine gun volley at Alpha, Carson pulled the Lynx in the direction of the ship. He knew full well the destroyer had no better than even odds against a torpedo. And there it was, dropping off the hard-charging Haze and into the water, straight and true for *Cambridge.*

Could he make it in time? He'd have to; if the ship went down, it would be a devil of a long flight home. Carson coaxed every ounce of speed from the Lynx as he vectored it on an intercept course.

"Peter, fire on the torpedo!"

"Too far away, Harry," McNally said rather calmly. "Get us within two hundred meters."

"They might not have that much to spare, damn it to hell," Carson growled, but he pressed on. The torpedo was closing quickly on the ship. Carson could see the froth of her screws at the stern. The Goalkeeper battery at the bow began firing, its seven-barrel 30mm Gatling gun sending shells into the water at a murderous rate of seventy rounds per second, but the system wasn't designed to engage targets below the surface. Plus, the angle was all wrong; Carson knew the Goalkeeper would miss. Was the ship going in reverse? Smart move by the skipper, and turning hard aport was swinging the bow away from the path of the torpedo, but from this angle Carson could see it wouldn't be enough. He did the geometry in his mind, and the result told him the torpedo would hit about ten meters from the bow. He knew that would probably spell doom for the ship.

"Fire the guns, for Christ's sake, Peter!"

McNally squeezed the trigger and the Lynx's twin machine guns chattered to life. Carson saw the tracers streaking toward the torpedo, too far behind it, and brought the nose up and a bit to the right to compensate.

Dodging from cover to cover, Schmidt was fifteen meters from his lines when a Chilean bullet creased his shoulder. Staggered by the hit, the Wehrmacht veteran went to one knee, but knew from old experience the wound wasn't bad. Gritting his teeth, he struggled toward the forward line as bullets flew through the air, searching him out.

"Herr Oberstleutnant!" a man shouted. Up ahead, someone was directing the Argentines' fire onto their right, from where the first shot of the engagement had come. Two men scrambled from the relative safety of their trench and grabbed Schmidt under the arms, hustling him back to their comrades. They almost threw him into the trench and dove in next to him. "Medic! Medic!"

"It's just a scratch," Schmidt said, breathing hard. "Get me a radio!"

A young obergefreiter handed him a transceiver, and Schmidt punched the transmit key angrily. "Winkler, this is Schmidt! Come in!"

The captain's voice could hardly be heard above the sound of barking guns and shouting men. "Herr Oberstleutnant! Are you all right?"

"Never mind that. What's our situation?"

"The English have us outflanked, Herr Oberstleutnant, but they are not advancing. The first shot came from our right. We think that's where the Chileans are."

"Spread the word, everyone is to hold their fire unless the enemy tries to advance on us. Are the mortars ready?"

"Yes, sir. Shall I order them to fire?"

"No, damn it! They are to fire only if the enemy fires first. We must conserve our ammunition in case of an assault on our position."

"Jawohl, Herr Oberstleutnant."

Schmidt keyed his radio again. "All units, this is Schmidt. Cease fire, hold your positions. Unit feldwebels, watch out for enemy advances, return fire only if they start moving on your position." The sergeants in charge of the individual squads were all hand-picked men, sons of Wehrmacht veterans, many of them trained in West Germany. They would keep their wits about them. Already the volume of fire from his men was decreasing to a few scattered shots. "Winkler, what is the situation with the helicopters?"

"Herr Oberstleutnant, I have Leutnant Brunner's aircraft in sight now. He has fired a torpedo on the Englishman and is taking evasive action. I believe there's been a missile launch from the ship." There was some shouting from the higher positions. "Oh, no!"

"What happened?" Schmidt struggled to the top of the trench, just in time to see something crashing into the sea, well off shore.

"Brunner was struck by at least one missile, Herr Oberstleutnant," Winkler said grimly.

Damn! "What about Speth?" A medic was fussing with Schmidt's shoulder, but the colonel let the man continue despite the irritating burn of the antiseptic.

"Leutnant Speth has attempted to engage the English helicopter but his guns are jammed. He requests permission to return to the island."

"Tell him—" There was a roar from far off shore. Schmidt squinted, trying to focus his weary eyes. Was that some sort of explosion on the destroyer? The front of the ship was obscured by rising water and smoke.

Schmidt knew he had little choice about the other helicopter. If Speth's helo was shot down, and the English ship survived Brunner's attack, the Argentines would be at the mercy of the enemy's offshore guns. At least with one helo, he could make another run at the ship, or at least some of his men could be evacuated should he be forced to give up the island. "Order Speth to return immediately," Schmidt said, trying to keep the resignation out of his voice. "What of the destroyer?"

"We're observing it, Herr Oberstleutnant. It appears to be in trouble."

Sailors near the bow of the ship dove for cover as the torpedo closed in. Stone watched them from the bridge. The bow was swinging to the right, but not quickly enough. Someone shouted, "The Lynx!" Then the morning was sundered by a terrific explosion, throwing the captain and nearly everyone not strapped into a chair onto the deck.

Two rounds from the Lynx's machine guns found their mark, detonating the torpedo's quarter-ton warhead barely ten meters from the ship's port side. The concussion of the explosion slammed into the ship, lifting its bow almost completely out of the water. Three sailors near the starboard rail were pitched overboard. The bow settled back into the ocean and surged a huge wave outward as the ship listed hard to starboard. Sirens began to sound, alerting damage control parties. Men screamed as they were flung against bulkheads. A few suffered broken bones and separated shoulders, their agonized shouts adding to the chaos. The list peaked at nearly fifteen degrees, dangerously close to the vessel's limits, but *Cambridge* valiantly recovered, and the ship tipped back to port, throwing more men in that direction.

"Jesus, Mary and Joseph," a young Scottish corporal breathed as he watched the torpedo blast rock the destroyer. Even from three kilometers away, it was an awesome sight, one they had never seen outside of a cinema. The lad crossed himself.

"Easy, O'Toole, easy now," Sergeant Powers said. He had alternated his view from watching the Argentines over the top of his covering boulder, and looking back out to sea. So had Ian, after making it safely back to British lines. They'd seen the torpedo launch, then the missile hit on the Argentine helicopter, and now this.

"It appears the enemy has ceased fire, sir," Powers said.

Ian looked back at the Argentines, dug in on the hill. "I believe you're right, Sergeant." He keyed his radio. "All units, all units, this is Masters, you are ordered to hold your fire, I repeat, hold your fire. Hodge, Arroyo, acknowledge." His captains radioed "aye, ayes" back within seconds, and an eerie silence took hold over the island, broken only by the sounds of distant helicopter rotors and the sirens from the destroyer.

It took Ian a moment to adjust his field glasses, but then he got *Cambridge* in clear sight. "She's taken a hit, but she's still afloat," he said finally.

"Thank God," Powers muttered.

CHAPTER SIXTEEN

10 Downing Street, London

January 1982

"Beg pardon, ma'am, you have an urgent phone call from the Defense Ministry. Secretary Nott."

Margaret Thatcher put down her reading glasses and rubbed the bridge of her nose. What now? John Nott wasn't prone to surprise phone calls. "Very well, put him on," she said into the phone.

"Good afternoon, Madame Prime Minister, this is Secretary Nott."

"What can I do for you, Mr. Secretary?" Thatcher's tone was frosty; she did not get along with Nott, although he was competent enough.

"We have a situation off the coast of Argentina." Nott rapidly sketched out the developments on Carpenter's Island.

Thatcher sat back in her chair. "Are there casualties?"

"No reports as of yet, ma'am, but likely so, on both sides."

"I must call the Foreign Secretary immediately. Order the ship to cease all offensive actions against the Argentines."

"Shall we leave the Argentines in possession of a British island, ma'am?" Nott's tone was almost disrespectful.

"I didn't say that, Mr. Secretary. We will find a diplomatic solution to this situation, but first we must get the shooting stopped. Is that understood?"

"Perfectly, ma'am."

***

Island of the Penguins, Southwest Atlantic

"Order Speth to search for survivors from Brunner's helicopter," Schmidt told his adjutant. "He can make himself useful that way, at least." The oberstleutnant knew he shouldn't be too angry at Speth. Guns jammed, after all, but it was frustrating nonetheless.

"Herr Oberstleutnant, Leutnant Speth requests permission to launch his torpedoes on the English destroyer."

Schmidt glared at Winkler. "*Nein!* If he is shot down we are completely at the mercy of the destroyer! Order him to search for Brunner and his crew."

"Jawohl, Herr Oberstleutnant."

Schmidt was making a quick inspection of his position. Including himself, four men had been slightly wounded in the exchange of fire with the English and Chilean marines. His forward observers saw no indication that the enemy troops were preparing to attack. They hadn't moved out of their initial positions. Schmidt had his mortar teams ready to fire at a moment's notice, but he felt sure the English commander on the ground would ask for fire support from the destroyer before making any kind of assault on the Argentine breastworks. Schmidt vividly recalled what Russian artillery had been able to do and did not look forward to taking incoming fire from the English ship. None of his men had been subjected to that kind of bombardment in real combat; none could possibly be prepared for the sheer terror. Would their discipline hold?

Schmidt considered his options. They could always retreat to the interior of the island, such that it was. A delaying tactic at best, it would allow the enemy to take the high ground Schmidt's men now occupied. He'd already lost one helicopter and his other aircraft might well be useless as a combat asset. Air support from the mainland was at least a half-hour away, and that was assuming the Air Force would react quickly to such a request.

If the ship started shelling, he would have to withdraw or he and his men would be decimated. A well-placed barrage from the ship would take half his men, Schmidt estimated, and the rest would be routed by the enemy troops. He could not allow that to happen. "Winkler, pass the word, prepare to withdraw to Hill 206 on my order."

The adjutant looked at him with wide eyes. "Sir? Withdraw?"

Schmidt looked away, bringing up his field glasses for another look at the destroyer. "You heard my order, Hauptmann."

Stone had climbed up the ladder to the bridge, but not without pain from a twisted ankle. Fields was hanging on to the command chair and doing his best to bring order out of near-chaos. "Captain on the bridge!"

"Damage reports, Mr. Fields?"

"Just coming in sir. Two reports of minor flooding in some forward compartments. Chief Bostwick is there now." The growler phone buzzed, and Fields listened to a brief message. "Lookouts report four men overboard, sir. We're lowering a boat now."

"Very good," Stone said, fighting to stay calm. The men needed him calm now, firmly in command. He turned to the talker. "Helm, come about to course 030. Engine room, all ahead one-quarter." The young sailor relayed the commands. "Let's get our starboard side facing the island," Stone said. "If they come at us again we don't want another hit on the port bow. Radar, what's the other Haze doing?"

"He's over the spot where the second one went down, Captain." Stone grabbed a pair of binoculars and quickly picked up the Argentine helo, hovering over the ocean some two kilometers distant. There was some wreckage in the water, but he couldn't see any swimmers. A yellow life raft popped out of the chopper and floated to the surface.

"Looks like someone survived, sir," Fields said.

"Appears that way, Mr. Fields." Stone took a deep breath. "Send a message to Masters, order him to withdraw to the beach. When we get our men out of the water here, send the boats ashore to pick up the landing force."

"Sir?" Fields was wide-eyed. "Are we withdrawing?"

"I'll not risk further loss of life for that bloody rock," Stone said. "Not without orders from London. I'm off to the radio room." He handed the binoculars to his XO. "Let's not tarry, Mr. Fields."

"Aye aye, sir."

"What's the word, sir?"

Ian grimly handed the handset back to his radioman. "We are to withdraw, Sergeant."

"Is the ship in distress, sir?"

"Not at the moment, but if I know Captain Stone, he's concerned about another torpedo run." Surviving one attack had probably used up all the ship's luck for this particular engagement.

"The ship could bring down that other Haze, sir," Powers protested.

"The Argie appears to be trying to rescue his comrades," Ian said. "Shooting him down now would really play bloody hell with the diplomats, and our friends up on the hill would no doubt call in fast-movers from the mainland. Then it would be bollocks for sure, for all of us." Powers shook his head, but Ian knew the veteran had to agree with him. A squadron of fighter jets could sink the ship and leave Ian and his command at the mercy of the Argentines, on land and from the air, and he had a feeling they wouldn't be too inclined to show much mercy by then.

Ian clicked on his short-range radio. "Hodge, Arroyo, this is Masters. Prepare to withdraw. I repeat, prepare to withdraw, stagger your retreat back to the landing area."

Hodge responded with a reluctant aye-aye, but nothing came from the Chileans. "Arroyo, this is Masters, report your situation, over." Nothing.

"Could be his radio's out, sir," Powers offered. His tone was respectful, but his eyes betrayed his cynicism.

"Possible," Ian said. "Sergeant, you're in charge here until Mr. Hodge and his men arrive. Stay under cover and wait for the boats. I want to see what's happening over there with the Chileans."

"Let me send a man with you, sir," Powers said. Before his C.O. could object, Powers whistled a rifleman over. "Garrett, you're going with the major."

"Right, sergeant," the young man said, his voice carrying a Welsh accent. "Right with you, sir," he said to Ian.

"Very well. Carry on, Sergeant. Corporal, let's move out. Keep to the cover as best as possible."

"Something's moving out there," Winkler said. Like his commander, the young hauptmann was observing through binoculars, his head barely above the level of their defensive position. "Movement by the enemy on the left, Herr Oberstleutnant," he said. "They appear to be heading back to the landing area."

"Yes," Schmidt said, also observing through binoculars. He swung his back to the center of the English formation and picked up two figures scampering to the right. Going further in that direction, he saw the enemy troops dug in. The closest one was only 150 meters from the Argentines' right flank. Crouched behind a spray of rocks, Schmidt caught a flash of color from the marine's shoulder. A patch of some sort...There it was again. A flag, but not the Union Jack.

"The Chileans are on the right," he said confidently. Unlike the English on the left, the Chileans weren't pulling back. Was the enemy commander considering a mass assault on his right flank? That would be madness. He could focus his fire, cut them to pieces even before the destroyer could open up on them. Perhaps they were consolidating their position to give the ship a wider field of fire.

"Be on the alert," Schmidt said. "They may be preparing an artillery barrage."

"Should we begin our withdrawal, sir?" Winkler asked.

"Not yet. If they see us reveal our position, that may prompt them to open fire. Let's see what they're really up to. Pass the word to the forward positions on the right. Any movement forward by the enemy brings a warning shot from our best marksman. Just a warning shot."

"Jawohl, Herr Oberstleutnant." Winkler grabbed his radio.

The nearest troops on the right flank of the Chilean position were now about a hundred meters away. The ground was rough here, and Ian had to push uncooperative penguins out of the way more than once. The corporal had been nipped on the arm, prompting a colorful Welsh profanity. Ian had tried to raise Arroyo twice more, to no avail. The Chileans had a backup radio, didn't they?

At fifty meters, the nearest Chilean marine spotted them, swinging his rifle around. Ian gave the "friendly" signal, hoping Arroyo had been diligent in showing his men the signals they'd agreed upon while aboard ship. They were virtually the same in every language, and now this Chilean waved them forward. Ian and Garrett scrabbled the last few meters and hunkered down next to the Chileans.

"Where's Capitan Arroyo?" Ian asked in his limited Spanish.

"About fifty meters that way, mi Mayor," the private said, gesturing to his left.

"Gracias."

It took another three tense minutes to reach the center of the Chilean line. Ian recognized Arroyo's lieutenant, Gomez. "Where's Capitan Arroyo?"

Gomez pointed to a forward position, about fifty meters away. "Our man out there at the observation post was wounded, mi Mayor. Capitan Arroyo and a corpsman went to retrieve him. I believe they were both hit as well."

"Is your radio working, *Teniente*?"

Gomez held up his comm unit. "Damaged by a ricochet during the shooting, mi Mayor. Capitan Arroyo has our other main unit."

Ian looked through his field glasses. Three bodies were down by some rocks and bushes. One of them moved slightly. "At least one of them's alive," he said. "Teniente, you and your men will cover me. Corporal Garrett and I will go out there and see what we can do."

"Si, mi Mayor." Gomez began giving orders to his nearby troops in Spanish. Ian radioed a report to Powers, then looked over the ground between them and the wounded Chileans.

"Where are you from, Garrett?"

"Llangollen, sir," the Welshman replied. Ian could hear the nerves in his voice.

"Up in the Dee Valley, isn't it?"

"Yes, sir, that's right. You've been there, sir?"

"Once or twice. Ever get out into the fields and clear away the bracken and gorse?"

"That I did, sir. Not much different than what we have around here, I'd say."

"Well, keep your wits about you now, lad, and you'll be back there soon enough." Ian gave him a grin and a wink.

Garrett smiled back, but Ian could see him swallowing back his fear, and perhaps something a bit more bilious from his stomach. "Right, sir. I'm with you, Major."

"All right, we're at it, then. I'll lead the way, follow me position by position."

"Aye, aye, sir."

The Argentines were only a hundred meters, maybe less, beyond the Chileans. Ian took one last look at the enemy through his binoculars. There were four or five men there, and they were looking right at him.

Oberschutz Rudolf Henkel saw the enemy soldier leave his protective cover and scuttle a few meters to some low rocks. "One of them is moving out," he said to the *Stabsgefreiter* lying next to him.

193

David J. Tindell

"I see him," the staff lance corporal said, looking through field glasses. "He's English. Probably an officer." He radioed a report back to the command post.

Henkel was only nineteen, but had already risen to the rank of Chief Rifleman thanks to his proficiency with long-range weapons. His father, a decorated veteran of the *Afrika Korps*, taught him how to shoot at the age of seven, plinking at cans and bottles on their farm in Pomerania with a .22-caliber bolt-action rifle. The family emigrated to Argentina a few years later, and on his eighteenth birthday young Rudolf enlisted in the Army. His father's influence helped him get into the Werewolves. This was his first combat operation, and his heart had just started to calm down from the firefight. His brand-new HK PSG-1 semi-automatic sniper rifle had proven to be just as accurate in the field as it was on the target range. It was a little on the heavy side, but Henkel was a strong young man, and taking out the three Chileans was easier than he'd imagined. Now another enemy soldier was coming out—wait, there's another one—and they were big as life in his powerful Hensoldt scope. He made sure a round was chambered and then rested his finger outside the trigger guard, waiting for the order.

"Two of them now, Herr Stabsgefreiter," Henkel said.

"Confirmed," the young lance corporal said, excitement touching his voice. "Our orders are to fire a warning shot."

Henkel was disappointed, but he was a proud young German soldier and would do exactly as he was told. "Jawohl, Herr Stabsgefreiter." He sighted on a patch of scruffy ground two meters in front of the lead Englishman's position, held his breath, found the spot-weld, where his cheek and the stock of the rifle came into contact, and squeezed the trigger.

Ian was thirty meters from the three downed Chileans when the ground in front of him erupted, followed immediately by the crack of a rifle. Sniper, he knew immediately. Had to be a warning shot, or he'd have been dead. Ian waved at Garrett, motioning him to get down under cover, and the Welsh corporal hunkered behind the rocks Ian had left seconds before.

Two of the Chileans were still alive, that was clear now. He had to get to them. He considered trying to raise the Argentine commander on the radio, maybe ask for a truce to retrieve the wounded men. He reached around to the radio clipped to his web belt.

Ten meters behind him, Corporal Garrett saw the major moving. Is he hurt? Is he reaching for his sidearm? The young Welshman shifted his eyes toward the Argentine position. The shot had come from that bunch of rocks, and now he saw the barrel of a weapon moving slightly. He's getting ready to fire again! Garrett raised his M16A1 to his shoulder, sighted on the enemy position, and fired a three-round burst.

Behind him, Teniente Gomez saw the SBS corporal firing. He'd already passed the word that all the Chileans were to hold their fire until further orders, except for the three men he'd selected to support the Englishmen. "Selected fire! Pin them down!" Gomez yelled, and his three marksmen began shooting. Gomez aimed his own rifle but held fire, waiting to see what the Englishmen would do.

Henkel saw the flashes from the muzzle of the second Englishman's rifle and ducked, just in time. Bullets snapped overhead and slammed into the rocks guarding his position. The Stabsgefreiter cried out, then slumped to the ground, unconscious. An enemy round had creased his Kevlar helmet, not enough to penetrate but enough to knock him out from the impact. The corporal's radio chattered angrily.

Ian reacted instinctively to the sound of the covering fire from behind. His radio forgotten, he leaped over the covering rocks and sprinted for the Chileans, zigzagging and snapping off two quick bursts with his own M16. A part of his brain noted that no Argentine fire seemed to be coming his way, but he couldn't take time to contemplate the thought. In seconds he had reached the wounded men and dropped heavily onto the ground beside them.

"Feldwebel Koch reports he is taking fire from the Chileans," Hauptmann Winkler reported.

"Let's get over there," Schmidt said. "Are they advancing on his position?"

"Two men coming out, Herr Oberstleutnant," Winkler said, running beside his commander, his radio to one ear. They heard the sounds of gunfire. A few of the Argentine troops were looking in that direction, but Schmidt noted with pleasure that most were still keeping eyes forward, watching the enemy's center.

"Two men? Only two?" What was going on here? A recon? That would be madness. Not even Chileans were that stupid.

"Jawohl, Herr Oberstleutnant. Koch is returning fire now."

One of the Chileans, a young corporal, was dead, shot in the throat. The corpsman had been hit in the left leg and had managed to field-dress his own wound after helping Arroyo, who had taken two rounds, one in the left shoulder, the other a grazing shot along his right ribcage. The corpsman was conscious, but Arroyo had gone into shock. Ian had to get him back to the ship as soon as possible, or the Chilean captain might not make it.

"Can you run?" Ian yelled at the corpsman above the chatter of gunfire.

"Si, mi Mayor," the Chilean gasped. "My wound, it is not too bad."

"Right, then, I'll take Arroyo. We'll make a break for that pile of rocks over there." Ian pointed at the jumble some twenty meters away. "Follow my lead."

"We must take the body of Corporeo Hernandez," the corpsman said. "We cannot leave him here!"

Garrett dived to the ground next to them. "You all right, Major?"

"So far." Ian quickly sketched the plan to the Welshman. "Can you bring this body back with you?"

"Yes, sir. We'll get him home."

"All right, then. Corpsman, you're with me. Garrett, we'll cover you when we get to the first spot of cover." As best he could, Ian struggled to get Arroyo into position, looping the Chilean's left arm over his shoulders. Ian grabbed Arroyo's left forearm with his left hand, snugged the arm around his neck, and reached around Arroyo's back with his right arm, hugging him tightly. Arroyo groaned in pain. "Go!"

Garrett fired a long burst at the Argentines as Ian hefted Arroyo and ran for all he was worth, knowing every meter was bringing him closer to safety, but was also exposing him to the Argentine sharpshooters.

Schmidt jumped down into the foxhole next to Koch. The sergeant was calmly directing his squad to fire on the Chilean position, covering the forward Argentine sniper's post. Schmidt could see that the sniper was still in action, but the man next to him was down.

"What's your situation, Feldwebel?"

"The enemy sent two men forward, Herr Oberstleutnant, possibly to retrieve their wounded. My sniper fired a warning shot, as you ordered. The enemy returned fire a moment later."

Schmidt brought his grimy field glasses up. Three figures in enemy fatigues had just gotten behind some covering rocks, several meters behind the forward position. Now, there was the flash of rifle fire from the rocks. Schmidt saw another man, carrying someone, leave the forward position and run for the second.

"Hold your fire!" Schmidt yelled. "They're retrieving their wounded! Cease fire!"

Koch repeated the order to make sure everyone in the squad understood. "Get some men down to that sniper post!"

Henkel crouched down as another volley of enemy fire ripped into his rocks. Thank God they were sturdy ones. If there was one thing this island had aplenty, it was rocks, plus the infernal penguins. Peering out between two of them, over the barrel of his weapon, Henkel saw some figures rise up from their cover. Were they going to open up on him? No matter, he was a sniper, and he would bring them down. He sighted on the middle of the three. They were moving, but away from him—

"Henkel! Hold your—"

The voice from behind startled him, and he jerked the trigger. The gun erupted, but Henkel knew it had not been a perfect shot; he'd moved just a centimeter or so when he'd heard his comrade's voice from behind. But maybe it was good enough.

The sound and the pain registered on Ian's brain as one. The sound was like the buzz of an angry bumblebee, Dopplering in with a high pitched whine and then passing him with a low burr. The pain was like nothing he'd ever felt, a hammer blow to the back of his left shoulder. It was like someone had rammed a hot poker into his flesh and through his body. He didn't even hear the scream that escaped his lips, and his vision was already turning fuzzy when he saw the ground rushing up to his face.

***

Five kilometers out to sea, a periscope turned slowly, then vanished beneath the surface. Inside the submarine, the scope hissed its way downward. "Dive master, make your depth one hundred meters," the captain said. "Helmsman, bring us about to course 045 degrees. Increase speed to one-third."

The executive officer made sure that the orders were followed, then approached his captain. "What is happening, sir?"

"The English destroyer took a torpedo hit, but she is still afloat," said Mikhail Ivanovich Govanskiy, Captain of *K-251*, attached to the Red Banner Black Sea Fleet. "Did we intercept any signals?"

"*Da*, Comrade Captain," the XO replied proudly. "There has been some significant radio traffic between the ship and its headquarters, ship to shore, and from the Argentines ashore to their headquarters on the mainland. As well as short-range transmissions between the troops themselves."

"Very good. When the transcripts are ready, send them to my cabin. Ask Lieutenant Commander Nevsky to bring them, in fact. I'm sure he will have some insights to offer." Nevsky was the ship's political officer, most certainly a KGB agent, but otherwise a likable fellow. He would look over the transcripts with the captain and might actually have something interesting to say about them, before they would be sent on to Moscow.

Well, something was happening down here indeed, Govanskiy thought as he walked through the narrow passageway to his quarters. This might not be a wasted cruise after all. He tried not to think of the long voyage back to the Black Sea and their home port of Sevastopol. It was a pity they could not make a stop first in Cuba to visit their fraternal socialist allies. In Cuba, the sun was warm, and so, as Govanskiy and his crew well knew, was the comradeship.

CHAPTER SEVENTEEN

Ascension Island, Central Atlantic

February 1982

The Air Force C-135 touched down with a mild thump, jolting several passengers out of their naps. Captain Jo Ann Geary was awake and alert well before the jet started its descent. She'd seen the volcanic peaks of Ascension Island from the small window next to her seat, and the sight of the island actually brought a lump to her throat. Ian was down there. Until that moment, she hadn't really believed she would see him again. But he was down there, and she was coming to him.

It had taken some doing to hustle a seat aboard this bird, but she'd managed. Colonel Reese pulled a string or two; he'd been glad to do it, since he'd gotten some very favorable comments from the Pentagon about Jo's work in the capital a few weeks ago. A particularly troublesome member of Congress had quieted down considerably, and hearings that might've embarrassed the military had in fact turned quite favorable. So it was that Reese arranged for Jo to get a seat on this particular flight, which was stopping at Ascension only long enough to off-load two officers for the local Air Force base, then continuing on to Turkey.

Rain was falling on Wideawake Field as the plane landed. Jo hadn't thought to bring an umbrella and her jog across the tarmac left her close to drenched by the time she reached the small terminal building. At least it was warm; she recalled that Ascension's sub-tropical climate kept temperatures around seventy virtually year-round. It took her a few minutes before she found a way to get from the base to the island's hospital, in the so-called capital of Georgetown. Half an hour after landing, she climbed aboard a converted school bus for the twenty-minute ride.

Three months ago she'd left Hong Kong thinking that her relationship with Ian, such that it was, might have run its course. By the time she'd arrived back in Florida, she was starting to think it was just a fling, a very pleasurable one to be sure, but a fling nonetheless. Then his first letter had arrived, and she'd written back, and their correspondence, uneven as it was because of Ian being at sea so much, kept Hong Kong alive for her. Much to her surprise, she found her feelings for him growing.

Then a friend in the base signals office alerted her of a battle in the far South Atlantic involving Ian's ship, and even got hold of a message from the destroyer's captain detailing the list of wounded men. Ian's latest letter said it wasn't serious, but of course she knew it could've been much worse. He'd been in combat. The thought of Ian being killed nearly brought her to tears. Was she really in love with him? She'd left Hong Kong knowing that she might be, but had worked hard to suppress that frightening emotion. Really, though, how hard had she worked? She'd answered Ian's letters, she'd dated no other men—in fact, she'd refused a couple of quite tempting offers. "You're hooked," Kate Simmons told her. "Give it up, girl. Ol' Cupid done shot you straight through."

Jo had tried to get in touch with the ship, but the Royal Air Force liaison officer at Eglin who tried to help her ran into a brick wall. "The ship's virtually blacked out," he told her. "Only official communications with Admiralty are allowed until she reaches port. Something serious happened down there, to be sure." He had, however, been able to find out when *Cambridge* would arrive at Ascension.

The small, two-story hospital came into view around a bend in the road. Jo tried to keep her heart from racing, but it was a losing battle. The rain had stopped and the sun was out. She really should have checked into her guest billet at the base and changed into a fresh uniform, but that would have meant another hour or two, and she just couldn't wait any longer.

***

The pain was never far away, and after three days on medication he'd told them no more, he'd have an occasional aspirin and that was it. The nurses clucked at him but let him be, exchanging knowing glances that told him all he needed to know about what they thought. Another balls-to-the-wall officer, wants to tough it out. Well, he'll see.

His meds finally wore off in the middle of the night, the third night after the surgery, his fourth on the island. It was like someone had stuck a combat knife into his shoulder and twisted it, slowly but surely, and his screams brought the nurse and then a doctor, who knocked him out with a shot of something. The next morning, the pain was back, but a bit duller now, and every few hours he'd pop a couple aspirin to keep it somewhat under control.

There was a patio of sorts here, and he came out after the rain shower and sat down wearily, his robe and gown sopping up the water. He didn't care, not about the wetness or even the pain. He cared about his men, and his career, and Jo Ann, not necessarily in that order. The week on board *Cambridge* en route to Ascension had passed in a fog of pain only occasionally thinned by the drugs, but he'd been lucid enough to learn that his unit had sustained three casualties, including his, which was the most serious. The Chileans lost two men; Hernandez, the corporal, and Capitan Arroyo, who'd gone into cardiac arrest on the beach. The night he heard that news, Major Ian Masters, Special Boat Squadron, Her Majesty's Royal Marines, waited until the ship's sick bay was dark and quiet, and then he wept for his Chilean comrade.

As for his career, where that would go was probably being determined in London right now. Foreign troops had taken British territory, and the British force sent to retrieve it had failed. Someone had to take the fall for that, and Ian suspected that his neck, and Captain Stone's, would soon be on the chopping block. In the past three days Ian had gone over the operation in his mind time and again. Could he have done anything differently?

He'd finally come to a conclusion. Given the tactical situation, and the political limitations he later learned were placed on the British captain, the answer was no. Ian's mission was doomed from the start. Only a full-scale artillery barrage from the ship would have saved the day, and Stone had confided in Ian that orders from London to disengage had come through just as he was preparing to give that very command. The SBS and Chilean commandos on the island could not possibly have dislodged the dug-in, determined Argentines without supporting fire from *Cambridge*. Ian was forced to accept this last, and did so very reluctantly.

Acceptance of that conclusion didn't mean he felt any better about it. Underlying it all was his anger at his own leaders. Sovereign British territory had been seized, and Her Majesty's Government had the means at hand to rectify that situation. London had decided not to. Who had given that bloody order? Nott, the defense minister? The P.M.? Ian found that last easier to believe. "What can you expect from a woman, after all?" he muttered.

A voice came from behind him. "I hope you're not talking about me."

***

"Were you..."

"What?"

"Were you afraid?" she finally asked.

They sat on a bench, on a breakwater overlooking the Atlantic. Discovering that there were no taxis in Georgetown, Jo had borrowed a car from Ian's doctor, who reluctantly gave his patient permission for a two-hour leave.

They were tentative, at first. The embrace on the hospital patio was tender, yet delicate, concerned as she was about his healing shoulder. Their kiss was warm, but lacked the fire she'd imagined it would bring. Her feelings for him were—what? She'd thought she might be in love with this man, back in Hong Kong and through his letters over the long winter, and she'd been frightened at the news of his combat and his injuries, but now that she was actually with him...was it really there?

Their conversation quickly steered to the battle on Carpenter's Island. Ian was hesitant to speak about it at first, but she prodded him with a few gentle questions, sensing that he needed to talk about it, and then it came spilling out. He got to the part about his being shot, and then fell silent, looking out at the ocean, clutching her hand in his.

"Yes, I was afraid," he said. "But I have to say, I was more afraid for my men than for myself. I feared the possibility of losing them, even one of them, through some bad decision of mine. And it happened."

"You said you took only three casualties, including yourself," Jo said.

He looked at her, his eyes sad. "The two Chileans," he said. "They were under my command, too."

"You deployed all your men as best as you could," she said, trying to defend him to himself. "You just told me it was a no-win situation for you, without support from the ship."

Gazing back out at the ocean, he said, "Yes, that's true, I think. I don't know what Admiralty will think about it, when they hear Captain Stone's report. This was a bollocksed mess from the start, Jo, and somebody will have to take responsibility."

"It won't be you," she said, taking his arm and pulling herself close to him. "You did the best you could. So did your captain. Neither one of you determined the rules of engagement. Somebody in London did that."

"And you expect the politicians to admit fault, when they can blame the military? My, what a foolish girl you are." He patted her hand. "Speaking of rules of engagement," he said, "what are ours?"

"What do you mean?"

"We have one hour until I'm due back at hospital," he said. "I'm rather tired of looking at the ocean." He turned to her, touching her chin, tilting it upwards. "I'd much rather look at you."

She looked into his eyes, and her heart began to race. It was there. "Perhaps we can find a place with a little more privacy," she said.

He was dozing, and she lay in the crook of his arm, the late afternoon sun slanting through the blinds, painting them with irregular bands of shadow. She'd pulled up the sheet to partially cover them, but she still felt the room's wheezy air conditioner chilling the patina of perspiration on their bodies. Resting her head on his uninjured right shoulder, she gently ran her fingers through the silky hair on his chest. He stirred, mumbling something that sounded like, "That feels good."

"I was afraid to see you again, Ian," she whispered, thinking out loud more than anything. "Afraid of my feelings for you, what they wanted to be, to grow into. I—"

His breathing stopped, then started again, and she realized he was awake now. When she didn't continue, he gave her a gentle squeeze. "Go on," he said. "Please."

She had to tell him, even if it meant opening the old wounds. If they were to have any future together, he had to know. "I was hurt before," she said, her voice almost trembling. "Twice. There was this boy at Stanford, a young man, really, I was only nineteen..."

"Your first?"

"Yes," she said. "He was a poli-sci major, very much the leftist, very much against the Vietnam War, and there I was, the prim and proper daughter of a CIA officer, and in Air Force ROTC to boot."

"Opposites attract."

"We were together for most of my sophomore year, and in spite of everything I fell in love with him."

"And it ended," he said for her.

She suppressed a shudder as the memory spun out again. "At the end of the academic year, my ROTC battalion was holding an honors ceremony. I was scheduled to get two, my parents were there, it was a big evening, and then some protestors got into the hall." Through her sudden tears, she told him about the ugly epithets, "baby-killer" and much worse, and the rotten tomatoes sailing through the air and spattering on her dress uniform and her shock at seeing Jimmy's bearded face as the protestors were rushed by a group of angry cadets.

"He tried to explain it to me later," she said. "How it had to be done, in the name of the revolution."

"What were they revolting against?" Ian asked.

"The war. President Nixon, the Establishment, the military, anyone in authority. He said sacrifices had to be made, and if our love was the cost, that's what had to be. He asked me to quit ROTC, join his group. I said no. I never saw him again."

He held her close. "That was difficult, I'm sure," he said.

"I was heartbroken." She sighed heavily, pushing the memory aside.

After a quiet minute, he said, "There was another?"

"Yes," she said. "The second was Franklin, a few years later. I was doing graduate work at the Academy in Colorado Springs. He was...well, he was one of my instructors."

"Oh, my," he said, unable to keep a tinge of mirth from creeping in.

She slapped him on the chest, but not very hard. "Franklin was just about everything a woman could want," she said. "Oh, God. I'm sorry."

He squeezed her. "You did say 'just about', didn't you?"

"Yes," she said, relieved. "He was good-looking, well-educated, an officer—a major, Marine Corps, a visiting lecturer for a course I was taking. He was also in my tae kwon do class. We dated for three months."

"Not very long," he said.

"It was pretty intense," she said. "Franklin was like that. He was on his way up. Wanted to be Commandant of the Corps someday."

"And then?"

She sighed. "Then the semester was coming to a close. He was taking a post in the Pentagon. I thought he might ask me to come with him, that he could arrange my transfer..."

"But he didn't," Ian said.

"No. He..." The searing memory of that night in Vail came back to her. She shuddered. "He told me he couldn't see me anymore. You see, he was black, and I'm not, of course, and he didn't want—didn't want his children to be of mixed heritage."

"Cheeky bastard."

She didn't respond to that. Franklin had possessed a raw power that she found intoxicating. It wasn't just his supremely conditioned body, the one he'd built as an All-American cornerback at the Naval Academy. It was the force of his personality, his intensity, and even his arrogance as a black man striving to succeed in a white man's world. He was an immensely proud man, and she suspected that his pride called for him to be careful in his selection of a mate. Some would have called it racism, and perhaps there was some of that in there, but deep down she knew Franklin was just being the kind of man he was driving himself to be, unwilling to let anything stand in his way. And while she admired him for that, her admiration had not stopped the pain.

She sighed again. It felt good to tell Ian about them, and as he held her tight, she sensed he knew what kind of pain she must have gone through, how it had affected her relationship with him, right up to this very day, this very hour. He understood.

"And what about you, kind sir? How many birds have you let fly away?"

He chuckled. "Oh, I suppose there were one or two fairly serious flings in there, but honestly, Jo, the Royal Marines have been it for me since I was a lad. A family thing, you know. Dad was in the last war, Gramps in the one before that. Fortunately, they both came home. Never talked about it much. I knew I'd be making the military a career. Went to a Royal Marines recruiting office when I was eighteen and a crusty old sergeant asked me if I was tough enough. That did it for me."

"Not much room for romance," she said, knowing full well how the demands of active duty played havoc with relationships.

He rolled onto his side, facing her. "I've decided it's time to make room," he said, as he lowered his lips to hers.

CHAPTER EIGHTEEN

Estancia Valhalla, Argentina

February 1982

Ernesto saw the ad in the classifieds of *Clarin*, one of several newspapers delivered to the estancia daily from Buenos Aires and other major cities in Argentina. The staff was free to peruse them on their own time the day after their arrival, when it was presumed the Baumanns and their frequent guests would have finished with them. There was also a weekly shipment of newspapers and magazines from West Germany and the United States, along with *The Times* of London and *Le Figaro* from Paris. Ernesto made a point of reading three papers a day. *Clarin* was a tabloid and a bit too sensational for Ernesto's tastes, but they did have an excellent cultural section on Sundays, and he always checked the classifieds in Wednesday's edition.

Most of the time, his search was fruitless, but today a small box in the Personals caught his attention. It was a simple, two-sentence entry: "Manuela, you are the reason I live. Please forgive me. Guillermo." Anyone who paid close attention to the listings might possibly note that Guillermo seemed to be in trouble with Manuela five or six times a year.

The ad held a different meaning for Ernesto. This Sunday evening, he would leave the estancia and drive one of the Baumann vehicles to Buenos Aires to visit his parents. As he had Sunday evenings and all Mondays off, the trip to the city was a regular occurrence, and he would usually stay the night with his elderly mother and father. Sometimes when he visited, he would place a votive candle in the window of his bedroom. The aroma helped him sleep, and also served as a signal for a certain individual who walked his dog along the street flanking the apartment building. The next morning, Ernesto would take a stroll to a nearby park and sit for a spell next to a fountain. He would be joined by a certain man, perhaps the same one who had walked past his parents' building the night before, and they would talk. Ernesto would occasionally leave his newspaper on the bench, and the other man would courteously retrieve the paper and take it with him upon his own departure, dropping the newspaper into a trash receptacle after carefully removing whatever documents or other materials it had been hiding.

On other occasions, like this one, Ernesto would see the ad from the lovelorn Guillermo and know that the man with the dog wanted to see him the following Monday morning in the park. Every meeting with the man was tense, although over the past year Ernesto had grown a bit more at ease, especially as he saw his bank account grow. His parents were getting older, and the medicines they needed were expensive.

The following Monday was clear and warm. Ernesto breakfasted with his parents, listened to them tell the latest news from the family again, repeating many of the stories he'd heard the night before, and then took his leave of them for his constitutional. By ten o'clock he had found a seat on an empty bench. His companion joined him a few minutes later.

"Good morning, my friend," the man said in flawless Spanish Lunfardo.

"Good morning," Ernesto said. In three years of these meetings, he had yet to find out the man's name. He was probably English—it stood to reason, really, and he was most certainly not Brazilian—and about his age, which was near fifty. Whereas Ernesto was slender and dark haired, this man was somewhat plump with streaks of iron gray in his hair. He wore nondescript slacks, a long-sleeved white shirt and a straw fedora.

"Thank you for coming," the man said. "I needed to ask you a question. Have you ever heard of Pilcaniyeu?"

"I have never been there," Ernesto said cautiously. "It is very far away."

"A thousand kilometers to the south," the man said conversationally, as if discussing the weather or the latest football scores. "An interesting place, so I'm told. A small town, nestled in the foothills of the mountain range, and a large research and development facility nearby. A military facility. Have you heard of it?"

Ernesto fidgeted on the park bench. "I've, ah, overheard some conversations," he said.

"I would be very interested in any other details you might come across," the man said. "This information is quite important. It would be worth double your usual payment."

"I am a loyal Argentine," Ernesto said, trying to control his anger. He was angry at the man, and his employers, for the hold they had on him. The Baumanns paid him well, but not well enough to care for his parents, too.

"I know you are, my friend," the man said, giving Ernesto a comradely pat on the arm. "We believe that the information you can provide about this place may actually save lives. Perhaps a great many of them."

Ernesto took a deep breath. He could get up and walk away now. The man had made that clear when they'd first met, nearly a year ago. Ernesto was under no compulsion to cooperate. However, it went unsaid that without their expensive medications, his parents' health would steadily decline. They probably would not live another two years, and he would then be alone. Forever. The Englishman not only paid him more than enough to cover the cost of the medicine, but had arranged for certain drugs to be made available to Ernesto at an exclusive pharmacy. If he walked away now, that would all vanish overnight.

"All right," the butler said. "I will see what I can do."

The man watched Ernesto walk out of the park, then took his own leave. Nothing but words had passed between the two men, but even so there was risk of arrest. The Bureau of Internal Security was stepping up its surveillance of British nationals in Buenos Aires, and the man—Donald Travis was listed on his passport, but that was false—took the appropriate measures as he made his way back to the embassy. When he arrived, confident he had not been followed, he reported to the second floor office of the Assistant Director of Cultural Affairs, a man who in reality was the head of the MI6 intelligence office in Argentina.

"Will he cooperate?" the Chief of Station asked Travis.

"I think so," Travis said. "His information has always been valuable." He had been running the butler, code-named "Jeeves", since his recruitment the previous year. Travis would never have believed that a sprained ankle would be a stroke of luck, but his slip on the stairs had put him in the hospital emergency room that day when the butler had brought his mother in. She'd taken a fall and was treated for a bruised shoulder. Travis recognized Ernesto from photos he'd been examining in connection with the Siegfried Bund. Once a year the staff at the Baumann mansion posed for a group photograph, and the photographer, for a small fee, agreed to provide a copy of the picture to an interested foreigner, who said he'd heard that his long-lost sister was working there as a maid. It was a simple matter to find out the name of the patient that night, and that of her son. An additional fee was required to provide details of the woman's condition, and that of her husband, but Travis had a rather comfortable expense account for such purposes.

A week's worth of surveillance on the couple's apartment building turned up Ernesto, and a week later Travis had occasion to share a park bench with the butler. Small talk about the weather and families over the course of three meetings led to the opening, and Travis dangled the bait. Ernesto was reluctant, but he took it. Reluctance was good; informants who eagerly accepted were often the most unreliable, and occasionally were working for BIS. More than one British agent had been burned over the years for being too quick to close such a deal.

"Are we sure the list of pilots he provided a few weeks ago is connected to Pilcaniyeu?" Travis asked now.

"Someone in London believes it, so we must, also," his superior said. "All of the pilots in question are native Argentines, sons of German immigrants. We think all of their fathers are members of the Bund. The pilots trained not only here but also in West Germany, with the Luftwaffe, for six months as part of an exchange program."

"What is the connection with the facility down in Pilcaniyeu?" Travis asked. He was persistent, but knew when to stop pushing. While he was on good terms with the chief, he had no desire to offend the man and risk losing this particular posting. A widower, Travis enjoyed Buenos Aires, particularly its beautiful women.

The man on the other side of the desk gave a slight shrug. "Apparently there's one somewhere," he said. Travis sensed he was not being told everything the man knew, but of course that was common. Field agents had need-to-know only to their own pay grade. "Let me know when you are next to meet with Jeeves."

Travis stood up. "I'll look for his signal on my walk Sunday night."

The MI6 station chief watched Travis exit the small office. A good man, perhaps a bit too curious, but if the butler found out anything about Pilcaniyeu, the agent would be able to put two and two together. Then he might have to be brought further into the loop. That could prove beneficial, though; the butler wasn't the only agent the man was running, and the others might be able to provide additional information about this Bund outfit.

The MI6 man reached for a file on his desk. He'd been re-reading it when Travis came to make his report. Now he picked it up again. The first page was the list of the six pilots provided by the helpful gentleman's gentleman. Various other sources of information had provided fairly complete details of each man's background. All of them had trained with the West German Luftwaffe, as the man had told Travis. What he had not mentioned was the name of one particular unit each Argentine pilot had worked with while in Germany. It was *Jagdstaffel* 72, based near Hopsten in northwestern Germany, near the Dutch border. The squadron flew the American F-4 Phantom and was the only Luftwaffe unit tasked to train pilots in the delivery of unconventional munitions, including nuclear weapons.

CHAPTER NINETEEN

Bermuda

March 1982

Jo Ann wondered if she had a right to feel this good, with the warm sun, the sand, the ocean gently surging into Warwick Long Bay, and Ian beside her, flipping through a soccer magazine. She sat up, sighing with contentment.

"You are allowed to take the top off, you know," Ian said.

She smiled at him. "I take it off at night for you," she said. "Why do you want me to take it off now, in public?" Although this wasn't one of Bermuda's most popular beaches, there were still a good number of people here today, and Jo had noticed that most of the women were going about without their bikini tops. She had no doubt that Ian had noticed that, too.

"Coward," he said, rolling back on his stomach and pretending to read the magazine again. Jo knew he was a big fan of Manchester United. This was the fourth day of their vacation here, and it hadn't taken that long for Jo to discover that British men weren't too different than their American cousins when it came to football, regardless of the shape of the ball.

Well, what the heck. Jo reached behind her, unsnapped the bra, and peeled it off. Reaching into her beach bag, she found the bottle of sun screen and began applying some to her breasts. She heard a muffled "Hmm" beside her. Something told her that soccer had suddenly lost its hold on her marine.

Done with the sunscreen, she lay back, propping herself on her elbows, and stretched her legs out. She noticed that two men walking nearby glanced at her appreciatively, in spite of the presence of their own topless companions. One of the men smiled at her and winked. She smiled back.

"Well, how does it feel?" Ian said. He was on his side now, the magazine forgotten. Jo glanced over at him. Like most of the men on the beach, he was wearing a Speedo; unlike most of the men, he had the body for it. By the look of his suit, it seemed Ian was enjoying Jo's altered appearance.

"Probably not as good as it feels for you," she said playfully. Really, though, she felt almost liberated. This was something she would never do on an American beach, not that there were any that would allow topless women in the first place, as far as she knew.

"You may be right about that," he said. He rolled another ninety degrees onto his back. Jo saw a couple of passing women giving him the eye. Good for the goose, good for the gander, she supposed. "Where would you like to go for dinner tonight?"

"How about that place down the road from the golf course, the one we saw yesterday?" They'd played nine holes at Belmont Golf Club, not too far from Warwick Bay, and a few kilometers west of the town of Hamilton and their hotel.

"Sounds fine," Ian said. "You know, I rather like this. Deciding where to go for dinner is the most difficult decision of the day. I could get used to this."

"Me, too," Jo said. She laid back, her hand finding Ian's. The sun felt good on her newly liberated breasts.

Their two-day reunion on Ascension Island had been too brief for them. A week after returning to England, Ian called her with the news that he had arranged for a week's leave. Could she join him in Bermuda? Jo didn't need to be asked twice. It took a bit of doing for her to arrange her own leave on such short notice, but the Washington incident was still proving useful for her, and with Colonel Reese's strong recommendation, her leave was approved.

Ian's wounds had healed nicely, although his shoulder was still tender and the bright red scar wasn't the most attractive thing in the world. Jo didn't care, though. She knew now she was desperately, gloriously in love with this man, and being with him was all that mattered. That he was rounding back into top shape physically was just a pleasant bonus. Very pleasant indeed; she had not even bothered to count the number of times they'd made love since arriving on the island.

In the month since Ascension, Jo had gone about her daily Air Force business with a zest that surprised even Kate, who knew her better than anyone. "You be glowin', girl," she said one day at lunch. "That man of yours, he must be somethin' else."

"He sure is," Jo replied with a smile.

When the lights were out in her quarters at night, though, Jo couldn't help thinking about the future. Where was this relationship going? Where could it possibly go? On the surface of it, there were so many obstacles—both of them in the service, and not just different branches, but different nations. Military romances were difficult enough under the best of circumstances, and these were far from the best. Of course, they could always resign their commissions, or at least one of them could and join the other. Ever practical, sometimes annoyingly so, Jo had begun to think about what she would say if Ian proposed to her. While her heart shouted at her to accept, her brain caused her to hesitate, think it through. Could she give up her Air Force career to marry Ian, move to England? What if he stayed in the Royal Marines? What if—

"You're thinking again," he said. Without even knowing it, she'd sat up, bringing her knees to her chest. It hadn't taken Ian very long to figure that one out. She was in her deep-thought mode. She'd been able to stay out of that so far on the trip, but here it was again.

"Sorry," she said, relaxing. She lay back down and rolled over to face him. "Ian?"

"Yes, love?" He leaned over and planted a gentle kiss on the tip of her nose.

"I was thinking about...about us."

He kissed her left cheek. "That's good," he said. "Are they good thoughts?"

"Yes," she said. "Some of them are confusing, though."

He stopped kissing her. "Such as?"

"Well...where are we going with this, Ian?"

He looked at her. "Is this what American men call 'The Big Talk'?"

She couldn't suppress her grin. "I suppose it is," she said. She reached out and touched his face. "I love you, Ian. More than I thought I could ever love a man again."

He took her hand and kissed it. "You know that I'm positively daft over you," he murmured. "I can't stand being away from you."

She felt her heart starting to beat faster. "I feel the same way."

"Jo..." With a sigh, he lay back down on the beach towel.

"What's the matter?" Panic suddenly surged through her. Was he going to break it off? Concede to the obstacles?

"There is something I haven't told you," he said.

Oh, boy, here it comes, she thought. Another woman. Maybe he's married...no, that couldn't possibly be. Could it?

"Before I left London, I was told that I'm to be promoted to lieutenant colonel," he said, pronouncing it "lefftenant", in the very British way. "Apparently some of the higher-ups at Admiralty had high marks for my performance on Carpenter's Island, regardless of how it turned out."

This one caught her right out of left field. "Ian, that's wonderful," she said. "I told you they'd see what really happened."

"Captain Stone and some other members of the crew are to receive commendations," he said. "You know the Argentines have been making political hay out of the whole thing."

"Yes, I saw it on the news," she said. Making hay, indeed. There had been jubilant demonstrations in Buenos Aires, bellicose speeches by President Galtieri, and a triumphant parade for the troops who took the island. One odd thing Jo noticed: the officers of that commando force all had German surnames. She meant to ask the Intel folks about that when given the chance, just out of curiosity. Ian had told her about his confrontation with the Argentine commander, Schmidt, but she hadn't known about the men under his command. Neither, apparently, had Ian, until returning to London.

"We didn't win the battle for Carpenter's Island," Ian said, "but we didn't really lose, either. The Argies left the island the day after we did. There are apparently some influential people at Admiralty who think that punishing anyone from Cambridge for leaving the island in Argentine hands would make things even worse than they are. The newspapers are already raking the P.M. over the coals for not providing us with any support. Not that there was any to provide," he added in a wry tone. He sat up, staring out to sea, to the south, as if he were trying to somehow see that wretched little island out there.

"Before I left for this trip, I had a very serious chat with a friend of mine in MI6," Ian said. "Something's up, Jo." He turned to face her again, and his eyes were hard. "A lot of people in the know in London believe the Argentines will move on the Falklands soon. Their success on Carpenter's just fueled the fire. Taking over a rockpile full of penguins for a day is one thing. Seizing islands settled by British subjects is quite another."

"That would mean war," Jo said, unable to keep the chill out of her voice.

"Indeed," Ian said with a serious nod. "My C.O. told me before leaving that I should enjoy myself here because things might start happening when I returned. He wouldn't tell me much more. My intelligence friend filled in more of the blanks. The Argentines are getting set up to move on the Falklands, Jo, and when they do, that's where I'll be going."

In spite of the Bermudian sun, a chill ran down her spine. "How soon?" she managed to ask.

"I don't know," he said. "My friend thought May at the latest. It's winter down there in our summer, you know. Once June arrives, the weather will be too foul to conduct naval operations. It will take us at least a month to assemble the fleet and get down there. If the Argentines move just before winter strikes, we may not get down there at all, at least until the fall. Our fall, that is."

"That would be too late," she said.

"Quite. By then, they will have consolidated their hold on the islands, and the cost of retaking them might be too high for some in London to stomach."

"Your Prime Minister wouldn't allow that, would she?"

He shook his head. "She wouldn't want to. She's full of brass, she is, but she might have little choice. Given three or four months to fortify the islands, the Argentines might be judged too entrenched to move them out without a large assault. Very large and very costly. Some in the House of Commons will certainly argue against doing anything."

Jo the woman was now transformed into Jo the warrior. "Why don't you just reinforce the islands now?" she asked. "Make it too costly for them to invade."

"Logical, but not very practical, considering the logistics and the politics," he said. "No, this will be a situation where we will react, rather than act. If we have time, that is." He lay back down again, hands behind his head. "That means my lads and I will be going back down there."

The woman came back, and she lay down next to him, holding him close. "Ian, I'm worried for you," she said.

"I have a job to do," he said. "I'm a marine in Her Majesty's Royal Navy. I will go where I'm ordered and do what they tell me to do." He looked at her. "Just like you would if your president ordered your wing into action somewhere. Just like you did on Fonglan Island."

"That was before we met," she said. "That was different, somehow..."

He stroked her hair. "You know that's not true," he said gently. "We're soldiers, Jo, you and me. It's what we do."

She took a deep breath. "Yes," she said softly. "It's what we do." She tried to imagine what her own reaction would be if some foreign power took over, say, Guam, or some of the Marianas, far-away American-held islands that few Americans on the mainland ever thought about, if they even knew of their existence. Well, it had pretty much happened once, hadn't it? Jo's father had answered the call then.

They lay together quietly for a while, lost in their own thoughts. Finally, he stirred. "What say we get back, get ready for dinner?"

"Okay," she said. Wordlessly, they gathered up their things, and she put her bra back on. But she knew that when they got back to the room, she would be taking it off again, and she would be making love to this man with a passion that she'd never known before.

Jo awoke the next morning to the sound of the surf coming through their partially opened balcony door. She stretched herself out gloriously, still feeling the glow from last night—the wine, the dinner, and the sex. Did anyone have a right to feel this good? The thought occurred to her just as she became aware that Ian wasn't next to her. Then came an urgent message from somewhere inside, telling her it was time to take care of essential business.

The clock on the nightstand said 7:45, and there was a note from Ian. Out for a quick run. Jo had always joined him for morning P.T., keeping with her routine from back home, but he'd let her sleep in today. Well, that was fine, anything he wanted was fine with her. She decided to hit the shower after answering nature's call.

Ten minutes later, she was out on the balcony, taking in the ocean view, wearing only the terrycloth robe provided by the hotel, and toweling the last of the water from her hair when she heard the door sliding open behind her. It was Ian, clad in his Royal Marines tank top and shorts. She turned to embrace him, but his expression stopped her.

"What is it?" she asked, fearing the answer.

He held up a yellow sheet of paper. "A wire from my base," he said, his voice flat. "I have to get back. Today."

"Oh, no..." They had planned to leave the next day. "Does this mean...?"

He nodded grimly. "He closes with the word 'Tallyho'. That's a war signal. It can only mean the Argentines are ready to move."

CHAPTER TWENTY

Buenos Aires

March 1982

The students gathered slowly, tentatively, some of them laughing at jokes that weren't very funny, but they needed a way to release the tension. Theresa Gasparini felt it, too, and not for the first time she asked herself why she was here on this mild fall day, a day when she should be in her international economics class at the university, or at the very least at home with her bambinos. Why was she here, in the Plaza de Mayo, with the intimidating façade of the Casa Rosada staring down at her, a squad of policemen protecting its front entrance, all staring right at her?

She saw reason entering the plaza now, drawn to him by the applause, even a few harried cheers from the knot of students gathered around the makeshift speakers' platform. Flashing his dazzling smile, Hector Guzmán shook hands as he made his way toward them. He looked younger in person than his newspaper photographs or the film she'd seen on television. Longish brown hair, a thin mustache, moving smoothly toward them in his pinstriped blue suit, Guzmán did not appear to be the leftist rabble-rouser so often denounced by the right-wing, government-approved newspapers. This close, he looked more like the graduate student in political science that he actually was—or had been, until he'd dropped out of school two months ago to devote all his time to the infant anti-war movement.

"Impressive, isn't he?" Beside her, the tall man with the goatee and studious round eyeglasses gave her a smile and then turned his attention back to Guzman. Franco Caciagli, Ph.D., professor of political science at the university, was as much responsible for Theresa's presence here as anything else. Since beginning his class in January, she had been spellbound by his lectures, inspiring thoughts she never had before, questions she had never considered asking. Professor Caciagli asked her personally to attend this rally. Theresa the woman knew that his interest in her was not entirely academic, but Theresa the student, exploring a world that was opening up more and more to her every day, accepted his invitation. Antonio, watching a report of Guzmán on television just last weekend, had denounced him as a dangerous threat to the country's stability. Perhaps, she thought with an illicit thrill, her husband's disapproval was part of her reason for coming here as well.

Guzmán's movement had stalled in the aftermath of the so-called "great triumph" over the English on the Island of the Penguins, but in recent weeks he'd picked up some steam. The same newspapers that trumpeted praises of the junta were also alarming many people with their incessant drumbeat over the Malvinas. Even novice political science students could see what was coming. War over the Malvinas would be a catastrophe, Professor Caciagli said in class.

What if the English refused to back down? The Argentine military was not strong enough to capture and hold the islands against a determined, battle-tested enemy. What if the Americans intervened on behalf of their English allies? What if the Chileans or the Brazilians seized the moment to strike at their old enemy? Theresa's mind whirled with the possibilities as the debate raged around her in class.

She tried discussing the war threat with Antonio, who scoffed at her fears. The junta leaders may be a bit reckless, he said, but they are not idiots. The Malvinas would be theirs eventually, but through negotiation, not open conflict. The trend in the world was away from colonialism; the old European powers were retreating all over the world. It would be no different here. Eventually the U.N. would pressure the English to give the islands back.

Theresa remained concerned, though. If war came, Antonio might have to fight, especially if their untrustworthy neighbors attacked Argentina. Although she didn't know a lot about what was going on at Pilcaniyeu—Antonio had only told her the work was top secret—it was obviously a military project of some kind, and so she sensed the facility would be high on the target list for Chilean or Brazilian bombers, or even American missiles, if it came to that. Her fear for her husband made her agree more and more with Professor Caciagli, and with Hector Guzmán. Something had to be done to help common sense prevail.

Guzmán jumped up the steps of the podium and held his hands up to quiet the applause. The microphone squeaked as he adjusted it. "My friends, fellow Argentines," he began, in a surprisingly deep voice, "we come here today, in the shadow of the Pink House, to say two things to our leaders: No to war! Yes to peace!" Cheers rang out.

Theresa cheered with them. She looked around and saw that the crowd now numbered around a hundred people. More were wandering over from inside the park, and from the nearby streets. The police in front of the Pink House looked more numerous now, too.

"We are called traitors, but we are not," Guzmán said. "Is it traitorous to want peace for your country? Is it treason to wish that the young men of Argentina never have to fire a shot in anger at the young men of another nation? I say it is not treason, but the highest form of patriotism!" The cheers were louder this time. Guzmán was an impressive speaker, naturally gifted. His looks entranced women, and some men, too, and the cameras loved him, it was said. He had what the Americans called charisma. No wonder the junta feared and hated him.

The thought made her shudder. She remembered very well what happened during the Dirty War not so long ago, when people the junta feared and hated tended to disappear. Her own second cousin vanished after helping organize a labor union at a paper mill. Rodolfo had left a wife and four children.

"Today we stand together for peace!" Guzmán shouted, holding his right hand aloft, displaying the V-sign borrowed from the Americans. "Today we stand together and call upon our leaders to renounce war, to seek peace. Peace with England, peace with Brazil, peace with Chile!"

Amidst the cheers, Theresa heard a shriek of fear, then another. She looked toward the Pink House, and there were the police, a long line of helmeted men, some carrying shields, some truncheons. They were advancing through the plaza, toward the crowd. Guzmán saw them, too. "Stand together, my friends! Are we not free Argentines? Do we not have the freedom to assemble, to speak our minds?"

"Not really," Professor Caciagli muttered. "This isn't America."

"Will the police attack?" Theresa asked.

"I don't know," the professor said. Suddenly, the university seemed very far away to Theresa. Inside Caciagli's classroom, it was all theory. This was reality, in the form of determined, armed men coming their way. No doubt there were more uniformed men watching it all through the windows of the Pink House, and to them the people in the park would appear very small indeed.

"We should go," she said. "I'm frightened, Professor."

"Stand fast!" Guzmán shouted. "Stand together for peace!" Many in the crowd echoed him, facing the police, shaking their fists.

One of the policemen raised a megaphone. "You are assembling illegally," came the amplified voice. "You are ordered to disperse. Go back to your homes. This is your only warning." The line of policemen halted about fifty meters from the protestors.

"We have a legal permit!" Guzmán shouted back at them. "We are peaceful! You have no right to order us around!" The crowd began to draw strength from Guzmán, and from the seeming hesitation of the police. Guzmán began a chant, quickly picked up by the crowd: "Yes to peace, no to war! Yes to peace, no to war!"

Theresa saw one of the policemen, perhaps the commander, holding a radio to his ear, listening to something, and then he shouted an order. The line began to move toward the protestors. Some on the outer fringes of the crowd lost their nerve and started running, but one young man took two steps toward the advancing line and threw something. Theresa gasped as the stone struck a policeman in the face, cracking his visor, knocking him down. The officer yelled an order, and his men charged.

"Run!" Caciagli shouted. He grabbed Theresa's hand and pulled her along. She needed no encouragement. They made it past the podium as the first wave of policemen collided with the edge of the protestors, truncheons rising and falling, bringing screams of pain.

Caciagli was heading for the center of the plaza. Theresa could see the Pyramide de Mayo, an obelisk built over an earlier monument to the Revolution of 1810. Somehow it occurred to her that the very next day, the Madres de la Plaza de Mayo would be holding their weekly Thursday afternoon march, calling once more for a full accounting of the Dirty War atrocities. That would be tomorrow; today, protestors were running for their lives. Past the pyramid, Theresa saw something that gave her hope. "The cathedral!" she yelled, and Caciagli saw it, too: the tall edifice of the Catedral Metropolitana. If they could make it inside, the police would surely not follow, not into the shrine that held the remains of the legendary patriot Jose de San Martín, who had liberated Argentina from the Spanish.

But they wouldn't make it that far. A flying squadron of policemen, anticipating the crowd's rush toward the safety of the cathedral, outflanked the protestors from the eastern part of the plaza. Pedestrians and bystanders, even those who'd ignored the assembly, ran from the police in panic or fell to their clubs. Caciagli and Theresa tried to double back toward the obelisk, but they were fighting against the tide of fleeing civilians. Screams and shouts filled the air. Cars and trucks on the nearby streets blared their horns. The peaceful afternoon of the plaza had descended into chaos.

A policeman appeared to their right. Caciagli held up an arm to ward off the blow, but the officer's club smashed him to the ground. Theresa screamed in terror as the policeman turned to her, club held high. "No!" someone shouted. "Do not harm the women!" The policeman hesitated, then grabbed Theresa's arm, twisting it painfully behind her, snarling, "You come with me, you leftist *puta*."

***

"Do you know why you are here?"

Theresa tried to summon words out from under the crushing fear. She had no idea how much time had gone by since her capture in the plaza. She remembered the pain of her arm pinned behind her back, the terror of the hood pulled down over her head, the hard floor of the van as she was thrown inside. There was moaning and wailing from other prisoners during the short ride, then they were manhandled out of the vehicle and taken inside whatever this building was. She was thrown down roughly into a stiff wooden chair, her wrists and arms tied behind its back. She waited for what seemed like hours, crying until tears would come no more.

"I asked you a question, Jewish bitch!" The man's voice dripped with hatred.

"I—I don't know," she managed. "I am not Jewish. I am Catholic."

"Tell me what you know about Guzmán."

"I don't know anything about him."

"Do not lie to me." The voice came from behind her, and then a hand reached down and grabbed her hair through the bag, pulling her head back. She gagged in pain. "You were seen in the plaza with him. You have been seen elsewhere with him."

"No...no...I've never met him. I just saw him today."

The hand shoved her head forward, pressing her face against the inside of the bag, sticky and wet from her tears and the mucous from her nose. She sobbed again. Antonio, my love, I'm sorry. She thought of her children, convinced she would never see them again.

"I am First Sergeant Hector Julio Simon," the voice said, now in front of her again. "Some call me the Turk. Do you know who I am, whore?"

Her frazzled brain managed to call up one reference, something she'd heard whispered somewhere. *El Turco Julian.* Julian the Turk. Something about being renowned for torture...Oh, God! She began to whisper a prayer, her brain calling on its native Italian as it began to shut down all external stimuli. "*Ave, o Maria, pienna de grazia, il Signore e con te...*"

"That will do you no good," the Turk said. "I have had many Jew whores here. I know how to deal with you." She kept mumbling the rosary prayer, but stopped when she felt something grab the front of her blouse. Hands. Unbuttoning her blouse, pulling it apart. With horror she remembered she was wearing the new brassiere Antonio had ordered for her, the red one that fastened in front.

The Turk's fingers expertly flicked the clasp, and she felt the cups peeling away from her breasts. Simon's breathing became louder, heavier. "Does Guzmán suck your nipples?" Now he was behind her again, whispering in her ear, telling her things he would do to her, horrible things. She felt cold, calloused hands on her breasts, the ones no man but her beloved Antonio had ever touched before. So proud he was of them, that she had nursed two bambinos and still they were full and firm. And now, being fondled by this thug...She felt the urge to vomit, and used what was left of her strength to fight it back.

"You will tell me what I want to know about Guzmán," the Turk breathed into her ear, "or you will not leave this place alive."

CHAPTER TWENTY-ONE

Estancia Valhalla, Argentina

March 1982

The telephone in the Baumann study rang for the twelfth time in the past two hours. "Oberst Baumann," Willy answered.

"I have something else about the protestors," Heinz Nagel said. He had been giving regular reports to Willy since the police attack on the rally. "Several of them are in custody of the federal police. There are three women among the prisoners."

Willy felt a chill. This was bad. He had no doubt that Galtieri or one of his henchmen had ordered the rally to be dispersed. Why now? Guzmán had been making public speeches for weeks. Why this one? Perhaps it was because of his audacity to appear within sight of the Pink House that finally pushed the junta over the edge. Willy had no love of the peaceniks, but he deplored senseless violence against them even more. Films of the riot would be on the television news in Europe and America within hours, if they weren't already. The government of Argentina may have struck a body blow against the infant antiwar movement, but it was about to suffer a massive defeat in the court of world opinion.

"Who is conducting the interrogations?" Willy asked, fearing the answer.

"The Turk," Heinz said. "He has them in Club Atletico. Seven men, three women."

"God help them," Willy said. The Bund was quite familiar with Sergeant Simon's work, especially because of the torture-master's high regard for Nazis. Simon was openly anti-Semitic, had a swastika tattooed on his chest, and frequently played old recordings of Hitler's speeches while he tormented his victims. Even Günther Nagel could not stomach the man's excesses, but Simon had too much protection within the junta for the Bund to move against him. Perhaps it was time for that to end.

"Do you have the names of the prisoners?" Willy asked.

"Yes," Heinz said, and began reading them off. One of the women's names flagged something in Willy's memory. He asked Heinz to repeat it. "Theresa Gasparini," he said. "I thought it sounded familiar. Do we know her?"

Willy tried to think. "No," he said slowly, "not her. Her husband, perhaps?" He was sure now that he had seen the Gasparini name on some sort of list, very recently, a military list...He reached for a file at the bottom of a stack on the credenza behind him. The Pilcaniyeu file. "I might have something here, Heinz," he said. "Hold on." Willy placed the phone on the desk and quickly riffled through the file. Yes, there it was, in a report by the installation's commandant,

Oberst Reinke, mentioning the promotion of his second in command, one Major Antonio Gasparini. Willy gasped. Could it be? He quickly pulled out a nearby file drawer, the one with the service jackets of the Pilcaniyeu security officers, and found Gasparini's. Yes, he was married, two children, wife's name is—

Willy grabbed the phone. "Heinz, are you there?"

"Yes, Willy. You found something?"

"Gasparini, the prisoner, is the wife of Reinke's second."

There was a moment of silence at the other end, and then, "Scheiss!" It hadn't taken long for Heinz to make the same leap that Willy had. The wife of an important officer at the nation's most vital military installation, in the hands of that sadistic bastard! The security implications were almost beyond comprehension.

"Get over there immediately and get her out of there," Willy said, trying to remain calm, even as his anger built to a rage. "Shoot that *verfluchtes Arschloch* Simon if you have to."

"I'm on my way."

***

It was half-past ten when the Chief of Station returned to the embassy. David Travis was waiting for him outside his office. "How was the party?" the agent asked.

"Rather lively," the MI6 man said as he unlocked his office door. Travis followed him inside. The chief tossed his coat on a chair. "All the talk was of the demonstration today in the plaza." The dinner party at the Bolivian Embassy was still going on, but the chief had left early, anticipating Travis. "You have something for me?"

Travis handed him a file. "Some rough notes of reports from our BIS contacts. I'll have a more detailed report for you in the morning. You might want to look at the third page."

The station chief thumbed through the papers. "Holy Jesus Christ," he said a moment later. He looked up at Travis. "Is this confirmed?"

"It will be within twenty-four hours," the field operative said. "It's not every day that Julian the Turk has a prisoner snatched from him at gunpoint, wouldn't you say?"

"And the man who rescued the lady..." He looked down at the paper again. "It was Heinz Nagel?"

"Our contact is certain. The de facto security chief of the Siegfried Bund handled this personally. I wish he'd shot the bastard."

The MI6 man nodded. "Indeed. But she was the only prisoner rescued, you say? Why only her?"

Travis handed the man another file. "I was curious, too, so I played a hunch and did a little checking in our records. It appears her husband is an important officer in their Army."

The chief flipped through the two-page dossier. "How important?" he asked, already knowing the answer from what he'd read.

"Second in command of the Pilcaniyeu security force," Travis said. "My guess is that he will be given emergency leave to come home and be with his wife. Probably here for several days."

"Can you contact him?" The chief knew an opportunity when he saw one.

So did Travis. "Yes, I think so," he said, "but it would be nice to know why."

The chief closed the files and leaned back in his chair, contemplating the man across the desk. He made a decision. "What I'm about to tell you is Most Secret," he said.

"I assumed it would be."

***

Major Antonio Gasparini did not wear his uniform on the day he went to the market for Theresa. He had not worn his uniform since the day he'd arrived home, the day after his wife's arrest. Now, three days later, he was wondering if he'd ever put on the uniform again.

Hatred burned within Gasparini like a cold flame. Hatred of the man who had defiled his wife. Hatred of the men above him who had given the beast his orders. And even some hatred of himself, for those same men gave Gasparini his own orders, and the work he was doing at Pilcaniyeu would, if successful, bring even greater glory and power to those same men.

Not for the first time, Gasparini considered going to the Pink House and using his sidearm. He would die, of course, but he would take as many of the *bastardos* as he could. It was tempting, but he knew it would not happen. For one thing, security at the Pink House was undoubtedly high these days, and the Gendarmaria might very well be on the lookout for Antonio Gasparini. For another, more important thing,

241

he could not bear to leave Theresa and the children. It would be hard enough to leave them in a few days, when his emergency leave expired.

Blessed be the Virgin, Theresa seemed to be recovering from her ordeal. Physically, her arms were a bit sore, but that was all. Psychologically, Antonio knew it would take longer for her wounds to heal. Perhaps he might arrange for her to see a counselor. She had told him about her time in the room, and Gasparini's anger had been tempered only slightly when she had assured him she'd not been sexually assaulted, beyond the Turk's fondling of her breasts, which was bad enough; one of them was still bruised around the nipple. He could only imagine the terror she had felt, the humiliation. His first three nights at home, she merely clung to him in bed and sobbed, but the crying had settled down and sleep was coming more easily now. This morning they made love, very gently, and this time her weeping was of gratitude when the "little death" claimed her and she held him like she'd never done before.

Theresa insisted on doing her normal household chores, and Antonio relented, thinking it would be good therapy for her. He held the line, though, on venturing to the market. He was concerned what the sight of a policeman might do to her. It was hard enough for him to look at one without thoughts of murder. He sighed now as he examined the melons. So much anger to overcome. Could he do it? His manhood cried at him to strike back at his wife's assailants. That was impossible, though. Going to a lawyer and asking that charges be filed was lunacy. This was Argentina, after all, not America, where such things happened all the time, where people had rights.

A man bumped into him, jostling the melons and causing one to fall from the counter. The stranger caught it and replaced it in the pile. "Excuse me," he said in Italian.

"Think nothing of it, *signor*," Gasparini answered, also in his native tongue.

"My condolences on what happened to your wife," the man said.

Gasparini was immediately on his guard. "Do we know each other, signor?"

The stranger, who looked like any other Argentine of Italian extraction, smiled and shook his head. "No," he said. "But I heard about what happened. A terrible thing."

"Yes," Gasparini said, feeling uncomfortable.

"If something like that had happened to my wife, I would want to do something about it," the stranger said, holding up a melon and looking at it carefully.

Gasparini said nothing. His heart seemed to double its pace. Who was this fellow? Could he be connected with the federal police somehow? Were they trying to goad him into saying something foolish, so they could lock him up?

The stranger looked at Gasparini. "Do not fear, Major. We are your friends. We wish only to help." He handed the melon to Gasparini. "This one looks about right, don't you think? *Arrivederci*." The man walked away, leaving the bewildered major holding the melon. Before setting it down, he turned it over and saw a piece of paper sticking to its surface. Gasparini quickly pulled the paper free and put it in his pocket.

When he arrived home, he helped Theresa unpack the groceries and then excused himself. In the small bathroom he pulled the paper from his pocket and unfolded it. His hands were trembling. The message was in Italian: *Tonight, 11pm, The Sardinio. A friend.*

The Sardinio was a small *cerveceria,* a café with a full line of beers, which the Gasparinis had sometimes visited. Normally, Antonio Gasparini enjoyed a stroll down the Calle Necochea, an area just beginning to emerge from its notoriety as the red-light district of La Boca. Tonight he was nervous. He had made his first decision in what he felt might be a new direction in his life. He felt guilty leaving Theresa and the children, even for a short time, but he told her he'd met an old Army comrade during his marketing and the man invited him for a drink. It was close enough to the truth. Theresa insisted he go, saying she was tired and would be going to bed early anyway. With a wink he found surprising and very welcome, she told him to wake her when he got home. Maybe things would get back to normal after all.

Gasparini found an empty table in the back and ordered a beer. The restaurant was still nearly full; Argentines had a habit of dining late, even on weeknights. He looked for the man he'd met in the market, but couldn't spot him. The waitress delivered his Quilmes beer and a *picada*, a plate of munchables. Gasparini took a sip of the beer and some of the popcorn and nuts on the plate. A minute later, a man came up to his table, but not the man from the market. "Major Gasparini?" he asked in Spanish.

"Si," Antonio answered. "How can I help you?"

"Our mutual friend from the market would like to know if you liked the melon he picked out for you."

Gasparini made his next decision. "Yes, very much so," he said. "Please, sit down."

Donald Travis pulled out a chair and sat. "Thank you," he said. "That beer looks good." He signaled the waitress and ordered a Quilmes. "I won't take up too much of your time," he said. "I know you have a wife and children at home, and your time with them must be precious."

"It is," Gasparini said. He would trust this man a bit further, but he would commit himself to nothing. The man's accent gave Gasparini an idea who this might be—or at least, whom he might represent—but just in case he was BIS, Gasparini would say or do nothing that could possibly implicate himself.

Travis normally took a lot longer to recruit a prospect, but time was of the essence. "Major, I heard about what happened to your wife. Dreadful business. Deplorable. We want to help."

"Who are you?" Gasparini asked, taking a sip of beer. His trained eyes flicked around the room. Nobody seemed to be paying them any attention. Of course, the man could be wearing a listening device, or carrying a tape recorder.

"Let's just say I represent people who have a common interest with you in this particular matter. If you are interested in finding out what we can do to help each other, perhaps we can meet tomorrow."

Gasparini thought it over. He had nothing to lose by taking it a step further, without actually committing himself. If these people were who he thought they were, they wouldn't have a problem confirming their identities; if this was a BIS setup, they would find out Antonio Gasparini wasn't the fool as they assumed. He thought of the Turk's hands on his wife. "Where and when?" he asked.

***

In the end, it was not such a hard choice at all. Two more meetings over the next three days settled the matter, and on the day of his departure, Gasparini packed his bags and put on his uniform, preparing for the arrival of the Air Force car that would take him to the base and his lift south. One last walk with his lovely Theresa that afternoon gave him the time and privacy to explain his decision, and what would happen next. She was quiet, but where he had expected to see fear, he saw only determination. Like him, Theresa's allegiance to their adopted homeland had vanished, thanks to the Turk.

She had only two questions. "You are sure about these people?"

"Yes," he said. "The English gentleman showed me very convincing evidence of his identity. As to his promise, well, much of that we shall have to accept on faith."

For her last question, she stopped their walk and looked him in the eyes. "You are sure this is what you want to do, my husband? It is very dangerous."

"Yes," he said firmly. "I will no longer serve a nation ruled by thugs. We will do this one thing, and then we shall go back to Italy, and raise our children in a civilized nation."

No words passed between them for a few fateful heartbeats. If she refused, he didn't know what he would do. But he knew his Theresa.

THE WHITE VIXEN

"Very well," she said. "Tell me what I must do."

CHAPTER TWENTY-TWO

Estancia Valhalla, Argentina
March 21st, 1982

Tobacco smoke hung below the ceiling in a haze. Willy Baumann did not smoke, but three of the men in the room did, and one of them preferred pungent Cuban cigars. He gestured to Ernesto, pointing to the side windows of the library. The butler nodded, finished serving the after-dinner drinks, and discreetly opened the windows enough to allow the smoke to start drifting out.

The butler's departure left seven men in the room. They'd dined on sumptuous Argentine steak, talked of the weather and crops and horses and business and politics, the typical dinner table conversation of wealthy Argentines, and since no women were dining with them, the subject of the fair sex came up once or twice. Reinhard Schacht told a ribald joke, bringing peals of laughter from everyone, even the younger men, Willy and Heinz. The old Nazi could still spin a tale or two.

Now they had retired to the library, where the real business of the evening would take place. Dieter Baumann quickly assumed command, handing out copies of three different reports. None of the copies would leave the room except in Willy's hands; he would take them to a special incinerator in one of the outbuildings for burning, with Heinz carefully observing.

"Gentlemen, these reports are the latest information about the status of Project CAPRICORN," Dieter said. "Referring first to the top document, I can summarize it by saying that Pilcaniyeu has two devices ready for deployment. The second document notes the readiness of Wing 45, the Air Force squadron that will carry out the strike. And finally, a report from our sources in Europe about the status of the English fleet."

Willy had helped prepare the reports, and so didn't need to see them again. He watched the other men as they read through the briefing papers. Schacht skimmed them with nods of his head and a few grunts. Foreign Minister Müller peered at them carefully, taking in every word as he puffed on a pipe. Günther Nagel flipped through the papers almost casually, a French cigarette dangling from his lips.

The man whose reaction most interested Willy was taking his time, occasionally sending a smoke ring skyward after a drag on his Montecristo. General Alfonso Sarmiento of the Argentine Army, the Bund's man inside the junta, appeared to be just another South American tinpot general, swaggering about with a chest full of medals and bellicose attitude. But Sarmiento's bluster hid an extremely shrewd and clever mind, and his loyalty did not necessarily go to the man in the president's office. Some years before, he had been approached by the Bund and a deal was struck. Sarmiento would keep the Bund informed of the junta's thinking, and perhaps try to influence it in certain ways; in exchange, the Bund made sure the general was very well taken care of. So far, it had been a mutually profitable relationship.

Sarmiento's current position was especially fortuitous, as he was involved in the military planning for the invasion of the Malvinas. He was working closely with Captain Jorge Anaya, the head of the Navy. Dieter had said Sarmiento might have word of the junta's immediate plans, and Willy found it hard to remain patient.

"Impressive, very impressive," Sarmiento said at last. "My compliments to you and your people, Señor Baumann. You are quite thorough."

Dieter nodded at the recognition. "Thank you, mi General," he replied in Spanish, the language of choice for the evening, in deference to their special guest. "At last, gentlemen," Dieter said, addressing everyone in the room, "we are ready to initiate Project CAPRICORN. All we require is forty-eight hours' notice. In that time, a weapon can be shipped to the launch point and Wing 45 can prepare its mission." He looked back at Sarmiento. "Mi General, do you have any information that might prove useful to us?"

A rather delicately phrased request, Willy thought, considering that the Bund owned Sarmiento lock, stock and barrel. For appearances' sake, though, it was wise to show proper respect to the general. He was, after all, a member of the junta that supposedly ran this country.

Sarmiento took a deep breath, leaned back in his high-backed leather chair, and steepled his fingers in front of him. The cigar smoldered in a nearby ashtray. He looked around the room dramatically. "Gentlemen, Davidoff's ship arrived off South Georgia two days ago. His men are ashore as we speak. As for the Malvinas, the date has been set. We launch our fleet on the twenty-eighth of March. Two weeks from today, the Malvinas will be ours."

There were several audible sighs, and the tension in the room eased a bit. Willy could almost feel it being replaced by the electricity of the announcement. Action, at last. The Malvinas, at last! Argentina's honor, restored at last! For a few brief moments, he allowed his Argentine blood to rush through him, carrying the import of the historic news. He looked over at Heinz, who grinned at him, eyes bright. Seven days from now...

Willy forced himself to consider the realities of South Georgia first. This operation was one of the Bund's most delicate projects yet. Constantino Davidoff, a scrap-metal merchant, had been negotiating with the English for over a year to salvage the abandoned whaling station at Leith on South Georgia, some 900 miles to the east of the Malvinas. Davidoff had even contracted with a firm in Scotland to buy the scrap and received permission from the English embassy in Buenos Aires. Their only requirement was that he call on the South Georgia port of Grytviken and get formal authorization from the British Antarctic Survey team stationed there. Davidoff chartered the Argentine naval transport *Bahia Buen Suceso* to take his force of some forty workmen to South Georgia. Only a few people knew that the entire operation was financed by the Bund, and that Davidoff's workers were actually Argentine marines, who would be ready to move on Grytviken within days after being reinforced by two more naval vessels that were now at sea.

The South Georgia operation had been in the planning stages for years, but the success at the Island of the Penguins gave the junta the confidence to allow Davidoff to proceed, with Anaya's assistance. Willy had little doubt the operation would work; the English had no troops at Grytviken yet, and he'd received word only yesterday that their ship *Endurance* had set sail from the Malvinas with some two dozen Royal Marines from their small garrison at Stanley. Too little, too late.

Dieter Baumann, German-born and bred, did not have his head anywhere near the clouds. Willy forced himself to remember that Dieter, and the two Kameraden with him, had been part of a struggle so epic that anything the Argentines would do seemed almost trivial by comparison. What was the takeover of a few sparsely populated islands compared with the invasion of Russia? The conquest of France?

"That is very good news, mi General," Dieter said now. "On behalf of the Bund, I offer my congratulations to the leadership of our nation for its boldness. I am confident we shall be successful."

"The Malvinas will fall, Señor Baumann," Sarmiento said. "The English fleet will sail to reclaim them, and then it will be time to raise the curtain on your act of this drama."

"Considering your date, mi General, we can anticipate the English will sail no later than the tenth of April, probably sooner," Nagel said. "They have some units at Gibraltar that may deploy early. Most of their capital ships and troop transports are in the North Atlantic or their home waters. Once they assemble, they will require about three weeks to reach the vicinity of the Malvinas."

"How will we know when they're in position?" Schacht asked.

"When they are south of the equator, our Air Force will be able to track them with modified Boeing 707s," Sarmiento said. "Prior to that, though, we will be in the dark."

Dieter glanced at Willy. "The English Admiralty will know the fleet's position at all times," Willy said. "They will have constant radio communication, and the English will have access to the Americans' spy satellites. We have assets in place in London which will relay the pertinent information to us."

"Spies, you mean," Sarmiento said, eyes gleaming. Like all of these military men, he was intrigued by the idea of espionage. The Argentines imagined themselves to be quite adept at it, Willy knew. He also knew they were amateurs compared to the real players in the game. But at least Sarmiento was smart enough to admit it. "My friends, you accomplish things our own Secretariat cannot. My compliments now go to you." He raised his glass.

Heinz winked at Willy. Within the Bund, especially those connected to the SD, Argentina's foreign intelligence service was not much more than a joke. The *Secretaria de Intelligencia de Estado*, or Secretariat of State Intelligence, known by its Spanish acronym of SIDE, did a decent job keeping track of events in neighboring countries; Willy doubted whether the general staffs of Brazil or Chile could get orders to their divisions fast enough to beat the news to Buenos Aires. But compared to professionals like those in the English MI6, the American CIA or especially the Soviet KGB, the men who worked for SIDE had a lot to learn. Fortunately, the Bund's SD had learned those lessons long ago.

The discussion lasted another hour. Sarmiento told what he knew of the junta's military plan. It was simple enough, Willy concluded. Sail the fleet, land the troops, seize the islands, and wait for the English to arrive. If diplomatic efforts failed to resolve the situation—in Argentina's favor, of course—the Royal Navy would be crushed by the intrepid pilots of the Argentine Air Force and the sailors of her Navy. The troops ashore would have a month to dig in and would easily repel any English marines that might survive the battles at sea. "That is the overall plan," Sarmiento said. "Of course, President Galtieri and Capitan Anaya do not know of CAPRICORN. I believe that your plan's success will change the equation somewhat."

"In what way, mi General?" Muller asked.

The Army general looked seriously at the Bund Foreign Minister. "A successful attack upon the English with the scale you envision, my friend, will cause panic among the more cautious of my colleagues," he said. "Indeed, many would be terrified of an English response in kind."

"That will not happen," Müller said confidently.

"How can you be sure?" Sarmiento asked, his voice taking on a tinge of anger. "The English have the capability of striking any target in Argentina. They could launch missiles from their submarines. Their bombers could destroy our cities. They could even launch ICBMs from their home island!"

Dieter looked at the elder Nagel. "Günther, do you have any information which might help alleviate the general's concerns?"

"The English have no ballistic missile submarines," the SD chief said with confidence. "They are at least ten years away from putting one of those to sea. The Americans and Russians have many of them, of course—the Americans call them 'boomers'—and the Chinese also have some in

254

development. The English do have nuclear-powered submersibles, but none that carry missiles. The SALT Two treaty between the United States and Soviet Union forbids the deployment of nuclear weapons aboard what are termed 'fast-attack' submarines, which the English do have."

"The English did not sign SALT Two," Sarmiento pointed out.

"True," Nagel said, "but they abide by its general principles. It is a political issue, mi General. Should the Americans let the English arm their fast-attack submarines in such a way that would circumvent the treaty, the Russians might start putting similar weapons aboard Polish submarines."

"The Poles have submarines?" Schacht asked.

Dieter waved a dismissal at the question. "It doesn't matter. The point is, mi General, we do not need to worry about an English nuclear response against us."

"Their bombers—"

"Their Vulcan strategic bombers have a limited range," Nagel said. "They are not like the American B-52s. They will have to fly from their base on Ascension Island. Just to reach the Malvinas, they will require mid-air refueling. To strike our mainland, even with conventional weapons, they would have to stage from a much closer location. There are no such facilities in the English possessions in the Caribbean. To stage out of an American base in Panama would cause too many political problems for them. Even more so if they were to approach any of our neighbors. As to their land-based missiles, they do not have the range to come anywhere near us. They are designed to attack the Soviet Union."

"The point is," Dieter said, "the English will not attack our mainland, even if CAPRICORN succeeds. Such an attack would fall outside the purview of Article 51 of the United Nations Charter, which allows a member state to use military force in self-defense. That is what the English will use to justify their attempt to re-take the Malvinas. Any kind of attack against the Argentine mainland, especially one which would target civilians, would be an escalation that would be unacceptable to the U.N."

"Remember, mi General," Müller said, "CAPRICORN will strike at a strictly military target. No English civilians will be harmed, other than those unfortunate enough to be on board any of those ships. Even the English civilians in the Malvinas will not be harmed. Our troops will be very careful about that, won't they?"

"But of course," Sarmiento said, somewhat mollified. "Those that wish to stay will be allowed to stay. Those that wish to leave for England will be allowed to leave. There are many Argentines who wish to settle there once the islands are firmly in our hands again."

Willy had a hard time stifling a laugh. Who would want to go live there? To banish the thought, he said, "Mi General, these possibilities have all been carefully considered. While anything is possible, if you would examine each contingency, you would see that our position really is quite strong."

"Precisely," Dieter said with a grateful nod to his son. "Mi General, when these questions come before the junta, you will be able to argue persuasively against the fear of an English counterattack to CAPRICORN. The political considerations Thatcher must take into account are enormous, much greater than ours. She will be prepared to move against us, but only to a point. She will not cross the nuclear line, even after we have crossed it. Rest assured on that."

Sarmiento took a deep breath, brow furrowed in thought. "Very well, my friends. I know these questions will come up when my colleagues learn about CAPRICORN. I hope I will be able to allay their fears."

"If not," Dieter said, "there is a contingency plan."

"And that is?"

Dieter glanced at Schacht. "Mi General," the Bundesführer said, "in the event the junta leadership disregards your calm advice and begins to panic, cooler heads must be prepared to seize the moment and save the nation from catastrophe."

Sarmiento was no fool. "Are you suggesting a...change of leadership might then be called for?"

Schacht shrugged. "We must be prepared for all contingencies."

Dieter jumped in at just the right moment. "If President Galtieri loses his grip, you must be ready to assume command. We will give you our full support. We will have the proper assets in place at the time, just in case." Willy was aware of that plan, and hoped it wouldn't have to be implemented. Any kind of *coup d'etat* was perilous, even in Argentina, where they sometimes seemed as common as the change of seasons. There would be no guarantee that commanders friendly to the Bund would be able to keep their units together and successfully disarm those led by loyalist officers. If a coup failed, it would mean the end of the Bund, and its leaders would find themselves facing firing squads.

Sarmiento blinked, and then he smiled. "I understand," he said.

"Tomorrow, my son and young Nagel will be going to Pilcaniyeu for one final inspection," Dieter said. "Assuming their report to us is positive, we will initiate the next phase of the operation. In the meantime, the Army and Navy will proceed with the successful seizure of the Malvinas." He raised his glass. "Gentlemen, to success!"

CHAPTER TWENTY-THREE

Langley, Virginia

March 22nd, 1982

Jo Ann straightened her blue Class-A uniform jacket as she stepped out of the car. The young man in business suit and sunglasses who'd driven her here from the airport was holding the door open for her. "You can leave your luggage in the trunk, Major," he said politely.

"Thank you," she said. "So this is CIA Headquarters. It looks like an ordinary parking garage to me." The man gave her a thin smile. So much for humor.

Another man in a suit was waiting for them at an unmarked door. "Major Geary," he said, "welcome to Langley. Please attach this to your uniform." He handed her a laminated card with a clip attached to the back. She gave it a look, saw that it was an official guest card, but also had her name, rank and photo prominently displayed. "Right this way," he said.

The door led to an elevator, and the man pressed the button for the fourth floor. Nobody else was aboard and the car didn't stop at any other floors, reinforcing Jo's first impression that this was the way special guests entered the headquarters of the Central Intelligence Agency outside Langley, Virginia.

At one time, her father's call yesterday would have been a surprise. Before her visit back in December, Joseph had rarely called her, preferring an occasional brief letter. Jo had more regular contact with her mother, usually a weekly letter in Korean and a phone call twice a month. Since the visit, he'd started calling her more often. This was the first time that her father had ever called her on official business, though. "I need you to come to Langley tomorrow," he said. "I've already spoken to your C.O. His office is arranging your flight."

"What's this all about, Daddy?" she asked, knowing the answer in advance.

"I'll tell you when you get here," he said. "See you tomorrow."

Jo's father had always been an imperious presence to her, from the days when she was a little girl all the way through adolescence, college and now into her Air Force career. When she visited her parents, her father always made time to talk to her, but his affection only went so far: a hug, a kiss on the cheek, a warm smile. Behind his eyes, though, Jo could sense a barrier around his innermost feelings. Things had started to change, though. Even with all her accomplishments in the Air Force, Jo sometimes wondered if Joseph was really proud of her. That was nonsense; of course he was proud of her, he'd said so more than once. But her role in helping plug that Pentagon leak was different. For the first time, she had taken part in something her father was involved in, something in his world, and she had proven herself in it.

They exited the elevator into a well-lit hallway, with smartly dressed people walking with papers or files or briefcases, all in civilian clothes, all intent on where they were going. Her guide led her down the hall to an office suite that appeared to be in a corner of the building.

A fortyish woman behind a desk looked up and smiled as Jo and her escort entered the suite. "Major Geary, welcome to Langley," she said, rising and offering her hand. "I'm Phyllis McGreevy, Director Geary's executive assistant. I'm glad I can finally meet you."

"Thank you," Jo said. It struck her that this woman had probably worked for her father for some time. When was the last time Jo visited this office? With a shock, she realized that she never had. Joseph Geary had been named DDO in 1979. Before that, he served in various overseas postings, interspersed with one or two tours at Langley. Jo couldn't remember the last time she'd come to see her father at work, but it hadn't been here. Her cheeks colored a bit with shame.

McGreevy led the way to an inside door. Jo couldn't help noticing that she was tall and attractive, her suit conservative but stylish. She felt a pang of jealousy, almost as if she were her mother. Did Umma ever come here? What did she think of the tall and shapely Ms. McGreevy? Jo shoved that thought out of her mind. She had never known a man more honorable than her father.

The executive assistant knocked on the door and opened it. "Director, your guest is here," she said. McGreevy stepped aside and bathed Jo with a warm smile. "Enjoy your visit." Jo nodded to her politely and entered her father's realm.

Joseph Geary came around his dark oak desk with a smile that was loving and happy but still somewhat reserved. The bags under his eyes seemed a bit more severe. But he was still her father, he most certainly was, and she came forward gladly to be enveloped in his embrace. "JoJo, it's so good to see you," he said. He unwrapped his long arms and held her at their length. "Well, I should be saluting you instead of hugging you. Congratulations on your promotion." He looked at the ribbon bars on her uniform, peering at the newest. "And a Bronze Star. Well done, young lady. Very well done indeed."

"Thank you, Daddy. It's good to see you again." She offered her cheek, and he bent to kiss it.

"Have a seat," he said, motioning to a couch in the small sitting area. She took a quick glance around the office, noticing some familiar photos and mementos, including her Stanford graduation portrait, and another of her and her parents next to a T-33 jet trainer on the day Jo was awarded her pilot's wings. Otherwise, the office was surprisingly subdued. Wood paneling, a nice credenza, the desk, leather furniture, light brown carpeting. On one wall hung a portrait of Theodore Roosevelt, one of her father's idols. On the credenza was a picture of her father and President Reagan. It was a man's office, definitely, but Jo suspected that her father didn't spend a lot of time here. He'd always been a man on the move, and there were probably several other places here at CIA where Joseph Geary spent considerable amounts of time.

"Well, I have to say that your name keeps popping up around here," he said. "It appears that little business with the congresswoman's chief of staff—I should say, former chief of staff, sent more than a few ripples through the Pentagon."

"I've heard a few rumors," she said. Several officers had been cashiered or transferred as a result of the investigation, but the brass had managed to keep most of it out of the press.

"That, and your commendation for the Fonglan Island mission," he said. "So, when we became aware of some very important things our British friends are involved in, your name came up."

That made her hesitate a little. She hadn't yet told her parents about Ian. "A military operation?"

"No," he said. "This is a field op, but not strictly Agency work." He glanced at his watch. "Let's head down the hall," he said. "There are a couple people I want you to meet, and then we'll talk about what's going on."

As they walked together down the hallway, Jo noticed how her father carried himself. "Posture is the currency of leadership," he'd once told her, and Joseph Geary was a leader. He smiled and nodded to everyone he passed, saying hello to several, using first names. The people returned his greetings with obvious respect and even affection. Jo's heart filled with pride. Here was a truly honorable man, doing important work for his country. Not for the first time, she prayed she could live up to his example.

They came to a door that opened into another suite, and then another one into a small conference room. Two men were sitting at the table and stood as Jo and the DDO entered. She thought she recognized one of the men.

"Gentlemen, my daughter, Major Jo Ann Geary," Joseph said. She could hear the pride in the voice.

The older of the two men, a bit heavy-set with white hair and glasses, stepped toward her and offered a hand. "Major Geary, welcome to CIA. I'm Bill Casey, DCI." The name clicked with the face now. William Casey was Director of Central Intelligence, her father's boss, and one of the heavyweights in the Reagan Administration. "And may I introduce Sir David Blandford, of Her Majesty's Secret Intelligence Service." Blandford held out a hand, and showed a gold crown on one upper tooth when he smiled.

"A pleasure," he said. Blandford was of medium height, a bit heavy around the waist, but splendidly turned out in what Jo assumed was a suit from one of London's finer tailors. He wore wire-rimmed glasses and a thin mustache. "I believe we have a mutual friend, a certain Royal Marines lieutenant colonel."

Another relay clicked in Jo's mind: Ian's MI6 friend. "I believe we do, Sir David," she said. She glanced at her father, and could tell from his eyes and hint of a smile that he would have a few questions for her about that over dinner. Perhaps, she thought, he already knew. His business was finding things out, after all.

Casey motioned everybody to seats around the table. "We should get started," he said. "Sir David has an early flight back to London tomorrow morning." He looked at Jo. "Major, we asked you here because your name was mentioned as a possible candidate for a special project we are putting together. I regret to say that I can't tell you much about it, and will have to ask you to make a choice about participating before you hear all the facts. All I can tell you beforehand is that this involves a matter of national security. It would require that you accept temporarily detached duty from the Air Force for the duration of the mission."

"May I ask for how long?"

"Almost certainly less than six months, perhaps considerably less," Casey said. "Before we can proceed, I must have an answer from you."

She looked at her father, but couldn't read anything on his face. Looking back at Casey, she said, "If my country needs me, I'm ready to do whatever I can."

Casey smiled, as did the Englishman. "Excellent. Major, you will be TDY to the SIS for this mission. Sir David?"

"Thank you, Director." Blandford produced a file and set it on the desk before him. Jo could see it was bordered in red and bore the words MOST SECRET. "Major, may I call you Jo Ann?"

"Of course."

"Very good. This is not a military mission, after all. Well. I trust that Colonel Masters has provided you with some background on the current situation in the South Atlantic, has he not?"

Jo looked at her father. "Ian is a...friend of mine." Joseph nodded, and she turned back to the MI6 man. "Yes, when we were in Bermuda, he mentioned it." She didn't want to say anything about Ascension Island, but undoubtedly these men knew about that, too. They certainly knew about Fonglan and Hong Kong after that. She felt a pang of regret at not telling her parents about Ian before now. It was almost like she was a teenager again, sneaking around with a boy she thought might not rate her father's approval. Well, she would rectify that later.

"We have reason to believe that an Argentine attack on the Falkland Islands is imminent," Blandford said. "There have been the usual diplomatic maneuverings between London and Buenos Aires, and we've endeavored to involve the United Nations in the matter. In the meantime, Prime Minister Thatcher has ordered the Firm, as we are known, to find out all we can about Argentina's intentions. As you might imagine, we have in fact been quite active down there for some time."

The MI6 man opened the file. Jo could see the first page was actually a black and white photograph, but she didn't recognize the subject. "In the course of our various activities in Argentina, we came into possession of some rather interesting information regarding a certain group of men who appear to be working rather diligently behind the scenes, and indeed, have been doing so for many years. Tell me, Jo Ann, have you ever heard of the Siegfried Bund?"

Jo shook her head. "I'm afraid not."

"Not surprising," Blandford said. He cleared his throat. "A brief history lesson, then. During most of the Second World War, Argentina remained neutral, even though its neighbor and rival, Brazil, joined the Allies. As Argentina has large ethnic German and Italian populations, sympathy for the Axis cause was high, especially within its military. Britain considered Argentina a vital trading partner, especially for its food, and was satisfied with its neutrality, although your President Roosevelt did not trust the ruling junta and pressured them to formally join the Allies against the Axis. It nearly came to war; in early 1944, Washington broke diplomatic relations with Buenos Aires and for a time considered supporting a Brazilian attack upon Argentina. There was also the possibility, and it surely was difficult to consider, that the Allies might have to seek an armistice with Hitler. To have an Axis partner in South America would have been completely unacceptable, and American troops would have eventually been sent down there to fight. Not a pleasant prospect, but the Argentines eventually gave in and declared war on the Axis in March 1945. They never sent troops into the fight, although there were efforts made to reduce the considerable influence of the country's ethnic Germans. Efforts we now believe were half-hearted for a very good reason."

Blandford shuffled the papers in the file, warming to his subject. "By 1943 it had become clear to many of the Nazi leaders in Germany that the war was probably lost. Their invasion of Russia had been stymied and they were being rolled back in North Africa. They knew there would be no refuge for them in Europe, so they looked to Argentina. They set up not just one, but two organizations to effect the evacuation of Nazi officials from Germany. One was called *die Spinne*, or 'the Spider', designed to operate an escape route through Austria to Italy. The other, perhaps you've heard of: *Organisation der ehemaligen SS Angehörigen*, the Organization of Former SS Members, better known by its acronym, ODESSA. This group brought people out through Spain. Both were designed to get the fugitives to Argentina. In the fall of that year, they sent this man to pave the way."

Blandford passed the top photograph to Jo. It showed a dark-haired man in the black uniform of the Waffen-SS, unsmiling, with intense eyes. "Dieter Baumann," Blandford said. "Born in Hamburg, 1907. Joined the Nazi Party in '31, rose through the ranks, and when war came he became an officer in the SS. Rose to the rank of SS *Standartenführer*, or colonel, saw action in France and Russia. In mid-'43, he was personally selected by Heinrich Himmler, the head of the SS and one of the leaders of the group that was interested in

Argentina, to go to that country and set up what became the Siegfried Bund."

"I was posted in Buenos Aires in '43," Joseph Geary said. Jo was surprised; she had always thought her father had spent the war in the Far East. "It was my first assignment for OSS, the Office of Strategic Services, the predecessor of CIA. I worked with our people there, and Sir David's people, to try to figure out what the Germans were up to. I met Baumann at a dinner party one evening. A very smooth operator."

Blandford took up the story again. "Himmler and his partners began shipping the booty from the death camps to Argentina on U-boats. It was a critical phase of the operation and Baumann built up the contacts in Buenos Aires to receive the cargo, convert it to cash and deposit the money in various banks." The MI6 man consulted a sheet from the file. "The Germans were meticulous record-keepers. They extracted a great deal of wealth from the Jews and others they murdered in the camps. This part of the plan used six U-boats to ship over half a million ounces of gold, thirty-five hundred ounces of platinum, over four thousand carats of diamonds, and millions in gold Reichsmarks, British pounds, American dollars and Swiss francs, as well as hundreds of works of art. The submarines all arrived safely in Argentina in early 1945. The Argentines took the crews into custody, but the loot managed to somehow get past the authorities."

"That wasn't all of the money," Joseph said. "A lot of the Nazi money went to banks in neutral European countries, and from them to Argentina. We believe they worked largely through Portugal, Sweden and Switzerland."

Blandford consulted his list again. "The biggest deposit was by the Banque Nationale Suisse, the national bank of

Switzerland. In November 1944, it deposited twenty gold bars in Buenos Aires. Less than two years later, early '46, the bank's holdings in Argentina were up to 470 bars. That was more than six tons of gold."

"My Lord," Jo said, trying to grasp the enormity of that much money.

Casey spoke for the first time since asking Jo to commit to the mission. "With the financial base established, the Nazi big shots started making plans to escape from Europe and get to Argentina before it was too late. Baumann had done a masterful job of creating close ties with Juan Perón, an Argentine Army colonel who was part of a junta that took over the country in '43. By '46, Perón was the president. Much of his financial support came from the Nazis. After he was elected, we believe he created some ten thousand blank passports and identity cards for Nazi fugitives."

"Ten thousand!" Jo exclaimed.

"Not nearly that many managed to escape," Blandford said. "The last few months of the Thousand-Year Reich were very chaotic. The Western Allies were invading Germany from the west and south, the Russians from the east. Things were falling apart quickly. The escape routes they'd planned were starting to break down. Some were afraid to leave for fear Hitler would have them hunted down and shot as traitors, which of course they were. Others were captured by the Allies before they could get out of Europe. But several hundred did make it, and they wasted no time in establishing themselves as businessmen, using the money to finance their purchases. They invested heavily in industry, the media and real estate. They were very shrewd, very circumspect."

"Where did the name come from?" Jo asked.

Blandford pulled another paper from his file. "*Bund* is the German word for 'union', as applied in this case. Siegfried harks back to German mythology. The *Nibelungenlied* is an epic poem from the thirteenth century. The main character is the warrior Siegfried, who has captured a hoard of gold from the Nibelungs, an evil family. It is rather involved, but the condensed version, one might say, finds Siegfried betrayed by his relatives and murdered. His wife seeks vengeance for him and there's a great deal of mayhem and death, but in the end Siegfried's chief, Etzel, is one of the few survivors. The poem is said to be a classical representation of the German ideals of fate and loyalty to the chief."

"Did Baumann become the leader of the Bund?" Jo asked.

"No," Blandford said. "What I'm about to tell you is something I have not yet shared with Director Casey." He turned to the DCI. "My apologies, sir, but I was under strict orders not to discuss this aspect of the situation until we had secured the services of the agent."

Casey nodded understanding. "Go ahead, Sir David."

Blandford fished in the file for another photograph. He looked it over, took a breath, and passed it to Casey. "Good God in heaven," the DCI said. "Not him. Are you sure?"

"Quite certain," Blandford said.

Casey passed the photo to Joseph. "Oh, Lord."

"Who is it?" Jo asked. Her father passed her the picture. It was of a man in a slightly different style of uniform, but definitely Third Reich-era German. This man was stocky, with a thick neck, thin slicked-back hair, a protruding chin, and eyes that were almost hidden by a thick-boned brow, but they were eyes that held a particular cunning. Jo didn't recognize the photo.

Blandford spoke in a voice that had seemingly taken on a darker timbre. "That, my dear, is one of the few surviving photographs of Martin Bormann, the Reichsleiter of the Nazi Party, personal secretary to Hitler himself. When the Nazi regime collapsed he became the most wanted man in Europe. He was thought to be dead, shot by the Russians as he tried to escape Berlin in the final days of the war. He was not shot. He escaped, and today he is living in Argentina, and he is the head of the Siegfried Bund. As we speak, he and his men are preparing to launch a nuclear weapon against the British fleet when it arrives at the Falklands. He is the reason we are sending you to Argentina, to find him and eliminate him, before they can attack."

CHAPTER TWENTY-FOUR

Langley, Virginia
March 22nd, 1982

The enormity of Blandford's words slammed into Jo with almost physical force. Her heart began to race. She forced herself to calm down, drawing upon her inner ki, and within a few seconds she felt fine, physically. Emotionally, that was another thing.

"Why me?" she managed to ask. "Surely you have more experienced agents who can carry out an assassination. For that matter, why can't you just launch a military strike?"

"A military operation is out of the question," Blandford said. "Regrettably, I might add. Bormann lives near the city of Bariloche, in western Argentina near the Chilean border. There are serious political obstacles in the way of a strike, either by air or on the ground. Launching an operation from Chile might very well ignite hostilities between the two countries, which we do not want to see, and most surely your government do not, either. An air strike from the east would require an overflight of Argentine territory that would be most hazardous, and short of using a nuclear weapon of our own, which of course is completely out of the question, a bombing run would not guarantee success. The decision has already been made on Downing Street that our forces shall refrain from any action against the Argentine mainland. Let me amend that: any overt action. There are other cards we can play to preclude a nuclear strike, should it come to pass."

"As to your inclusion in this mission, Jo Ann, you're not going in alone," Casey said. Jo sensed that the DCI was a bit miffed, perhaps at the way he learned about Bormann. Casey had acted surprised to learn about the Reichsleiter. She knew there was a friendly rivalry between CIA and SIS, and surely neither side liked to be one-upped by the other.

Blandford was fingering another photo from his file. "At the Firm, we had decided to send a man to Buenos Aires to infiltrate the Siegfried Bund and lead us to Bormann. At that time, we would employ other assets to complete the job. This is the man we chose." He handed the photo to Jo. It was a color portrait of a middle-aged man, obviously of Nordic stock, but otherwise undistinguished. "He is Walter Schröder, age fifty-two, an assistant to the Economic Minister of the East German government. He has been working for us for six years, since his first wife and two children died in the crash of an Aeroflot airliner. They were on their way home from holiday on the Black Sea. Schröder had been called back to East Berlin two days earlier, but insisted that his family remain to finish their visit. The official cause of the crash was mechanical failure, but the actual cause was shoddy work by the ground crew preparing the flight. Like just about everything else in the Soviet Union, their airline is horribly inefficient and prone to such tragedies. Really, it's amazing there haven't been more. In any event, we found Herr Schröder to be, shall we say, receptive to the idea of providing us with information."

"We became aware of Schröder ourselves a few years ago," Joseph said. "By and large the information he's been supplying to our British friends has been solid stuff. Not spectacular, but useful. Here at CIA we had some doubts about him, though. One of our people reported a contact between Schröder and an upper-level officer of Stasi, the East German intelligence service. We had previously confirmed a connection between this officer and the Siegfried Bund."

"CIA informed us of this contact," Blandford said. "We've no other reason to believe Schröder is involved with the Bund. However, when this particular operation was in the planning stage, this raised a flag. Our CIA liaison in London suggested that an American agent be sent to Buenos Aires along with Schröder, to ensure his loyalty, so to speak." The MI6 man pulled yet another photo from the file and passed it to Jo. This one showed a casually dressed Schröder with a dark-haired, Asiatic-looking woman.

"His wife?" Jo guessed.

"His current one," Blandford said. "Schröder remarried in 1980. His wife is of Armenian heritage. They met while he was on a trip to that area of the Soviet Union. Their courtship was rather swift and she was allowed to immigrate to East Germany once they married. Her name is Larisa, maiden name Kocharian. No children, age thirty. She works in a small office that manages cultural exchange missions between East Germany and the Armenian Republic. As you might imagine, she is not very busy."

"SIS has already tasked Schröder for the operation," Joseph said. "In exchange, they will help him to defect to our side once the op is done. For now, he's managed to arrange an official visit to Argentina for himself and his wife. The two of them will go to Budapest, where you will meet him. The real Larisa will be taken in hand by our people and smuggled into Yugoslavia and then here."

"Major, your assignment is to accompany Schröder to Buenos Aires, posing as his wife," Casey said. "While there, you will monitor Schröder's activities and alert us or SIS if it appears he is indeed involved with the Bund, and if so, you will try to learn as much about their nuclear plan as possible. It appears that Sir David's people hope he can lead you to Bormann. It's a long shot, but time is of the essence, so it's the only shot we really have."

"Our latest intelligence estimates place an Argentine invasion of the Falklands within one week," Blandford said. "I regret to say that we will not be able to oppose the landing. We have only a small garrison of marines on the islands and no appreciable naval assets in the area. By the time we have assembled our own fleet and sent it to the war zone, several weeks will have elapsed. Our intelligence indicates that the Bund is planning to strike the fleet when it is within two hundred miles or so of the Falklands."

Jo turned to Casey. "I'm assuming that there are reasons why we can't really use our own assets to do this, Director."

Casey nodded solemnly. "Unfortunately, that's true, Major. The President is in a delicate political situation. Argentina is a nation friendly to the United States. We have some serious concerns about human rights violations there in recent years, but they are, after all, a nation of our own hemisphere. Their president, General Galtieri, visited here last year and made quite a few friends in Congress. We anticipate that he will ask us to invoke the Monroe Doctrine to prevent European interference in this hemisphere. We won't, of course; officially, I expect, we'll remain neutral as long as possible. Certainly no American military forces will be employed on either side. We're quite confident the British can defeat the Argentines in a conventional conflict. It goes without saying, however, that we simply cannot allow the Argentines to launch a nuclear attack on the Royal Navy."

"We have to worry about the Russians," Joseph said. "Right now we're very concerned about what they're up to in Nicaragua, El Salvador, elsewhere in Central America and the Caribbean. If we take up arms alongside a European power against a Latin American nation, the Russians will exploit that and make things quite difficult for us. The last thing in the world the Latin American countries want is for the Yankees to come down there and take over, and frankly, we don't want that, either. But the destruction of the British fleet would be catastrophic. The Royal Navy is vital to NATO defense plans. Its sudden loss could very well prompt a Soviet move in the Mediterranean. The political turmoil might even give them ideas about doing something on the continent, such as seizing West Berlin. So we have to play this very carefully."

"My government also have some serious political considerations," Sir David said. "Besides the obvious, of course, that the Falklands are sovereign British territory and a foreign occupation of them cannot be tolerated. We are concerned about indications that Guatemala may want to move on Belize, to whom we granted full independence last year. The Spaniards have been talking about wanting Gibraltar back. We simply must make a stand over the Falklands. At the same time, the prime minister's position is not completely secure. Should it become known that the Argentines have nuclear weapons and may be willing to use them, there will be many in Parliament who will argue that the Falklands are simply not worth that cost. And should she then proceed anyway, and should the worst happen, her government would fall." He spread his hands. "We are, as you can see, in somewhat of a bind."

Jo nodded her understanding. She looked at the Englishman. Was there a plaintive look in his eyes? She thought of Ian, preparing to go back in harm's way to help the people on some faraway islands who would soon have their freedom taken away. "I'm honored that you have asked me to help, Sir David. But I do have a question. If I remember, wasn't Bormann's body found in Germany several years ago?"

Blandford shrugged his shoulders. "Everyone thought so," he said. "The historical record is fairly clear about Bormann's attempted escape from the *Führerbunker* at the Reich Chancellery. Around midnight on May first, 1945, Bormann and several others decided to make a break for it, through the Russian lines to German units in the outskirts of the city that were still engaging the enemy. From there, it is assumed they would try to contact one or both of the escape organizations. Witnesses have placed Bormann near the Admiralpalast when, supposedly, he was killed when the German tank he was walking behind was hit by Russian shells. One of the other Germans in the escape party claimed to have buried Bormann and the other victim, a Doctor Ludwig Stumpfegger, Hitler's physician, very close to the site."

Blandford withdrew another photo from his file. This one showed human bones exposed in a crude grave. "In 1972, during construction work, the remains of two men were found. One was the correct height for Bormann, and had a collarbone that had once been broken. Bormann's sons testified that their father had broken a collarbone in 1939 when he fell off a horse. What supposedly clinched the identification were dental records. Hitler's personal dentist had also treated Bormann. The dentist was captured after the war by the Americans and made a chart of the teeth of both men. The lab technician who prepared bridgework for Bormann was still alive in '72, and when presented with the charts and photos of the corpse's teeth, he confirmed that it was Bormann. The investigators went further, however, and ordered a forensic reconstruction of the face based on the skull. The result was remarkably similar to Bormann. That was enough for the West German authorities, who closed the case in 1973 by declaring the remains positively identified as those of Bormann and Stumpfegger."

"But they were wrong?" Jo asked.

Casey picked it up. "Sir David knows that we've never really accepted that judgment. We have reason to believe that the dental records, which had been in U.S. custody since the interview with the dentist right after the war, had been altered since they were first drawn up. The forensic workup was fairly convincing—I've seen the pictures myself, and there's a strong resemblance—but that alone doesn't prove the remains were those of Bormann. What we think happened is that sometime in the early fifties a man similar in appearance to Bormann was located by the Bund in West Germany, taken to West Berlin, and murdered. They buried him at that spot, along with a corpse resembling Stumpfegger. The dental records of the victim were used to alter the records drawn up by the Nazi dentist. The broken collarbone, of course, could have been easily arranged. It was a very well-conceived and executed operation, designed to do exactly what it eventually did: provide so-called evidence that Bormann never made it out of Berlin alive."

"I see," Jo said. She took a deep breath. Her fears had subsided. She had a chance to help right a wrong. She remembered what little she'd read about Bormann: an evil man, undoubtedly responsible for a great deal of suffering and death, and he was still alive, planning to cause more of it. He had to be stopped. "Tell me what you'd like me to do," she said to the MI6 man.

Blandford seemed to relax just a bit, and smiled. "Very good, Jo Ann." He reached under the table and produced another folder, this one thinner than the first. He slid it across the table to Jo. "This is a file on Larisa Schröder. Once you read it, I'm sure you'll understand why we wanted you for this mission. You bear a striking resemblance to her, for one thing. You have experience in the field and have proven capable of taking care of yourself. I read the after-action report of the business on Fonglan Island. Quite impressive, I must say. Plus, you have a proficiency in foreign languages. How many do you speak, may I ask?"

"I'm fluent in English, Korean and Japanese, conversational in French, Spanish and Mandarin Chinese." When Blandford's eyebrows rose in astonishment, she smiled. "My mother is Korean, and we lived for a few years in Japan, so it was easy to pick those up." She didn't mention the long hours of study all through her academic career, and the half-hour a day she devoted to reading something in one of her other tongues, just to maintain proficiency. It wasn't quite as easy as it might have appeared. "I'm assuming Larisa speaks German and whatever language they speak in Armenia," she said.

"She speaks German, of course," Blandford said, "and her native language, which is indeed Armenian. She's conversant in Russian as well. What we want to do is take you to London straight away and give you a crash course in German. You'll get enough Armenian and a smattering of Russian to get by in the event someone down there decides to test you, which is unlikely, but could happen. It's a tall order, I'm afraid, but again, we have no other assets that provide the combination of qualities you possess."

Jo managed a smile. "I'm a quick study, Sir David. I'll be fine with the languages." She wished she felt as confident as she sounded.

"Excellent," the Englishman said. "Well, I see I shall have a seatmate when I return to London tomorrow." He looked at Casey, then at Joseph. "Gentlemen, it appears Operation EMINENCE is underway." To Jo, he said, "Bormann was known as the 'Brown Eminence', for his brown Nazi Party uniform."

"I suppose I'll need a code name," Jo said.

"Yes," Sir David said. "Any suggestions."

Jo looked at her father, then back at her new boss. She remembered a story her mother had told her long ago. "How about 'White Vixen'?"

CHAPTER TWENTY-FIVE

Pilcaniyeu, Argentina

March 22nd, 1982

Brian Jamison was surprised at the size of the facility. He had toured nuclear weapons plants before, and this one was half the size of the smallest he'd seen. For a moment, he thought he might have been led to the wrong place, but the soldiers standing guard at the main gate convinced him that this was likely where he was supposed to be. Once he was inside, he knew for sure.

Major Gasparini was nowhere to be seen, and that was as it should've been. The Argentine had risked much already; there was no need to compromise him by being seen together, in the event this little trip went bollocksed. The way this one was slapped together, Jamison was giving no better than fifty-fifty odds about that.

Contrary to what was shown in the cinema, MI6 normally devoted lengthy and meticulous planning to its field operations. Not this time. Jamison had taken two weeks' leave after his return from Asia in November and then was put to work studying Argentina. The Firm was anticipating some sort of dust-up with the Argies, and scuttlebutt around Century House, the SIS headquarters in London, had it that something was afoot concerning the Falkland Islands. Jamison had learned much about this part of the world in the past three-plus months. He'd never visited Argentina, but talked to other agents who had, and they all spoke glowingly about the country's great food and beautiful women. It was a pity that he wouldn't be around long enough to sample much of either.

Just a week ago, he received hurried orders to depart for South America, orders signed by "C" himself, the chief of SIS, in the traditional green ink. That made this op very important indeed, as his briefing emphasized. He flew from London to New York on the Concorde, from there to Los Angeles, and then down to Santiago, Chile. Given a blessed twenty-four hours to rest, he was then more thoroughly briefed by the MI6 chief of station at the British Embassy and a representative of the Chilean security service, *Centro Nacional de Informacion*. The Chileans, it seemed, were quite concerned about what was going on just across the border at the place Jamison was tasked to visit. They supplied him with a BIS captain's uniform and appropriate identity papers.

It then became a matter of waiting until the right time. Jamison spent three pleasant days in Santiago and then was driven to Osorno, a city about seventy-five miles from the border. The next day he crossed over into Argentina using the identity of an Irish businessman with contacts in the nearby city of Bariloche. His luggage passed the border guards' cursory inspection, which didn't come close to finding any incriminating clothing or weapons, as those had been smuggled across the border ahead of him by a Chilean agent. Jamison then met the Chilean in Bariloche for the handoff.

The agent checked into a Bariloche hotel as Duncan MacPherson, Dublin antiquities merchant, made a phone call, had dinner alone at a nearby restaurant and then drove his rented car to the village of Pilcaniyeu. Still playing the role of an Irishman, Jamison checked into the town's only hotel, having reserved a room with his call from Bariloche. A friendly man-to-man inquiry to the bellhop, along with a few pesos, produced a name that Jamison already knew. Within a few minutes he found his way to a cantina that also served as one of the town's sporting houses, catering primarily to soldiers from the base.

In the small bar Jamison saw the man he'd come there to meet. Without letting his gaze linger on the man, Jamison gave the recognition signal, rubbing the right side of his nose with his right index finger. He sat at the bar and ordered a local beer, and while taking his first sip he looked around the barroom again. The man, wearing civilian clothes, was nervously twisting the wedding ring on his left hand. Good, he hadn't been followed. A few minutes later, the man rose and went over to a swarthy local sitting near an inside door, had a brief word with him, and was allowed into the next room.

Ten minutes later, after checking one more time for any possible surveillance and concluding he was in the clear, Jamison asked a discreet question of the bartender, who nodded to the local near the inner door. The agent paid for his beer and left a hefty tip. A minute later he was inside what appeared to be a sparsely furnished living room. Four young, world-weary women were watching television. An older woman appeared from another room, bringing the aroma of food with her. "How may I help you, señor?"

Jamison produced a hundred-peso note. "I believe Pedro is expecting me."

The woman took the bill and motioned down a hallway. "Second door on the left, señor. Thirty minutes, please."

Half an hour later, Jamison left the brothel by a side door, five minutes after a nervous Major Antonio Gasparini departed through the cantina. The young lady who had thought she'd be part of some three-way fun with the two interesting gentlemen was sent out for a walk, two hundred pesos richer.

The Argentine was quite uncomfortable during the meeting, causing Jamison to harbor his own concerns about the officer's reliability. "I was told to come here every few days once I returned from leave," he told the Englishman. "I have always been faithful to my wife, señor. Your people said this would be a good place for us to meet, and I had to establish a pattern by visiting it once or twice ahead of time. But I paid the whores and then had them listen to me spin a tale of woe about my poor wife and how she is coming unhinged. I rejected their offers for physical release from my torment."

A good cover story, Jamison told him, in the event his superiors at the base were suspicious of him, which would have been quite understandable, considering the circumstances. Jamison had been briefed on the ordeal forced upon Gasparini's wife. He reassured the major that deliverance for him and his family was quickly approaching. Once his inspection of the base was done, Jamison would return to Chile and file his report, then wait there until he would return to help the Gasparini family across the border to freedom. A matter of a week or two, he was told.

Somewhat reassured, Gasparini gave Jamison the critical documents he would need to gain entrance to the compound. He would be conducting a cursory inspection of the facility under the auspices of BIS. Gasparini assured him there was no regular BIS presence at the base, security being the purview of the Army, but occasionally the agency sent a man down for a look around. Jamison was advised to be discreet; should a suspicious security officer make an inquiry to Buenos Aires, Jamison's cover would not hold up. The MI6 agent assured the nervous Argentine that he would be in and out within two hours. With luck, Gasparini's superior would never know a BIS man had purportedly been looking around.

The dicey part of the op came the next afternoon, when the MI6 agent, now posing as BIS Capitan Eduardo Concepción, drove his rented car the three miles from the village to the nuclear facility. The Argentine Army-standard .45 automatic in his hip holster did what little it could to bolster his confidence. Relying on his training and experience, Jamison used the short drive to compose himself, and when the gate came into view, he was as ready as he'd ever be.

The guards at the gate were thorough, inspecting Jamison's papers and searching the car. Gasparini had assured him they would not report his presence to the security office; BIS insisted that its inspectors be allowed in unannounced and given free reign. They were permitted inside, but certain areas were off-limits. The BIS inspectors never raised a fuss about it, being content to quickly complete what they viewed as a boring assignment.

David J. Tindell

There was always an exception, though, and Jamison did his best to push that thought away while at the gate. The man who searched the car reported to his sergeant that it was clean, and the sergeant of the guard gave Jamison's documents one last look and handed them back without a smile. "You may proceed, mi Capitan," he said.

"*Muchas* gracias." One big hurdle leaped, more to come.

Nobody paid any attention to him once he entered the facility. Armed soldiers were everywhere, greatly outnumbering the civilians in business suits or lab coats. Jamison had memorized the rough map of the facility drawn up by Gasparini, and made his way casually around the grounds and through the four interconnected buildings, carefully avoiding the people while not seeming to. Inspecting an enemy military base or research facility was not normally undertaken by active MI6 operatives; Century House much preferred to get its information from people who worked there. Much safer, and the foreigners generally were eager to cooperate when given proper incentive. This time was an exception, but Jamison had been on hostile ground before and doubtless would be again. Like many of his fellow agents, he'd come close to death enough times to give it a healthy respect, always taking proper precautions. James Bond could infiltrate Blofeld's headquarters with nothing more than a Walther PPK and a willing female accomplice, shoot several dozen ill-trained guards and bring down the entire place with a handful of well-placed explosives. In real life it was a bit more complicated.

The compound consisted of six buildings, four of which were connected by enclosed aboveground walkways as well as underground tunnels. One of the outbuildings was a large barracks for the security troops, the other a warehouse and repair shop. Jamison ignored these and entered the central complex by a side door. A guard stationed inside inspected his papers and waved him through.

The danger increased with each step further inside the facility. At any moment, a security officer could ask to see his credentials, perhaps tipped off by a suspicious employee, perhaps just practicing due diligence. Jamison was fluent in Spanish and able to handle himself in a pinch, but his experience in China not too many months ago had reinforced the belief that he was far from infallible. If it came to a confrontation with any of the security force here, the game was up. The challenge, then, was to avoid such a confrontation.

One of the buttons on Jamison's khaki jacket was not the standard brass. It concealed a tiny but powerful camera, capable of shooting up to thirty photos, activated by a tug on a certain spot of the hem of the garment. One of MI6's clever tools that would serve to enhance his report, assuming he lived to deliver it. He'd already taken three shots of the exterior of the main building.

Jamison's briefing had told him what to look for, but not why. That would not be difficult to figure out. Considering the tensions over the Falklands, inspecting a suspected enemy nuclear facility could lead to only one conclusion: the British intended to destroy this place rather than risk a nuclear attack on the fleet. It quickly became evident, however, that a British assault on this base, short of a nuclear strike of their own, was out of the question.

From the size of the troop barracks alone, and the proliferation of armed men, Jamison concluded that the Pilacaniyeu facility was guarded by at least three hundred soldiers, perhaps as many as five hundred. He had seen a few sandbagged bunkers, doubtless for machine-gun emplacements. It was likely some light armored vehicles were concealed somewhere. Reinforcements from the Army post near Bariloche were only a couple hours away, and their helicopters even closer. An assault by SAS or SBS commandos would be suicide; infantry and armored tactics were not his specialty, but Jamison could still estimate that it would take at least a battalion-strength assault with armor and air support to take the base. The Chileans might be able to muster something like that here, but it was not within the realm of possibility for the British.

He followed a series of hallways, remembering Gasparini's map. Some of the civilians nodded to him, and he nodded back with what he hoped was an appropriate air of superiority. Some of the security guards gave him a look, but none challenged him. His destination was in the middle of the large building, and he knew he was getting closer by the increasing numbers of guards and the decreasing numbers of civilians.

Gasparini told him the entrance to the top-secret bomb-assembly section was heavily guarded. Even the BIS inspectors never entered unless in company of a senior security officer. Jamison didn't want to risk exposing Gasparini, so he asked about an alternative. The Argentine major told him about a circuitous route sometimes used by the scientists, who delighted in outwitting the security force in such small ways. This "back door" was known to Gasparini's people and regularly checked, but they let the scientists think they could come and go relatively unscathed.

The MI6 agent saw the double-doored entrance to the central lab complex, guarded by four soldiers with automatic weapons, plus an officer with a sidearm who was checking the identity cards of each person entering and leaving. Jamison quickly continued on his way down the connecting hallway. One glance had told him he would never get through that gauntlet. Plan B it was, then.

He knew he was somewhere near the scientists' changing rooms. A fiftyish man in a white lab coat was going past him. "Excuse me, señor," Jamison said politely, "can you tell me where the nearest lavatory is located?"

"Certainly, mi Capitan," the scientist said. "That would be the changing room. I was just going there. I'd be happy to show you."

"Gracias, señor."

They exchanged small talk about the weather in the half-minute it took them to reach the appropriate door. The scientist led Jamison into a cramped room, lined with lockers and smelling of sweat intermingled with various colognes and cigarette smoke. "The side door, mi Capitan," the scientist said, gesturing. Jamison thanked him again and went into the lavatory. He presumed this was the changing room for the male scientists; Gasparini had told him there were about a dozen women working on the project, and they had their own separate changing room. Jamison entered a stall, closed and latched the door behind him, dropped his drawers and sat down. He waited an appropriate length of time, stood and pulled up his pants, flushed the toilet and left the stall. The lavatory was still empty.

Emerging into the changing room, Jamison saw that he was alone. Moving quickly, he went to a large cabinet he had seen when he first entered the room. Opening it, he caught his first break: it was, as he hoped, a laundry closet, containing freshly-washed towels and, thankfully, a dozen plain white laboratory coats. He quickly took one, closed the cabinet and put the coat on over his service jacket. His cap went into a nearby trash receptacle, hidden underneath some slightly damp paper towels. From an inside pocket of his service jacket he took a pair of eyeglasses and put them on. Another inside pocket produced an identity card similar to those used by the scientists; Gasparini had provided a standard blank ID card upon his first visit to the town sporting house, and a Chilean agent had retrieved it so it could be properly doctored with Jamison's photograph.

A nearby desk produced a clipboard, into which he inserted some papers he found in a wastebasket. An inside drawer of the desk revealed several pens and pencils, and even a clear plastic pocket protector. His luck was holding. Forty-five seconds after emerging from the loo, Jamison left the changing room by its back door, looking like most of the other scientists he'd seen in the hallways.

He had to control his breathing, force himself to stay calm. The hallway he entered had a few civilians, but no soldiers. He'd found the entryway he was seeking. A dozen paces led him past large rooms containing a myriad of computers and lab equipment, with several men and women busily engaged in their work. Nobody paid him any attention. Jamison picked up a sense of urgency, as if things might be coming to a head soon and there was a deadline that had to be met. He'd seen it often enough in various facilities, at home and abroad. Regardless of nationality, people were the same when dealing with stress in the workplace. They all took on the same tense appearance.

The first radiation sign told him he was getting close. The universal yellow and black triangle needed no explanation, but the door next to the sign had an additional warning: AUTHORIZED LEVEL-3 PERSONNEL ONLY.

Jamison hesitated. Gasparini had not told him if personnel accessing more secure levels needed special ID badges. Typically they were different colors. A glance through the door's window showed a woman coming his way. Jamison bent over a handy water cooler to drink, keeping one eye on the door. An attractive woman with lustrous dark hair flowing over the shoulders of her lab coat emerged, carrying the ubiquitous files. Her ID badge was trimmed in red.

Jamison stood up and turned to the woman, pretending he didn't see her, and bumped her as he went past. The woman's files spilled. "I beg your pardon, señora," Jamison said. "How clumsy of me. Please let me help you."

The harried woman was already bending over to pick up the scattered papers. "Think nothing of it, señor," she said. As he was counting on, she was too busy to notice that his was an unfamiliar face. Ordinarily Jamison would have been dismayed to have an attractive woman ignore him, but not this time. He knelt down to help her.

"I believe there's one more over there," he said, gesturing over her right shoulder. She turned her head, saw the stray paper and moved to retrieve it, giving Jamison a chance to expertly unclip her ID badge and slip it into his lab coat pocket. The woman grabbed the last paper, stuffed it into a file and flashed a quick smile at Jamison as she stood. "Thank you for your help," she said.

"Again, my apologies," the agent said, keeping his eyes averted and hunching over slightly, hoping it would hinder her attempt to identify him. "I must be going myself. Good day, señora." He walked past her to the door and quickly went inside. Stepping into the first doorway he saw, he quickly took the woman's ID badge, slipped her card out of it and replaced it with his own.

Time was of the essence now. The woman would eventually discover her ID badge was missing, and she would retrace her steps. If it happened quickly enough, she might recall the collision with the man in the hallway. She might report it to security. It all depended on how soon she acted and how diligent she was. No doubt the scientists here had a heightened sense of security.

Jamison passed a few more labs, this time recognizing some of the apparatus inside. He parted the lab coat enough to expose his button camera and shot a few frames, being as unobtrusive as possible. This was definitely a nuclear weapons facility. Radiation signs were everywhere, although he'd yet to see anyone wearing protective clothing. He looked at the stolen ID badge, and saw a white circle in one corner he'd missed on first glance. A radiation detector. If he were exposed, it would turn color.

He'd seen enough to confirm his own suspicions, but SIS would want a bit more. It was a gamble, but he knew from Gasparini that he must be close to the central warhead assembly area. It would likely be two rooms, a smaller one where the warhead's components would be assembled, and a larger room where the warheads would be mated with bomb or missile casings and readied for transport. This section was probably capable of being sealed off in the event of radiation leaks. A minute later, he saw a man garbed in a light blue "clean suit" emerging from a doorway. The man stopped to adjust his own ID badge, then proceeded down the hallway and took a right. Jamison knew he was close now. He went into the room the man had emerged from, found it to be a small changing room with racks of the sterile, hooded suits, and quickly found one his size and started climbing into it.

He was starting to perspire, not a good sign. He doffed the lab coat and hung it in an empty locker, retrieved his ID badge, then zipped himself inside the radiation suit and clipped the badge to an exterior pocket. Carrying his clipboard, he made his way back into the hallway and followed the path of the man he'd seen. The suit, he discovered, was designed to include its own oxygen supply; the oxygen tanks were doubtless inside the assembly room. He put on his hood but kept it slightly unfastened to allow for air.

Jamison turned the corner and saw another set of double doors in front of him, with an armed guard, a sergeant. His first instinct was to hesitate, but that might make the guard suspicious. He continued at a brisk pace, intending to go right on through. The guard held up a hand. "A moment, please, señor."

The agent stared at the guard through the clear plastic visor of the hood. "I'm in a hurry, *sargento*." It did no good; the guard carefully examined Jamison's ID badge, then pointed to his hood.

"Please remove your hood, señor."

With a deep breath, Jamison pulled the hood back. The guard peered at his face, then at the ID badge again. "You are new here, Doctor Concepción?"

"That's right," Jamison said, holding up his clipboard as if it held very important papers. "I'm new here, just in from Buenos Aires, and my flight was delayed, and I can't waste any more time." He tried a small grin. "You know how they are here."

The guard smiled knowingly. "Si, señor. You may proceed."

"Gracias, sargento." Jamison nodded, put his hood back on and pushed through the doors.

CHAPTER TWENTY-SIX

Pilcaniyeu, Argentina

March 22nd, 1982

Willy was tired, but there was one more important task to perform before they could finally leave this oddly depressing place and go back to their hotel in Bariloche. Heinz, as usual, appeared to be as fresh as he had been that morning. Willy knew that his friend stayed in shape with a daily regimen of calisthenics, plus he rode horses and swam whenever possible; for Willy, on the other hand, it was all he could do to spend even a half-hour every other day or so in the estancia's small gymnasium. The paperwork he had to deal with seemed to be growing by the hour.

The numbers in the report he was staring at started to dance around. Willy closed the file and handed it back to the nervous adjutant. "These look fine," he said, as if he really cared how many pounds of potatoes and corn the mess hall was consuming. The Bund had long ago ensured that Pilcaniyeu would get whatever resources it wanted, including the best food for the staff and guards. Duty here was lonely work, but it was work, and it paid well, and there was something to be said for that in these uncertain times. Willy knew that the Germans stationed here were grateful, at least, especially those few who knew the true meaning of the work being done. While they might not know the ultimate fate of the devices they were making here, they could read the newspapers, and they could think, and their conclusions gave them a sense of pride.

He'd spent the last hour with the base accountants, while Heinz toured the security perimeter with Oberst Reinke and his second in command, Major Gasparini. Willy had made sure to speak to Gasparini, inquiring about the health of his wife. The Italian-born officer replied rather stiffly that she was doing as well as could be expected. If the major knew that the men responsible for rescuing his precious wife from the Turk were standing before him, he didn't indicate it. Well, what could you expect from Italians, after all?

Willy glanced at his watch. Nearly 1600 hours. He was due to meet Heinz at the entrance to the assembly room in fifteen minutes for the conclusion of the inspection. No harm in getting there early. "Let's go, Herr Leutnant," he said to the young security officer who'd been assigned as his aide for the day. Willy put on his high-peaked officer's cap. He and Heinz had worn their Army uniforms today; they were still reserve officers, after all, subject to recall to active duty in the event of a national emergency, but today they'd chosen to wear their uniforms for effect.

He knew the way, having been here several times before, and a few minutes later he came into view of the guarded double-doors leading to the largest room of the main building. It was here that the warheads, produced in nearby laboratories, would be mated with their bomb casings. Although the scientists repeatedly assured everyone there was no chance of an accidental detonation, this room was avoided by anyone who didn't have a good reason to be here, as if being on the outer edge of the building would give them any protection if something went seriously wrong. He decided to go ahead and wait for Heinz and Reinke inside.

The large room, almost warehouse-sized, never ceased to impress Willy. In some ways, this was the most important room in all of South America. The men and women who worked in it seemed to realize that, and kept it meticulously clean and orderly. It was very nearly square, about fifty meters on each side, with a large garage door at the far end where trucks could be brought in. A complicated series of racks and tables took up most of the nearby space. The floor was about five meters below ground level, and Willy and the aide now stood on a metal landing, with elevated walkways leading in both directions along this wall and then down the sides. A stairway led to the floor. No guards were present here, but Willy knew that when the weapons were ready to be loaded onto trucks, the walkway would hold a dozen or more armed men, with orders to shoot anyone who appeared intent on damaging the precious devices.

Many of the workers on the floor were wearing the self-contained clean suits, and those closest to the main array of tables had their hoods on and sealed. Willy could see they were working on a small silver canister, about a quarter-meter long. Nearby, sitting in a yet-to-be-assembled crate, was a longer white cylinder, about three meters in length. At one end were four red fins. The other end was open. A nose cone, its tip also painted red, was on one of the tables.

"You're early," Heinz said from behind him. Willy turned and saw the SD officer, along with Reinke and Gasparini.

"I was anxious to have a look at it," Willy said. He turned back to the assembly area. "I'm surprised at its size. I imagined something larger."

Reinke stepped forward. "It is truly an amazing device, Herr Oberst," he said, pride in his voice. He was, after all, the commanding officer of the facility. Reinke was also the only man here who knew the details of CAPRICORN. In his early forties, Reinke had been born in Hannover just before the war. His father, a Panzer commander, died at Normandy, and a few years later his uncle brought Reinke and his family over the ocean to the new land of opportunity. His uncle's Bund connections helped Reinke get this posting, but he'd proven worthy of the challenge. "It is based on the American B-61 gravity bomb. Our version is as sophisticated as any weapon in the American or Soviet arsenals."

Willy doubted that, but said, "Not as powerful, though."

"The yield of this device can be altered depending on the parameters of the mission," Reinke said. "Anywhere from a third of a kiloton up to perhaps three hundred kilotons, the scientists tell me. While not as powerful as the strategic warheads in the American and Soviet inventories, it is a very respectable tactical weapon." Willy shook his head slightly, amazed that the man could discuss this infernal thing's specs as if he were talking about a simple artillery shell. Three hundred kilotons. If he remembered his history, the Americans needed only a twenty-kiloton weapon to destroy Hiroshima.

"The Super Etendard will be able to deliver the weapon quite efficiently," Heinz said. "The pilots have rehearsed a similar attack many times with the same aircraft and dummy weapons. If the pilot executes the mission properly, we will succeed."

"I have every confidence our pilots will prove worthy of the mission," Willy said. He wished he felt as confident as he sounded. Something had been eating at him ever since they'd left Valhalla that morning aboard a Bund private jet. Heinz had told him that he wanted to discuss something of importance, but after the inspection. Willy had a feeling he knew what the subject would be.

"What are they doing now?" Willy asked.

Reinke answered. "They are in the midst of the warhead assembly, Herr Oberst." That produced the usual reaction, a sharp intake of breath, from his guests. "There is nothing to fear, I assure you. The weapon is not yet armed."

Willy swallowed and said, "I'm sure they are taking every precaution."

"I really must compliment our scientists," Reinke said. "The weapon has almost six thousand parts. Once assembled, it will weigh about five hundred kilos."

"A remarkable achievement, to be sure," Willy said, fighting back against an almost unbearable urge to flee the room.

One of the blue-suited figures on the floor below was next to a rack of equipment, checking items off on a clipboard. The movement on the landing near the main entrance caused the figure to shift its gaze slightly from the rack to the landing. The pen kept moving on the clipboard, a bit slower, but nobody noticed. After a half-minute, the figure turned back to the rack, and a minute later moved casually to a side door and left the floor.

Sweating inside the clean suit, Brian Jamison quickly made his way up the stairs and through the short maze of halls and doors that had led to the lower-level side entrance to the final assembly area. He'd recognized four of the men on the landing. The fifth man, the youngest, was unimportant, but two of the others were Gasparini and his commanding officer, Reinke, whom Jamison recognized from a photograph produced during his briefing in Santiago. The other two faces hadn't registered immediately, but when they did, he knew he had to leave, right now. He'd seen enough to confirm MI6's suspicions about the place anyway. Now there was new information to be brought out. Vital information.

Back at Century House, Jamison had been told of the existence of the Siegfried Bund, and given a rough outline of what SIS had learned was called CAPRICORN. He was shown photos of several men said to be high-ranking Bund members, including one man whose mere existence surprised Jamison and required further explanation. Two of the other photos were of middle-level but important Bund officers. Those were the men he'd seen in the assembly room. They certainly weren't here on holiday. They were here to make sure everything was going according to plan. CAPRICORN was a fact, and from what Jamison had seen in the building, it was near completion. And if Germans were involved, especially the man who should've been long dead, that was very bad news indeed. Century House didn't like bad news, but it had to hear this.

***

The Bund private jet, a new Messerschmitt Blitz model, lifted off from Bariloche three hours later. Heinz had insisted on treating Willy to dinner at the city's best restaurant. He was pleased with the security at the facility, and impressed with Reinke. "We'll have to keep him in mind," he said while carving his steak.

"For what?" Willy asked. His friend just smiled and changed the subject.

They were the only two passengers on the jet. The lone female attendant served them each a cognac, and then retreated to the small steward's cabin, leaving the men alone. Willy was tired and decided he didn't want to wait any longer. "You said on the way down we needed to discuss something, Heinz. What is it?"

Heinz reclined back in his comfortable seat, his jacket off and draped over a nearby chair, his tie loosened. He swirled his cognac in his glass. "Do you remember that conversation we had back at your estancia, Willy? Christmas time, it was."

Willy thought for a moment. It came back to him clearly. "Yes. What of it?"

"Have you thought any more about it?"

Of course he had. "Some," he said. "Please come to the point, Heinz. It's been a long day."

Heinz sat up and leaned forward, looking his old friend directly in the eyes. "Very well. CAPRICORN is within a few weeks of execution. Everything appears to be ready. The pilots will be ready. The bomb will work. The English fleet will vanish; in one blinding moment, thousands of brave men will die, without ever knowing what happened. The war for the Malvinas will be over practically before it starts."

"If all goes according to plan, yes," Willy said, taking a sip of his drink. He had an uneasy suspicion he knew what was coming.

"Willy, a nuclear weapon has not been exploded in anger in nearly forty years. I'm sure you have thought about what the reaction will be in London. In Washington, Moscow, Brasilia. Everywhere."

"Am I worried about an English counterattack, Heinz? No. Will the Americans move against us? They'll scream at us, their doddering old president will go on television to condemn us, but they will not move against us. The Brazilians will run to the U.N. for protection." He let his irritation seep into his voice. "This has all been thought through." Was Heinz getting cold feet? He wouldn't have thought it possible.

"Yes, it has been thought through. More than you think," Heinz said. He took another drink. "Willy, have you heard about an operation called VALKYRIE?"

"No," Willy said. "What is it?"

"Something I became aware of only a few weeks ago myself," he said. "I would have told you sooner, but I wanted to confirm some details. Then I had to discuss it with...certain individuals." He looked at Willy. "Forgive me for not bringing it up sooner, but you'll understand when I explain."

"Please do."

Heinz finished off the rest of his glass and re-filled it from a nearby bottle. "Our dear fathers have been working on something for some time now. Here and back in Germany."

"West Germany?"

"Both East and West," Heinz said. "They have put together a plan they call VALKYRIE. Its goal is the reunification of our beloved Fatherland. They will achieve this through a *putsch*."

Willy had to blink at that. "What? Reunification, through an uprising? How could such a thing be done?" Among the older Germans in Argentina, reuniting their old country was a common topic. The general belief was that it would never happen unless one side triumphed over the other on the field of battle. A very few thought that reunification would eventually be possible through political means. Like most of his generation, Willy hadn't paid much attention. Whether or not Germany ever reunited would mean little to faraway Argentina. Or so he always thought.

"Consider the political turmoil that will result among the western powers when CAPRICORN is executed," Heinz said. "The English will be almost out of their minds, with their precious fleet gone. For hundreds of years, their fleet has been the only thing protecting their islands from invasion. The psychological impact alone will be devastating. Do not forget that the Royal Navy is an important part of the NATO defense plans. The English and the Americans will immediately begin to worry that the Soviets will take advantage of the situation by moving against West Germany."

"Heinz, a land war in central Europe will involve infantry, armor and aircraft, not ships."

"Naval forces wouldn't be involved immediately, that is true," Heinz countered. "But NATO's plan to defend West Germany from Soviet invasion relies on quick reinforcement from North America. That reinforcement will have to come by sea. Without those troops and equipment, the American forces on the continent will not last two weeks against a coordinated assault by the Warsaw Pact. The NATO war plan calls for naval reinforcement to begin within days after the outbreak of hostilities."

"All right, but how does this involve us?"

"The U.S. Navy, while powerful, is not invincible. In the North Atlantic, they must rely on the English to help safeguard the sea lanes from Soviet submarines. There is also the prospect of Soviet air attacks against Allied convoys, operating from bases they might seize in Norway or Iceland. Removing the Royal Navy from the equation will leave those countries virtually defenseless. Using them as platforms for air strikes, plus their submarine attacks, will allow the Soviets to interdict the Allied convoys and destroy them. That is critical to the Soviet plan for winning a war in Europe. This we know from our sources in Moscow and other Warsaw Pact nations."

"Again, I ask—"

"Don't you see?" Heinz set his glass down on the end table rather forcefully. "When the realization of CAPRICORN sinks in, there will be panic in London and Washington. Likewise, there will be panic in Moscow. The Soviets are not prepared to exploit such an advantage, but the western powers don't know that. The Soviets may think the Americans will launch a pre-emptive strike. Both sides will come to a war footing very quickly. But until they do, there will be confusion. This will create a brief window of opportunity."

Willy's heart seemed to slow down as the realization sunk in. "An opportunity..."

"Yes," Heinz said. "Even as we speak, there are men in positions of importance in both West and East Germany. Men who have control of army and police units. In the critical hours after CAPRICORN, they will move. The Red Army has a large supply of tactical nuclear warheads in East Germany. The Americans control the warheads in the West. The men on both sides of the border involved in VALKYRIE will seize these warheads, as well as the communications centers in both countries. The Soviet and NATO forces in the field will be cut off from their headquarters. Their most powerful weapons will be in the hands of the putschists."

"Heinz, this cannot possibly work. Don't you think the Americans have prepared for such an eventuality? Certainly the Soviets have. They've never trusted the East Germans."

Heinz stood up and began pacing the cabin. "The plotters believe they only need a few hours. Yes, the enemy units in the field have alternate communications. They will know something is afoot, but they won't know what. The Soviets in particular will do nothing without hearing from Moscow. Their command-and-control structure does not allow for initiative in the field. The Americans are more flexible, but they will still want to hear from NATO headquarters in Brussels. The public airwaves will be full of news about the destruction of the English fleet. By the time the Soviet and NATO field commanders re-establish links with their leadership outside the country, VALKYRIE will have succeeded. Once the rebels have the weapons under control, they will arrest the political leadership in East Berlin and Bonn. They will throw open the gates in Berlin and rebel forces from both sides will join up. So will units along the border between the two countries." He sat down again, looking intently at Willy. "Imagine the power of those scenes on television, Willy. The Wall finally coming down. After more than thirty years of suspicion and fear, the German citizenry will see their soldiers, young men from East and West, embracing and flying one flag. The emotional impact of that scene is impossible to underestimate. What do you suppose the people will do when the rebels go on the air and announce that they have united Germany under one government? Do you think they will demand a return to the status quo?"

Willy could easily see it. He'd spent enough time in the Federal Republic to know the deep longing the people had for a reunited country. Once the genie had been let out of the bottle, it could not be put back in. "The warheads will be their trump card," he said. "The Soviets and NATO will have to back down."

"Of course they will," Heinz said. "Is Reagan willing to risk nuclear war with the Soviets over Germany?"

"Perhaps," Willy said. "He has called them 'the Evil Empire'."

Heinz snorted. "Rhetorical claptrap! He is showing the Soviets he can't be intimidated by them, as his predecessor was. The Russians understand power, Willy. You can only negotiate with them from a position of strength. With nuclear weapons, the new Germany will be able to do that. Within a month, all foreign troops will be off German soil for the first time in nearly forty years."

"They're using us," Willy said slowly as the truth bloomed within his mind. "CAPRICORN, the Malvinas, it's all just a part of the overall plan."

"Of course!" Heinz stood again. "Willy, that's always been the plan: to reunite Germany, under their leadership. Who do you think will be running the new Germany? What do you think the Reichsleiter will do once Berlin is secure and the Russians are gone?"

Willy looked up at him in alarm. "He means to return? To re-establish the Party? Heinz, that's madness! The Russians will go insane!"

"Exactly," Heinz said, kneeling in front of Willy. "At first, the new German government will be officially neutral between East and West. There will be not a whisper of Nazis returning. That will change once the foreign troops are gone. Weapons or not, the Russians will never allow the Nazi Party to rise again. They lost millions to Germany in the last war, Willy. They will fight to the death to prevent that from happening again. There will be another war in Europe, and when the dust has settled there, what do you think the Americans will do about us? They will see us as just an extension of the Nazis. Do you think Reagan will allow a nuclear-armed Nazi nation in his own hemisphere?"

Willy looked out the nearby window at the night. Thousands of feet below him, dark and sleeping, lay Argentina. His country, the land where he had been born, the land he was risking everything to build into a major power in the hemisphere. For so long, he'd believed the only way to do that was with CAPRICORN. They were so close. It would work. But it would be a trigger for something far more horrible. He looked at Heinz. "What can we do?"

Heinz sat down again and leaned forward intently. "There are several others within the Bund who have come to the same conclusion," he said carefully. "Men of our generation. Argentines first, Germans second. We have decided there is a need for action."

"I'm listening."

"It is too late to stop CAPRICORN, but not too late to prevent it from touching off a catastrophe in Europe. The invasion of the Malvinas will go forward. The English fleet will sail to recapture them. We will launch the CAPRICORN attack, but we will make sure the pilot is one of our people. He will detonate the weapon well away from the English. At the same time, we will move on the government here. Sarmiento is with us. We will announce to the world that we have more weapons but do not wish to use them. Instead we wish to negotiate with the English over the Malvinas. At the same time, we will alert the Americans, and the Soviets, about VALKYRIE."

Willy stood now as well, as agitated as Heinz. "What about the leadership of the Bund? What about the Reichsleiter? What about our own fathers?"

Heinz gripped Willy by the shoulders. "Sarmiento will have the Kabinett arrested. The Reichsleiter as well. Our fathers...well, we will do all we can for them. They may spend time in prison. The Reichsleiter, though, will be handed over to Israel. Sarmiento will be a hero. Argentina will gain enormous prestige. Think of it: we will have prevented World War Three, and given the Jews one of the men who planned the Holocaust. The English will probably sign over the Malvinas with gratitude."

"This is a dangerous game you are playing, Heinz. What if the Reichsleiter finds out? Or your father?"

Heinz held his head down, heavy with emotion. "It pains me greatly to work against my father, Willy. But I have to think of Argentina first. We have to think of our country." He looked back at Willy. There was a fire in his blue eyes. "Germany will reunite eventually, Willy, with a democratic government. The Soviets will fall. Their economy can't possibly compete with the Americans. Reagan intends to build up his defenses and the Soviets cannot match America. It's inevitable. But that doesn't mean we cannot make our own country strong and free, instead of a vassal of a new Nazi Germany. Or, worse yet, a pariah nation, blamed for touching off a nuclear war that kills millions." He stood up as much as the cabin allowed. "But we need you, Willy. Are you with us?"

Willy's heart was hammering. Everything he'd worked for, everything the Bund had worked for, all these years, supposedly for a strong Argentina...all a sham? A front? He thought of his father. Dieter had always been a good father to him, and Willy truly loved him. But, if Heinz was right, what Dieter and the rest of the Kameraden were doing was wrong. It was a betrayal of everything they'd been told the Bund stood for.

He looked straight at Heinz and made the toughest decision of his life. "I'm with you, my friend."

CHAPTER TWENTY-SEVEN

Munich, West Germany
Thursday, March 25th, 1982

"Any plans for the evening, Heinrich?" Colonel Johann Becker of the ASBw asked his adjutant.

"Not really, Herr Oberst," Captain Heinrich Altmann said. "Dinner and then home for a good night's rest."

"Are you sure you're not married, Heinrich?" Becker asked with a chuckle as he stuffed the last papers from his desk into his briefcase. He did not notice one file that had been partially hidden under the day's edition of *Suddeutsche Zeitung*. It had, after all, been a long day. "I believe my Greta has *sauerbraten* on the menu this evening. Then I will have to help the boys with their homework. Then to bed, and tomorrow we do it all over again, eh?"

"As you often say, Herr Oberst, the excitement never stops," Altmann said with a wry grin. In truth, he was often more than a little bored with his job. Serving in the Army of the Federal Republic had been his idea, but he'd dreamed of assignment to a front-line combat unit, perhaps ultimately as a Panzer commander as his grandfather had been in the last war. But here he was, twenty-seven years old and a staff officer in Military Intelligence. Interesting work, sometimes, but not thrilling. For thrills, lately, he'd come to seek out other things.

Becker reached for his overcoat on the nearby coat tree. "Well, Heinrich, if it's excitement you crave, bear with me. Soon we may have more than we bargained for."

That perked up Altmann's ears. "Oh, Herr Oberst? Something is brewing?"

The question brought only an enigmatic smile from his superior. "Perhaps," he said. "Perhaps not." His coat and cap on, Becker picked up his briefcase. "See you tomorrow, Heinrich."

"Good night, Herr Oberst."

Paperwork occupied another half-hour of Altmann's time. When the last paper had been put in his *Ausgaben* tray, it was nearly 1830 hours. As was his habit, Altmann got up to take a look around Becker's inner office, just to make sure nothing was out of place. Like most German officers, Becker was efficient and neat, but occasionally he left something lying about that Altmann would put in its proper place. Tonight he could see nothing amiss except the newspaper. Becker normally read his paper right away in the morning, over his first cup of coffee, and then gave it to Altmann. Today something must have caught his superior's eye; he'd probably laid it aside in the morning and come back to it later in the day.

Altmann picked up the paper and casually flipped through it. One item drew his attention. It had a small blue check mark next to it, Becker's way of marking something of interest in a document. This story was a piece about a planned exercise by Bundeswehr troops in the vicinity of Baumholder, a city in the Rhine Valley west of Frankfurt. The U.S. Army's 2nd Brigade, 1st Armored Division, was stationed at a large base outside of the city. The article noted that the base had recently been targeted by Green Party protestors who demanded that the stockpile of tactical nuclear warheads supposedly housed on the base be removed from the country. A Green leader was quoted, saying that the Bundeswehr maneuvers were the government's way of disrupting the peaceful anti-nuclear protestors who only wanted a nuclear-free Germany.

Two other bits of information registered with Altmann. One was the planned date of the exercise: it was set to begin about three weeks from now. Another was a listing of participating German units. *Panzergrenadierbrigade* 32 was one of them, and Altmann recognized it because he knew it was commanded by a close friend of Oberst Becker's, another oberst, what was his name? Oh, yes, Richard Mainz. The oberst had spoken of him before. Well, perhaps that explained Becker's marking the story.

Altmann put the paper back on the desk and noticed the file that had been hidden underneath. It was bordered in blue, but it wasn't an official ASBw file, that was certain. The markings on it were different. Not terribly so, but to a trained intelligence officer, they were apparent. Altmann quickly looked back at the door. Nobody there. He picked up the file.

Fifteen minutes later, Altmann put the file back on Becker's desk and replaced the newspaper on top of it. His hands were shaking.

Altmann's despair grew over his dinner, taken at a small restaurant in the Schwabing district. Why would his trusted superior completely exclude him from such an operation? The file on Becker's desk had detailed the orders to Mainz and his unit of motorized infantry. During the upcoming maneuvers near Baumholder, Mainz was to break off from the main Heer battalion and assault the American base, securing the warhead storage facility and the base's command-and-control structure. It was a daring and risky plan, but feasible. The Americans would never suspect brother NATO troops of such a thing. Becker's notes suggested that similar strikes were to be made against the two other American nuclear strongholds in the Federal Republic and similar Soviet bases in the East. The whole operation was code-named VALKYRIE.

Altmann didn't need to think hard about the overall aim: the overthrow of the government of the Federal Republic. And if such a thing were also happening in the East, then reunification would be the only possible logical goal. Reunification! *Ein Volk, ein Heer, ein Vaterland!* One people, one Army, one nation! The thought was staggering, but intoxicating.

But Altmann had been left out of the picture...

After his third beer, Altmann paid his bill and left the beer hall, somewhat unsteadily. Anger was starting to mix in with his anguish. How could Becker do this to him? After five years of faithful service. He'd made Altmann privy to many other sensitive ASBw and NATO operations. He said more than once that Altmann held great promise as an intelligence officer. And now this. The most important operation of all, and he was cut out of the picture.

Perhaps the oberst meant to bring him in later? There were still some three weeks to go, after all. Altmann shook his head and muttered as he passed a laughing, drunken American soldier with his arm around a pretty young German girl. No, he would've been in on the planning right from the beginning. Altmann was smart, he was inventive, Becker had told him that before. He could have contributed much to the planning of this VALKYRIE business.

Altmann began to feel the hunger deep inside him, as he did whenever he felt lonely or depressed. It was a hunger he'd first fed as a teenage boy, and despite its risks, its public veneer of disapproval, he'd felt moved to satisfy it several times since then. Now was one of those times.

He found the small storefront on the same side street it had been the last time. Of course it was. He entered, had a word with the woman behind the counter, paid his marks and was shown through a curtain and down a hall to a door. He knocked and entered. Lying seductively on a divan, the young man waited. "Hello, Heinrich," he said. "It's been too long."

***

Becker was in his private study, after a pleasant dinner with his wife and children, when he opened his briefcase and discovered the VALKYRIE file was missing. The cold needles of panic momentarily gripped him, but he took a deep breath and shrugged them off. He rapidly considered the possibilities. He knew he'd been studying the file that afternoon at his desk, after seeing the newspaper article he had planted. Stirring up the Greens was part of the plan; if the anarchists caused problems near Baumholder during the maneuvers, it would be only reasonable for the Heer commander in the field to detach a unit to assist the Americans with security. Richard's unit would be the one for the job.

After checking his car and failing to turn up the file, Becker went back to his study and placed a call to the head of ASBw internal security for the Munich station, ordering him to seal off Becker's office immediately. No one was to be allowed inside except for the oberst himself, who would be there shortly. After hanging up, Becker changed back into his uniform and placed another call. Altmann's private phone rang several times before Becker broke the connection and called the security office again. "Hauptmann Altmann is not answering his phone," he said. "Locate him and bring him to the office. You know where he's likely to be found." He hung up again, had a brief word with his wife, and left the house.

***

Matthias could hardly wait for the *Schwuler* to leave. This was only his second time with the young ASBw officer, and he'd struck gold long before he expected to. As during the first visit, Altmann requested certain services, which Matthias supplied with feigned enthusiasm. This time, though, he offered his guest a "popper", a small bottle of butyl nitrate that produced a quick high when inhaled. One of its effects was the relaxation of the sphincter, which made it popular among homosexuals. This particular dose,

315

provided to Matthias by his real employer, contained an additional chemical that acted almost like sodium pentothal.

Altmann gladly took the popper and squealed with delight as Matthias completed his performance. He'd been told that if the drug took hold, he would notice it within a few minutes. Sure enough, Altmann began to get drowsy, and was barely able to pull his pants back up before falling into a nearby chair, his eyes half-closed, his breathing slow. "Can you hear me?" Matthias asked.

"Yes," Altmann answered slowly.

"I am going to ask you some questions, Herr Hauptmann. You will answer them truthfully."

"Truthfully..."

"What is your name and rank?"

Altmann's mouth moved, but it was as if his tongue had thickened. Momentarily fearful, Matthias repeated the question, and the young officer finally answered. "Hauptmann Heinrich Altmann."

"What is your current posting?"

"I am adjutant to Oberst Becker, Amt für Sicherheit der Bundeswehr."

Matthias looked at the door. It was still closed. He knew he only had a few minutes. "Tell me about Oberst Becker. What is he working on?"

***

At the moment, Oberst Becker was working on keeping his fear and anger in check. He was angry at himself, for

316

leaving the vital VALKYRIE file on his desk. What a stupid mistake! The file was right where he'd left it, underneath the newspaper, but he couldn't be sure whether Altmann or anyone else had disturbed it. Normally the file never left his briefcase except for those times he was actually working on it. He thought it had been about 1600 hours when he'd been examining it, and then some unrelated matters suddenly came up, requiring his immediate attention, and the file was left on the desk.

Becker knew that Altmann had stayed late, as was his habit, and he was sure the fussy young adjutant had also come into his office, which was also his habit. So it was likely Altmann saw the newspaper, and then the file underneath it, and he would have read it. Altmann had a high security clearance for normal ASBw work, after all. He would've assumed it was something rather routine.

The oberst picked up his phone and called the security desk. "Have you found Altmann yet?"

"No, Herr Oberst. My last report from the field units said they had checked his apartment and the public library. No one has seen him there this evening. He did, however, dine at his customary beer hall in Schwabing, and left around 2000 hours."

Becker checked his watch. An hour ago. "You know where to look next," he said.

"My men are scouring the neighborhood as we speak, Herr Oberst."

"Very well. Keep me informed."

Becker made another effort to compose himself. He would find Altmann, and then he would find out if he'd read the file, and then if he'd told anybody. At that point, the oberst knew he might have to make a very difficult decision.

***

Matthias left the brothel shortly after Altmann had recovered his senses, completed dressing and left with hardly a word. Matthias had carefully turned back the hands on the intelligence officer's watch a half hour. Eventually Altmann would discover the time discrepancy, but by then it would be too late to do anything about it. As to their conversation, Altmann would remember nothing about it, or so the young man had been told.

The prostitute went to a public phone and placed a call. After a short conversation, which included a specific code word that Matthias had been warned to use only if he had extremely sensitive information, he hung up the phone and hailed a cab. Thirty minutes later, he was walking through a darkened public park. When he got close to the statue of Frederick the Great, he saw the man in the long coat waiting for him.

"Johann, you old fart, is that you?" Matthias asked.

"Johann went to Berlin last week," the man replied. The identification code established, Matthias went up to the man. He spoke a few more whispered words, and the two of them went off through the park. Matthias hardly dared hope that this might be the time his information would actually earn his freedom, and that of his elderly mother back in Dresden. They'd told him they would do that, eventually; the Stasi officer who talked to him after his arrest six months ago made it clear that cooperation would be beneficial for him and his mother. Resistance, he said, would not be.

***

Johann's friend knew he had something hot when the fag finished his story. The man had nothing but contempt for the little queer, but he had to run him anyway. The man was an officer of MfS, the *Ministerium für Staatssicherheit,* the Ministry of State Security for the German Democratic Republic. Commonly known as Stasi, it was primarily responsible for internal security within East Germany, but also maintained a foreign intelligence directorate for operations in the Federal Republic and other NATO nations. Generally they passed their information on to the KGB, and the officer knew this particular report would quickly find its way to Moscow. First, though, he had to get it to his own people in East Berlin. What they would do with it was not his concern. He hoped, though, that the report's sensitivity, and his efficiency in handling it, would pay off for him. Perhaps a promotion, but not a transfer back home. Like virtually all Stasi agents posted outside the worker's paradise of the East, he had no desire to actually go back and live there. The West was decadent and its society was doomed, but in the meantime, it was a pretty nice place to live.

Unlike most government bureaucracies, intelligence agencies tended to move rather quickly when the information they received was deemed important. Stasi was no different. Among its ranks were men, and a few women, who were dedicated communists and loyal to the state. Most of them, though, were in the game for reasons other than service to the men in East Berlin who allegedly ran the country. Many were in it for the money and the perks, which for high-ranking Stasi officers were considerable, by comparison to the average worker in their gray, humorless nation. A fair number were in it for the excitement, and more than a few were there to satisfy certain base instincts that came into play whenever they uncovered individuals who were planning treason against the state.

Whatever their motivations, every one of the 90,000 people who staffed the agency, and their quarter-million informants who were in every city and hamlet in the East and most of those in the West, knew who was really running the show. That was why Matthias' report, forwarded by the man in the park, quickly worked its way up the ladder in Stasi's East Berlin headquarters once the coded message was received from Munich.

At seven o'clock the next morning, as a frightened and exhausted Heinrich Altmann was being interrogated yet again by ASBw security officers in Munich, the general who was the head of MfS was reading the file that had been handed to him by a high-ranking officer of the Bavarian desk just minutes before, upon his arrival at his East Berlin office for another long day. The general read the file carefully twice through, asked some questions of the nervous colonel, was satisfied of the document's authenticity, and dismissed his subordinate. The colonel breathed a silent sigh of relief and returned to his own office, thinking of a telephone call he would have to make later that day, which would undoubtedly lead to a very risky meeting sometime that night. In his own office, the MfS general read through the file one more time and reached for a certain telephone on his desk.

One hour later, at 0930 hours Moscow time, the general in charge of the KGB's First Chief Directorate climbed a flight of stairs at Number 2 Dzerzhinsky Square, carrying a red-bordered file whose contents had upset him greatly. He went directly to the office of the chairman and was waved inside by the secretary. Yuri Vladimirovich Andropov, who was two months away from his fifteenth anniversary as head of the most powerful intelligence and security agency the world had ever known, was sitting behind his desk. He'd been forewarned of the general's visit and was expecting to read something interesting. This file, however, was much more than interesting. Andropov read it twice, asked three questions of his subordinate, ordered him to verify the information with other sources in West Germany as quickly as possible, and dismissed him. The chairman then told his secretary to cancel his appointments for the rest of the day and hold his calls. He had to think this one through.

CHAPTER TWENTY-EIGHT

Fort Monckton, England

Saturday, March 27th, 1982

Jo Ann Geary pulled the headphones off and slumped back in her chair. The reels of tape kept turning on the machine in front of her, and after a moment she mustered the energy to reach forward and turn it off. The German voices in the headphones ceased, giving her a respite she knew would be short-lived.

She had to get some rest, that was all there was to it. She'd been in England only four days and her body was just now coming to grips with the jet lag. It hadn't helped that she'd insisted on jumping right into orientation and training upon her arrival in London. Sir David gently suggested she rest for a day, but Jo would have none of it. Now she wished she'd taken his advice. Fatigue pulled at her eyes like cat's paws.

Not too many people on the post seemed to be resting, though. Word had come through the previous day that

Argentine marines had landed on South Georgia, part of the Dependencies, east of the Falklands. The Royal Marine garrison was outnumbered five to one, and it was said the Argies had warships ready to support their marines. The British position on the island was untenable, and there was no way to send in reinforcements. When the fighting started, it wouldn't last long. The Falklands garrison had been put on war alert. The invasion was only days away, it was said, perhaps hours.

No formal training sessions were scheduled today or tomorrow anyway, and she suspected that was Sir David's doing. Jo had decided to come to the language lab on her own. She was picking up the German pretty quickly and had no doubt that she would be fairly conversant in the language by the time she arrived in Buenos Aires. The Russian and the Armenian, however, would be another matter. Like Russian, Armenian did not use the Roman alphabet, but it didn't use the Russian Cyrillic, either. Not only that, she had to learn a specific dialect, Eastern Armenian, since the woman she would impersonate had grown up in the capital, Yerevan. An Armenian from closer to the Turkish border would use the western dialect. She had no doubt that, given time, she could learn both Armenian and Russian, but time was one thing in short supply. Her instructors said it would be enough that she learned some common phrases in both and hope for the best. Most of the people she would be dealing with in Argentina would, after all, be speaking Spanish or German.

She glanced at her watch: nearly three p.m. She decided to knock off for the day and head to the gymnasium. A workout always served to energize her, and on her previous visits she'd noticed some of the personnel here at the MI6 training center were practicing martial arts moves. Perhaps she could find someone to spar with.

She'd asked permission to contact Ian, whom she thought was at his base in Poole, but had yet to get an answer. Security was obviously of the utmost concern here, but if anyone should have checked out as a good security risk, it was a decorated lieutenant colonel of SBS. But when she arrived back at her quarters, the message light on her phone was dark.

She had almost finished changing into her workout gear of tank top, shorts and sneakers when the phone rang. Her small room came with a double bed, a desk and nightstand, a radio and a television set. She'd found a classical music radio station and kept it on in the background when she studied, and she ignored the TV except for the nightly BBC newscast. The phone jangled again, and she picked it up. It was the duty officer in the commandant's office, asking her to stop by as soon as possible.

Brigadier Reginald Paulson was British Army through and through; he was in command of Fort Monckton because it was, officially, an Army installation, although it was used almost exclusively for the training of MI6 agents as well as those from MI-5, its domestic counterpart. Paulson had met Jo Ann upon her arrival at the post two days ago. Now he welcomed her back into his office with a friendly smile. He was in uniform, and that made her feel a bit self-conscious.

"My signals officer received an urgent message from Century House a short time ago," Paulson said. "I was ordered to present it to you personally." He handed her a sealed file marked MOST SECRET, EYES ONLY, with her name underneath. "When you finish it, I'm to escort you to the burn room, where you are to destroy the file and its contents." Paulson moved to the door. "Take your time, I'll be outside."

Jo broke the seal and opened the file. Inside was a single typewritten, single-spaced page. The FROM line featured her father's name. It bore today's date, and was marked RECEIVED only two hours before.

JoJo:

Some vital information has been received which impacts upon your assignment. This message stems from a discussion late last night with the DCI and the NCA...

Jo's eyebrows rose. NCA was the National Command Authority. She had assumed her father might meet with the president every now and then. She kept reading. Five minutes later she closed the file, but one word from it stuck in her mind: VALKYRIE.

She wished Joseph could've been more specific. *"We don't have a lot to go on at this point,"* he wrote. *"The source in Germany apparently only knew something vague about a suspected plan to move against the NATO nuclear armories. There were no dates, but we believe it's too great a coincidence that reactionary Germans in Argentina are planning CAPRICORN at the same time reactionaries in Germany are working on this VALKYRIE. Be very careful when you're down there."*

Her father hadn't referred to anything happening in East Germany, but Jo knew enough about geopolitics to conclude that if something like this was being planned in the West, something similar had to be going on in the East, too. That meant the Soviets would be in the game very soon.

She stood up and gathered herself. Well, she knew this would be a dangerous assignment to begin with. Now it looked even more so. She refused to reconsider her decision, though. Too much was at stake. Ian would be going to the South Atlantic again very soon. He would be doing his part to prevent war. She could damn well do hers.

***

RM Poole, England

"The Brigadier will see you now, gentlemen," the secretary said. Ian and Hodge nodded at the prim but stern woman wearing Royal Marine sergeant's stripes and knocked at the door of Brigadier Robert Chandler, then went inside. "Lieutenant Colonel Masters and Captain Hodge, reporting as ordered, sir," Ian announced as they snapped to attention. He still wasn't quite used to his new rank. Hodge had been promoted, too.

"At ease, gentlemen," Chandler said. The C.O. of 42 Commando was a no-nonsense marine who had seen plenty of action in his day. The word was he had personally dispatched five Japanese soldiers during an SBS operation in Malaya near the end of the war, and that was just the start of his illustrious career. Someone seeing him out of uniform might have assumed him to be an accountant. Short, slender, with thinning hair and a wisp of a mustache, Chandler would never have appeared on any Royal Marines recruiting posters, yet here he was, decorated many times over and in command of one of his country's most important military units.

Chandler motioned them to an easel near one wall. "We haven't much time, I'm afraid," the brigadier said. "I am about to give you a broad outline of an operation to which your unit has been assigned. Ian, how is your shoulder doing?"

Even hearing the word brought a painful twinge, but Ian didn't let on. "I can't say that it's in top shape, sir, but I've been cleared for duty."

Chandler looked at him sternly. "This mission will require maximum physical effort, Colonel. If you are unable to perform your duties fully due to an injury not yet completely healed, it could jeopardize the mission and your men."

"I'm ready to go, sir," Ian said confidently. He pushed the full truth away from the front of his mind. When the doctors told him he needed at least another month of light duty and physical therapy, he bullied and cajoled them into giving him full clearance. But Chandler had undoubtedly seen their report, and wouldn't have Ian in his office now if he didn't think the younger man was up to the task.

"Very well," Chandler said. "Gentlemen, I apologize for the short notice, but time is of the essence across the board. We anticipate hostilities to break out with Argentina at any moment. They have landed on South Georgia, as you know. Their fleet will likely set sail for the Falklands within days, perhaps hours. Because of your unit's experience on Carpenter's Island, you have been assigned this mission. Its code name is GALAHAD."

Ian noticed that a symbol was at the top of the page Chandler now revealed on the easel. He recognized it as the symbol Joseph of Arimathea, a red cross—originally drawn in blood, according to legend—on a white background: Galahad's shield, which he had used on his quest for the Holy Grail. Ian was glad he'd paid attention to his university lectures about King Arthur and the Knights of the Round Table.

Next to the symbol was a map. Ian immediately saw it as a slice of the Argentine Atlantic coast. "You are to consider this information Most Secret," Chandler said. "You will receive a more complete briefing on board ship during your journey. There will be ample time to flesh out your plan and brief your men. This is merely an outline."

Chandler picked up a pointer. "I'm sure you have heard talk of our fleet sailing to the Falklands should the islands fall to the Argentines. You may rest assured it is not idle talk. Plans for the expedition are being drawn up in London even as we speak. We have come into some information that indicates the Argentines intend to strike the fleet when it is within two hundred miles or so of the Falklands. We believe they will launch the strike from their Air Force base near here." The pointer touched the map on the coastline of Patagonia. "The base is on this gulf, Golfo San Jorge, about ten kilometers north of the town of Comodoro Rivadavia. The gulf is rather large, as you can see, but ship traffic is somewhat light, as there are no significant ports on its shoreline. Your landing will, hopefully, be unnoticed."

"What type of landing, sir?" Ian asked.

"You will sail day after tomorrow aboard HMS *Cambridge* and rendezvous at sea with the submarine *Reliant,* which will take you close to shore. I'm presuming you will then make an E&RE." It was what Ian expected. Exiting and Re-Entering was a hazardous procedure in which the entire SBS troop would disembark the submarine underwater. They'd practiced the maneuver a few times in Scottish harbors but had never done it in combat. Still, it made sense, this deep inside enemy waters.

"And while we're ashore, sir?" Hodge asked.

"Our information is that the enemy will launch a squadron of aircraft from this base to attack the fleet. One particular member of the squadron will be your target."

"Begging your pardon, sir," Hodge said, "but surely the fleet will be able to defend itself against air attack. Is there something special about this one aircraft?" It was a question Ian had thought of, but even as it had coalesced in his mind, he sensed the answer. Chandler confirmed his suspicion.

"This aircraft, Captain Hodge, will be carrying a nuclear weapon. Your mission will be to shoot that aircraft down as it launches from the base. We must do everything we can to ensure that it will never get near the fleet."

***

Fort Monckton, England

Hanna, dool, set, net...

Jo did a dozen knuckle push-ups before realizing she was counting in Korean, as she always did. She switched to German. "*Ein, zwei, drei, fier, funf...*" She did thirty-eight, giving her an even total of *funfzig*, and was panting hard when she brought her knees up underneath her and stretched upward. The man leaning against the weight-lifting apparatus a few feet away smiled at her.

"Hope I didn't startle you," he said.

"No, I knew you were there," she said. She reached for her nearby towel and wiped the perspiration from her forehead and chest. With a touch of embarrassment she saw that her nipples were thrusting against the thin, sweat-soaked fabric of her tank top. Well, it wasn't as if he hadn't seen such things before. She stood up, feeling the pleasant fatigue a good workout always produced.

The man extended a hand. "Louis Archer," he said. He was a bit on the short side, lithe but powerfully built, with dark brown hair and green eyes that regarded her with a look Jo had seen before. He was wearing shorts and an Army tee shirt.

She took the hand and let him give it a quick, gentlemanly pump. "Lucy Wong," she said, giving him the cover name she'd been assigned by MI6. "Archer" was probably not the man's real name, either. At times Jo found the secrecy comical, but she knew it all had a purpose. Many of the men and women training here were learning to employ deception not only to do their jobs but to stay alive.

"I'd ask what brings you to the Monk, but I'm sure you'd say it's classified," Archer said with a rakish grin.

"That's right," Jo said. She had looped the towel around her neck and was holding the ends to conceal her breasts. The last thing she needed now was for a man here to express an interest in her that went beyond the professional. Unfortunately, it looked like that's exactly what Archer had in mind.

"I just finished up, and if you have, too, how about sharing a pint? Have you been to the pub just down the road from here?"

She smiled politely. "Thank you, no," she said. "I'm really kind of tired. I think I'll head back to my quarters and curl up with a good book before turning in."

He stepped closer to her. "Well, I could bring something around and we could have a nightcap. Perhaps give you something a little more interesting to curl up with than a dry book."

She wasn't sure whether she should be amused or irritated, but it had been a long week, and so irritation took over. "Really, Mr. Archer, I would think your instructors could teach you a better line than that. Or have you been watching a few too many movies?"

Archer's eyes narrowed a bit, but his smile stayed put. "That's not very polite, Miss Wong," he said. "You're American, aren't you? I can tell by the accent. I'm just trying to be hospitable to a guest." He reached out and touched her towel. "Just trying to be—"

He never finished the sentence. Without thinking, Jo reached across with her own right hand and grasped Archer's, peeled it easily away from the towel and twisted it 180 degrees, producing a gasp from the Englishman. She bent forward, forcing him almost all the way to the floor. "If it's all right with you, Mr. Archer, I'll go find my book now." She tossed Archer's hand away and walked past him, picking up the sweatshirt she'd worn over to the gym.

"Yank bitch," he hissed at her. She didn't look back.

Jo tied her sweatshirt around her neck, letting it drape over her shoulders, and left the gym, shivering as the evening air hit her. Her quarters were only a quarter-mile away, an easy jog, but a man standing near a parked car waved to her first. "Good evening, Miss Wong."

"Sir David," she said, recognizing him. "What brings you here?"

Blandford came over and offered his hand. "Well, I thought I might have to prevent my charge from disabling one of MI-5's most promising operatives. Was it something he said?"

"Let's just say it was the wrong thing at the wrong time," she said.

"It's been a stressful week for you, I'm sure."

She nodded wearily. "Yes, it has. But I'm making progress with the languages."

"So I'm told," the MI6 man said. "I have another assignment for you, though."

She looked at him in surprise. Was she being pulled out of EMINENCE?

"Don't look so shocked," he said with a chuckle. "It's something you need to do. I'm ordering you to take the day off tomorrow. Go back to your quarters, get a good night's sleep, and enjoy the day. It will be Sunday, after all."

She couldn't conceal her relief. "Thank you," she said. "But really, Sir David, I'll just keep studying, if you don't mind. I'm not much for shopping or the movies."

"Perhaps not, but I believe there might be someone nearby you may wish to visit. A certain marine lieutenant colonel at Poole. Not that far away, you know. I've arranged for a day pass and a car for you."

***

Ian and Hodge were going over equipment requisitions the next morning when a corporal knocked on the office door. "Begging your pardon, Colonel, there's a visitor asking to see you."

The two officers exchanged a glance. "A visitor, Corporal?" Ian asked. "For me?"

"Yes, sir. A lady, sir."

"Well, then, we know she's not waiting for me," Hodge said with a grin. "Almost lunch time, anyway, isn't it?"

Ian checked his watch. They were due to board the ship in some twenty hours and he still had two days' work to do. Who in the hell would want to see him now? His sister lived in Manchester...no, too far away, unless something had happened to their mum or dad, but wouldn't she ring him first with that kind of news? "All right, Corporal, where to?"

"The Officers' Club, sir."

The O-Club was busy with the luncheon crowd. The base was buzzing anyway, with war talk dominating the conversation. An informal betting pool had been established to predict when the enemy would hit the Falklands, another for the date when the fleet would sail. There was no doubt at all that it would indeed sail; the debates that were even now raging through the government offices in London had a far different tenor than the energetic discussions underway at RM Poole.

Holding his green beret, Ian scanned the crowd. All of the women were uniformed marines or sailors...except one. She was sitting at the bar, a marine on either side, and all Ian could see were a pair of shapely legs, but there was a bit more leg showing than a typical marine bird. The pumps she was wearing were definitely a bit more stylish than regulations would allow. The legs looked awfully familiar.

"How about a pint, then?" one of the marines was saying to the woman, just as Ian made his appearance in front of her.

"Are you really here?" Ian asked, flabbergasted.

"Yes, I am," Jo said.

The marine who'd offered her a drink had already had a couple himself, by the look of him. A major, wearing a paratroop badge. "Shove off, mate," he said to Ian. "Find your own fun."

"It's too early in the day to get snockered, Major," Ian said. He turned to the marine on the other side of Jo, a captain wearing the same unit insignia as the major. "Better get your mate here a cup of coffee, Captain."

"Aye aye, sir," the captain said, thoroughly intimidated.

Ian offered his arm to Jo. "It's a beautiful day. How about a stroll?"

"Love to."

When they were outside, Ian pulled her into a secluded doorway and embraced her fiercely. Their kiss burned with a passion that threatened to consume them right there. "God, I could hardly believe my eyes," he said, when they finally came up for air. "How did you ever get—"

She touched a finger to his lips. "Hush," she said. "I'm here. How much time do you have?"

His pained eyes told her the answer before he spoke. "Not a lot. We—I have a lot of work to do and not a lot of time in which to do it. Damn it all."

"I understand," she said. "Let's take a walk."

The base hummed with activity around them, but for the next hour they might as well have been strolling through a silent park. They talked about what had happened in their lives since Bermuda, but they didn't talk about what they were doing next. "I'm in England on official business," she told him. "That's all I can say."

"I assumed as much," he said.

Finally, he glanced at his watch. "I hate to say this, but I have to get back to work," he said. "I'd much rather take you off the base to the nearest bedroom."

"I understand," she said, at the same time feeling a heat deep inside her that longed to have Ian lying next to her. "Ian, I won't ask you what you'll be doing, you know that, but in case we meet...somewhere, we should be careful."

His eyes widened with understanding. "I agree," he said. "It might be...a bit dicey. Perhaps a password."

She nodded, thinking. "Fonglan Island," she said.

"And the response is, 'Not a good place for swimming.'"

She looked at him with a smile. "It wasn't, was it?"

"In the event you use a radio, use this frequency first," he said, then rattled off a number. "Memorize it, Major."

"Roger, Colonel. But how will you know to listen on that one?"

He grinned at her. "We have our ways in the SBS." His eyes suddenly showed great sadness. "Time for you to go," he said softly.

They had somehow wound their way back to the Officers' Club. Marines and sailors were coming and going, more than a few glancing at Jo. "Ian—"

"Before you say anything, I have to tell you something," he said. "Oh, Lord..." He looked away, then back at her. "When this is over, I want to see you again, and I'll want to put a ring on your finger."

She felt awash in his eyes, felt his strength through his hands as he gripped hers, and she surrendered her heart to him. "I'll want to wear it," she said.

He embraced her, and she wanted to stay in his arms forever. They kissed, ignoring the whistles and cat-calls around them, and then he said, "I have to go."

"I know." The tears were coming, and she turned away. "God be with you, Ian."

"I'll make it through," he said. "We both will. We have too much to live for, now."

CHAPTER TWENTY-NINE

HMS Cambridge, *North Atlantic*

Monday, March 29th, 1982

Spray whipped across the ship as the bow knifed through the waves. *Cambridge* was making twenty-five knots against a westerly wind, but the weather forecast was promising. England was fifteen hours behind them, Argentina twenty days away. The morning briefing, four hours out to sea, had revealed that they could expect reconnaissance overflights by Argentine aircraft while still a week away from their destination. The Argentine Navy was known to have submarines, diesel boats that didn't roam too far from home, it was said, but that might change.

Ian held onto the railing and stared into the setting sun. He'd resisted taking a last look at the green hills of Cornwall as *Cambridge* rounded the peninsula and entered the open sea. He didn't want to think about the odds against him returning to his home county. Hadn't even had a chance to take Jo Ann there, introduce her to his parents, show her their modest estate.

He sighed. The mission would have to come first, as usual. Before now, he hadn't really thought about how much his career, his service in SBS, controlled his life. It had been everything he'd known for a dozen years and more. The Royal Marines gave him purpose and direction when he had none, and a physical challenge that forced him to push himself beyond anything he'd ever done. The money wasn't the greatest, but his needs were few.

That's what he always told himself, anyway. There were women over the years, as he'd told Jo, but none he allowed to get too close. He didn't need a wife, he'd always thought, as long as he had the service. Things were different now, though, indeed they were. A woman had come into his life that was unlike anyone he'd ever met, and he found himself head over heels in love with her. Planning marriage, even.

Marriage. The whole idea was rubbish, wasn't it? An American, a military officer, a career woman. What did he expect, that she'd marry him and move to England, tending his hearth and home and raising his children while he was off serving Queen and country? Was he daft?

But another part of him knew that this woman was different, so special that to lose her was unthinkable. Somehow, he had to make her part of his life, had to make it all work out. If it meant leaving the service, well, he would be doing that eventually anyway, wouldn't he?

"Beautiful sunset, Colonel," a voice beside him said, slicing into his reverie.

"Captain, good evening," Ian said, straightening.

"As you were," Stone said. "Pardon me for interrupting your thoughts. You appeared quite at sea, so to speak."

"Well, sir...there's a woman, sir," Ian said, suddenly anxious to tell someone, anyone besides Hodge, who already suspected more than he actually knew. "I've just been doing a lot of thinking about her, lately."

"I quite understand," Stone said. He raised a lighter to his pipe and cupped the bowl against the wind with a hand as he puffed it to life. "I heard she's American."

Ian laughed in spite of himself. "Word gets around, evidently."

"It does," the captain agreed. He fished into a pocket of his jacket and brought out a flimsy. "This was for my eyes only, and that of my exec, but I have some discretion in who I share it with." He handed the message to Ian, who read it and handed it back. Stone crumpled the paper and tossed it to the waves below.

"So the Argentines are at sea," Ian said.

"Indeed," Stone said. The message relayed the news that American spy satellites had confirmed British intelligence reports: the Argentine fleet had set sail the previous day, heading east. The governor at Stanley was told to prepare defenses. "We estimate they should arrive in another three days."

"Not much we can do about that, is there, sir?"

Stone sighed. "Not at the moment, Colonel. We've been caught with our knickers down this time. The fleet is assembling, however, and some elements are already at sea. Besides ourselves, I understand that *Fort Austin* sailed today from Gibraltar. She's a frigate; I know her captain. A good man, and a good ship."

Ian was quiet for a moment, and then asked, "What of the enemy submarine force, sir? Is it a threat?"

"The Argentines? Perhaps," Stone said. "We shan't have to worry about them for several days. In the meantime, we have another problem."

"Sir?"

Stone looked at him, eyes hard. "One hour ago, our sonar picked up a submerged contact some two miles back, pacing us. My sonarman, Sanders, swears it is the same contact that was with us near Carpenter's. He's one of the best sonarmen in the fleet and I trust his judgment."

"A Soviet sub, sir?"

Stone nodded grimly. "Undoubtedly, Colonel. Ivan is very interested in our mission. I notified Admiralty, of course, and was told to take no offensive action against the Russian for the time being. Once we're close to enemy waters, though, all bets are off."

"What do you think he wants, sir?"

Stone stared out to sea, turning his gaze aft. "With Ivan, one never really knows," he said. "I rather doubt he's out there just for something to do, though."

***

Stanley, East Falkland

Thursday, April 1st, 1982

Rex Hunt was nervous. The Governor of the Falkland Islands paced his small office in Government House, fretting over the cable he had just received from London. He had earlier been warned that the Argentines had sent a submarine to his waters, purpose unknown, although it didn't take an Oxford graduate to figure it out. Now, the news was even worse: a large Argentine fleet had sailed from the mainland and presumably was destined for his islands. He should prepare defenses immediately to repel an invasion.

Hunt had to laugh at the mere thought. Repel invaders? He had about a hundred Royal Marines to defend over two hundred islands covering more than twelve thousand square kilometers. Nearly thirteen hundred kilometers of coastline. Almost all of his two-thousand-odd subjects were on the two main islands, East and West Falkland. The territorial defense force, supposed to number about 120 islanders who had drilled a few times and allegedly knew how to handle a rifle, was a joke. How many would actually show up if called to muster? He had no aircraft, and his only warship, *Endurance*, had just been ordered to reverse course and head back to South Georgia, where the Argentine flag flew over Leith and a handful of British marines and civilians huddled in Grytviken, waiting for the enemy to show up.

"Governor, the officers are here," his secretary announced at the door.

"Show them in, please," Hunt said.

The two Royal Marines entered the office and saluted the governor. They were young, serious, attired in full battle kit, but had kindly left their weapons outside. Hunt returned their salute. Major Gary Noott was in command of Naval Party 8901, the remaining original troops of the garrison, and Major Mike Norman led the relief platoon that had just arrived. Together they had about one hundred marines. "Majors Noott and Norman, reporting as ordered, sir," Noott said.

Hunt shook their hands grimly. "Gentlemen, our situation is grave and not about to get better." He outlined what little he knew from the recent cables. "It looks as if the buggers mean it," he said.

"We should begin preparing defenses," Noott said. "Time is of the essence, sir."

"Indeed," Hunt said. For the next fifteen minutes, the three men pored over maps and discussed what could be done. The final consensus was that nothing could prevent the Argentines from coming ashore if that's what they decided to do. Norman, who had assumed overall command of the marine force, would send men to guard the airfield, the single road into town and Government House. It was agreed that the level of resistance offered by the British would depend largely on the enemy's tactics. While none of them mentioned surrender, they all knew it was only a matter of time.

"I shall order the defense force to muster, which I will then turn over to your command," Hunt said. "Gentlemen, deploy your men as you suggested. This evening, I will go on the radio to announce the imminent invasion to the population. We must strive to avoid panic. My overriding concern is to prevent loss of life if at all possible, civilian as well as military."

"If the Argentines shell the town, sir, there could be many casualties," Noott said. "Might I suggest an evacuation?"

"I regret to say, gentlemen, that our civil defense procedures are rather incomplete," Hunt said. "I fear that ordering an evacuation would produce the very panic that we seek to avoid. I should hardly think, though, that the Argentines would want to destroy the town and kill civilians. That would strike me as a very poor way to begin their administration of these islands."

The marine officers shared a quick glance. "Very well, sir," Norman said. "Should the enemy sail his ships into the harbor and open fire, we have very little with which to counter. We have no artillery, as you know, and no combat aircraft."

"I realize that, Major," Hunt said defensively. "It has never been London's desire, nor mine, to turn these islands into a fortress. Such a thing would surely have been viewed by the Argentines as a provocation."

"Well, with all due respect, sir," Norman said, "it appears they've been provoked anyway. I suggest we get about our business."

***

HMS Cambridge, *mid-Atlantic*

Saturday, April 3rd, 1982

Ian opened the door to the ship's briefing room and entered, followed by Hodge. They had been finishing their breakfast in the mess when word came to report to the captain. The marines found Stone and his exec, Fields, examining a map on the table. Ian saw it was a map of the southwest Atlantic, showing the Argentine mainland and the Falklands. That could only mean one thing.

"You asked to see us, Captain?"

"Yes, gentlemen, good morning." Stone's expression was grim. "I'm afraid there is bad news. Admiralty has cabled that the Falklands have fallen to the Argentines. It is also reported that the enemy is engaging our marines on South Georgia. It is expected that they shall soon surrender as well."

"It's war, then," Hodge said.

"Indeed, Mr. Hodge," Stone said. "Other than *Endurance*, we are the closest British warship to the Falklands. However, as there would be little good we could do there until the rest of the fleet arrive, we are ordered to proceed with our mission. The only good news is that there evidently were no casualties among our troops or the civilians. Governor Hunt has surrendered the islands to the Argentine commander."

"What of the marines, sir?" Even though Ian had expected this, the thought of his comrades being defeated in the field, being held prisoner, left him thunderstruck.

"I am informed that the governor and the garrison are being airlifted to the mainland," Stone said. "From there it is expected they will be repatriated, probably through a neutral party, perhaps Uruguay. The Argentines evidently have no wish to hold British prisoners any longer than absolutely necessary."

"Public relations," Hodge grunted.

"Our fleet is gathering and the main task force should sail from England within three days," Stone said. "One

344

strategy that is being seriously discussed is the implementation of a Maritime Exclusion Zone, two hundred kilometers around the islands. Any Argentine ships or aircraft entering the zone would be subject to attack."

"We don't expect this to go into effect until the tenth or the eleventh, at the very earliest," Fields said. "By then we should have submarines in the area that could enforce the zone, at least against enemy naval assets. The body of the surface fleet isn't expected to be inside the zone until the twenty-eighth soonest."

Stone indicated a circle on the map, drawn around the Falklands. He used a pen to touch the northern edge of the circle. "We should arrive here on the twenty-fourth," he said. "We could make better time but to linger too long in the war zone would draw the enemy's interest and quite possibly bring us under attack. It is imperative that we make our rendezvous with *Reliant* on time and unmolested." GALAHAD called for Ian's SBS commandos to transfer to the submarine shortly after midnight on the twenty-sixth. They would go ashore some twenty hours later, anticipating the Argentine air strike against the fleet to be launched within forty-eight hours of their landing.

"I realize that three weeks is a long time to wait, Colonel," Stone said. "We shall arrive at Ascension Island tomorrow for a two-day stay. Your men and the rest of the crew will have some liberty ashore. It's likely to be the last for all of us for some time."

"I'll give the lads some time off, sir, but we'll also be rehearsing. Wideawake Field should make for a good practice target."

Stone nodded. "Very good." He looked at his men. "Gentlemen, we are at war. In a short time I shall make that announcement to all hands. Once we leave Ascension we shall be at general quarters on all watches. Our rules of engagement will be different than they were during our last voyage to these waters. Pass the word that the men should prepare themselves for action."

Nobody responded for a few seconds. No man aboard had been old enough to see action in World War Two or Korea. Ian wondered how the men would react to the news that British territory had been seized and British troops taken prisoner. It would be a new feeling for all of them. He was grateful for the combat experience he and his troops had gained on Carpenter's. They had seen the elephant, and he knew they would meet the challenges to come. He thought quickly of Jo. She would be down there, somewhere, risking her life for England, for him. He said a quick, silent prayer, asking for her protection. It was the best he could do for her now.

CHAPTER THIRTY

MI6 Headquarters, Century House, London
Sunday, April 4th, 1982

Sir David Blandford did not like the look in "C's" eyes. "He wants to come out? Now?" the director asked again.

"I'm afraid so, sir," Blandford acknowledged. "Our station chief in Santiago was quite specific in his cable. Tuscany requests extraction for himself and his family, as quickly as possible." "Tuscany" was the code name for the Argentine Army major, Antonio Gasparini, who had so daringly provided access to Pilcaniyeu for MI6's agent.

"I would say it is completely out of the question," grumped Sir Alec Hyde-Watters, the service's Director of South American Operations. "It is much too early. EMINENCE won't be initiated for another, what, fifteen days?"

Blandford nodded. "Vixen is scheduled to be in Buenos Aires on the nineteenth. It will take her at least two or three days to get oriented and provide any useful information."

"And GALAHAD?" "C" asked.

"Some eight days after Vixen's insertion," Blandford said. "That is the backstop operation, as the Americans would say. Should EMINENCE fail, the SBS will have to thwart the attack. The last line of defense, of course, is the fleet itself. Properly warned of the threat, I should think they could muster a credible effort to deter the strike."

"We can't be sure of that," Hyde-Watters said. "We don't know the exact particulars of the Argentine plan. Suppose they use more than one aircraft, more than one weapon? We know they have at least two ready to deploy. What if there's a diversionary strike? I must tell you, gentlemen, Admiralty is in an absolute dither about this."

"If Tuscany defects now, I should think that would alert the enemy that Pilcaniyeu has been compromised," "C" said. "It might move them into a contingency plan, of which we're not aware. It is vital that we be able to track the deployment of the weapons. Without that knowledge, GALAHAD would be an utter failure, perhaps a suicide mission."

"Tuscany may already be in trouble," Blandford said. EMINENCE was his operation, and he was fighting desperately to keep it alive. There was pride involved, of course, but he truly believed that the plan provided the most reasonable means to foil what the Argentines called STEINBOCK, and which was referred to as CAPRICORN in the few offices at Century House that were aware of it. "We know that the arrest and torture of his wife alerted Siegfried. They extracted her from custody at some political risk. Surely they realized there was a potential security problem with Tuscany. I should think they have had him under observation since then. Yet he was able to successfully assist our man in his infiltration of the facility. That was nearly two

348

weeks ago. It could be that Tuscany fears he is in danger of exposure. Surely the security is tightening there as they move closer to activating their plan."

"Or perhaps he just has cold feet," Hyde-Watters said.

"Gentlemen, there is risk either way," Blandford said, hands spread helplessly. "If we extract Tuscany now, that will certainly alert Siegfried that Pilcaniyeu may have been compromised. On the other hand, that might not necessarily lead to a change in their plans. Unless they fear that we will take military action against the facility, why would they move the weapons ahead of schedule?"

"Downing Street has strictly ruled out a pre-emptive strike against the facility," "C" said. "The logistical and political problems are simply too great."

"That's what they say now," Hyde-Watters said. "But if we tell them the weapons might be deployed early, and that we might very well lose track of them, perhaps that could change their minds. Do they just trust the Argentines to sit tight and adhere to their original schedule, or might the enemy initiate an alternate plan, perhaps to move one of the weapons to a naval base and install it in a submarine? A sub could intercept our fleet well before it reaches the war zone and launch the weapon in a missile. The fleet would be virtually helpless. There is no way they could deter that threat without direct help from the Americans."

"And as long as Mr. Haig is flitting back and forth, they are not likely to provide such assistance," "C" noted, referring to the frenzied diplomatic efforts of the American Secretary of State, Alexander Haig.

"Let us examine the other possibility," Blandford said. "Suppose we deny Tuscany's request for extraction, somehow persuade him to sit tight for another, shall we say, two weeks? And he agrees, with great reluctance. He would have no choice. There is risk with this course of action, as well."

"We are at war," Hyde-Watters said. "There is risk in everything we do, or don't do."

"Please continue, Sir David," "C" said, with a look at his DSAO.

"If Siegfried is caused to suspect Tuscany of working with us, they could arrest him and extract the truth. Without question, that would compromise everything. They would know for a fact that their facility has been penetrated. They would have no choice but to move the weapons. There is no guarantee, after all, that Downing Street won't decide to strike the plant rather than risk losing track of them."

"Or, he could crack on his own and tell what he knows voluntarily," "C" said. "If he feels we have abandoned him, he may believe he has no alternative. They could double him."

The risk of having a double-agent at work against them in such a critical juncture brought them all pause. "That would be a disaster," Blandford said. "As of now we are trusting him to let us know when they deploy the weapons. If they turn him back, he could give us all sorts of damaging misinformation."

"And if he does leave, then how are we to track the weapons?" "C" asked.

"Sir Alec has a backup in place for that," Blandford said, eyeing Hyde-Watters with a bit of satisfaction.

"Indeed?" "C" turned to the other man. "And that is?"

Hyde-Watters shifted uncomfortably in his chair. "We have a man on the inside, in addition to Tuscany," he admitted. "Not as highly-placed, by any means. His code name is Mercedes. He is a sergeant in their motor pool. If they move the weapons overland by truck, he would know."

"So if we extract Tuscany now, the fate of this entire operation would be in the hands of a mechanic?" "C" asked.

"Basically, yes," Hyde-Watters said. "We didn't use him for the infiltration because Tuscany was there and had access to the proper documents for our man. We have had Mercedes in place for several months now, ever since we became aware of what they might be doing down there."

Blandford couldn't suppress a smile. "There we are, then. Even if they deploy the weapons early, we will know."

"Hopefully," Hyde-Watters said. "There are no guarantees. Keeping Tuscany in place would give us a much better chance to track the deployment."

"C" looked back at Blandford. "During the war—and I suppose that now we should be more specific, World War Two—there were many very important decisions made in this office. Some of them resulted in people from occupied countries being handed over to the enemy. Sacrifices had to be made, we were told. The important thing was the mission. Dozens of French Resistance fighters, and even a few Allied agents, were given death warrants to preserve the secrecy of D-Day. And all along they thought we would get them out, as we had promised." His voice was barely a whisper now. "C"'s eyes were far away, to a desperate time four decades before. The director was silent for a moment, and Blandford thought he saw the man's lower lip tremble, just barely. Then those cold gray eyes turned back at him, and then at Hyde-Watters. "We shall not do that again, gentlemen. We shall not abandon those who have served us, served us at great risk."

He turned back to Blandford. "Sir David, you shall signal Santiago station to pass the word to Tuscany as soon as possible. Extraction shall occur one week from today, April the eleventh. He will have one opportunity."

"Thank you, sir," Blandford said, slowly exhaling his sigh of relief.

"Sir Alec, make the appropriate arrangements with our people in Santiago," "C" ordered. "Is Jamison still there?"

"I believe he is in Belize, sir, but he can be back in Santiago by tomorrow."

"Well, he knows the chap. He shall handle the extraction. Santiago is to render him whatever assistance he requires. That is all, gentlemen."

***

Fort Monckton, England

Jo Ann tossed the Russian-language book against the wall and lay back on her bed, staring at the ceiling. Her head felt as if it would explode if she tried to shove anything more into it, especially if it was Russian or Armenian in origin. The German had gone fairly well, and while she was far from fluent, she felt confident enough to pass for a German in casual conversation. Her cover story would help; Larisa Kocharian knew German only as a second language, and one recently acquired at that. Still, Jo hoped most of the people she encountered in Argentina would use Spanish, which she had learned in high school. She'd kept up on the Spanish and used it on previous trips to Mexico and Spain.

She'd been here only ten days or so, but it felt like ten months already. Her instructors were top-notch, her few fellow students were friendly, as were the other personnel she met on the post—sometimes a bit too friendly, although she hadn't spoken with Archer after that incident in the gym. The food was good, her quarters adequate, but she was tired of the training and wanted to get on with the mission.

It hadn't all been languages, though. The SIS people gave her basic lessons in tradecraft, some of which she was already familiar with, some that were pleasantly new. Even the familiar material served to bring her up to speed, so it was helpful. The self-defense lessons were avoided entirely once she had demonstrated her martial arts prowess. She was grateful for the weapons training, though; she had been falling behind with her firearms proficiency and the post's firing range and instructors gave her a welcomed chance to catch up.

She'd gotten a few hours' leave to go into nearby Portsmouth a couple times, including a six-hour junket yesterday that was wonderfully refreshing. She did some shopping, browsed through a museum and art gallery, and generally enjoyed being outside the confines of the post. At her instructors' suggestion, she used the opportunity to practice a little bit of her tradecraft, such as following a suspect individual, which she found harder than she expected. Before she flew to Budapest, she was told, she'd be taken back into the city for some more serious training, including an exercise in which she would have to evade an

MI-5 surveillance unit. She found herself looking forward to that.

For now, though, fighting the boredom was her number one priority. The post had a movie theater—"cinema", as it was called here—but she'd already seen this week's feature, *Tootsie*. Dustin Hoffman was hilarious in the lead role, but she had no desire to see it again. Her time was too valuable to waste seeing a movie she'd already seen, or reading a book she'd already read.

She told herself she had to loosen up a bit more. The iron discipline which she'd used to rule her life had gotten her this far and would take her further, but she was starting to wonder if there wasn't more in life than duty. Duty to her country, to her service, to her martial arts training, even this duty to learning new languages and espionage skills. With a sigh, she rolled over on one side, thinking that a nap might be in order. At least it would take her mind off things.

Ian's face drifted into her thoughts, not for the first time that day. She remembered with crystal clarity the words he'd last spoken to her, a week ago now at RM Poole. He wanted to marry her, and she told him she'd accept. There was a part of her now that shuddered at the mere thought of tying herself down like that. Was there room in her life for someone else, someone with whom she'd share everything? She'd never had to share anything with anybody.

That was the problem. She had lovers over the years, after Jimmy and Franklin, but when they started to get too close, she pushed them away. The two she'd told Ian about were years ago, when she was much younger, more undisciplined. Since then, she'd dated a handful of men, slept with a very few of them and enjoyed their company, but once they'd started pressing into her life, her personal space that had room for only one, she pushed them away. She had to. Intimacy, she could handle. Companionship, she usually found welcome. But long-term partnership? Marriage? That would mean exposing too much of herself, sharing too much, and she didn't want to do that.

Well, she was thinking of doing that with Ian, wasn't she? And why the hell not? He was a wonderful man. Loyal, honest, dedicated, and very much in love with her. Not to mention damned attractive and wonderful in bed. What more could a girl want in a man? He wasn't wealthy, by any means, but Jo had never cared much about material things. Certainly she could've made a lot more money working a civilian job someplace than she was making in the Air Force. She took after her father in that. She knew Joseph Geary had turned down offers from private industry that would've tripled his CIA income, but he was out for more in life than accumulating money. He'd told her once that more than money, he craved challenge, and helping defend their country against its enemies was certainly more challenging than selling stocks or running a company.

Her father had dedicated his life to serving his country. That brought up an interesting question: what exactly was his daughter out for in life? She didn't see herself ever wearing general's stars, so promotion, which drove so many of her fellow officers, wasn't a driving force for her. Proficiency in her area of expertise? She'd come a long way on that score, that was for sure. A person with her skills, her military training, was going to be in demand in years to come. She paid attention to geopolitical trends, and something told her that the Cold War was going to wind down in a few years, and something else was going to start winding up. The Iranian hostage crisis should have tipped everyone off. Islamic extremism might very well replace communism as the West's primary threat, and those people operated with a different set of rules than the ones followed by Moscow. Under those new rules, someone with her skills would be an even more valuable commodity.

Rising to the peak of her profession, though, wasn't exactly at the top of her priority list. What was the peak, after all? A desk job someplace? Her father's work in the field for OSS, and then CIA, had led to his current job. She was much too young to consider administrative work, although something like that could be interesting ten or twenty years down the road, when life in the field became a bit too strenuous, as it undoubtedly would. Becoming the foremost linguist around, the best martial artist, now those were real challenges to be sure, but leading where? There would always be another language to learn, another art to master, and as she well knew, nobody ever mastered the martial arts; she was on an infinite journey that would always leave her with more to learn.

Looming over everything was the long shadow cast by a certain Royal Marine. She remembered his touch, and suddenly she felt a twinge from deep inside. Not a sexual longing, but something far deeper, more profound. She placed a hand on her abdomen. Children? They'd not discussed that, of course. Over the years, Jo felt maternal longings every now and then. That was only natural. No childless woman could see a baby without thinking of having one of her own. But now, for the first time, she seriously considered the prospect of becoming a mother, of having Ian's child. She expected the thought to be scary, but it wasn't. It was...comforting, perhaps. She sighed pleasantly.

In her heart of hearts, Jo Ann knew that she loved Ian Masters. But she also knew that something was keeping her from making that final leap into marriage. She was trying to figure out what that was when she dozed off into a slumber blessedly free of dreams.

***

Estancia Valhalla, Argentina

It was time to finally call it a night. Willy closed the last file on his desk and sat back, rubbing his eyes. There was a time when Sundays were days of rest at Valhalla, as they were throughout Argentina. Those days, at least for a while and at least on this estancia, were gone.

The work was going well, really. The nation was still celebrating yesterday's news that the English had surrendered the Malvinas. Thankfully, casualties were very light. The fighting was more intense on South Georgia, but the English marines finally gave up there, too. The dancing in the streets of Buenos Aires would go on well into the night. Tomorrow, reality would start to intrude. People would go back to work, they would start to slowly realize that their lives hadn't really changed that much, and the newspapers would start reporting on the movements of the English fleet. Galtieri would put up a brave front, but anyone in the know about the comparative military strength of the two nations would quickly realize that the Argentine occupation of the Malvinas was likely to be short.

Unless, of course, something happened to the English fleet before it could land its marines.

Willy stood up and stretched. The house was quiet, except for the muffled sounds of music coming from the library. Dieter was spending this Sunday evening as he spent them all, in the library with his books and Bach. Today he had seemed quieter than usual at dinner, forcing Willy to carry the conversational ball with their guests, the Carmaños. Giselle was particularly bewitching, and Willy smiled as he remembered their afternoon ride, which included a stop at their favorite spot, a secluded glade featuring a picturesque babbling brook. Dieter had first shown it to Willy when he was six. Ten years later he showed it to Giselle, and it had always been their special place. A few years later it became even more special, for it was the place where they'd first had sex, when she was seventeen. They were shy, hesitant, fumbling. Not today. She was almost fierce during their lovemaking, challenging Willy to match her passion, a challenge he gladly met.

On their ride back to the estancia, he caught himself thinking that when this was all over, he would marry her. She would have his children and they would live a happy life in Valhalla—provided, of course, he could avoid being lined up against a wall and shot.

He entered the library, expecting to find his father asleep, but Dieter was just putting a volume back on its shelf. Willy saw that it was *Mein Kampf.* He'd read it in the original German as a teenager, dismissing it as the ramblings of a fanatic, but re-reading it ten years later impressed upon him the writer's cunning and twisted genius. Fortunately, the men who had survived their leader's demise and made it here were much more sensible, more pragmatic. In their own way, though, they were just as ruthless. Not for the first time today, the word VALKYRIE crossed his mind.

"I've come to say good night," Willy said.

"Ah, yes," Dieter said, returning to his favorite chair. "I apologize for not speaking much during dinner," he said, reaching for his glass of schnapps. "I trust the Carmaños were not offended."

"Of course not," Willy said.

"You should marry that girl," Dieter said, eyeing him. "She's a fine one, even if she is half-Spanish."

Willy smiled. "I may surprise you yet, Father, and do just that."

Dieter grunted, taking a sip from the glass. "Make it soon," he said. "I fear I will not see another Christmas, much less grandchildren."

Willy almost blurted out his first thought: Is that why you're pushing this dangerous plan? Is reunifying the Fatherland so important that you must see it before you die? Instead, he said cautiously, "The Malvinas are ours, Father. CAPRICORN is on schedule. It will all happen soon. Next Christmas we will have much to celebrate."

"Let us hope so," Dieter said, draining his glass. He rose unsteadily to his feet. Willy stepped forward quickly to help him.

The younger man wanted desperately to tell the older man what he knew, how VALKYRIE had to be stopped, that it was insane and could bring down the wrath of the Americans upon them all, but he remembered Heinz and his cautionary words: "You must not tell your father what you know. As hard as it is, you must seem ignorant of what they're doing. If the Reichsleiter finds out about us, we are finished, and so is Argentina."

But Willy knew he could not bear to see his father rot in prison. He helped Dieter to the door and down the hall to his bedroom. No, he would not see him put before a firing squad, either. Somehow, he had to find a way to save his country, and save his father at the same time.

CHAPTER THIRTY-ONE

Bariloche, Argentina

Sunday, April 11th, 1982

Bryan Jamison was pleasantly surprised by Bariloche on the occasion of his first visit. The city reminded him of Salzburg, in the Austrian Alps, and indeed it was the center of the Argentine lake district, in the foothills of the Andes. Bustling with some eighty thousand people, the city was on the southern shore of Lago Nahuel Huapi, one of the largest lakes in the country and the centerpiece of a sprawling national park. Bariloche was designed in the Central European style, but now Jamison could see modern, garish apartments and office buildings crowding the city's architectural skyline. It wasn't very pleasing to the eye.

Today there was no time for that, though. After spending two days browsing through antique shops and chatting up the dealers, even buying a few pieces and arranging for their shipment to an MI6 cover in Dublin, it was time for business. Dangerous business, to be sure;

extracting a subject from his country was always dicey, but this was wartime, and there was not one person to extract but four.

He was fairly confident he wasn't being followed, but couldn't be sure. Hopefully, BIS just considered Duncan MacPherson to be a harmless Irish businessman, not worthy of their attention. One couldn't count on that, of course, so precautions had to be taken. Not very obvious ones, but he'd already established on his previous visit that MacPherson was a man on the go, and this morning was no exception. He rose at seven, breakfasted at his hotel, Las Piedras II, and spent an hour strolling the busy sidewalks before hailing a cab. This particular cab was driven by a Chilean agent. Once they'd exchanged identifying code phrases, the two men went over the plan once more as they headed east along Avenue Bartolome Mitre. The driver turned left on Beschtedt, and Jamison saw it ahead: Iglesias Catedral, where Mass would begin in about twenty minutes, and where Duncan MacPherson, a good Irish Catholic, would celebrate it.

Oscar, the driver, nodded as Jamison exited the cab and handed a wad of pesos through the window. The MI6 agent nodded one last time, and the Chilean responded by staring ahead, as if looking for his next fare. He would be where Jamison wanted him in one hour.

Jamison joined the crowd of worshipers entering the cathedral and paused as he came into the sanctuary. Scanning the pews in a certain area, he quickly found who he was looking for. Antonio Gasparini and his family were there, in the fifth pew from the front on the left. Theresa was wearing a tasteful but stylish blue hat, Gasparini's signal that they were ready. If she had been bare-headed, that would mean BIS had tumbled to the operation, and after Mass,

Duncan MacPherson would simply return to his hotel and prepare to leave for Chile later in the day, alone.

But the hat was there, and Jamison's heart started to beat a little faster. He found an empty seat and tried to concentrate on the service. It wasn't easy.

Fifty minutes later, Jamison slid out of the pew, excusing himself as he brushed past his fellow celebrants, and left the sanctuary. He found a men's room, relieved himself—not faking it, either, nerves again—and then, exiting the restroom, turned down a hallway that led away from the main entrance to the sanctuary. On his first visit to Bariloche he'd visited Iglesias and did a little unobtrusive scouting. He found the side double doors with no trouble. A minute later, they swung open, and a young man in assistant's vestments kicked the door stops into place. His eyes went a bit wide when he saw Jamison. The agent smiled and nodded, and the acolyte retreated back into the sanctuary.

Jamison took a sideways glance through the doors, confirming that they led past the choir loft to the altar, with a stage-left row of pews to the right. The Gasparinis were still there. The priest concluded the Mass and dismissed the congregation. Gasparini led his family against the flow of departing worshipers, heading for the choir loft, holding his hand out to the man and woman who'd sung a beautiful duet. The Army officer chatted with the singers, introduced his family, and shook hands with them again. Then he herded his wife and children toward the side doors. Jamison looked behind him, back down the hallway, and saw nobody coming. So far, so good.

Gasparini's eyes brightened as he recognized Jamison. "Señor MacPherson," he said in Spanish, "It is very good to see you again."

"And you, Major," Jamison said. "Please, come with me."

Two very long minutes later, they had wound their way through the rear of the cathedral and out a back entrance. There was a small park behind the cathedral, and they walked quickly along a path to Costanera Avenue 12 de Octubre. The Chilean's cab was waiting. "Inside, quickly," Jamison said, holding open the rear door. The Gasparinis piled in, with eight-year-old Arturo between them and five-year-old Maria on her mother's lap. Jamison got in the front passenger seat, and Oscar pulled out smartly into the traffic.

"Mama, where are we going?" Arturo asked.

"Just a little trip to see the mountains," his mother said. Jamison glanced at the boy, then at his father. Gasparini's eyes betrayed his nervousness. They were like the eyes of every defector Jamison had helped in the past: grim resolve alternating with regret, and always the nerves and fear underneath. It was a hell of a spot to be in.

"We proceed as planned, Señor MacPherson?" Oscar asked.

"Yes," Jamison said. He had trusted the Chilean to plot the escape route. In Santiago they told him the CNI agent had previously helped four Argentine defectors over the border safely. They hadn't told him if there'd been any that hadn't made it over safely.

***

Even though it was Sunday, Colonel Lothar Reinke was at his desk. Two days earlier he had been notified that

Project CAPRICORN's execution phase was underway. The first weapon, code-named X-1, would be shipped from Pilcaniyeu two weeks and a day hence, on the morning of April twenty-sixth. Reinke did not know its destination, but he was told to have X-2 ready for deployment by May fifteenth. That would be pushing things, according to the scientists, but they would do their best. No, Reinke told them, you will do what needs to be done to have X-2 ready on schedule. As a result, Reinke was far from the only person on duty this day.

His second in command, Major Gasparini, had asked leave to spend the weekend in Bariloche with his family, who were visiting him here for the first time. Bearing in mind the major's wife's recent...difficulties, Reinke granted the request, requiring his second to report back to the post by eight p.m. There would be no further leave for Gasparini, or any of them, for some time.

Reinke was concerned about Gasparini. The major's work was beyond reproach, his personal conduct impeccable, especially considering the strain the man had been under in recent weeks. Fortunately, he had told Reinke that his wife seemed to be dealing with her ordeal rather well. The colonel was glad to hear that. The last thing he needed now was to have any of his people distracted by outside concerns.

That was why the phone call he'd received yesterday was so disturbing. Colonel Hernando Malín of the BIS in Buenos Aires was on the other end of the line, inquiring about Major Gasparini's conduct and, in particular, his whereabouts. Reinke gave Malín a favorable report of the major's work and told him about Gasparini's weekend leave in Bariloche. The BIS colonel politely thanked his Army counterpart for the information and hung up.

Was Gasparini under suspicion of some sort? Reinke hadn't slept well the night before. If BIS suspected an officer of subversive or criminal activity, they might also suspect his superior. Reinke knew that his record was as pure as the driven snow that would be coming out of the Andes in a few weeks, but he also knew that certain members of the current government, and thus certain members of BIS, were not enamored of the men who were Reinke's patrons. Being a military man, Reinke always sought to steer clear of Argentina's turbulent politics; unfortunately, since the military was always involved in politics, that proved to be impossible. High ranking officers always had to choose sides, and hope that their side would stay on top. Reinke hoped he had chosen his side well.

He was going over a report from the officer in charge of the mess hall when his telephone rang. Colonel Malín, his aide announced. Reinke ordered the call to be put through.

"Coronel Reinke, good day to you," Malín said smoothly.

"And to you, Coronel Malín. I see we are both working today. How can I help you?"

"I am calling as a professional courtesy, Coronel. You will recall our conversation yesterday about Mayor Gasparini?"

A chill ran down Reinke's spine. "Of course." Reinke checked his watch. "He is due back here in just under eight hours."

"I must inform you that less than an hour ago, Mayor Gasparini was observed leaving Iglesias Catedral with his family, in the company of an Irish national named Duncan MacPherson. Does that name ring any bells, Coronel?"

"No, it does not." An Irishman? In Bariloche? Reinke had never met anyone from Ireland, but he knew it was close to England. He also knew that the Irish and English generally did not get along.

"After our conversation yesterday, I took the liberty of placing Mayor Gasparini under surveillance. His name had come up in connection with a security investigation."

Reinke began to sweat. "And this Irishman, do you know him?"

"In these rather turbulent times, we must keep tabs on Europeans who visit our country," Malín answered smoothly. "Especially those from the British Isles. So it was that I found it interesting that Mayor Gasparini should know this gentleman. Coronel, my office has obtained a photograph of this man MacPherson. One of my men will be bringing it to your main gate within the hour. He will want to show it to your people. I would appreciate it if you would extend him your full cooperation."

Reinke forced his hand to hold the telephone steady. "Of course, Coronel. When I see Mayor Gasparini I will question him with regard to this Irishman."

"Let us hope you have the opportunity to do so, Coronel Reinke. I will be in touch."

***

Jamison was watching Theresa Gasparini herd her children from the cab to the decrepit-looking station wagon when Oscar motioned the agent aside. "Señor, I believe we were being followed in Bariloche."

"I picked up your signal, Oscar. Were you able to lose them?"

The Chilean looked back past the farmhouse toward the city, ten kilometers to the east. "I think so, señor. But one never knows for sure. If they were BIS, they can quickly summon help if they truly wish to find us."

Jamison nodded. "How much further to the border?"

Oscar looked to the west. "About fifty kilometers. The road is a good one, although not as well-traveled as Route 231. We should make good time. When we get to within a few kilometers of Puerto Frias, I will use a side road I am familiar with." He unfolded a map and held it out so both men could see the route. The longer but more popular trip would've been to head east out of Bariloche and curve north along the eastern end of Lago Nahuel Huapi, then take 231 to the northwest through the national park to the border. Popular with the tourists for its magnificent scenery, it was also much longer. Oscar had suggested the shorter route along the south shore of the lake, toward the small town of Puerto Frias at the border.

"The checkpoint there will be hard to pass through if BIS has alerted it," Jamison pointed out.

"True, señor, which is why we will be taking an alternate route." He took a pencil from his shirt pocket and touched a point on the map just south of the village. "There is a mountain road here that goes near the border. There is no checkpoint."

"A fence?"

"Yes, but I doubt if it has not been fortified since my last visit."

368

"Let's hope you're right."

***

Traffic was moderate on the road to Puerto Frias. Despite the political tensions between Argentina and Chile, commercial and private traffic between the two nations remained brisk. Oscar mentioned that this was normal. The politicians might be angry at each other, he explained, but life went on. Many people living on one side of the border had relatives on the other.

"Ten kilometers to the turnoff," Oscar finally announced after what seemed an interminably long drive. The Gasparinis had been quiet in the back seat of the station wagon. The children were asleep, and Señora Gasparini gazed out the window. Jamison had seen the look before. She was looking at her country for the last time. The British agent knew something about that. Every time he left England, it hit him that this might be his last glimpse of home.

The major, on the other hand, stared straight ahead, with an occasional glance over his shoulder. Jamison admired the man's discipline. Defectors had been known to crack at the last minute, to insist on being let loose, willing to risk discovery and punishment in order to go home. Not this man, though. His hatred of the regime that so casually brutalized his wife had to be great indeed. Well, that was all right. Hatred was a good motivator, as long as one kept it in perspective.

"Any sign of pursuit?" Jamison asked the driver.

369

"I don't think so, unless they are using multiple vehicles."

"Is BIS that sophisticated?"

The Chilean shrugged. "Sometimes. They are not to be underestimated, señor."

A few minutes later Oscar turned left, cutting across the eastbound lane. The new road was paved, but just barely. The old wagon bounced over potholes. The dry weather meant that a cloud of dust was kicked up behind the car, adding to Jamison's unease. He reached inside his jacket to grip the handle of his Walther PPK. Still there. "How long?"

"Thirty minutes, señor, perhaps less, if the road stays good."

Ten minutes later, without having encountered another vehicle, the mountains began to close in around them. The old wagon's engine strained as they gained altitude. Just before rounding a curve, Jamison looked back and saw the glint of sunlight off glass. "There's a car back there," he said to Oscar, forcing calm into his voice. "Two, maybe three kilometers."

"Just one?"

"I don't know," Jamison said. Gasparini turned around to look, but the wagon had gone around the curve. "How much—"

"Two minutes. Be ready to move."

Gasparini didn't need to be told again. He roused the children, who'd been half-awakened by the bumpy ride. "Listen to me," he said to them. "We are going to stop very soon and you must do exactly as I say. Do you understand?"

"Yes, Papa," Arturo said. "Where are we?"

"We are going on a little adventure," the major said, smiling. "We might have to run for a bit."

"Okay." The boy looked at his father and smiled. His sister grasped her mother closely. Theresa looked close to tears. Her husband touched her arm, but she didn't look at him.

The road was curving to the left up ahead, and beyond it Jamison saw a thin stand of pines, with a tall wire fence running through it, about a hundred meters from the edge of the road. Oscar was looking closely at the trees. "Can we drive right up to the fence?" Jamison asked.

The Chilean shook his head. "The trees are too close together." He took the curve, drove another thirty meters and then swung the wheel to the right. The car thumped off into the grass, plowing over small bushes, before Oscar braked to a stop. "On foot from here," he said.

"Let's go, then," Jamison said. He was out the door quickly, looking back down the road. He could hear an engine. "They're coming!" He drew the Walther. Oscar had a gun out also, and the MI6 agent saw that Gasparini was armed as well. "Oscar, lead the way," Jamison said. "I'll cover the rear." He longed for the feel of a submachine gun, but it had been deemed too risky to bring any over the border.

The little girl began to cry. "I wanna go home!" Her mother shushed her, to no avail. Theresa was crying now. Gasparini supported her as they made their way through the brush behind the Chilean.

They were still thirty meters from the fence when Jamison saw the vehicles, a white sedan with a flashing blue light on the top, followed by two large pickup trucks. The three vehicles pulled to a stop next to the abandoned station wagon. An officer emerged from the sedan, pistol in hand, and started shouting orders. Soldiers leaped from the pickups, rifles at the ready. "Run for it!" Jamison shouted.

Oscar sprinted to the fence, just ahead of the major, who was carrying the little girl and pulling his son by the arm. Theresa was struggling behind him. Fifteen meters from the fence she tripped and fell awkwardly, crying out in pain. The Chilean used his gun to push aside strands of razor wire, finally finding the ones he'd carefully cut and then put back in place on his previous visit. "Here! Quickly, mi Mayor!"

Jamison ducked behind a tree and faced the oncoming Argentines. "Antonio! Save the children!" Theresa screamed through her sobs. The soldiers were fifty meters away now, and Jamison saw the officer aim his pistol. The shot was wild, ripping through the branches over the agent's head. Jamison looked back, saw Gasparini handing the children one by one through the fence to Oscar, then turned back to the soldiers.

Take down the officers first. See how disciplined they are. He aimed carefully and squeezed the Walther's trigger. The round caught the Argentine commander in the stomach. He grunted and fell to his knees. The soldiers hesitated. One raised his rifle and fired a burst in the direction of Jamison's tree, just as the agent pulled himself out of the line of fire. Rounds slapped heavily into the trunk just over his head, but a few zipped past. Jamison saw Gasparini take a hit to his left arm, spinning him around and to the ground as his wife screamed in terror. Jamison came around the other side of the tree and squeezed off four quick shots. Men yelled in pain, and more guns opened fire.

Gasparini struggled to his feet and staggered to his wife, managing to pull her up with his good arm, but he had to transfer his gun to his wounded left and wasn't able to return fire. Jamison quickly ejected the spent clip from his Walther and inserted a fresh one. They'd never make it, he saw. Oscar was beyond the fence, in Chile, hustling the children behind covering trees a few meters away. By the time he could come back and bring his gun to bear, it would be too late.

Jamison made a decision. He made it without hesitation, for if he'd had time to think about it, he might have made a different one. "Run! I'll cover you!" he shouted to Gasparini, in English. The major knew some English, didn't he? Gasparini looked back over his shoulder as he half-dragged his wife to the fence, now only a few meters away. Did his eyes convey his thanks? Perhaps they did.

The MI6 agent spun around the tree and ran straight at the startled Argentine troops. The Walther was up and blazing, and his aim was off a bit, but three more of the soldiers fell before the remaining troops overcame their surprise and took aim at the onrushing, screaming European in the tan suit. Jamison saw the flashes from the muzzles but didn't hear the roar. There was something else in his ears now. Was it music? Yes, music it was, and as six of the bullets thudded into him, the pain blazed through his nervous system and so he couldn't identify the song. A pity, it was so beautiful. He fell to his knees, the gun dropping to the ground, and as the blackness started to dim his vision he took one last glance backward. Were they through the fence? Yes.

CHAPTER THIRTY-TWO

Budapest, Hungary
Thursday, April 15th, 1982

The windows of her hotel suite gave Jo Ann a spectacular view of the hills of the western half of Budapest. She knew from her guidebook that the Hungarian capital had been created in 1873 with the unification of hilly, western Buda and flat, eastern Pest. The winding ribbon of the Danube wasn't too far away, just two blocks to the south with Castle Hill looming on the far side. She'd never been to the Continent, and on another occasion, and accompanied by a certain Royal Marine, she would've considered the city to be incredibly romantic. Even a third of a century under the heels of the Russians had not stopped the Hungarians from keeping their identity, with their capital's unique atmosphere holding at bay the stocky blandness of socialist architecture. Keeping the soldiers at bay was something else again; it seemed to Jo that the Hungarian Army was maintaining a high profile, with Kalashnikov-armed troops on every block.

The people ignored the soldiers as they went about their business.

She'd been able to use her German from the airport to the hotel, grateful that she'd not had to learn Magyar, the native language that was renowned for its difficulty. It was proving difficult enough for her to shape her mouth around the sounds of German and Russian, so different and guttural after the ease of English and the sing-song of her Oriental tongues. Hopefully, things would go as well in Buenos Aires.

There was a knock on the door of the bedroom. "Come in," she said in German.

The door opened and Walter Schröder said, "Would you like to take a walk, my dear?" He looked a bit older than his photograph, grayer at the temples, his eyes weary but alert. He cupped a hand to his ear, the signal to Jo that they had to assume the room was bugged. Jo nodded her understanding.

"An excellent idea," she said. "Let me get my jacket." A few minutes later and they were on the sidewalk, her hand inside the crook of his elbow. "The exchange went well, I thought."

"Yes," Schröder said. Just as London had arranged, Jo swapped identities with Larisa Kocharian Schröder in a rest room at the airport. Her flight from London arrived a half-hour before the Schröders' from East Berlin, and she spotted the couple at the baggage carousel next to hers. Taking her small suitcase with her, Jo went to the restroom and locked herself inside a stall. Surprised to find her hands shaking, she waited patiently until the stall next to her was entered. Jo dropped a lipstick tube onto the floor near the wall between the stalls, near enough to be seen by the next-door occupant. At the last second she had remembered to open the tube and extend the lipstick halfway out, the signal that she had not been followed. A similar lipstick dropped to the floor on the other side, also opened halfway. Within sixty seconds, the women exchanged coats, hats, purses and shoes. Leaving her suitcase, Jo left the stall and risked a glance in the mirror to make sure her hair, which had been around her shoulders, was now properly pinned up underneath the hat. The two other women in the restroom ignored her. Heart thumping, she left without ever taking a look back at the real Larisa, who would soon be on her way to freedom, courtesy of MI6.

"The resemblance is truly remarkable," Schröder said. He patted her hand. "Your German is good. Not excellent, but good."

"Thank you," Jo said. "It's an interesting language."

"We are an interesting people." They walked in silence for a while, taking in the sights. They stopped soon at a large café. "The Ruszwurm confectionary," Schröder said. "Founded in 1827."

"You've been here before?"

"Twice," he said. "Tonight, we shall have a quiet dinner in a nice restaurant I know. Tomorrow night, the symphony at the Zeneakademia. Are you familiar with the work of Bartok?"

"I'm afraid not," she said.

"Bela Bartok, one of Hungary's most famous composers," Schröder said. "Died some years ago, but still revered here. They celebrated his centennial last year. Tomorrow night we will hear his "Hungarian Sketches, for orchestra". The conductor is Ervin Lukacs. Truly one of the best in Europe." He glanced at her. "You do not know classical music?"

"Not as well as I should," she admitted.

Schröder shook his head. "We have much work to do. The people we meet in Buenos Aires are liable to ask you about it, especially if they hear we attended the symphony in Budapest." He sighed. "All right, let us begin over lunch." He led the way into the café.

She hoped the two days until they left for Argentina would pass quickly.

***

Buenos Aires, Argentina

"It took some doing, but I believe my father has finally calmed down," Heinz Nagel said.

"As has mine," Willy Baumann said. The files on his desk were starting to blur. He desperately needed a good night's sleep. No, what he really needed was for this whole business to be over. Once again he longed for the peace of the estancia; he imagined himself out riding with Giselle, a very pleasant image indeed.

The defection of Major Gasparini had thrown the Bund into an uproar. Willy heard the news hours after the family's escape into Chile, conveyed by a smug BIS colonel named Malín, whose not-too-hidden pleasure at discovering a traitor in the middle of the Bund's most important project quickly turned to concern when Willy reminded him that the BIS had, after all, allowed an English spy to wander around unmolested and then failed to prevent the defection. A very nervous Lothar Reinke was on the line next, offering his resignation. Willy declined it, and instead ordered the Pilcaniyeu security chief to lock down the facility. The scientists and all other civilians would stay on the premises until further notice.

"My father said the Reichsleiter inquired about an early deployment," Heinz said. The strain was beginning to show on him as well. "X-1 is scheduled to leave the facility in nine days."

"We must adhere to the schedule," Willy said. "There is no other place we can move the weapon without risking it falling into Galtieri's hands. Pilcaniyeu is the only facility where we can maintain control."

"There is talk we have lost control there," Heinz said.

Willy exploded. A file went flying into the wall, papers everywhere. "Damn it, Heinz! You were there with me, you met Gasparini, and you didn't read the man's mind any more than I did!"

"We should have anticipated this. After his wife's arrest, we should have put him on extended leave. He was a prime target to be turned by the English."

"Reinke said he could not spare him. We've been over this already."

Heinz leaned forward, elbows on knees. "I know."

"Nine more days, Heinz. That's all we need. Reinke can maintain tight security that long, can't he?"

Heinz shrugged his shoulders. "I would think so." He looked up at his friend. "I am told the Reichsleiter is concerned about an English air attack on the facility."

"Nonsense! The English can no more bomb Pilcaniyeu than we can bomb Liverpool. And the Chileans will not risk war with us by allowing a commando raid to be staged across the border. The Reichsleiter is worrying like an old woman."

"Careful, Willy," Heinz said. "He is not to be underestimated."

"So you are always telling me," Willy said. "I am more concerned about our glorious president. I'm sure he suspects what we are working on there. He may even get the idea of striking the English fleet himself and seize the weapons."

Heinz offered a thin smile. "He knows better than that," he said. "If he moves against us, he will not live to see the dawn of the next day."

"He may be willing to take that risk, with such a prize on the line," Willy said. He sat back in his chair and rubbed his eyes. They felt like sandpaper. "Reinforce Pilcaniyeu with a company of Werewolves," he said.

"Very well," Heinz said. "I can have a hundred extra men there within twenty-four hours."

"Assign Schmidt's unit. Tell him I want to talk to him before he leaves."

"Consider it done."

Willy leaned forward, elbows on his desk. "Wing 45 will be ready?"

Heinz nodded. "The commanding officer is Major Steinhorst. One of ours. He assures me the pilots will be loyal and carry out our instructions."

Willy looked at the calendar on his desk. "Nine days, Heinz. We must keep the lid on for nine more days and then we can bring this madness to a conclusion."

CHAPTER THIRTY-THREE

Buenos Aires, Argentina

Thursday, April 22nd, 1982

Jo Ann found the café right where her contact said it would be and selected a table on the sidewalk. It was a fine day in Buenos Aires, a city she had quickly found to be one of the most beautiful in the world.

She and Walter had arrived in the Argentine capital six days ago, after a flight from Budapest to Madrid and then across the Atlantic on Iberia Airlines. That leg took over twelve hours, all in coach. The long flight and the time change—Buenos Aires was five hours behind Budapest— exhausted them both, and it wasn't until Saturday that Jo felt human enough to venture outside their suite at the Gran Hotel Colón in the Microcentro district, a block away from the broad and very busy Avenue 9 de Julio. She discovered a city that surprised her with its European architecture and atmosphere, but after a few days of exploration, she had the feeling that try as it might, Buenos Aires could not match the great European capitals it sought so hard to emulate. Perhaps the political turmoil, which never seemed to end in this place, had something to do with that.

During their time in Budapest, she and Walter had come to an understanding. Although posing as his wife, she would not be required to sleep with him, something Jo was prepared to do if absolutely necessary. Her MI6 handlers in England made it clear that she would not be expected to be intimate with her "husband", and Schröder was perfectly fine with that. In fact, he told her with remarkable dignity, he and Larisa had separate bedrooms at home because of his snoring. On the few occasions they traveled together, they maintained the practice of sleeping apart, despite the added expense. On their first night in Budapest, even with her bedroom door securely closed, the rumbling from Walter's room convinced Jo that the German wasn't just being polite.

After another day of rest on Sunday, during which they visited the bustling pedestrian mall on nearby Lavalle Street and went all the way to the Pink House and Plaza de Mayo, Schröder began a series of meetings with Argentine government officials around the city. He made daily visits to the East German embassy, and every evening called for a dinner at a high-end restaurant or, as had happened just last night, at the private home of a corporate executive who was in negotiations to do business with Walter's government. Jo quickly discovered, somewhat to her irritation, the Argentine custom of dining late in the evening.

Jo had anticipated having her days largely free, but instead found herself invited to luncheons with the wives of many of the men Schröder was meeting with. "It is the way they do business here," he told her. "The men are in charge, but the women wield great influence through their social contacts. If they do not approve of someone's wife, they will pressure their husbands not to do business with her husband."

Jo found that interesting. "How do Argentine husbands feel about that?"

Schröder shrugged. "They allow it, to a great degree. In return, the wives generally give their husbands a good deal of latitude in, shall we say, seeking occasional pleasure outside the marriage bed."

"Ah." Jo wasn't sure she would be quite so tolerant.

She found herself liking her companion. Schröder was courtly in the old European way, gently corrected her German when needed, and never asked her personal questions. She could imagine that some men might try to take advantage of this kind of situation, but Walter had not even hinted at desiring intimacy. In fact, on the rare occasions he referred to the real Larisa, he did so with obvious fondness. Jo was beginning to wonder if this polite but rather dull man could really be the double agent MI6 and CIA suspected him to be. She was hoping that the person she was scheduled to meet here at this café would let her know that Walter was in the clear.

Before leaving England, her contact from CIA's London station gave her careful instructions for communication in Buenos Aires. Each day, she was to call a certain telephone number from a public phone. The call was to be placed anytime between ten a.m. and two p.m. She was never to use the same phone two days in a row. When the person on the other end answered the call, she was to ask, in Spanish, to speak to Señora Menendez, if she had nothing to report. The señora would come on the line and give Jo any instructions that were required. If, on the other hand, she had information that had to be passed to CIA, she was to speak in German and ask for Herr Zastrow. She would then be told of a time and place for a meeting. She also had to write a one-page daily report, on hotel stationery, and leave it each morning in a dead drop, which in this case was on the underside of a vending machine down the hall from her hotel suite.

This was her fourth "working" day in Buenos Aires, and so far she had not asked for Herr Zastrow. She did her best to get information from several of the women she met, women with German husbands, but so far none of them had said anything that even hinted at the existence of a Siegfried Bund. She was frustrated and getting a little bored. Not good traits for a field operative, she knew, but this was her first assignment which involved such a large amount of "soft" work. Today, finally, she had been told to meet a contact and receive instructions. Perhaps something was about to break.

At least the walk to this part of the city, Recoleta, had been invigorating. She left their hotel and walked north on Carlos Rellegrini about a half-mile, past the Brazilian consulate, and then headed northwest on Avenue Alvear. Another half-mile brought her to Ayacucho, and the Alvear Palace Hotel. Along the way she stealthily used the techniques taught to her at the Monk about how to detect and evade a surveillance tail. Without being obvious about it, she crossed the street several times, doubling back a half-block once or twice, ostensibly to check out an interesting store. She used the windows of stores as mirrors to watch who might be behind her, and whenever she emerged from a shop she carefully scanned the sidewalks, her eyes hidden by sunglasses. Once or twice she thought someone looked rather suspicious, but they didn't stay behind her long. If the Argentine BIS, or anyone else, was indeed following her, they were using multiple tails and being very cautious. There wasn't a whole lot she could do about that.

She went into the lobby of the Alvear Palace and asked for directions to the nearest ladies' room. Once inside, she entered the next to last stall and closed and latched the door behind her. Without removing her stylish, French-made slacks—she was using Larisa's luggage, and had to admit the woman had good taste—she sat on the toilet for thirty long seconds, then rose and flushed it. As the water gurgled, she reached behind the tank and felt for the small device Señora Menendez had told her would be there. It was. The plastic disc-shaped container, the size of a bottle cap, came loose from the ceramic tank without a sound. Prying it open, Jo withdrew the small piece of toilet tissue. *Café de la Paix* was written on it with a blue marker. *L Aya R Qui.* She memorized it and dropped the paper and container into the toilet, where it disappeared with the last of the water from the flushing.

Turning left outside the entrance to the hotel, Jo walked down Ayacucho, crossed Avenue Alvear, and a block later came to another cross street, Quintana. A right turn, and another block later the street ended at RM Ortiz, with a public plaza on the other side, and beyond that, the most incredible cemetery Jo had ever seen. It had to cover half a dozen square blocks, and the mausoleums seemed to outnumber headstones. All of them were large and ornate to varying degrees.

Tearing her gaze away from the cemetery, she looked to her left, then her right. There it was, Café de la Paix. She found an empty table and ordered a mineral water. Five minutes later, as she was perusing the menu, a plain-faced, brown-haired woman approached the table. "Excuse me," she said in French, "I believe I'm lost. I was told the French consulate is a few blocks away." She pointed back down RM Ortiz to the southwest.

"I'm sorry," Jo answered. "That would be the Uruguayan consulate. I don't know where the French consulate is." Actually, she did; it was back in the Microcentro district. The contact, however, had now been confirmed.

"Oh dear," the woman said. "May I sit here and rest for a bit?"

"Of course," Jo said. "Please join me."

The woman set her handbag and a folded magazine on the glass-topped table and dropped into a chair, scooting it around to be nearer to Jo. "*Bonjour, Renarde,*" she said, her voice a bit lower. "You can call me Marie. Do you mind continuing in French?"

"*Pas du tout,*" Jo said. Not at all.

"Very good," Marie said. "I knew the French I learned for Paris would come in handy again. There are a lot of people around here who speak German and English, not to mention Spanish, but few who speak French. So it is a bit safer." The waiter came, and Jo ordered a Caesar salad. Matching her Spanish, Marie said she would not be dining, but would like a bottle of mineral water. When the waiter departed, the CIA agent turned back to Jo. "I have been asked to pass along a 'well-done' for your German. It is remarkably good, for someone with so little training."

"*Merci,*" Jo said. "I presume, then, that one of the people I've met has actually been from your shop?"

"A good assumption," Marie said. "You passed with flying colors." The waiter brought her a bottle of mineral water and a glass. Marie took a moment to quench her thirst. "I can't stay long. As we talk, smile, relax. It is a polite conversation between strangers, no?"

"I'm sorry that I haven't been able to report anything useful," Jo said, trying to make it sound as if she were remarking about the weather.

"Nonsense," Marie said with a smile. "Your information has been welcomed. I know how easy it is to be frustrated in this business, Vixen. You must be patient."

"But time is of the essence," Jo said.

"It is a factor, yes," Marie said. She took another drink of her mineral water. "An opportunity has arisen, though."

"Yes?"

"Saturday night, you and Schröder will attend a party at the East German consulate. It is on the other side of Cementerio de la Recoleta. Not too far from the British consulate."

"That's the cemetery across the street?"

"Yes," Marie said. "Remember the luncheon you had Tuesday? One of the ladies was the wife of a consular official. She apparently liked you enough to get you on the invitation list. So your work the past few days wasn't at all in vain."

"That's good to hear," Jo said.

"Schröder will tell you about the invitation tonight. He is at the consulate right now, meeting with his Stasi contact."

Jo felt a chill. "Is he—"

Marie nodded slightly. "We're almost certain he is working for the Bund. Some members of the Bund hierarchy will be attending the party. We think they will give Schröder his final instructions for his part in their East German operation. The men are quite close to Eminence. We expect they will discuss him with Schröder. This is your chance to find out what we need to know."

Jo's salad arrived, and when the waiter had departed, she asked, "How am I to do that?"

Marie took another drink and set the empty glass on the table. "I'm going to leave now. Inside this magazine is a voice-activated listening device which can be attached to virtually anything. It transmits to a receiver that is also a recording device. There is a cordless earplug for you to listen in. Its range is about a hundred yards, so don't let him stray too far away."

Jo nodded. "How will I get the tape to you?"

"When you return to your hotel after the party, slip it to the red-haired doorman. He works for us. The next morning, between eight and nine, call in for further instructions."

"Our flight to Madrid leaves at four p.m. Sunday," Jo said.

"You won't be on it, and neither will Schröder," Marie said. "Wait for your instructions."

"I understand." She hesitated, then voiced the thought that had been trying to get out. "If Schröder is really a double agent, won't he expose me to the Argentines?"

"There is that possibility," the CIA agent said. "We can't be sure what his game is. If he'd meant to expose you, the Bund would have you already. You should be on your guard. Once you go into that consulate, we can't provide any assistance to you."

Marie stood up and picked up her handbag, but left the magazine on the table. *"Bon chance, Renarde,"* she said. Good luck, Vixen.

"Merci. Au revoir."

***

HMS Cambridge, *South Atlantic*

Friday, April 23rd, 1982

The mess hall had become a regular evening gathering spot for the SBS troopers. Ian's toughest decision—so far— had been the selection of men for the mission. The seven he had picked were here now, including Hodge, his XO. Colour Sergeant Powers was here, of course, as was Corporal Garrett, the Welsh rifleman.

Ian didn't feel real good about going into enemy territory with only eight men, but he felt good about the ones who were going. All of them had been Royal Marines for at least four years, with SBS for at least two, and with Ian's command for at least one. They'd all been on Carpenter's Island. They knew each other, knew their jobs, and they knew and trusted their commanding officer. As he looked them over now in the mess hall, he could barely suppress a grin of pride. It broke through just a bit, enough for Hodge to notice.

"They're good lads, aren't they?" Hodge knew exactly how Ian was feeling.

"Yes, they are," Ian said. "We'll have to make sure we bring them home safely."

Ian checked his wristwatch. Nearly 2100 hours. "Time for the briefing."

"All right, lads, let's have your attention for the colonel," Hodge announced.

Powers tossed down the cards he held in his hand. "Bloody well lucky for you, mate," he said to one of the three other men at his table. "Inside straight, I had."

"You'll have your chance to prove it, Sergeant," Ian said. Seven pairs of eyes were looking at him now. He took a moment to scan each of them.

"It's lights out at 2230," he began. "We're up at 0600 for morning P.T. on the deck. I'm told the weather will be acceptable." That brought a few good-natured groans. "Breakfast at 0730. Weapons check at 0830. At 1000 we meet here to go over the E&RE. Lunch at 1200. At the morning brief I'll have more info about our afternoon schedule." It was a challenge every day on this voyage to keep the men busy, but fortunately they were used to the downtime that came with a deployment at sea. They'd all been aboard Cambridge on the long trek across the Pacific, and had learned to keep occupied with letters home, books, and marathon card games. Some of them were quite proficient at chess. Garrett, the Welsh corporal, had organized a tournament on the Pacific run that involved half the men on board. Ian lost in the second round, but Garrett hung in until the championship match, when he was beaten by an ensign from Northumberland.

Ian held up a flimsy he'd gotten from the comms officer a short time ago. "Latest word on *Reliant* is that she's on

389

schedule for the rendezvous. We meet at 2200 hours Sunday night. At 2230 she surfaces and we transfer over to her. If the weather cooperates she'll be alongside. If not, we're in the boats."

"Here's to the meteorologist," Powers said, raising his glass of water. That brought nods from most of the men. Nobody wanted to make the transit to the submarine in a small boat battling rough seas.

"When do we go ashore, sir?" one of the men asked.

"If all goes according to plan, we disembark *Reliant* at 2330 hours Zulu on Monday. That will be 2030 local." The ship was on Greenwich Mean Time for this mission, even though Argentina was three hours behind. "Starting tonight, by the way, we're moving our lights-out time back an hour each night. Don't want any of you lads falling asleep as we get to the sub."

"Gor' blimey," Corporal Garrett said. "Twenty-odd hours on a submarine. Twenty hours too long."

"'Specially 'cause the squids don't use deodorant," another trooper said, bringing a laugh from the men. While all the men deeply respected Royal Navy sailors, especially submariners, they took pains not to be obvious about it.

"We'll have to make do," Ian said, grinning.

"Will we have bashers on board the sub, sir?" Sleeping quarters were of primary concern to an SBS trooper on the verge of beginning an operation. The men were skilled at grabbing shuteye whenever they could, but using something approaching a real bed was a plus.

"I'm told we'll have some hammocks strung up in the after torpedo room. They should be sufficient provided the boat doesn't have to go into action."

"Any sign of the enemy yet, sir?"

"We've had one overflight a day of what is probably an Argentine surveillance aircraft," Ian said.

"Why not shoot the bugger down?" Garrett asked.

"We're not yet in the exclusion zone," Hodge said. "And they could be civilian airliners." Someone snorted at that.

"What about submarines, sir?" Powers asked.

Ian glanced at Hodge, who gave him a slight shrug. "The Argentines have a few German- made Type 209 diesel boats," he said. "None are expected to be in these waters. However, that possibility cannot be ruled out. What we do know is that we've been shadowed off and on by a Soviet boat, as I'm sure you've heard."

Although the captain had made no official announcement to the crew about the Russian, word had spread, as it inevitably would. The marines picked up the word before Ascension. "What's Ivan up to, sir?"

"Hopefully, nothing except keeping an eye on things," Ian said. "However, the captain tells me he's not inclined to let the Russian interfere with our mission. He will do what he needs to do in that event." That brought some worried glances between the men. Taking on the Argentines was one thing. Tangling with the Soviet Navy was another. There had been talk on the voyage about which major powers might be playing on which side. Although the United States and Soviet Union had more or less declared their neutrality, everyone knew that might change once the shooting started.

Ian knew the men were concerned about that, and was about to address it, when the always-prescient Sergeant Powers spoke up. "Let's hope that won't be necessary, sir."

CHAPTER THIRTY-FOUR

Buenos Aires, Argentina

Saturday, April 24th, 1982

"You look exquisite, my dear," Schröder said, rising from the divan in the sitting room of their suite.

Jo Ann glided into the room, wearing Larisa's best evening gown, red silk with an intricate, Russian-inspired pattern sewn in gold thread. It was a bit more conservative than one would see in Paris or New York, but for the wife of a Communist bureaucrat, Jo imagined it was somewhat daring. A gold shawl and handbag completed her ensemble. For accessories, Jo wore a honey amber beaded necklace, which Walter had bought for Larisa on a trip to Estonia, and a matching pair of amber earrings, also from the Baltic. Her only ring was Larisa's plain gold wedding band, which Jo had found in her luggage, carefully wrapped in tissue paper. That particular discovery brought a lump to Jo's throat.

"Thank you," Jo said. Since Marie's warning two days earlier, Jo's time with Schröder had been difficult, although she didn't let on that she knew. Now, she approached him, smiling. He did look rather debonair, although East German men weren't known for their fashion sense. "You look very handsome tonight, Walter." She reached up to adjust his tie and then tugged at the lapels of his dark blue suit jacket. "There. All straight." When her left hand came away from his lapel, it left behind the wireless microphone, carefully attached to the underside of the lapel. No larger than a ten-cent piece and nearly as thin, Jo was confident it wouldn't be discovered. Tomorrow she would remove it on the pretext of brushing the jacket.

He smiled back at her, but his eyes were different than they usually were. They'd spent over a week together and she hadn't yet seen him really relax, but tonight he seemed to carry an underlying air of tension. "How do you feel?" she asked.

"I've been having a bit of indigestion," he said. "The food here is quite rich."

"Yes, it is," she said. She went over a quick mental checklist. The microcassette recorder was in her handbag, but the handgun she'd brought to Buenos Aires, a SIG/Sauer P210, was reluctantly left in her bedroom. She'd trained with the SIG at Fort Monckton and was quite pleased with it, after years of handling standard U.S. military Colts, but it wouldn't at all do to have the wife of a guest bringing a firearm to the party tonight. "Shall we go?"

"Yes," Schröder said. "By the way, I was informed that President Galtieri could very well be attending this evening."

"Really? How exciting!"

"Some fairly prominent members of the German community will be there as well," Schröder said. "I might have to spend some time in conversation with them. I hope you won't mind."

"Not at all, Walter."

***

It appeared to Jo Ann that the reception hall of the Consulate of the German Democratic Republic had probably been spiffed up within an inch of its life. The main floor of the four-story building on Avenue Pueyrredon—only a block from the British consulate, ironically enough—was the consulate's public area. The East Germans weren't known as the most popular hosts on the Buenos Aires party circuit, which was as active as any capital and probably more so than most. They had, however, put on their best face tonight. Not surprising; the Argentines were riding high, with a military victory over a West European power giving them huge prestige among those nations who had long felt they weren't quite welcome at the table. The Soviets, with their East German proxies, were always right there to give a hearty slap on the back to the little guys, usually followed by an invitation to their table.

Jo had to remember that down here, people didn't think about geopolitics in an East vs. West way; it was more South vs. North. One of the lecturers at Fort Monckton had stressed the difference. Southern Hemisphere nations looked upon those in the North as the "haves", and those in the South as the "have-nots". South Americans felt more of a kindred spirit with Africans than they did with Europeans or

North Americans, even though the great majority of South Americans were of European descent.

From what she had seen of the people in Buenos Aires, though, Jo had come to the conclusion that the average Argentine was like the average American or Briton, and probably the average Russian: they just wanted opportunity and security, and otherwise to be left alone. Geopolitics may be endlessly debated in ivory university towers and government offices, but the average man and woman worried about things like jobs and children.

The Argentines in this room, though, were not average. More than half of the men wore military uniforms, glittering with medals and draped with insignia. The women who accompanied the men were just as imperious, lavishly dressed and dripping with jewelry. Jo also recognized American, French and Soviet uniforms, and a few she concluded must be from other South American nations. Waiters circled the room with trays filled with glasses of champagne and plates of hors d'eourves. A string quartet was set up in one corner, playing something Jo thought might be from Mozart.

Walter introduced Jo to the East German ambassador, a stuffy bureaucrat named Schultz, and his even stuffier wife. A number of other consulate officials came and went, and Jo's German was put to the test constantly. Fortunately, she felt more comfortable in the language every day, and did well with it tonight. "You speak it like a native," one woman said, when Jo told her she was from Armenia.

"Herr Schröder!"

The hail came from a large, block-shaped man in the uniform of a Soviet Army general, who was making his way over to where Jo and Walter stood chatting with a couple from Austria. "General Maltov," Walter said to her. "Military attaché to the Soviet Embassy. We met in Moscow last year."

"I don't recall the meeting," Jo said, trying not to tip off the Austrians.

"You stayed home that time, my dear," Walter said, and Jo breathed a sigh of relief.

Maltov was moving through the crowd like a Red Army tank, a flute of champagne nearly invisible in his large ham of a hand. "Schröder!" He embraced Walter with a large bear hug. "So good to see you, comrade," the general said in passable German. "And I see you have your beautiful wife. You bring her to Buenos Aires, but not to Moscow, eh?"

"General Yevgeny Maltov, my wife, Larisa."

The Russian clicked his booted heels and placed a kiss on Jo's outstretched hand. "You are indeed more beautiful than Walter had described," he said. "Our fraternal socialist allies in the German Democratic Republic produce lovely women as well as steel and Olympic swimmers."

Jo smiled. Her first big test. She would have to answer this man in his own language, lest he find out later about Larisa's heritage and perhaps ask a question or two. "Фактическ, Я от Армении, Генералитет Камрада," she said in Russian. Actually, Comrade General, I am from Armenia.

Maltov's eyes widened, and he looked down at Jo's feet. The shoes, she thought, he's looking at the shoes, they told me that Russians always check out each other's shoes. Jo was wearing Polish-made open-toed heels. Black, to contrast with her dress, but she'd painted her toenails red. The general quickly looked back up at Jo, and his smile of surprise broadened. Jo hoped fervently that Maltov wasn't from

Yerevan. "Armenia!" he said, and then, in Russian, "I am from Latvia originally. A town near Riga. There are fine Armenian boys in the Army. They always boast of their women. Now I know why!"

Jo was rapidly running dry with her Russian. To get into a conversation with Maltov would be disastrous. "Excuse me, General," she said, then to Walter, in German, "Where is the ladies' room?"

Schröder gestured behind Jo. "Through that door, down the hallway, my dear."

"Thank you." To Maltov, she said in Russian, "So nice to meet you, Comrade General. Perhaps we'll talk later." Jo fled to the restroom, struggling to maintain her composure. By the time she reached the door she was trembling.

This would not do. She had to get a grip on herself. She went inside, nodded to the two other women standing at the sinks, and went into a stall. Latching the door, she sat down and focused on her breathing. A few seconds later, relying on her inner ki, she was calm.

When she returned to the reception room, Walter was free of the Russian. He was talking with two men in civilian clothes, one man in his seventies, the other much younger and rakishly handsome. There was a resemblance between the two men. Jo took a fresh flute of champagne from a passing waiter and joined them.

Schröder seemed momentarily startled when she touched his elbow, but he recovered quickly. "Ah, my dear," he said, in German. "Gentlemen, allow me to introduce my wife, Larisa. My dear, may I present Herr Dieter Baumann, and his son, Wilhelm Baumann, from Buenos Aires."

The Siegfried Bund operative. The face and name registered with Jo as soon as Walter spoke the words. The elder Baumann clicked his heels, bowed, and kissed her hand much more smoothly than Maltov had done. His son was just as elegant, but there was one difference: his eyes never left Jo's. She felt a tingling from her hand up to her elbow as his lips touched her skin. "Madame," he said. "A pleasure to make your acquaintance."

"The pleasure is mine, gentlemen," she said, tearing her eyes away from the younger Baumann and looking back at his father.

"Are you enjoying Buenos Aires?" Dieter Baumann asked politely.

"Very much so," Jo Ann said. "It's a beautiful city."

"I wish I could have seen more of it," Walter said. "I have had meetings every day."

"When do you return to Germany?" Dieter asked.

"Tomorrow, unfortunately."

"A pity. You really must stay longer next time."

Walter glanced at Jo. "We shall," he said.

The quartet began to play a waltz. "'The Blue Danube'," Dieter Baumann said. "Herr Schröder, were I ten years younger, I would ask your lovely wife for this dance."

"I am a terrible dancer, as Larisa well knows," Schröder said. "But perhaps your son might enjoy it."

Wilhelm clicked his heels. "Madame, I would be honored," he said.

The last time Jo had danced a waltz was at her Academy graduation ball. "I'd love to," she said, trying to sound sincere.

Baumann led her onto the dance floor and in seconds they were moving smoothly together. "Strauss is always better with a full orchestra," he said. "But this quartet is good."

"Yes, they are," Jo said. There was something about this man, something she hadn't felt from a man in a long time. A type of magnetism, almost. She worried that her freshly-learned German might not pass muster with this man, but Larisa did not know Spanish. She'd have to risk the German. "What business are you in, Herr Baumann?"

"Please call me Willy," he said. "My father's company has several divisions. Some newspapers and radio stations, some construction firms, primarily."

"And what is your role, if I may ask?"

He smiled. "My father is semi-retired. I find myself doing many different things these days."

"I see." She decided to venture a little probe. "Your people seem quite excited about the Malvinas. You must be very proud."

Did his eyes narrow just a bit? The smile didn't change, though. "Pride will not carry us through what is to come, I'm afraid."

"I am told the English fleet is on its way."

"Yes, it is," he said.

Could she risk another probe? "There are so many Germans here. Is there still animosity from the last war?"

His smile got a bit thinner. Jo knew she would have to be careful now. "We are Argentines first, Germans second," he said. "Or Italians, or Spaniards, or whatever."

They whirled past Schröder and the elder Baumann, engaged in conversation. Jo warned herself not to lose him. "When I married Walter and came to Berlin, I was surprised by how many people still talked of the last war," she said. "The division of Germany is still such a sore spot for them."

"I could tell you are not German," he said with a polite grin. "Eurasian, perhaps?"

"I am from Armenia," she said, hoping that Baumann didn't know Russian, or worse yet, Armenian. What would be the chances of that? Dancing an Austrian waltz in Buenos Aires with a German-Argentine who knows Armenian? "I have heard of it," Baumann said.

"It would be wonderful if Germany could be reunited someday," she said, trying to sound wistful.

"Perhaps it shall be," Baumann said. His eyes seemed to drill into hers. Jo caught a break as the waltz ended. They were on the far side of the room now from where they'd left Schröder and Baumann's father.

"Ladies and gentlemen!" At the main entrance, a man was speaking loudly in German. "The president of Argentina, His Excellency, General Leopoldo Galtieri!"

The quartet swung into something that must have been Argentina's version of "Hail to the Chief". Everyone faced the main entrance and burst into applause as President Galtieri, wearing a magnificent uniform, entered the room, an elegantly-gowned lady on his arm. Jo couldn't help but noticing that the Argentine First Lady wasn't introduced, unlike her American counterpart would've been.

She also noticed that Willy Baumann's applause was polite but not nearly as enthusiastic as most other guests'. "An impressive personage," she said, as much to gauge Baumann's response as to make conversation.

"He knows how to make an appearance," Baumann said.

Galtieri began to work the room, but with an imperious manner more in common with an old European potentate than a contemporary politician. Jo had to remind herself that this was a politician who wasn't beholden to the voters for his position. The East German ambassador was first to greet him, and then began to escort the president around the room, introducing him to the other guests. Jo watched people, as many women as men, begin to move into position from other places in the room.

"I should find Walter," Jo said. "He may be able to meet the president."

"*Necesito conseguir un poco de aire*," Baumann said, almost under his breath. Jo knew the Spanish: I need to get some air. Turning to Jo, Baumann smiled and bowed slightly. "Thank you very much for the dance, and the conversation, Frau Schröder," he said. "I wish you a pleasant journey home tomorrow."

"Thank you, Herr Baumann—Willy," she said. With a smile that would have melted almost any other woman, he was gone, working his way through the gathering crowd, heading for a doorway as far away from Galtieri as possible. Well, that was interesting. No love lost there. A personal thing, or political? Her briefing had been short on details about the Siegfried Bund's relationship to the Argentine leadership. One of the MI6 experts referred to the Bund as a virtual shadow government. Perhaps the new president was trying to shake off the shadow.

Jo looked for Schröder, but he wasn't where he had been before. Neither was Dieter Baumann. Without trying to be obvious, Jo scanned the room. There—she caught a glimpse of Walter's distinctive bald spot, disappearing through a doorway. She made her way in that direction, swimming upstream against most of the other guests who were moving toward Galtieri.

Reaching the doorway, Jo saw that it opened onto a short hallway, with a staircase heading down at the other end. Nobody else was about, but she heard a heavy door closing. Moving away from the door, she reached into her handbag and took out the microcassette recorder. The tape was running, so Walter was talking. She unclipped the wireless earplug and put it in her left ear, making sure her hair was swept down over it.

Schröder's voice came through, tinny but audible. "A beautiful evening."

"Yes, but winter is coming." Dieter Baumann's raspy voice came through, loud and clear. He had to be walking beside Walter, probably on his right, near the lapel that concealed the microphone.

"Your man wishes to meet in the cemetery?"

"Yes," Baumann said. "Inside was too risky. Too many ears, too many eyes."

Jo made her decision. She had to follow them.

***

Without her shawl, the evening air was chilly on her bare shoulders. Jo emerged from the main consulate building and saw Schröder and Baumann about seventy yards ahead, walking toward the main gate of the compound. Jo was glad she'd remembered to put her fake East German passport and her Argentine visa in her handbag. She wished now she'd put the SIG inside, too.

The two men passed through the gate and turned left. The compound fronted on Avenue Las Heras, a block away from the southwest boundary of Cementerio de la Recoleta. If Jo remembered her map correctly, they would have to turn right on Calle Azcuenaga to get to the cemetery.

She took her time getting to the consulate gate, paying attention to the idle conversation from her earpiece while trying to appear casual. The East German soldiers flanking the gate looked her over carefully, and she gave them her best smile. "Getting some fresh air," she said.

There they were, heading up Azcuenaga toward Recoleta. The street was well-lit, like most in Buenos Aires, and a number of people were strolling the sidewalks. Cars jostled for position on the street. Jo headed off in pursuit. Turning up Azcuenaga, she noticed that there seemed to be a number of young, heavily made-up women about. Ahead of her, she saw a man talking to one of them, and then the woman led him to a nearby doorway. Evidently she'd wandered into part of the red light district.

Schröder and Baumann reached the intersection with Calle Vicente Lopez, waited for the green light, and crossed the street. On the other side they turned right and crossed Azcuenaga. Jo ducked into a doorway, letting the shadows envelop her. The two men reached the other side of the street, where the high iron fence of the cemetery loomed. They turned left and began walking alongside the cemetery boundary.

"Hello," a voice next to her said. Jo turned, but the man was a stranger. Short and middle-aged, with breath that carried more than a hint of beer. "You're a nice-looking one. Haven't seen you around here."

"Excuse me," she said in Spanish. "I have to go."

"Wait a minute. You think you're too good for me?" The man put a pudgy hand on her right shoulder.

Jo didn't have time to be polite. She reached up with her left hand, grabbed the man's pinky finger, and twisted it up and over. The man gasped. A little more pressure and she felt tendons snap as the man went down on one knee. "*Santa Maria! Usted perra loca!*"

The signal in her ear was fading, and Jo moved quickly down the street to the intersection, thankful that the light was green, and ran across as nimbly as her heels would allow. At the far corner she jaywalked against the light, dodging cars with two other pedestrians, a young couple who'd had too much to drink. Schröder and Baumann had disappeared into the cemetery. When she got to the other side, she picked up the signal again.

The side gate was fifty yards up the street. As she walked briskly toward it, she thought ruefully that she was probably violating every rule of tradecraft that the patient instructors at the Monk had impressed upon her. She was tailing her targets but wasn't armed, had no backup, and wasn't exactly dressed to blend in with the crowd. Well, it couldn't be helped. She was formulating a cover story, just in case.

Jo came to the gate and let herself in. She seemed to recall hearing that the cemetery closed at six p.m., but someone had managed to leave this gate open. Probably not a coincidence.

A cobblestone path led into the cemetery, flanked by small trees and shrubbery. Noise from the street seemed more muted than it should have been, and the light from the streetlamps filtered through the leaves and around the mausoleums like dark yellow stains. Was it suddenly colder, as well? It had to be her imagination.

The path branched off into what she assumed was a grid pattern. Schröder and Baumann were still about seventy yards ahead, and she ducked into the shadow cast by the nearest monument. The men had slowed their pace.

"This is an impressive place," Schröder was saying.

"Recoleta is unlike any other cemetery in the world," Baumann said. "A writer once called Argentina a nation of 'cadaver cultists'. We celebrate the date of a person's death, not his birth."

"These crypts must cost a great deal of money."

"It is cheaper to live extravagantly all your life than it is to be buried in Recoleta, or so the saying goes," Baumann said. "Most of these mausoleums have several levels, extending underground. The most recently deceased occupies the ground level. See, this one here? The casket is before the altar. A child would be placed on the altar. When the next one in the family dies, this one will go underground. Many famous Argentines are here. Evita Perón is about a hundred meters that way." Jo saw Baumann gesture ahead and to their left.

"Indeed? I suppose Juan Perón's monument is enormous."

Baumann chuckled. "Not really. He's buried over in Chacarita, across town. A much less pretentious place. No,

Evita is here, in the Duarte family plot. You might find it interesting to know that her body was actually stolen once."

"What?" Jo could tell Schröder's astonishment was genuine.

"A general opposed to Perón, Aramburu, took the body to Italy and petitioned the Pope to have it kept in Milan, as a way to embarrass Perón's supporters."

"You must be joking, Herr Baumann."

The old man laughed. "I am serious. The Pope refused, and Evita was shipped off to Madrid, where Perón was in exile. Eventually she made it back here. Ah, our friend should be down this way." They turned left and disappeared around a corner. Jo crept gratefully out from the shadow. Gooseflesh had arisen on her arms and shoulders, and it wasn't just from the evening chill. Taking off her heels, she flitted barefoot down the path, ready to duck into cover if anybody appeared ahead of her. At the corner where the men had turned, she glanced around a mausoleum and saw them about fifty yards ahead, near a small plaza of some sort. Another man was sitting on a bench.

"Good evening again, Herr General," Baumann said.

"Gentlemen, what a wonderful place in which to meet," Maltov answered, also in German.

"Let's get down to business," Schröder said. "I don't want to keep my wife waiting."

"Certainly not, a beautiful woman like her in a room full of Argentines," Maltov said with a chuckle.

Jo worked her way closer, but avoided the path, stepping around headstones and hugging the sides of the enormous marble crypts. She got within about thirty yards of the men and dared go no further, but she was confident she couldn't possibly be spotted by them.

"Herr General, are you ready to move?" Baumann was asking Maltov.

"Yes," the Soviet general said. "When I receive the signal from Comrade Schröder, my men will take command of the installation's headquarters and turn it over to your people when they arrive."

"Can your men be trusted?" Baumann asked.

"They will think it is a drill," Maltov said. "I have brought none of them into my confidence. They are all Russians, the officers anyway." Jo thought back to the party. What had Maltov said, that he was Latvian? The Bund must have recruited him; he obviously was stationed at a critical installation in East Germany, probably a base that housed part of the Soviet tactical nuclear arsenal.

"When Oberst Koch's brigade arrives, the general's officers will all be arrested," Schröder said. "The general too, of course. A short time later, he will be separated from the rest and will be transported to Berlin."

"Your family?"

"They will be safe, Comrade Baumann. My son is attending your university in Dresden. I will be in contact with him when your people have the situation in hand. He will know what to do. My wife and daughter will be on holiday in Helsinki. They will be safe."

"Do they know what is to happen?" Schröder asked.

"Of course not," Maltov said. "But when I contact them, they will be told where to go. They'll be on the first available flight to Berlin."

"Herr Baumann, I trust your end of the operation here will be successful?" Schröder asked.

"We will be ready to execute CAPRICORN on the twenty-seventh," Baumann said. "I am authorized to tell you gentlemen that H-hour is 12 midnight Buenos Aires time. That will be three a.m. Greenwich Mean Time on the twenty-eighth. Four a.m. in Berlin."

"Six a.m. in Moscow," Maltov said. "It would be better if it could be earlier."

"The operation has to be carefully timed to avoid a launch during twilight," Baumann said. "The American spy satellites are not as efficient at night. The earliest we could launch the strike would be ten p.m. local time. Two hours' flight time to the target, I am told. It is as early as we can make it and ensure optimum security for the strike."

"Very well," Maltov said. "In any event, it will be several hours before Moscow gets a clear picture of what has happened. The same will be true for Washington."

"By noon that day, Germany will be in our hands," Schröder said. "Herr Baumann, what about Taurus?"

"I will be flying to Bariloche to meet with him on Tuesday," Baumann said. "I will be monitoring the operation with him from there. My son will be relaying information about CAPRICORN from his office in Buenos Aires. Reports from Germany will come directly to me."

"I look forward to meeting the Reichsleiter someday," Maltov said. "He must—"

"Code names only," Baumann hissed. "Even here."

Jo had heard enough. She had to get this tape to the American embassy as fast as possible. They must be nearing the end of their meeting; she had to beat Schröder back to the party. As quietly as possible, she began to wind her way toward the side gate of the cemetery, cutting across the grounds, avoiding the paths.

A few minutes later she emerged onto the path that paralleled the fence. She figured she had about a five minute head start on Schröder, and she could move faster than he could. The key would be staying out of his sight until she got back to the consulate.

The side gate was fifty feet away when a man stepped out of the shadows. Jo froze in place. The man took two steps into a pool of light from the street.

"A rather curious place to visit in the evening, Frau Schröder," Wilhelm Baumann said.

CHAPTER THIRTY-FIVE

Buenos Aires, Argentina

Saturday, April 24th, 1982

"Herr Baumann," Jo said, allowing herself to appear flustered. Now was the time to think fast. Cover story, stick to the cover story.

"I saw you leave the compound, and thought perhaps something was wrong."

She approached him. "Thank you for your concern, Herr Baumann."

"It's Willy, remember?"

She got closer. "My husband..." She brought a hand to her mouth, trying not to appear too melodramatic. "I am embarrassed to admit it, but I fear my husband has been seeing another woman."

"Oh?"

"Yes. There was someone else back in Berlin, and when I found out he swore he would remain faithful to me from now on. But here, in Buenos Aires, I...well, let's just say I had reason to believe he was not adhering to his word."

Baumann took a step closer to her. They were almost touching now, their voices barely above whispers. Jo had put her earpiece back into the recorder, so she didn't know whether or not Schröder was still talking with the other men, or whether he was heading back to the embassy. "I find it hard to believe that a man would betray a woman as beautiful as you," Baumann said.

She looked up at him. "I saw him leave the ballroom and thought he must be going to meet someone. I followed him here. Not the smartest thing in the world, I suppose."

"The city can be dangerous for women at night," Baumann said. "I must say, though, you seemed to handle yourself very well back there on the street, with that man who accosted you."

Jo gave him a nervous laugh. "Oh, that. I grew up in a rough neighborhood in Yerevan." She heard footsteps, back on the main pathway. The one she and Baumann were on, running alongside the perimeter fence, intersected with that path just before the gate. Schröder would walk right past them. They were about fifty feet away.

"You should really see Recoleta in the daylight," Baumann said. "At night it can be somewhat disconcerting, no?" He reached out and touched her shoulders. "You are chilled." His hands felt warm, but his grip was tightening. Jo felt she was about five seconds from a decision that might compromise her mission.

The footsteps—two sets—were getting closer. "My husband, he's coming," she said. She took Baumann by the elbow and pulled him out of the pool of streetlamp light. They would still be visible from the main path, but not clearly. Behind him, she saw two figures walking toward the gate. Reaching up quickly, she pulled Baumann's face to hers, bringing her lips to his.

Baumann brought his arms around her, pulling him closer to her. Jo could hear the footsteps passing them, the muttering of one of the men, a chuckle from the other. Then came the creak of the iron gate. She pulled away from the kiss, but remained enclosed in Baumann's arms. "Thank you, Willy," Jo said.

"Not at all," Baumann said. "May I escort you back to the consulate, Frau Schröder?"

"That would be kind of you, but I suppose that now you should call me Larisa."

When they emerged from the cemetery, Schröder and the elder Baumann were already a block away, across Vicente Lopez and heading down Azcuenaga. Jo knew she would never make it back to the consulate before Schröder, so she began working on a cover.

They were a block away from the consulate when Baumann broke the silence they'd held since leaving Recoleta. "I would not worry too much about your husband, Frau Schröder—Larisa."

"Why is that, Willy?" She was walking with her left hand in the crook of his right elbow, and she felt him tense ever so slightly.

"You impress me as a woman who can take care of herself."

Alarm bells started going off for Jo. "Oh, really?"

"Yes," he said. "Your willingness to follow him in a strange city, at night, and into a cemetery, of all places. Your obvious ability to defend yourself. There is more to you than you let on, I think."

She managed a laugh. "You overestimate me, Willy."

They were nearly to the embassy gate now. "Oh, I don't think so," Baumann said. "Before I take your leave this evening, I would like to ask you one question."

"And what is that?"

With the gate five meters ahead, he turned to face her. He reached up and touched her face. "Could you do an arithmetic problem for me?"

"A—what?"

The light was dim, but his eyes were steel. "Division, for instance. Anything at all."

Jo immediately locked onto something her German instructor had told her back at the Monk. Doing mathematical calculations in the foreign language is difficult. During the war, that's how the Germans would catch many of our people posing as native civilians. Learn one or two, just in case.

She smiled. *"Dreissig geteilt durch zehn ist drei."* Thirty divided by ten is three. "Would you like to hear it in Russian, or Armenian?"

Baumann's smile was wry and thin. He tilted her chin upward. "Very good, *liebchen*. Perhaps you are not as complex as I thought." He leaned forward and kissed her lips lightly. "It has been a pleasure getting to know you, Larisa. A pity you are leaving tomorrow."

"Yes, a pity," she said. "Good night, Willy." She left him and walked quickly to the consulate gate.

***

Jo didn't know whether she should be relieved or dismayed when they arrived back at their hotel suite. Fortunately, the handoff with the doorman went smoothly, and Jo assumed the microcassette was on its way to the American embassy. She would make a report to them in the morning, just to be sure. But spending another night here with Schröder didn't make her feel very comfortable. Well, she had just one more night with him. Tomorrow she would get the order to split up; they were scheduled be on the same flight to Madrid, but Marie had indicated neither would be making the flight. With any luck at all, she'd be flying back to the States, and Schröder would be facing whatever fate was in store for him.

"Excuse me while I use the bathroom," Schröder said as they entered their suite. He went off to his bedroom, while Jo took a seat on the couch, pulled off her wrap and slipped out of her shoes. She wasn't used to spending this much time in high heels. She was massaging her left foot when she heard the toilet flush and then Schröder emerged from his bedroom.

"Let me take that jacket off," Jo said, moving toward him. "You look uncomfortable. How about a neck rub?"

"Some other time, perhaps," Schröder said. He held out his left hand. "I'll save you the trouble. I believe this is the transmitter you must have planted earlier?"

Jo froze, three feet away. Recovering quickly, she said, "I don't know what you're talking about, Walter."

"You must not have been in this business very long, my dear. You're not a very good liar. A decent actress, though. Your performance with the man back at the cemetery was touching." Seeing her eyes widen a bit, he barked a laugh. "Your, ah, posterior wasn't quite out of the light. A man doesn't soon forget one like yours." He reached into his right jacket pocket and withdrew a handgun. "Please be so kind as to take a seat on the couch."

Jo deliberately avoided looking at the barrel of the gun as it pointed at her. "What's going on, Walter? We're supposed to be working together."

"Let's not play the game, shall we? Now, sit down. My associates will be here momentarily. I took the liberty of calling them from the phone in the lavatory. So bourgeois, a telephone in the loo, yet it came in handy. In retrospect, I should have informed them earlier about who you really are. A tactical error on my part, but one that I have rectified."

Jo knew now she had to act. Still three feet away, she took a cautious step forward, bringing her hands up toward her head. Schroeder brought the gun up, exactly the wrong thing to do. "Please, Walter, don't shoot me. Please! They told me to keep an eye on you, they—" Moving faster than Schröder's mind could comprehend, Jo slapped out with her right hand, knocking the gun aside, while bringing her left hand up to shield the near side of her face from the flash and powder burn. At the same moment, she lashed out with her right foot, catching Schroeder on the inside of his right knee. The gun fired, the bullet missing Jo's head by ten inches, as the German yelled in pain, his knee buckling, sending him off-balance.

He held onto the gun despite the pain. Jo leaped toward him and grabbed his gun hand with both of hers, bending the hand far to its right. Schröder swore as tendons popped in his wrist and Jo wrenched the weapon away. With a roar, the German launched himself at her, taking Jo by surprise with agility that belied his injuries. Schröder bulled into Jo, grabbing her around the waist with his left arm, driving her backwards.

Jo dropped the gun and let herself go with Schröder's momentum, pulling him forward and downward with a two-handed grip on his shirt front, and as she crashed to the carpeted floor, barely missing the sharp edge of the wooden coffee table, she brought both feet up and under the German, levering him up and over with her powerful legs. Schröder yelled as he sailed through the air, clearing the top of the couch and falling heavily to the floor with a strange cracking sound. Jo continued up and over, executing a perfect backward somersault, landing on her feet. She whirled and ran to Schröder, hands raised for another attack, but the German was lying motionless, his neck at an impossible angle. Jo reached down cautiously and felt for a pulse at the side of the broken neck. It was there, faint, and then a moment later it was gone.

She had to get out now and fought to remain calm. Larisa's clothing could stay behind, but she had to get her own gun and get to the embassy. Before she could move, though, the suite's main door opened. A tall, blond-haired man in an immaculate suit stood there, and when he saw Jo he quickly pulled a gun and stepped carefully into the room.

"Don't move, Fräulein," the man said. Another man came in behind him, then another. All had guns drawn.

Schröder's weapon lay on the floor, near the first man. He knelt down and picked it up.

"Who are you?" Jo asked in German.

"My name is Heinz Nagel," the blond man said. "Herr Schröder warned us there might be some difficulties with you. We were in the lobby. A shame we did not arrive a few minutes sooner." He glanced past her and shook his head. "Some very important people are going to be very disappointed with this news."

Jo tensed inwardly. If they were going to shoot her now, she would have to do what she could to save herself, despite the odds. This Nagel was no fool, though. He motioned with his gun. "Please don't attempt anything foolish, Frau Schröder, or whoever you really are. You have a choice: cooperate, or be shot now. Choose wisely."

***

"Well, Larisa, we meet again," Willy Baumann said.

The Siegfried Bund executive was sitting behind a plain desk in a small, sparsely-furnished office. Jo Ann stood before him, her wrists handcuffed behind her. Nagel stood off to the side, between her and the desk, and his two men were behind her, doubtless still with guns drawn. "I see you have changed into something a little more casual," Baumann said.

"I trust your flunky here was entertained," Jo said, glancing at Nagel. The Bund security officer had watched her closely, his gun at the ready, while she changed clothes in her hotel bedroom. With as much dignity as possible, Jo took off the gown, regretting her decision to wear one that had not required a bra, and put on a pair of loose slacks and a simple blouse. Nagel maintained his distance, never giving her an opening. The handcuffs were applied before they left the suite. There were still some things Jo could do despite this handicap, but not against three armed, well-trained men. She knew she had to let this play out a little further.

"You are a beautiful woman, but also a very dangerous one, as our late friend Herr Schröder discovered," Willy said. "Heinz took proper precautions. Now, we must put that aside and discuss your particular situation. I don't suppose you will cooperate by giving me your real name?"

"You're right about that."

Willy nodded, smiling grimly. "I thought not. Well, you are obviously not Larisa Schröder. That much we knew already, thanks to your 'husband'. We have had you under surveillance since your arrival in Buenos Aires. I must say, you have proven yourself to be a clever adversary. It wasn't until your meeting with the CIA agent at the Café de la Paix two days ago that we were able to make some progress. Oh, don't look so surprised. We are a nation at war. Don't you think we would have our enemy's people, and those of their biggest ally, under surveillance?"

Jo felt a sinking sensation in the pit of her stomach. She had worked so hard that day, all week in fact, at sticking to her legend as Larisa Schröder. The one meeting she'd had with someone from the embassy, and somehow she'd fouled it up. What had they told her back at the Monk? Even the best agents make mistakes. They're only human, after all. Recover as best you can and stick to your mission. In any event, they'd been following the CIA agent, not her. She saw

Baumann open a thin file on his desk. She could see a pair of photographs, and even upside-down she recognized herself.

"This file arrived here just a short time before you did," Willy said. He nodded at Nagel. "Heinz and his staff are very efficient. Still, it took two days after you were photographed at the café before they could finally identify you. Jo Ann Geary, newly promoted to major, United States Air Force. Obviously chosen for this assignment because of your resemblance to the unfortunate, newly-widowed Frau Schröder. Now, the only question is, Major Geary, why are you here in Buenos Aires?"

"I am an American citizen," Jo said defiantly, in English. "I demand to be allowed to call my embassy. You have no right to hold me. I've committed no crime here."

The Argentine switched to English as well. "The police might have a different opinion of that, once they find the body of your supposed husband," Willy said. "You are also in our country under false pretenses, traveling with a fake passport. I am sure that is in violation of one or two statutes." He looked at Nagel. "Did she have anything else incriminating?"

The security officer shook his head. "Only a handgun, plus the recording device in her handbag. The tape was missing. We searched her suite thoroughly. She must have passed it between the consulate and the hotel."

"I would venture to say that I know whose voices are on that tape," Willy said, eyes narrowed. "I blame myself, Heinz. When the good major here passed my little math quiz, I let her go on her way. I'm sure she had the tape on her person at that point." He sighed, sitting back in his chair. "A weakness of mine, Major, to be swayed by a beautiful woman. A weakness, you will find, that is not in the makeup of the next man who will interview you, should our discussion prove fruitless. Now, one last time: what was your mission in Argentina?"

Jo mustered up her inner strength. "*Gehen Sie zur Holle.*" Go to hell.

Willy shook his head. "Very well." He stood. "Heinz, we shall be taking Major Geary on a trip. I spoke with my father before your arrival. He instructed me to bring our guest to Bariloche if she were to prove uncooperative here."

Did the slightest trace of unease pass over Nagel? "I'll have the jet prepared," the security officer said stiffly.

"We will depart at 0800 hours. Make sure our guest is comfortably secure for the rest of the evening." Baumann looked back at Jo. "Tomorrow we will see how our American friend here fares with Taurus."

***

Pilcaniyeu, Argentina

Saturday, April 24th, 1982

Colonel Reinke checked his wristwatch for the fifth time in the past half-hour. Nearly midnight, and they were still on schedule. In another ten minutes, thank God, the infernal thing would be on its way.

The security chief stood on the platform in the assembly room of the research facility, watching the activity below. A white-suited man was cautiously directing a forklift as it approached a large, rectangular crate, resting on a wooden pallet. A company of hand-picked troops stood several meters away, surrounding the activity in the center of the large room. Their assault rifles were held at port arms. Reinke expected no trouble here, but the men had to maintain vigilance at all times. When they got outside, things might be different. Reinke would not put it past the English to attempt some sort of commando assault on the convoy, which was why the man standing next to him was here.

"My compliments on the efficiency of your men, Herr Oberst," Lieutenant Colonel Gerhard Schmidt said. The Werewolves commander was in full battle dress, camouflage fatigues and soft cap, which he would exchange for a helmet when he boarded his vehicle outside. One hundred of his troops were waiting for him.

"Thank you, Herr Oberstleutnant," Reinke replied. "I must confess that I am not at all reluctant to pass this responsibility over to you."

That drew a glance from Schmidt. "I understand completely, sir." Schmidt didn't reveal his true thoughts. He had been briefed on the defection of Reinke's subordinate, Gasparini. The Bund had not lost complete confidence in Reinke, but they had lost enough to assign Schmidt to take charge of the convoy that would carry the weapon to its destination.

The forklift operator, beads of sweat on his forehead, deftly maneuvered his machine and slid the tines into the pallet. At a signal from the white-suited scientist, the forklift engine revved up and the pallet carrying the crate which housed X-1 began to rise. When it was a meter above the floor, the operator stopped the lift and turned his steering wheel, swinging the load toward the back of the large truck that was parked several meters away. The rear gate of the truck was lowered, and soldiers stood on either side, watching the inbound cargo as the forklift inched its way toward the truck. Everyone in the room was tense. The scientists had assured him that nothing would happen should the crate be bumped or even dropped to the floor, but Reinke had his doubts about that. The sooner it was gone, the better.

Ten minutes later, Reinke sighed in relief as the loadmaster signaled that the cargo was successfully secured inside the vehicle. The soldiers locked the rear gate in place and fastened the burlap flaps to conceal the interior. Reinke nodded to the major standing next to him. "You may proceed, Haus," he said. He offered his hand. "Godspeed." Major Haus would be second to Schmidt on this mission. Reinke was pleased that he and his men had not been cut out of the operation entirely, but he was also glad that Schmidt's Werewolves, and their impressive array of armored vehicles, would be taking part. If X-1 ultimately was effectively used, it would be to the credit of the men and women who had constructed the device here, under Reinke's command.

The major gave his commanding officer's hand a quick, firm shake. "Thank you, Herr Oberst," he said, snapping to attention and saluting. "You can count on us."

"I know I can, Friedrich," Reinke said. He liked the young man, recently promoted after the unfortunate departure of the treacherous Italian, Gasparini. Haus was German, though. He would get the job done. "I want reports every hour on the hour until you reach your destination."

"I don't wish to disturb your sleep, Herr Oberst," Haus said.

"Don't worry about that. What's another sleepless night, eh?"

Five minutes later, the truck's diesel engine rumbled to life and the vehicle made its way slowly out of the room, through the large door and out into a light drizzling rain. Standing at the doorway, the sergeant who had hours before given the truck one more last inspection watched it roll away. He knew the vehicle would do its job, even though he had no idea how far it would have to travel with its special burden. Now, he would have to complete his own job. That might prove difficult to do, with the base still locked down, but he would have to find a way.

***

HMS Cambridge, *southwest Atlantic*

Saturday, April 24th, 1982

Ian took a moment to drink in the brilliant vista of stars overhead. Here in the southern hemisphere many constellations were different, but somehow the stars themselves seemed brighter, the panorama more awe-inspiring. He thought again of Jo Ann, somewhere in that dark and invisible land a few hundred miles to the west, and breathed yet another prayer. *Watch over her, please. I don't care what happens to me down here, but keep her safe.*

The ship was blacked out, all running lights extinguished, everything subdued on the bridge. Cambridge's CIC was manned around the clock as the ship stayed at general quarters. There had been no sign of enemy air or surface activity, but there was always the possibility—the likelihood, even—that a stray patrol aircraft would spot them and call in air or naval forces to investigate. Captain Stone had confessed to Ian that he was more concerned about Argentine submarines. Admiralty had been unable to pinpoint their location. They were probably not this far north, he was told. Probably.

Hodge joined his commander at the rail. "Latest word is that Ivan is still on our tail, about four miles back," he said, keeping his voice low, as if the Argentines might be able to hear him even at this distance.

"I'm wondering what that will mean when *Reliant* shows up," Ian said.

"Could be trouble, you think?"

"We'll have two capital ships virtually linked together during the transfer, with a possibly hostile warship within torpedo range," Ian said. "I rather think the captain will be somewhat reluctant to trust Ivan in that case."

"Might get dicey indeed, us challenging the Russian," Hodge said with a worried glance aft.

"Things tend to get dicey all around in wartime."

The men were silent for a minute, and then Hodge spoke again. "Well, anyway, I came to report that we're on station, right on schedule. Now we have to wait for *Reliant*. I have to say I'm not very happy about having to muck about out here for twenty-four hours."

"Nor am I, Stephen," Ian said. "We'll just have to treat the day as another day at sea. Keep the men busy, make sure they get fed and rested. *Reliant* will be here by this time tomorrow night and then things will get a bit more interesting."

"Let's hope so," Hodge said. He looked aft again, although they had no idea exactly where the Soviet submarine was lurking tonight. "Damn, I hope that Russian doesn't get too nosy."

"I agree. One problem at a time."

CHAPTER THIRTY-SIX

Rio Negro Province, Argentina

Sunday, April 25th, 1982

Jo Ann got her first glimpse of their destination from the air. The sleek, German-engineered jet came out of the clouds and banked to port over the city of Bariloche. The Andes rose majestically to the west, nearly blotting out the patch of morning sky visible from Jo's window. She felt the aircraft descend and then the landing gear came down, barely audible in the quiet of the main cabin.

She sat alone in a section of four seats, her left wrist handcuffed to a chain that was bolted to the floor, doubtless an aftermarket feature added by the jet's buyer. The chain allowed her enough maneuvering room to be able to sit comfortably and eat the breakfast that had been served, but not much else. When she asked to use the restroom, she was told she could do so only with the door open and under observation by an armed guard, so she decided to wait till they were on the ground, not that she thought it likely to bring more privacy.

The flight from Buenos Aires had lasted about two hours. Baumann told her their destination was about a thousand kilometers distant. Ever observant, Jo calculated that the cruising speed of the jet had to be around three hundred miles per hour, very impressive for a private aircraft. She filed that fact away. She'd have to get out of here somehow, and a jet would be the fastest way to get back to Buenos Aires, or better yet, over the border to Chile.

She was one of five passengers. Nagel was just as efficient as he'd been the night before, and perhaps a bit more apprehensive. Something was wrong here. He didn't like where they were going, or maybe it was who they were going to see. Two of his men were also along, the same pair who had helped him with her capture. Willy Baumann was the fourth, clearly the one in command. While the other men wore business suits, Baumann was more casually dressed, wearing a pair of riding boots, gray slacks, an open-necked white shirt and navy blue sport jacket. Completing the ensemble was a dark red silk cravat known as a *foulard*, an accessory favored by young Argentine men of means. That Baumann would deliberately choose to avoid an austere business suit told her something, confirming a feeling she sensed the night before at the consulate: this was a conflicted man, one part German, one part Argentine, and something inside him went back and forth between the two.

Jo had spent the night locked in a sparsely-furnished room in the Bund office building, sleeping on a cot, and in the morning was led to a bathroom where she was allowed to take a shower, all the while under the gaze of the Luger-toting Nagel. He displayed no emotion whatsoever as he watched her disrobe and bathe. Swallowing her pride, she went about her business quickly and dressed in the same clothes she'd worn from the hotel.

Ten minutes after flying over Bariloche, the jet touched down on an airstrip surrounded by the pampas, dotted here and there with clumps of trees. One of the guards, the one she'd heard called Hans, unfastened her handcuffs from the chain, then slapped the empty cuff around her right wrist. Luger at the ready, Nagel motioned her to the cabin door, preceded by Baumann and Hans. Two Mercedes sedans were waiting for them. Jo saw a cluster of buildings about a half-mile away, surrounded on three sides by trees, the mountains rising behind them in the distance.

The short ride in the car to the compound gave Jo another chance to collect her thoughts. Since her capture the night before, she'd fought hard to keep the fear at bay. It was logical to assume that the odds were against her being able to get out of this alive. She'd been in other threatening situations before, of course; Fonglan Island, most recently. The fear was always been a part of those, too. From the beginning of her special ops training, her instructors told her that fear was to be expected, even welcomed, to a certain extent. The agent without fear, they said, was an agent who was a fool, and foolish agents tended to wind up dead.

She'd always been able to control her fear, to channel its energy into proper caution, and she always came out alive. How many times, though, could she do that? Was it all just playing the odds, anyway? She'd known other operatives who were fatalistic about that. When your number's up, that's it, they'd say. Nothing you can do. She didn't really believe that. Her parents had taught her to believe in God, and as a teenager she'd become a Christian, so she was secure in her belief that eternal salvation would be hers. Still, she was afraid sometimes, and one of those times was now. Taking a deep breath, she steeled herself for whatever was to come.

***

HMS Cambridge, *Southwest Atlantic*

Sunday, April 25th, 1982

"You asked to see me, Captain?"

"Yes, Colonel, please sit down." Stone motioned Ian into the only empty chair in his cabin, which doubled as his personal office. The captain was starting to show the strain of the mission. Ian noted the bags under the man's eyes, and did his hair appear a bit more silver than it was a few months ago? "How are your men holding up?"

"They're impatient, of course, but ready to go, sir," Ian said. "Hodge and I are keeping them busy today."

"I wish we could provide better exercise facilities," the captain said. "In any event, this just came in and I felt you should be informed." He held up a communications flimsy. "Admiralty have given me permission to deal with the Russian at my discretion. I am not at all comfortable with a potentially hostile nuclear attack submarine being so close to me while I rendezvous with *Reliant* and transfer you and your men. Therefore, I intend to take action."

Ian felt a tightening in his chest. "I understand, sir. For what it's worth, I totally agree."

Stone gave him a nod. "I appreciate that, Colonel. Your mission is vital to the war effort. The Russian could cripple it with one torpedo at the wrong moment. We cannot be sure he will remain neutral. If, somehow, Moscow is aware of our mission, and they decide to intervene to support the Argentine strike against our fleet, this would be their best opportunity to engage us without widening the war. So, we must be proactive."

"What do you intend to do, sir?"

Stone glanced at the clock on his desk. "The scheduled rendezvous with *Reliant* is set for 2200 hours, with your transfer thirty minutes later. The weather looks good. I am expecting a radio contact from her at 2100. At that time I will inform her skipper of my intentions."

"May I ask, sir, do you plan to actively engage the Russian?"

Stone didn't answer for a moment, then said, "I will do what I can to convince him to withdraw without firing a shot. If, however, it appears he intends to shoot first, I will not hesitate to do whatever is necessary to defend this ship. I'll be honest with you, Colonel, it is liable to get very dicey indeed. You should prepare your men."

The SBS troops would all be assigned to damage control if the ship went into combat. While they all would've preferred to help with the fighting, their weapons wouldn't be much good against a submarine, so they'd do what they could to help. "I understand, sir. Will *Reliant* be assisting us?"

Stone nodded. "I trust that she will. Her skipper is Tom Bentley, an old friend of mine. We participated in an exercise against a French boat a few years ago. It worked then. Let's hope it works again tonight."

"Aye aye, sir."

***

Rio Negro Province, Argentina

Sunday, April 25th, 1982

There was a knock on the door, bringing Jo quickly out of her meditative calm. She got to her feet, noting by the clock on the night stand that she'd been meditating for nearly a half-hour. As always, the ritual had quieted her nerves, helped clear her mind of distractions, and refreshed her physically.

This building, the largest of the half-dozen that comprised the compound, seemed to be the main living quarters. She'd been led inside and locked up in what was obviously a guest bedroom. The only window was latched tight, and through it she saw a man armed with a submachine gun walking the grounds only a few yards away. She was sure an escape opportunity would come, but it wasn't here yet.

She heard the tumbling of the lock, and the door swung open. Willy Baumann stepped inside. "It is lunchtime," he said, using the traditional German word, *mittagessen*. "Our host requests us to join him."

"I'm not hungry."

"Come now, Major, we'll have none of this nonsense." A Luger appeared in his hand. "Shall we?"

The dining room was large, with walls of dark burnished wood. A heavy oak table dominated the room, with seating for ten. Places were set for four diners, one at the head of the table with its back to a large fireplace, one at the opposite end, and one on each side. A set of double doors were in the side wall across from Jo, who had followed Baumann into the room through this wall's single door. In one corner was a suit of armor, one hand gripping a double-bladed, long-handled axe. The wall opposite the fireplace held a portrait of a stern-looking man with a curled, white eighteenth-century wig, tri-cornered hat, and riveting eyes.

Jo knew that Heinz Nagel, Luger at the ready, was right behind her, close enough for a killing shot, far enough away to avoid any sudden attack from her hands or feet. Baumann had likewise kept his distance to her front. He saw Jo looking at the painting. "Recognize him, Major?"

"Friedrich *der Grosse*," Jo said. Frederick the Great. "King of Germany during the 1700s."

"*Sehr gut*, Fräulein Major," a deep voice said, and Jo turned to the double doors. A silver-haired, barrel-chested man stood in the open doorway. He was wearing a plain brown jacket, an open-collared white shirt, and charcoal slacks. "Actually, he was king of Prussia, from 1740 to 1786. A very cultured man, preferred to speak French, composed music. A great military leader. Many consider him the founder of the modern German state."

Baumann snapped to attention, heels clicking, and Jo heard Nagel's click behind her. Baumann bowed. "Herr Reichsleiter."

"Welcome to my estancia, Herr Baumann, Herr Nagel." The stocky man walked around the table and faced Jo. He wasn't much taller than her, but she immediately sensed an aura about him. The man radiated power and strength, almost a kind of sexuality. Jo steeled herself. "And this is Major Jo Ann Geary, United States Air Force. You have caused us no small amount of trouble, Major. Herr Schröder was an important part of our operation in the Fatherland. He will be difficult to replace on such short notice."

"That's too bad," Jo said.

"Please, sit down," Martin Bormann said, gesturing to the place at the end of the table. "We have much to discuss."

***

10 Downing Street, London

Sunday, April 25th, 1982

Margaret Thatcher considered the choices the men sitting before her had just outlined. "I do not care for any of these alternatives, gentlemen," she said. "Not at all."

The man in the army uniform was General Sir Terence Lewin, Chief of the Defense Staff. "In war, there are rarely pleasant alternatives, ma'am."

"I realize that, Sir Terence," she snapped. "Our best choice is for an Argentine withdrawal from the Falklands, but I don't suppose that is likely to happen."

"Not without a fight, I'm afraid." This was from the man to Lewin's right. Defense Secretary John Nott was trying

434

hard not to enjoy Thatcher's predicament. His country was, after all, at war, and she was its leader.

"There is the good news from South Georgia," said the third man, Admiral Sir Henry Leach, First Sea Lord. He had opened this meeting a half-hour ago with word that the Argentines had surrendered to his Royal Marines, hours after an enemy submarine, *Santa Fe*, was caught on the surface by a British helicopter and forced aground.

"Not enough, I fear," the prime minister said. "Galtieri will not take this defeat lightly. If he gives up the Falklands now, his government will fall." The men looked a bit nervous at that; everyone knew that if the British failed to retake the islands, Thatcher's own government might not survive. The difference was, if Thatcher were forced out, she wouldn't wind up facing a firing squad.

Lewin looked at Nott. "What of the MI6 effort?"

Nott cleared his throat. "C" was being his usual cagey self with this one, even though Nott was, strictly speaking, the man's superior. "I am told that Operation EMINENCE has hit a snag. The operative we sent to Buenos Aires was found dead in his hotel room this morning. The American agent who accompanied him as his wife is missing."

"We must assume the worst, then," Lewin said, turning back to Thatcher. "The enemy will launch the attack against our fleet, unless we strike him first."

"Mr. Nott, have you any indication of when they plan to attack?" Thatcher asked.

"Our source at their assembly facility reported today that the weapon has been moved out. Unfortunately, we don't know its destination, or their exact timetable."

"Probably an air base on the coast, or close to it," Lewin said. "I would estimate a launch within three or four days. By then our fleet will be at the exclusion zone, will it not, Sir Henry?"

"That is correct," the First Sea Lord said. He was clearly uncomfortable with the thought that his ships and sailors were so close to being atomized. "The enemy shall want to strike when the target is well away from the islands. I would say Thursday at the latest, probably sooner by a day or so."

"And what of your backup plan, GALAHAD?" Thatcher asked the admiral.

Leach looked at his watch. "The SBS platoon should be ready to transfer to *Reliant* in about six hours. They go ashore twenty-four hours later."

"That's cutting it quite close," Nott said.

"These things take time," Leach shot back. He decided not to say anything about the complication involving the Soviet submarine. Thatcher already knew, and had authorized Admiralty's cable to *Cambridge*, giving Stone a free hand to deal with the threat.

"Time is one commodity we do not possess in abundance," Thatcher said. "I should feel somewhat better, Sir Henry, if the SBS men were to be in position sooner."

"Our best intelligence indicates the strike won't be launched earlier than Tuesday night," the admiral said. "The men will need time to reconnoiter the area and select their positions. They obviously cannot move openly during the daylight. Going ashore Monday night gives them about eight hours of darkness to locate the target and evaluate the situation. Assuming they are successful in avoiding detection during the day Tuesday, they'll be ready to intercept the strike aircraft that night."

"And if the strike isn't to be launched until Wednesday night?" Thatcher asked.

"Then they wait another twenty-four hours. If there is no launch by 0600 hours Zulu Thursday, they are to make their way to the coast and rendezvous with *Reliant* for extraction. I shan't risk them any longer than that," the admiral said, anticipating the PM's next question. Nott asked it anyway.

"So if the Argentines wait until Thursday night, or if the SBS are discovered before then and are killed or captured, where are we?" Nott asked with a touch of sarcasm. He was tempted to ask how Leach could be sure the commandos would even find the right air base, but didn't.

"We are then left with a much more difficult situation," Lewin said. He turned to Thatcher. "Ma'am, time is of the essence, as you yourself stated. I recommend we initiate LION'S FURY."

Silence filled the room, except for the tapping of Thatcher's pen on the blotter of her desk. She sighed, and turned to Leach. "Admiral, is your vessel in position for this?"

"*Vanguard* will be on station within twelve hours, ma'am." HMS *Vanguard* was the newest Churchill-class submarine in the Royal Navy, and had been one of the first vessels deployed from Gibraltar after the fall of the Falklands. The boat's six torpedo tubes were designed to fire Mark 24 modified Tigerfish torpedoes. The forward tubes could also launch SUBROC weapons, which would exit the submerged boat as torpedoes and break the surface as guided missiles. The Royal Navy arsenal included versions of the American UUM-44 short-range weapon, modified to increase their range to 100 miles and to explode the warhead up to 500 feet above ground. Two such missiles were on board *Vanguard*, each armed with a twenty-kiloton nuclear warhead. Thatcher had agreed with Lewin's recommendation on that one. It was something she had not told President Reagan about, and she wasn't looking forward to that particular phone call.

The prime minister breathed in deeply. "Gentlemen, I ask for your help here. Is there any alternative to this choice? Any at all?"

Nott spoke first. "We must assume EMINENCE has failed. GALAHAD has a chance, but frankly I do not like the odds. Colonel Masters and his men are first-rate, but they will have to be lucky as well as good. Should they also fail, and should the enemy strike aircraft evade the fleet's combat air patrols..."

"We cannot take that chance," Lewin said. "We must strike first, ma'am. To lose the fleet would be a catastrophe of the first order. Then there would be the matter of what might happen in Germany."

"I'm aware of that, General," Thatcher shot back.

"And what are we doing about that?" Nott asked, unable to restrain himself.

"What do you suggest, Mr. Nott? That I should ring up Chancellor Schmidt in Bonn and pressure him into rounding up suspected insurrectionists? And just whom would you suggest he round up? We simply do not know enough about these rumors."

"There have been rumors like this for thirty years," Leach said dismissively. "The Germans. Always the Germans at the heart of the trouble." It was no secret that Leach was not fond of that particular NATO ally.

Thatcher pounded a fist on the table, startling the men. "I will *not* be the first person in the history of the world to launch a pre-emptive nuclear attack. It is simply out of the question. If Galtieri launches one, then history will forever blacken his name and that of his nation."

Leach sighed heavily. History would also record the deaths of thousands of British sailors at Galtieri's hands, and the crippling of a once-mighty nation. He sat up straighter, thrusting out his chin. "Then, at the very least, ma'am, strike the bastards after they hit us. One of *Vanguard*'s SUBROCs up Galtieri's arse should teach them a thing or two."

Thatcher looked at each of the three men. Without a word, she opened a drawer of her desk. Inside was her purse, and she opened with a flick of her wrist. From inside the purse she withdrew a card, inserted into a paper sleeve. On the sleeve was the royal coat of arms.

The Americans called their version of this card "the biscuit". Thatcher did not know whether the British had ever given their card a nickname. She suspected not. Officially it was the Prime Minister's Defense Information Card, a rather innocuous name, she thought now, because this card contained the specific codes that would enable her to launch a nuclear weapon from the British arsenal. Outside her office right now sat a Royal Army captain with a small suitcase at his feet. The Americans called their suitcase the "nuclear football". Inside the British case, like its American cousin, were detailed instructions for launching all manner of terrible weapons. Also inside were evacuation plans, updated for whatever city the prime minister happened to be in at the time. Thatcher had always thought that file might as well contain blank paper. Should the proverbial balloon go up, she doubted whether she would have time to do much more than sit down and give a few hasty orders before the first Soviet warhead exploded overhead.

"Admiral, what is the selected target?" she asked, barely above a whisper.

"The enemy naval base at Ushuaia, ma'am."

She took a deep breath. "You may begin your preparations, Admiral. May God help us all." Silently, she added a request for special help to Colonel Masters and his men. She had completely forgotten about the missing American agent.

CHAPTER THIRTY-SEVEN

Rio Negro province, Argentina

Sunday, April 25th, 1982

The guard was still outside her bedroom window when Jo Ann was escorted back and locked inside. Once, the man outside glanced in her direction, and their eyes met. She saw no sympathy, no curiosity, just discipline and attention to duty.

They were all like that here, even the man and woman who served their food during the meal. Jo was pretty sure they were native Argentines, but they didn't speak unless spoken to and were as efficient as well-oiled machines. As for the Germans...

Among her history classes at the Academy, Jo had taken a course on the history of Germany between the world wars. Just how could a rag tag, extremist political party led by a lunatic take control of a civilized nation? She found some answers in class, particularly when they had a guest lecturer who served as a major in the Waffen-SS. The man was in his

441

seventies but still a commanding presence, and he mesmerized the class. The Q&A session got heated as the cadets questioned their guest about Nazi policies. To her surprise, the man actually defended many aspects of the detestable regime, to the point where some of the young cadets nearly lost control of themselves. Others, however, spoke later about how persuasive the old *sturmbannführer* had been. Yes, the Germans got carried away with the concentration camps and all that, but they were well-organized, highly disciplined and had a hell of an air force. They were proud of their country and what's wrong with that? Plus they had cool uniforms. Some of the men nearly came to blows over it. As they found out later, this was exactly what their instructor wanted them to experience. "Now you have an idea of how seductive it was," he told them. "You gentlemen and ladies are well-educated, clear-thinking individuals, raised in a free and prosperous nation, and yet some of you were ready to start goose-stepping. Imagine how it was back then for the common, ordinary German, defeated in a war and then struggling to get through an economic depression, looking for anything that offered hope for the future."

Jo hadn't fallen under the spell of the old SS officer back then, but after spending just an hour in the company of Martin Bormann, she understood a lot better.

Bormann was a charming host, carrying the conversation and drawing in Baumann and Nagel, and eventually Jo Ann. They discussed literature, music, South American and European politics, and their respective estancias. To her surprise, Bormann spoke fluent English, something he said he'd learned since coming to Argentina, along with Spanish. He insisted they converse in English, for the benefit of their guest. It was all she could do to keep herself from coming under his spell, and now, she wondered whether she had truly succeeded in that.

They'd finished their meal and Jo was taken back to her room, without any word about what would happen next. She knew it was part of the game, trying to keep her off-balance. She wondered if they would've treated her differently if she were a man. Probably. More than once she'd caught Bormann looking at her with eyes that seemed to be undressing her. She remembered from her briefings that he had been considered quite a ladies' man, taking mistresses even with his wife's approval, so powerful was his influence.

Forcing herself to concentrate on her mission, she examined every inch of her room and its adjoining small bathroom, looking for anything that might help her escape. There wasn't much. Her bed was queen-sized, with a mattress and box spring and a wooden head board that had seen better days. A chest of drawers contained fresh clothing, nondescript white blouses and dark slacks, plain white cotton panties and even some brassieres. One glance told her the bras were too big, but they had underwiring. That fact might prove useful, and she filed it away. The bathroom cabinet contained towels and washcloths, extra toilet paper and soap. The medicine cabinet held a tube of toothpaste, but no toothbrush; she'd been told to request one when needed, and she would have to return it immediately afterward. No tweezers, no shaving materials, and of course no razor blades. She was used to shaving her legs every evening when she bathed, and she was irritated for a moment when she realized she'd have to forego that for a time. Then she angrily shoved that venal thought away. There were more important things to worry about.

What could she possibly use as a weapon? Well, she could stuff a wet washcloth down someone's throat, or squirt toothpaste in his eyes, but she doubted those tactics would take her very far. On her second sweep through the bathroom, though, she found something she'd missed the first time: a small paper box containing half a dozen Q-tips. An idea started to tickle the back of her mind. She took three of the Q-tips into the bedroom and slid them between the mattress and box spring of the bed.

It was four p.m. when the next knock came. Baumann unlocked the door and peeked inside carefully. "Major Geary? Am I disturbing you?"

Jo had been reading through one of the three German-language novels she'd found on the nightstand. "No."

The door opened wider and Baumann stepped into the room. "The Reichsleiter requests your presence in his library."

Jo's senses were on full alert as she was escorted to another part of the house. She thought this might be her only chance, yet something told her it was still too early. She decided to hear him out. She'd know when it was time to move.

With Nagel in the rear, Baumann led her to a set of double doors, knocked, and opened them. "Herr Reichsleiter, we have brought Major Geary."

"Please, show her in."

The library was lined on three walls by bookshelves overloaded with old volumes. On the far wall was a large fireplace, with flames dancing in the hearth. A statuette of a bull dominated the mantle. Bormann was sitting in a stuffed chair, a newspaper in his lap, wearing bifocals, which he quickly took off as he set the paper aside and stood. Jo knew she had to observe him, discern his strengths, his weaknesses. He was stocky and probably a powerful man in his day, but he was nearly eighty-two now and certainly couldn't move very quickly. All she would need was a split-second. And then what? A Luger bullet in her back, probably, but at least the mission would be accomplished.

Baumann discreetly took a position midway between the Reichsleiter and Jo. Taurus pushed himself out of the chair, knees cracking like gunshots. "Ach," he said, and gave Jo a sheepish grin. "It is truly hell to get old." He motioned to an empty chair about ten feet from his. "Please, Major Geary, sit down."

Jo could smell the rich leather of the chair, which seemed to mold itself to her as she settled in. A glance told her Nagel was just inside the doorway, Luger still pointed at her.

"Gentlemen, I would like a few minutes alone with our guest," Bormann said.

"Herr Reichsleiter—"

"It's all right, Herr Baumann," Bormann said as he sat back down. Another Luger appeared in his right hand. Jo had been watching him carefully, but didn't see the move. Wait, he'd had the newspaper in his lap. The gun must've been underneath. Still, quite good. He was not a man to be underestimated. "You may wait just outside the doorway. Don't close them all the way, if it makes you feel better." Baumann clicked his heels and left the room. Nagel followed, but left the doors about a foot open.

Bormann switched to English. "Now, Major Geary, I am told you are quite the expert in hand-to-hand combat. I would hate to shoot such a lovely woman, but rest assured I will if you make a threatening move." He waved the Luger in emphasis. "I'm sure you are quite fast, but you must know my bullet will be faster."

"What do you want?"

"On Wednesday morning, you will be flown back to Buenos Aires. My men will escort you to the American Embassy, and you will be allowed to go inside and make a report to your CIA superiors. I trust they will quickly forward my message to Washington."

Jo's heart started beating a little faster. Could it be possible that he was going to let her go? This had to be a trick somehow. "What message is that?"

"Quite simply, that the Republic of Germany wishes to have peaceful relations with the United States, and with all nations, but we will tolerate no interference in our internal affairs."

"Don't you mean the Federal Republic?"

Bormann smiled. "A slight change. By the time you get to your embassy, you see, the Federal Republic will no longer exist. Nor will the German Democratic Republic. The new Republic of Germany will be one united nation, under one flag, one government. A nation that will be prepared to defend itself against aggressors, from any direction."

Jo said nothing. Bormann waited a moment and then continued. "My decision to release you will be a sign of my good faith. We have no quarrel with the Americans."

"Just the British, this time," Jo said.

Bormann laughed, a deep chortle that sent a chill through her. "A means to an end. Of course, we speak of

Argentina's quarrel with the English. One way or another, that will be over quickly. I suspect that my good friend Leopoldo may have bitten off more than he can chew. Still, thanks to our help, he should prevail in this little dispute." He picked up a glass from the table next to his chair, took a sip of the clear liquid. "You know, the real enemy is Bolshevism. Communism, as you say today. We should have fought them together, us and you Americans."

"Oh, please."

Bormann slammed the glass down on the table, spilling some of the schnapps. "You think not? Even as we speak, your country has thousands of nuclear weapons targeted on the Soviet Union. The Bolsheviks have thousands of their own targeted on you. Twenty years ago you nearly went to war when that fool Kruschev sent missiles to Cuba. Cooler heads prevailed then, but what of the next time there is a provocation? All of that could have been avoided had your President Roosevelt simply been reasonable."

"Your government was a threat to the world. It had to be destroyed."

"We offered the world order! Discipline!" Bormann glared at her, his face reddening. "You have no idea how things were. There was chaos in the streets. Money was worthless. People were starving. We changed all that. We rebuilt a nation virtually overnight, Major. We became strong and proud again. The Führer was ready to lead the world in the battle against the real enemy, Russia."

Jo was surprised by how calm she was. Sitting not ten feet from her was a man who had been instrumental in one of history's most monstrous crimes, a man who could end her life in an instant, yet her ki was at peace. "Your Führer

447

was a madman. Six million Jews could testify to that, if they were still alive."

Jo expected that to bring a strong response, but Bormann seemed to calm down. He smiled, and took another sip from his drink. "Ah, yes, the precious Jews. It always comes back to them, doesn't it? You know, Major Geary, it amuses me to be lectured by an American. Your people, after all, enslaved Africans by the millions. How many, eh? Your country nearly tore itself apart over that. And your own Indians. How many did your people slaughter? Even today, your own native citizens rot on reservations, drinking themselves blind because they have no hope of becoming real Americans. And your Africans, can you honestly say they are equal to whites?"

"That's not a fair comparison—"

"History is written by the winners, Major. Is it not just a matter of perception? What of your own heritage? Part Korean, I understand. What about the Asians in your country? Equal? Your country brought Asians in by the thousands to build your railroads and didn't care whether they lived or died. When you fought the Japanese you rounded up all your own loyal citizens of Japanese descent and put them in concentration camps, did you not?"

That was too much for Jo. Her ki gave way to emotion. "None of them were led into gas chambers, you monster!"

"And I also find it interesting that your country can still lecture us Germans about what we did with our Jews forty years ago, when your own people today are allowed to kill their unborn children. Tell me, Major, how do you justify that, eh? How many millions of your own babies have your people murdered in the last nine years? In the name of what, convenience?"

Jo forced herself to calm down. "We could argue this for years and not change each other's minds. I would rather spend the next three days locked in that bedroom."

Bormann nodded. "I appreciate intellectual debate as much as the next man. Or woman," he said, with a gleam in his eye. "One last point about the Jews, though. Something I would like you to keep in mind, because unlike me, you are young enough that you will see this day dawn."

Still holding the Luger, Bormann rose and walked over to the fireplace. Jo saw him looking at a small photograph of what appeared to be some German soldiers. Bormann turned back to Jo, and his eyes were hard. "After the war you helped the Jews create their own nation, Israel. We all know what has happened since then. Four wars between the Jews and their Muslim neighbors. Tens of thousands dead. Now we understand that the Jews have nuclear weapons. The Muslims know this, and so they make overtures for peace. They still want to destroy the Jews, of course, but from now on they will try different means, more subtle. Not as direct as military action, not as swift. The Muslims know they cannot defeat the Jews in battle, because they know you Americans will back Israel, you will allow her to use the nuclear option if she is pushed too far. At the same time, you make friends with some of the Muslims, the ones who have the oil, because their oil, you want that very much. The Muslim leaders hoard their wealth and treat their people like serfs. Already we see how their resentment of America is building. Their hatred of Israel translates into hatred for America. They consider you one and the same." He wagged a finger at her. "Mark my words, Major, your country's blind support of the Jews will one day lead you into conflict with the Muslims, and that will be a very long and bloody conflict indeed, for there are a great many Muslims. They breed like rabbits and their priests teach them to kill the infidel. Are your people up to it? Will you have the discipline to prevail? I have my doubts. The Americans who fought us forty years ago, they could do it, they were tough and disciplined, but today's Americans? Tomorrow's? We shall see."

Taurus went back to his chair and tossed down the rest of the schnapps. "You may go now. I will make your visit here as comfortable as possible. You understand, of course, that I cannot allow you some privileges that my guests might normally have."

Jo stood up. "I'm not asking for any."

He looked at her, and Jo saw the eyes of a man who was quite sane, and quite dangerous. "Tomorrow morning we will talk again." He smiled, once more the charming host. "I hope that by the time you leave here, we shall have become, shall we say, better acquainted?"

"Don't count on it."

***

HMS Cambridge, *southwest Atlantic*

Sunday, April 25th, 1982

"I have the bogey, Captain!" Sonarman 1st Class David Sanders yelled with something akin to delight. Everyone in the CIC heard him.

"Very good, Mr. Sanders," Captain Stone said. "Are you sure it's the Russian?"

Sanders' fingers danced over his computer keyboard. On a monitor screen, jagged lines seemed to match. "Definitely, sir. It's our friend Ivan, all right." Soviet submarines had their own definitive sonar signatures, distinct from those of NATO submarines. Royal Navy computer technicians were working on software that would enable sonar operators to fine-tune their readings and identify individual signatures, once a database had been built up. Right now, though, Stone could be sure that this particular boat was the one which had shadowed him all this way south, and that was enough for him.

"Very good. Send his coordinates to the ASW station. Mr. Bender, you may begin your pursuit when ready."

"Aye aye, sir." Lieutenant Philip Bender was the ship's antisubmarine warfare officer, and would direct the engagement from his station. Stone, Bender and their counterparts on *Reliant* had already discussed the operation. "Helm, make your course 047. Mr. Fields, increase speed to one-third, please."

The destroyer and its companion submarine now began an intricate and hazardous dance. With the Russian boat's position pinpointed, the British vessels would attempt to outflank the target. Once in position, they would be ready to implement the next phase of the operation, something they hoped Ivan would not find to his liking.

Captain Mikhail Govanskiy of *K-251* was dining with Lieutenant Commander Nevsky in his quarters when there was a rapid knock on his cabin door. Before Govanskiy could give permission, the door opened and a man leaned inside. "I beg your pardon, Comrade Captain," Lieutenant Commander Boris Myshkin said. His eyes were shining.

"What is it, Boris?"

"The English vessels are both moving, sir. They have reversed course and are heading in our direction."

The captain wiped his lips with his napkin. He understood his executive officer's excitement, but he had played with the NATO navies more than a few times. "Indeed. What is their range?"

"Six kilometers and closing, sir."

Govanskiy set his napkin down on the table and took one last sip of his vodka. He noticed the political officer staring at him. "Well, comrades, it appears our Sunday evening will not be a dull one. Boris, bring the boat to general quarters, please. I'll be at the conn shortly."

"Yes, Comrade Captain." Myshkin nearly slammed to door behind him.

"What do you intend to do, Captain?" Nevsky asked.

"I will follow my orders, comrade," Govanskiy said, rising. "Moscow was quite specific. I am not to fire on the Englishmen unless fired upon."

"And if they shoot first?"

Govanskiy shot the man a glance he normally reserved for imbeciles and fresh-faced officers. Nevsky, he had long ago decided, qualified on both counts, although he made pleasant dinner conversation. "Then I shall sink them, of course. Would you care to join me in the control room?"

"The Russian is diving," Sanders said. "Passing one hundred meters."

452

"He's going for a thermal layer," Fields said. The ocean was not simply one vast container of water. It was layered, like a cake, with temperature variations, ranging from twenty-five degrees Celsius at the surface in the tropics to ten degrees a kilometer down. If a submarine could get underneath a layer of colder, denser water, into what was termed the "shadow zone", it could more easily hide from sonar searches. Provided, of course, the sonar doing the searching was above the layer, such as aboard a destroyer on the surface.

"*Reliant* is diving as well," Sanders said. "She is at 150 meters, staying below the Russian."

"Good man, Tom," Stone said. *Reliant*'s sonar, not having to go from warm water to colder, would be more effective at depth than *Cambridge*'s. "Active sonar, if you please, Mr. Sanders."

"Aye aye, sir!" Sanders punched a command into his panel, sending out a powerful pulse of sound toward the position of the Russian submarine at a speed of 1.6 kilometers per second. The men could hear the "ping", but that was a sound effect added by the computers for their benefit. The men on board the submarine would hear the real thing.

Almost immediately, Sanders yelled, "Got him!"

The sound reverberated throughout *K-251*. "Are we below the layer yet?" Govanskiy asked calmly.

"Not yet, Comrade Captain," his sonar officer said. "Another hundred meters, perhaps."

"And what of the English submarine?"

The sonarman swallowed. "I lost contact with her a few seconds ago, sir. I believe she is under the layer."

Govanskiy made a decision. "Diving officer, level off. Make your depth 175 meters. Helm, come to course 165."

"The destroyer has us pinpointed, Captain," Nevsky said nervously. At that moment, another ping echoed through the boat. "Will you not go below the layer to evade him?"

Govanskiy didn't look at the political officer. "That is where the English submarine is waiting, comrade, perhaps with a torpedo ready to fire at us. Sonar, what is the range to the destroyer?"

"Four kilometers and closing, sir. His course is 047 degrees." The English destroyer was sailing in a northeasterly direction, and the Soviet submarine was moving to the south-southeast. Within a very few minutes, their paths would cross, giving the Englishman a good opportunity to launch depth charges, if he was one of the few NATO destroyers that still used those weapons. More likely he would fire a torpedo. Govanskiy, however, would have a very poor angle from which to counterattack. Then there was the matter of the English submarine. Her last known position was five kilometers to the southwest of *K-251*. Then she had gone below the layer.

The Soviet captain realized that his position was quickly becoming untenable. He could evade a destroyer on the surface, something he had practiced many times, and he could also dance with an enemy submarine below. But both, at the same time?

Another loud ping sounded through the boat. Then another one, not quite as loud. "Comrade Captain," the sonarman said, "the English submarine has just pinged us."

"Do you have a fix on her position?" Govanskiy asked quickly.

"Yes, it—no, wait, she has dropped below the layer again," the sonarman said. "I had her briefly at three kilometers northwest of us, sir, off our starboard rear quarter." He wiped the sweat off his brow with one sleeve of his drenched uniform. The temperature in the boat seemed to have gone up in the past several minutes.

"This English sub captain, he is a smart one," Govanskiy said. "Comrades, a lesson: the English are very good sailors. They have been fine sailors for centuries." He looked at his XO. "Boris, what is your assessment of our tactical situation?"

"The English vessels have us boxed in, Comrade Captain," the XO said. "It would be prudent to withdraw."

"Withdraw! That would be cowardice!"

Nevsky's outburst drew a hard look from the captain. "It is not cowardice," Govanskiy said. "Comrade, I expect frankness from my officers. On a submarine, lives depend on it. We have no time for foolish games. Comrade Myshkin has quickly analyzed our situation and made a professional judgment. One I agree with," he said with a look at the XO. "The Englishmen could have fired on us by now had they wanted to."

"You can defeat them, Comrade Captain!"

"Perhaps, Comrade Nevsky," the captain said. "But that is not our mission, is it?" He looked around the control room at the tense, sweating sailors. They were all brave men, good men, and he had no doubt they would do their duty to the Soviet Union, but at this time their duty was not to die.

"Helm, come about to course 035. Maintain present speed. Diving master, maintain our depth at 175 meters."

"The Russian is changing course," Sanders said, his voice rising another notch. "Coming about to...035 degrees."

"Speed and depth?" Stone asked.

"Speed is unchanged, fifteen knots," Sanders said, looking at his screens as his fingers played the keyboard. "Depth remains 175 meters."

"He's withdrawing," Fields said. Several of the men in CIC visibly relaxed. Stone could hear one or two exhaling.

"Another ping, sir?"

"Negative, Mr. Bender," Stone said. "Ivan has gotten our message. He shall trouble us no further, I believe." The captain looked around the cramped room. "Well done, gentlemen. Sonar, keep me posted if the Russian deviates from his new course. I shall be on the bridge." He moved to the ladder but gave his XO one last order. "Take us to our rendezvous point, Mr. Fields. We have some anxious marines who want to get aboard *Reliant*."

"Aye aye, sir."

***

Willy Baumann watched the sun dip below the Andes. The chill he'd felt for the last few hours seemed to increase by a few degrees. Beside him, Heinz Nagel kicked at a pebble.

Willy looked back at the main house of the estancia, about a hundred meters away. Nobody else was in sight. "We have to move, Heinz," he said.

"When?"

"Soon. Before CAPRICORN."

Heinz looked at him with surprise. "You mean to abort the attack?"

Willy nodded. "Yes. Bormann is mad, but he is clever. I fear that if we allow the attack to proceed, events may spin out of our control. We cannot be sure the pilot will follow our orders and deliberately miss the target. We may be unable to prevent VALKYRIE. I have a very bad feeling about this, Heinz."

His friend sighed. "Without CAPRICORN, we have no chance to move on Galtieri, you know."

"There are things more important, Heinz. Our honor, for one thing."

"If the English fleet isn't destroyed, they will retake the Malvinas. Our navy is a joke. Our troops cannot stop them, even if we sent the Werewolves."

Willy shook his head. "I know. Galtieri's government will fall. Perhaps we will have an opportunity then. But at least then we will not be forever stained because we used the weapon. We will live, and so will our nation, Heinz. Argentina will live."

The SD man was silent for a moment. "Very well. Tomorrow, then. I shall take the first opportunity—"

"No, my friend," Willy said, looking at him, his eyes hard. "I will do it. Tomorrow morning, when we bring the American to him."

Heinz nodded. "Then we will have to move against the Kamaraden. They can still launch the attack, even without the Reichsleiter. Your father—"

"I will deal with my father." Willy took a deep breath and looked back at the mountains. "We should get back, get some sleep, my friend. Tomorrow will be a long day."

CHAPTER THIRTY-EIGHT

Rio Negro province, Argentina

Monday, April 27th, 1982

The dining room was empty when Willy entered on the dot of eight o'clock for breakfast. There was only one place setting at the table. Where was Heinz? Willy had knocked at the door of his friend's room, but after getting no response, assumed Heinz had gone ahead. For that matter, where was Bormann?

The opposite doors opened and two house staff members came in, carrying trays of food, one with steaming eggs and sausage, the other with fresh fruit. The butler followed them in, keeping an eye on the two women as they served. "Where is Herr Nagel?" Willy asked the butler.

"I don't know, Herr Baumann," the man said in flawless German.

"Well, then, where is the Reichsleiter?"

The butler's eyes flicked away for a moment. "The Reichsleiter has already eaten, sir. He asked me to have you join him in the library when you finish your breakfast. He will be there in half an hour."

Something was very wrong here. The house was quiet, as usual. The servants on Argentine estancias were always properly courteous, of course, but usually they were friendly and went about their work in a way that was pleasant as well as efficient. Things were different here. The service was meticulous, but Willy sensed no joy here, no happiness. The mood among the staff was as dark as the wood in Bormann's library. Willy wondered if the stories were true: servants who wanted to leave Bormann's employ could only do so under threat of death if they ever divulged his identity. Was it any wonder that these servants seemed older than most?

He ate his breakfast quickly and returned to his room to rinse out his mouth, then checked Heinz again. No answer to his knock this time, either, and the door was locked. Down the hall, Willy saw a large man standing guard outside the American's room. That, too, was different.

Precisely at eight-thirty, Willy knocked at the door of Bormann's library. "Come in."

Bormann was standing at the hearth, gazing at the old photograph of German soldiers in Paris. "Good morning, Herr Baumann," he said.

"Good morning, Herr Reichsleiter. You asked to see me?"

"Yes." Bormann made no motion toward a chair, but simply turned and faced Willy. "You have inquired after Herr Nagel, yes?"

"He wasn't at breakfast, and he doesn't appear to be in his room."

Bormann's eyes seemed to bore into him. "He is no longer at the estancia. I had him arrested earlier this morning. He is being held at a...secure location."

"What!"

Bormann took two steps forward until he was nearly at arm's length. Even though he was shorter than Willy, his presence was still commanding. "You are a fine young man, Herr Baumann, but you are still young. So is your friend. Did you think you could conspire against me? Hm?"

A ball of coldness formed in the pit of Willy's stomach. "Herr Reichsleiter, I—"

"Save your words," Bormann interrupted. His menacing gray eyes narrowed. "You little welp, you thought you could intrigue against us. We are the masters of intrigue, my young friend. We mastered it fifty years ago. We know all about your little plan to disrupt CAPRICORN. We know you intended to inform the Americans and the Russians about VALKYRIE. Did you honestly believe you could so easily stop an operation that has been running for a quarter of a century? Did you?"

Willy fought to get past the dread. "We want only what is best for our country."

"For Argentina? A beautiful land that is constantly endangered by the stupidity of the Spaniards and Italians? A land that would have been under the Brazilian and Chilean flags years ago were it not for the Germans who live here? That Argentina?"

Willy said nothing. Bormann turned and walked back to the hearth. "Germany is your true fatherland. What is best for Germany is to be united and strong once again. Not divided. One-third under the heel of the Bolsheviks, a drab and colorless place. Two-thirds given over to the decadent West. The people are lazy and undisciplined. They allow the Turks and other vermin into the country to do the work. Germany needs order and discipline, and we will give it back to them. It needs vision, and we will provide that, too. Germany will fulfill her destiny to be master of Europe!"

Willy felt the tendrils of fear reaching around his heart, but he summoned his courage. "Heinz and I are Argentines first, Herr Reichsleiter. We want what is best for *our* country. Do we want to be a vassal of a new Nazi Germany? Do we want to be forever known as the nation that started World War Three? Do we want our streets to be patrolled by American soldiers after our inevitable defeat?"

Bormann looked back at him, eyes glinting, a thin smile creasing his face. "Be careful, my proud young friend. Only my friendship with your father has kept me from having you shot."

Willy had left his sidearm in his room, but he could still rush Bormann and kill him with his bare hands, end this madness once and for—

The double doors behind him creaked, and he felt the snout of a pistol poking the small of his back. Bormann was still smiling. "As you can see, Herr Baumann, I am once again a step ahead of you." He shifted his gaze to the man behind Willy. "Fritz, escort Herr Baumann back to his room. He is to remain there until I send for him again. Then bring the American to me."

"Jawohl, Herr Reichsleiter!"

Jo had made up her mind that she had to escape. After eating breakfast in her room alone, she went through a half hour of yoga and taekwondo forms. A shower and change of clothes refreshed her, and she forced herself to meditate, in order to bring her adrenalin levels down and think clearly about her options. Some time later, a rapping on the door interrupted her. Quickly coming around, Jo felt energized. She reached under her mattress and found what she'd hidden there the previous night.

Jo's first option was to overpower the guards who would come to get her for her next meeting with Bormann. She scratched that, though, when she found two men waiting for her as the door opened, both armed with Lugers. One she could handle, perhaps two, even in close confines like the bedroom or the hallway, but these men were well-trained and professional. They gave her no openings, and she moved on to her second option as she was escorted to the library.

The lead guard, the one she'd heard called Fritz, knocked at the closed library doors. "Enter!"

Bormann was standing near a side table, a telephone in hand. He waved them inside. Jo noticed the Luger on the table next to the phone. "That is my decision," Bormann said into the phone, his eyes flicking back and forth between Jo and the guards. He was sizing her up again. As old as he was, he knew what he was doing. Once more, she had to warn herself against underestimating the man.

"Yes, that is correct," Bormann said. "Code Red, zero-two-hundred. I will explain when you arrive, Dieter. Sieg heil!" The handpiece clattered back into its cradle. "Ah, good morning, Major Geary." Jo was amazed at how easily Bormann was able to shift from stern commandant to cordial host. Everything she learned about him gave her a deeper understanding of his power, and how dangerous he truly was. Subconsciously, she ordered her nerve endings to search for the small item she'd hidden in the sock on her left foot. Yes, still there.

Bormann left the table and walked to the hearth, leaving the Luger. "Fritz, leave Jürgen here with the major. I would like you to inform Armando that all incoming telephone calls are to be routed to me. There are to be no outgoing calls without my permission."

"Jawohl, Herr Reichsleiter." Fritz hustled out of the room. Bormann motioned Jo to a chair. Jürgen, the other guard, kept his position, standing just inside the double doors. A quick glance told Jo that he held his weapon ready. Automatically, she measured the distance and angles between herself and the two targets. Jürgen first, then Bormann, because it would take him a moment to get his gun, and by then she'd have the guard's. Or she'd be dead.

"I have decided to send you back to your people a day earlier than originally planned," Bormann said. "You will be flown to Buenos Aires tomorrow morning."

Jo quickly put that together with the end of Bormann's phone call: The attack had been moved up. "Change of plans?"

Bormann only smiled. "Nothing of your concern, my dear."

"What are we going to discuss today?" Jo asked with a false pleasantness. "Your racial theories again?"

Bormann chuckled. He moved over to a bookcase and selected a volume. "You know, the Führer was a great believer in the racial superiority of the Aryan. He decreed that the Aryan depicted in our official artwork be tall and broad-shouldered, blonde and vigorous."

"Even though he himself was short, dark-haired and not exactly athletic," Jo said with a hint of sarcasm.

Bormann roared with laughter. "You are exactly correct, my dear major," he said finally. "Which is one reason why I never believed any of it. It was all so much *Pferdscheiss.*"

Jo sensed a slight movement from Jürgen, standing seven feet away to her left at the doors. A quick glance and she saw the startled expression on his face. "But you gave it lip service," Jo said.

"Of course! It was merely a means to an end, and the end was political power. Your politicians do the same thing. They tell the people what they want to hear in order to get elected. Mind you, I truly do believe that there is something in the German character that sets us apart. A sense of discipline that is rarely seen among other peoples. A product of our culture, our history, no doubt. Take young Jürgen, here," he said, gesturing toward the guard. "His father came here after the war. Your mother, she was born here, was she not?"

"Yes, Herr Reichsleiter," Jurgen said proudly. "Her parents came here from the Fatherland in 1921, after the first war."

"And so we see a native German, for all intents and purposes, who was born Argentine," Bormann continued. "A perfect illustration of my point. Even though he was born in this land of mongrelized peoples, Jürgen could walk the streets of Berlin or Frankfurt and pass easily for a native. You enjoyed Germany on your visit, did you not, Jürgen?"

David J. Tindell

"Immensely, Herr Reichsleiter," the guard said, his chest expanding. Jo glanced at Bormann. She wanted the old windbag to keep talking, as she crossed her left leg over her right. She casually reached down and scratched her left shin. In her peripheral vision, she noticed Jürgen glancing at her as he caught the movement, and his Luger came back up and pointed at her. She didn't take her eyes off Bormann as she moved her hand back to her lap. Jürgen relaxed again and the gun moved slightly away.

"So while our dear departed Führer expounded on his racial theories, I would handle the politics," Bormann said. "That is not to say he was a wild-eyed radical. No, in fact, he was very shrewd, he had a native intelligence that many underestimated, to their eternal regret." Bormann lectured on, replacing the book on shelf and peering at the other volumes. Jo risked a more direct glance at Jürgen. He was listening to Bormann intently, his Luger pointing away from her now, held lightly. She looked back at Bormann. He'd selected another book. "Now this one, I really recommend to you..."

Jo moved her right hand down her left leg, reached two fingers inside her sock, and found the sharp wooden point of the dart. She pulled it from the sock, hoping the feathers wouldn't come off. They didn't, held tightly in place by the wire she'd taken from a bra in her dresser and wound around the makeshift weapon. The three Q-tips, their cotton swabs removed on one end, provided the shaft that held the wooden needle, which she'd laboriously pried out of the headboard of her bed. The feathers from her pillow would provide just enough aerodynamic guidance.

Even if Jürgen had been looking directly at her, his eyes would not have been able to follow the movement of her hand. Still, he had seen something, and was pulling his attention away from Bormann, and something happened, but before he could react he felt a sharp pain in his throat. Crying out, he reflexively squeezed the trigger of his Luger and the gun discharged with a flat crack. The sculpted bull on the mantelpiece exploded.

Jo was moving before he pulled the trigger. She uncoiled from the chair and launched herself at the guard. She lashed out with her right foot in a knife kick, catching him on the wrist of his gun hand, smashing the delicate bones and sending the gun flying. Landing on her feet, she kept moving, spinning clockwise. Twirling on the ball of her left foot, Jo unleashed a turning side kick with all her force, catching Jürgen in the right ribcage. Her loud kiap yell almost drowned out the sound of ribs cracking and Jürgen's own shriek of pain. The guard crashed back into the library doors, but they held, and he slumped to the floor.

The guard was down but not out. He'd keep for a moment. She heard a roaring yell from behind her, and before she could move two brown-jacketed arms gripped her like a vise, pinning her upper arms to her side. "Fritz! *Kommen sie hier! Macht schnell!*" Bormann screamed. His strength was surprising, and he started to lift her. Jo knew she had to stay on the ground. She sucked in a deep breath and then exhaled sharply and bent forward, thrusting out her elbows to loosen his grip. She pistoned one elbow backward and then the other, connecting with Bormann's abdomen. Did a rib crack? She heard him grunt and felt his hot breath on her neck. Sliding to the floor through his weakened arms, she pushed him backward with her shoulders, propped herself with her hands, and shot her legs overhead and backward, catching Bormann squarely in his massive chest.

There were footsteps running down the hallway now, a man shouting. Bormann staggered back to the fireplace, his shoes crunching on the shards of the bull. He steadied himself with one hand by grabbing the mantle and holding on. Jo rolled to her feet and saw Jürgen's pistol on the floor. She dove for it, and when she rolled to her feet again, the Luger was in her hand and pointed directly at Bormann.

The Reichsleiter's knees were buckling, and his face was a dark gray. He gasped for breath, one hand clutching the mantle, the other pounding at his chest, trying to tear open the jacket. His eyes bulged as he looked at her, then at the fallen guard, then at the photo of the soldiers. "My—heart—" Jo fired once, twice, the rounds catching Bormann square in the chest.

"Herr Reichsleiter!" Someone was pounding on the doors from the hallway. The door handle moved and one door tried to move inward, but Jürgen was in the way. There were more steps in the hallway, more shouting in German.

Willy was pacing his bedroom when he heard the muffled sound of what had to be a gunshot, then shouting and a thudding crash. Instinctively he knew that the American was making a break for it. He went to his door, turned the knob—unlocked—and pulled the door open. The man standing guard outside was looking down the hallway toward the library, his face concerned, one hand on the holstered weapon at his hip. Willy slugged him in the stomach with everything he had, doubling the man up. Grabbing the Luger from the holster, Willy cracked the butt of the handle down on the back of the guard's head and ran for the library.

Fritz was pounding on the door, his gun in the other hand, yelling for the Reichsleiter. "Get away from the door!" Willy shouted. Fritz turned, brought up the Luger and squeezed off a shot just as Willy fired. He felt a searing pain in his leg as he watched Fritz spin around and fall to the floor, hit in the right shoulder.

Willy's leg burned like fire. He looked down and saw a ragged hole and rapidly spreading dark stain on his left thigh. He tried putting some weight on it, gasped from the pain, but concluded the bone wasn't broken. Lurching against the library door, he pushed it open with difficulty.

The Reichsleiter was slumping to the floor in front of the hearth, the American crouching a few feet away with a smoking Luger aimed at Bormann, then swinging quickly to take a bead on Willy. "Don't shoot," Willy said, panting.

"Drop the gun," Jo said.

"I—I am on your side," Willy said, tossing his Luger to the floor. "The Reichsleiter..."

"He was having a heart attack. I helped it along." Bormann's chest heaved once, twice, then stilled. His eyes were still bulging open, mouth slack. Willy limped into the room, stepping over a white-faced Jürgen, who was clutching at his throat. Blood was seeping through his fingers, his eyes were rolling back, and then he took one rattling breath and lay motionless. A large pool of blood was underneath him.

"*Gott in Himmel,*" Willy breathed. He had never seen a man die before, not even in the Army. He looked back at Jo. The American was carefully reaching down to Bormann's neck, her other hand pointing the Luger at the Reichsleiter's forehead. She felt for a pulse.

"He's dead," she said, standing up. A glance at Jürgen told her she'd hit his carotid artery. She'd killed two men in the space of a minute or two. That would be something she'd have to deal with later. "How many more guards are there?"

"At least three," Willy said. "Someone will come soon to investigate."

She looked at his leg. "You're hit," she said. "We've got to get that bandaged or you'll bleed to death." Willy slumped into a chair, pressing down on the wound. The butler's face appeared in the open doorway, peering around the closed door, eyes wide. "Are you Armando?" Jo asked in Spanish.

"Si, señora," the man said, his voice shaking as he took in the bodies on the floor. His eyes lingered on Bormann.

"Get a first-aid kit," Jo ordered. "If any more guards come to the house, tell them nothing's wrong. Hurry!" The frightened butler disappeared down the hallway, shouting for one of the maids.

"The guards will come here eventually," Willy gasped, as Jo looked at the wound.

"I know, but that'll buy us some time," she said. "Do you have a knife?"

Willy shook his head. Sweat was beading on his forehead. The pain, surprisingly, had quieted down into a dull, persistent throb. "On the bookshelf, over there," he said, gesturing with his head.

A ceremonial SS dagger sat inside a case on one of the shelves. Jo pried the case open, unsheathed the weapon and used it to cut away part of Willy's trouser leg, exposing the wound. She probed the underside of his thigh. "It didn't go through," she said. "The bullet's still inside."

Willy nodded. Footsteps clattering in the hallway brought Jo's weapon up, startling a middle-aged maid as she appeared in the doorway holding a white metal box with a red cross on the lid. "Thank you, señora," Jo said, putting the Luger aside as she gestured for the maid to come in.

Jo quickly field-dressed the wound as best as she could. "That'll keep for a while," she said, "but we have to get you to a hospital."

Willy shook his head. "Too risky," he said. He had felt himself going into shock, but Jo's treatment settled him down. "Bormann has men everywhere. We—we have to get out, somehow."

"I overheard him talking to someone on the phone, someone named Dieter," she said. "Would that be your father?"

"Probably. What did Bormann say?"

"I only heard the end of it. 'Code red, zero-two-hundred.' He said he'd explain it to Dieter when he arrived."

Willy's eyes widened. "My father is on the way here, then," he said, "to monitor the attack. Bormann must have moved up the launch time."

"Moved it up?"

The Argentine nodded as he struggled to stand. "It was to launch tomorrow night at ten p.m. If he said 'zero-two-hundred', that must mean he has moved it up to 0200 hours tomorrow morning."

"That explains why he wanted to send me to Buenos Aires a day early," she said. "What about the 'code red'?"

Willy tried putting weight on the wounded leg. It held, but the pain pounded against him. He had to hold onto the back of the chair. "An alternate launch plan," he said. "They will move the weapon to a secondary base and the plane will take off from there. Just one aircraft. The rest of the strike force will launch from the original base, as a decoy."

Jo looked at the clock on the wall. Nearly nine-thirty, less than seventeen hours before the attack. Somehow she had to get the information to CIA or SIS. She rapidly ran through the few contact procedures she'd been given in the event she'd have to leave Buenos Aires. Jo reached for the telephone but when she dialed O, she got another dial tone. "Only Bormann can make long distance calls from here," Willy said. "He has a code number that has to be dialed first."

"Is there a British consulate in Bariloche? An American consulate?"

Willy shook his head. "We can take a car across the border to Chile," he said. "You can contact your people from there."

"How far to the border from here?"

"At least an hour by car, I think, probably closer to two."

This time it was Jo who shook her head. "They'll get us before we can cross. Is your jet still here?"

"Yes, it is. We can order the pilot to take us anywhere."

"Too risky," she said. "He could fly us right into a trap, or right into the ground."

"What, then? I'm certainly no pilot," Willy said.

"I am," Jo said. "Let's go."

CHAPTER THIRTY-NINE

Rio Negro province, Argentina

Monday, April 26th, 1982

Jo Ann stepped out of the library, sweeping the hallway with the Luger. At the far end a man was walking quickly in her direction. She recognized him as the guard who'd been patrolling the grounds outside her window. "Stop there or I'll shoot," she said. The guard, caught by surprise, stopped in mid-stride and held up his hands. "Baumann, tie him up. Use his belt, and make sure to take his gun." Willy hobbled down the hallway and quickly subdued the grim-faced man, pinning his wrists behind him with his narrow belt. He took the man's Luger and put it in a pocket of his own jacket.

"How many more of the Reichsleiter's men are outside?" Willy asked him.

"I will tell you nothing."

"Sure you will," Jo said. She aimed the Luger and fired, hitting the floor inches from the man's shoulder, sending up

473

a spray of splinters. The man yelled in pain as two shards caught him in the side of his face. "Now, answer the man's question."

"Just one more," the man said, gasping. "He's outside, at the motor pool. I told him I would come in to investigate the noise."

A trembling Armando was at the end of the hallway. "I am sorry, señora, but he insisted on coming—"

"Never mind," Jo said. "Go to the back door and call for help. That will bring the other guard." As they followed the butler, Jo asked Willy, "What about the two men who came here with us?"

"They are staying in guest quarters near the hangar, at the airstrip."

"Can they be trusted?"

"They have worked for me for years. I'm sure of it."

"Well, I'm not," Jo said with a wary look. "They stay here, along with the pilot and co-pilot."

"You can fly the Blitz?"

"We're about to find out, aren't we?"

The lone remaining guard was suspicious, brushing past Armando with gun drawn, but when he saw Baumann limping toward him and rushed to help, Jo got the drop on him from behind. In a few minutes she was at the wheel of a Mercedes they found in the garage. She slowed down when they were within a hundred meters of the hangar.

"I don't suppose this place has an armory of any kind," Jo said.

"Why? We are armed. It's only a few minutes across the border into Chile. I presume that's where you intend to go."

"Actually, no," Jo said. "We're heading east, to Buenos Aires, but in case we have to set down elsewhere, we might need to have something a little heavier than these Lugers."

"I don't understand. We can be in Chilean airspace in minutes."

She glanced at him, leaving no doubt as to her determination. "I have to warn the British fleet somehow about the air strike. I don't know what I'll be dealing with if we go to Chile. If we head east, toward the Atlantic, I can get a message out over the jet's radio. If you have a problem with that, now's the time to say so."

Baumann swallowed hard. "No. We have to stop the strike."

"Good. Now, back to my question."

Willy waved toward a side door near the rear of the hangar. "I think there might be something in there that could help us."

Jo pulled the Mercedes to a stop near the door, which mercifully proved to be unlocked. Inside, a small room contained a variety of Soviet, European and American-made assault rifles, plus one surprised man, who recognized Baumann. "Herr Oberst, what is going on?" His eyes quickly shifted to the business end of Jo's pistol.

"Do not ask questions, Hans," Willy said. "Keep your hands in the air, please."

A minute later, they came out with a pair of M-16s, three clips of ammunition apiece, and a bonus: a pair of Bundeswehr-issue field radios. Jo's instinct told her to take them along, just in case. They left Hans on the floor of the armory, tied with his belt. It wouldn't hold him too long, but by then they should be in the air.

They walked another fifty meters to the side door of the main hangar, Baumann struggling with his throbbing leg. "We should've disabled the telephone line at the house," Jo said, angry at herself.

"It would make no difference," Willy told her. "Bormann has a short-wave radio transceiver somewhere in the house. It's what he would use to communicate in the event the phone lines were down."

"He thought of everything, didn't he?"

"Let us hope not."

They entered a side door unopposed. Inside the large hangar, Jo counted three aircraft, two small prop planes and the larger, sleek white jet. Two mechanics were working on an open side panel.

"We have to get moving," Jo said. "The servants will free those guards as soon as they see us take off."

"It is best to be assertive, then," Willy said. He hobbled toward the mechanics, Jo following, her gun hidden behind her. "Say there! Is there something wrong?"

"No, Herr Oberst," one of the men said, wiping his hands on a greasy rag. "Just routine maintenance."

"She is ready to fly, then?"

"Of course. We refueled the aircraft after you landed yesterday, per standard procedure." The man saw Baumann's bloodied pants leg. "What is going on?"

"We're taking the aircraft," Jo said, pointing the Luger. "Stand aside. One of you, open the hangar door."

"What is the meaning of this, Herr Oberst?" the older mechanic said, eyes narrowing.

"Do as the lady says."

The older man backed away, while the younger one scampered toward the hangar door controls. The door began to rumble open. Jo opened the forward passenger door on the port side of the jet and pulled the short stairway into position. She had a decision to make. "Do you still have a weapon?" she asked Willy.

"Yes."

"Keep it trained on these guys. I have to get into the cockpit and prep the aircraft for takeoff. When I yell for you, get aboard and shut the door." She looked at Baumann, trying to read his eyes. If she brought him inside with her, the mechanics could easily disable the jet. She had to trust him.

"All right," he said, reaching into his pocket and pulling his Luger.

Jo climbed into the jet and made her way to the cockpit. Everything was where she figured it should be. She thanked the Air Force for making sure she put in her training hours every year to maintain her pilot's certification. Most of her hours were aboard trainers, but her last trip had been an exhilarating two hours in the cockpit of an F-15 Eagle. The instruments of this Messerschmitt were in a few different locations, but within a minute she had started the engines spooling up.

She was going through the final pre-flight checklist when she heard a commotion outside, shouting voices over the whine of the engines, then the crack of a gunshot. Instinctively, Jo released the brakes and advanced the throttle, steering the aircraft toward the open doorway. The outer cabin door was still open, but if Baumann had been taken down, she had to get moving before anybody else got aboard. If she got far enough down the runway, she could unbuckle for a few seconds and close the door before takeoff.

There was a thump behind her, the sound of the cabin door closing, and she turned in the seat, her Luger ready, to see Baumann staggering into the cockpit. "Are you all right?" Jo asked.

"The pilot made an appearance," he said. His face was white and bathed in sweat. "He demanded to know if we had filed a flight plan. I fired a round to let him know we were dispensing with official procedure."

"Did you hit him?"

"No. The Reichsleiter's hangar ceiling now has a new hole in it."

"Buckle your harness," Jo said, applying more thrust. "This won't be the smoothest takeoff in the world."

Jo found the windsock as they emerged from the hangar. The single runway ran north-south, and she noted the wind was out of the west, but not too stiff. Fortunately, the Blitz was handling like a dream. She would've preferred a slight headwind, but this would have to do. "Here we go," she said, lining up the runway markings and pushing the thruster controls forward. The jet's twin turbofan engines whined and the aircraft seemed to leap forward. Watching her speed indicator, Jo waited till they'd achieved the minimum and pulled back on the stick. The Blitz nimbly lifted off the pavement. "Retract the landing gear, please," she told Baumann. "The red handle down there to your left." Responding to the Argentine's pull, the gear thumped into their wheel wells, and Jo felt the aircraft gain some trim. She began a slow turn to port as they climbed and used the compass to set a course due east. When the altimeter showed ten thousand feet and climbing, she finally allowed herself to relax a bit. With any luck at all, they could get close enough to transmit a message before the Argentines caught up with them.

***

Aboard HMS Reliant, *Southwest Atlantic*

Monday, April 26th, 1982

Captain Tom Bentley checked his wristwatch. "Time for our midday radio check," he said, looking at the men around him in the control room of the nuclear attack submarine. "Sonar, any surface contacts?"

"Negative, sir."

"Very well. Bring us to periscope depth, Mr. Travis."

"Aye aye, sir," the executive officer said, and began issuing orders. The boat tilted upward slightly. Lieutenant Colonel Ian Masters took hold of a nearby grip, noting that the submariners adjusted easily to the movement without missing a beat. He'd been on a few subs in his time and was always impressed with the efficiency of their crews. *Reliant*'s men were as good as any he'd seen.

"Periscope depth!" a man sang out.

"Raise the antenna mast," Bentley ordered. Somewhere above them, a thin mast containing the boat's sensitive radio and radar antennae broke the surface. In a small room just aft of the conn, two specialists went to work with their sensitive equipment, sweeping the skies for any radar emissions. A patrolling enemy anti-sub warfare plane that might detect the mast would need only a few seconds to lock onto their position and begin an attack run.

The speaker on the bulkhead near Ian crackled to life. "Conn, radar, no enemy activity. Shall we go active?"

Bentley picked up a microphone . "Negative. Sparks, let's get our mail and get below."

"Aye, sir," came the voice of the radio operator. A hundred miles further east, *Cambridge* was broadcasting its identification signal, right on schedule. The sub's radio operator acknowledged and quickly wrote down the coded message. This one took a bit longer than Bentley would've preferred. He was only fifty miles from the Argentine coast and he didn't feel comfortable with any part of his boat above the surface. Finally, the radio man reported in. "Conn, radio, message received. Any response?"

"Acknowledgement only, Mr. Weeks," Bentley ordered. "Up periscope." The captain walked the periscope a full 360 degrees. "Contact! Bearing, 135 degrees, range three miles. Looks like a merchantman." That was a bit surprising. They'd heard that Argentine merchant vessels were staying well clear of the MEZ, and in fact few were straying out of port at all, despite assurances from the Argentine military that they would be safe. "Down scope. Lower the mast. Diving officer, take us back down to 150 meters."

Men began moving again as the ship slid lower into the deep. "Colonel Masters, let's see what the news is today," Bentley said.

The radio officer had the decoded message ready on a flimsy when the two men entered the cramped cabin. Bentley frowned as he read, then handed it to Ian.

1510 ZULU 26APR82

COMMANDER, HMS RELIANT

RADIO MSG OVER EMERG FREQ RECD 1430 ZULU.

SENDER ID WHITE VIXEN. ADVISES ENEMY

MISSION ADVANCED TO 0200 ZULU 27APR82.

SENDER UNDER AIR ATTACK. WHITE VIXEN

ENDS. EXECUTE GALAHAD MINUS 3. CONFIRM

MSG REQ 2100 ZULU.

STONE, HMS CAMBRIDGE, COMMANDING

"A word, if you please, Colonel," Bentley said, motioning Ian into the passageway. Other than going aft to the captain's quarters, this gave them as much privacy as one could expect aboard a submarine. "Know anything about this?"

It took all of Ian's discipline to hide his feelings. "Yes, sir. White Vixen is the code name of an American agent in Argentina. I don't know what her mission was, but evidently she's discovered that the attack on the fleet has been moved up."

"'She'?

Ian looked the skipper straight in the eyes. "Yes, sir. It's a woman."

Bentley nodded, not fooled for a moment. He'd been told that the SBS mission was back-up for a classified operation in-country. Plus there was the scuttlebutt about Masters and a certain American woman. "I see. Very well. You go ashore three hours early, then. Not too long after local dusk. If the attack is set to launch at 0200 local, you won't have much time."

"We'll be all right, sir. If you can get us as close to shore as possible, we'll make it on time."

"I'll do what I can. Let's hope the Argies don't decide to bring some ASW assets around tonight. Right, then. Best inform your lads. I'll surface the mast at 2100 to acknowledge the mission being moved up, and I'll inform the galley to have a hot meal for you and your lads at 2000 hours."

"Thank you, sir." He looked again at the flimsy before handing it back to the captain. "'Under air attack'," he mumbled.

"Let's hope she made it," Bentley said.

"Aye aye to that, Captain." Ian blinked his eyes rapidly and headed aft to his men.

CHAPTER FORTY

Chubut province, Argentina
Monday, April 26th, 1982

They'd been in the air a full hour when Jo's worry level edged into the red zone. She had no complaints about the aircraft; the Blitz was a dream to fly. It even had radar that showed a sky mercifully clear of any potential threats, just the occasional civilian airliner above them or small plane well below. She kept the radio tuned to the commercial frequencies and heard nothing alarming. It seemed to be just another day in the skies of Argentina, and that in itself was enough to worry about. This was a nation at war, with an enemy fleet a few hundred miles off its coast, and by now someone should have figured out there was one potentially hostile aircraft up here.

Adding to her concern was Baumann's condition. She'd been able to look at the wound while the jet was on autopilot, and while his bleeding had stopped, he was losing strength and she knew he might not last more than another few hours without hospital care. He'd slept part of the way, his breathing a bit ragged but steady, and she made sure when he awoke that he had something to eat and drink.

She checked the map she found in the cockpit with landmarks below and determined they were about halfway between Bariloche and the Atlantic coast. The main body of the fleet, she figured, was about 300 miles north of the Falklands, which would put them about the same distance due east of the plane once she reached the coast. She would start broadcasting on a special Royal Navy frequency when she was a half-hour from the ocean, hopefully make contact and relay her message, then divert to the city of Rawson, where she could land and get Baumann to a hospital. She would certainly be arrested, but there didn't seem to be too many alternatives. Without Baumann, she would've been able to reverse course and make a run for Chile. He wouldn't last that long, though.

Baumann groaned and struggled to sit up straight. "Where are we?"

"About 300 kilometers from the coast," she said. "I'm going to get you to a hospital. We'll land in Rawson. Is that a good-sized city?"

"About thirty thousand, I think," Willy said. "What about you?"

"Don't worry about me," she said. "We crossed a river a few minutes ago. That would be the Chubut, wouldn't it?" She pointed to the river on the map.

"Probably," he said. He groaned again. "I'm sorry," he said.

"For what?"

"I am a burden to you. Without me you could make your report and escape to Chile."

She smiled at him. "Perhaps," she said. "But I might not have made it this far without you."

"That is likely true," he said, forcing a chuckle, which only brought another wince of pain. "You are a good pilot. You are good at very many things, in fact."

"Thank you." She decided the subject needed to be changed. "I'm curious about you, though. You're committing treason, Willy. Why?"

He looked out the window, and for a long moment she thought he wouldn't answer. Then he said, "You see the land down below? That is Argentina. It is my country."

She said nothing, and he continued. "My whole life, I have wondered: am I Argentine, or German? Can a man be both?" He looked at her. "You are both American and Korean, are you not? You must feel conflicted about that, as well."

"Not really," she said. "In America, just about everybody's from somewhere else, maybe several generations back, or maybe they just arrived, but we become Americans pretty quickly. There are many things about my mother's culture that I admire, but my loyalty is with America."

"That is it, exactly," Willy said. "There is much I admire about my father's country, but I have decided that my loyalty must be with Argentina." He gazed out the window again. "When my father told me about CAPRICORN and placed me in charge, I was proud. We would finally get the Malvinas back and establish ourselves as a world power. It would give our people self-respect, give them something to work for.

Then I found out about VALKYRIE. That changed everything."

"I've heard of that, but what is it designed to do, exactly?"

"My father's compatriots here and their colleagues in Germany will use the confusion touched off by the nuclear strike to forcibly reunite Germany. They will seize the NATO and Soviet nuclear arsenals and overthrow the governments in Bonn and East Berlin. Then they will demand that all foreign troops leave the country."

She looked at him keenly. "You realized that would touch off a wider war."

"Yes," he said. "My friend Heinz put it together first. He knew the Kameraden—Bormann and his men—were just using us. Using all of Argentina. They meant to restore the Nazi Party in Germany. It would be a catastrophe."

"I think you're right about that," she said, quickly putting it together in her own mind. The Russians would go out of their minds. NATO would have to respond. Things could spin out of control very quickly. "This 'code red' alternate launch site. Where is it?"

"There is a small airstrip about ten kilometers north of the Ninth Brigade base. Used mostly for training flights if it's used at all. The plan calls for the strike aircraft to launch from there. Once it is well out to sea, it will divert to the north and circle around to approach the target from the northwest. The rest of the squadron will launch from Ninth Brigade and head due east toward the fleet as a diversion."

"To draw the fleet's combat air patrol," Jo said.

"Yes," Willy said, wincing again in pain. "There are to be six aircraft in the diversionary strike. It was assumed the British would have suspected a nuclear attack and would throw everything they could against the squadron."

"Leaving the real bomber to come in clean," she said. A good plan, and it could very well work. "All right. In a few minutes, I'll try to raise the fleet on the radio. If I can get through and warn them, they can deal with the strike force. If the bomb doesn't go off, VALKYRIE doesn't happen."

"The wing commander is one of our people," Willy said. "He will order the pilot to launch the weapon early. It will go off, but not over the fleet."

"What do you mean?"

"The English will survive, but they will have to withdraw, and we will keep the Malvinas. The Kamaraden—Bormann's men, my father's men—would be arrested by the government. But..." Willy winced in pain again. "I fear Bormann has uncovered our plot somehow. If he has removed that officer, the pilot will carry out the attack as planned." He unbuckled his harness. "I must use the lavatory. Please excuse me." He got up and staggered back into the cabin. A minute later, Jo heard a shout. She flipped on the autopilot and rushed aft.

Willy was standing at the door to the lavatory. A body had been propped up inside and slumped to the floor of the cabin. Willy knelt down, his wounded leg barely bending, and touched the cold forehead. "It is Heinz," he said, his voice catching. "They shot him."

Jo saw the tears forming in Baumann's eyes, saw him try to hold them back, saw him fail. She reached down to touch him, give him some comfort. She was trying to think of something to say when the radio in the cockpit crackled to life. *"Flight SB435, come in. This is Ninth Brigade Air Force Command, calling on civil aviation frequency. You are ordered to respond."*

Willy fought to get a grip on himself. "That is our call sign," he said, wiping his eyes with his sleeve. "Ninth Brigade is headquartered near Comodoro Rivadavia, on the coast."

They made their way back to the cockpit. The voice, speaking in Spanish, came from the speaker again. *"Flight SB435, you are ordered to respond."*

"If we respond, can they get a fix on our position?" Willy asked.

"No, if they're looking for us they've already found us with radar," Jo said, her heart sinking. She checked their position again. Probably another hundred klicks to the coast.

"I will talk to them," he said. "Perhaps I can stall them." He picked up the microphone. "This is Flight SB435. Over."

"Identify yourself, SB435."

"This is Wilhelm Baumann. We are a private flight on commercial business."

"Stand by, SB435." There was a series of clicks, then a different voice, speaking German. *"Willy, this is your father. What are you doing?"*

Willy looked at Jo. She saw confusion in his eyes, and tried to give him strength through hers. She nodded. He nodded back, then stared straight ahead as he thumbed the mic. "Father. It is good to hear your voice. Are you well?"

"None of this nonsense, Willy. I order you to change course and land at Rawson, immediately."

"That is our destination, Father. We should be there shortly."

"Is the American agent with you? Please tell me you are not helping her escape."

"She is here, Father. So is Heinz," he said, his voice hard. "I would let him speak with you, but he will not speak with anyone ever again. Your beloved Reichsleiter made sure of that."

"Willy, I don't know anything about that. You must believe me. Please, land the aircraft and we will straighten everything out."

"I'm sorry, Father. We will land shortly, but I do not want the American taken into custody. She is under my personal protection."

"Wilhelm, if you do not divert to Rawson immediately, I cannot protect you." There was a pause. *"Please, my son. I ask you one last time to divert and land. You will not be harmed. Our people there will also guarantee the safety of the American."*

"As they guaranteed Heinz's safety?" Willy shouted, with as much strength as he could muster. "No more will die for your damned Party, Father! No more! The Party is dead. Argentina must live!"

Jo was watching the radar, and saw two bogeys appear on the edge of the screen, coming in fast. She flipped off the autopilot and took the stick. "Wrap it up," she told Willy. "We have company coming."

"Willy, I beg of—" There was a click, then a new voice, more menacing, in Spanish again. *"Baumann, this is General*

Mendoza of Ninth Brigade. If you do not divert immediately to Rawson, you will be shot down. Change course to—"

Jo reached over and switched the radio to a new frequency. "That's it," she said. "They're coming after us. I have to get word to the fleet and then we're going for the deck." She dialed in a frequency she'd memorized from her training, praying that it would find a listening ear out there in the South Atlantic. "Den Mother, this is White Vixen. Den Mother, this is White Vixen. Please respond."

A harrowing minute of silence went by. She tried again. This time she got a response. *"White Vixen, this is Picket Fence. Stand by for Den Mother."*

Jo heaved a huge sigh of relief. "Den Mother" was the fleet back-up for her land-based contacts in Buenos Aires. The Royal Navy was on the ball. *"White Vixen, this is Den Mother,"* another voice said. *"What is your position?"*

"I am in the air over Chubut province," she said. "Urgent information follows. Enemy has advanced CAPRICORN. Repeat, enemy has advanced CAPRICORN. Launch time set for 0200 hours Zulu tomorrow. Repeat, launch time set for 0200 hours Zulu 27 April."

"Copy that, White Vixen. The dogs are on the trail. Anything further?"

"Yes. Main strike—" The aircraft shuddered and alarms began to chime. Jo dropped the microphone and grabbed the stick, fighting to maintain trim. In front of them, a jet fighter screamed across their nose, barely a hundred meters away, banking to the right. She recognized it as a Mirage III. His wingman was probably right behind them. She thumbed the mic just as tracer shells proved it, crossing over the nose of the plane right to left. "I am under air attack," she said.

"Repeat, under air attack. CAPRICORN main strike is—" A thudding sound cut her off and the jet suddenly started to lose power. The radio went silent. "Damn! We're hit. They must've gotten the antenna and some of our avionics."

"Can you get us down?"

"Not much choice, is there?" She fought the stick and managed to regain some control, but the instruments were going crazy and they were losing altitude. "Strap in," she said. "This isn't going to be pretty."

The instruments were in an uproar. Their starboard engine was out, and the fire indicator flared red briefly before the fire suppressor kicked in. She tried to restart the engine, but it was a lost cause. Altitude was dropping fast, but on the plus side she still had one engine and some control over the aircraft. "We have to land," she said. "I might limp her to Rawson with one engine but they'll have soldiers waiting for us."

"If you don't land there, they will shoot us down!"

"They could've done that easily if they wanted to," she said. "That pilot out there is a good shot. They want us alive."

Willy was pale, but Jo sensed he had found some sort of inner peace. Maybe the exchange with his father had exorcised some long-hidden demon. "Do your best, then," he said. He reached over and touched her arm. Surprised at the gesture, she flashed him a grin, trying to hide her own fear. Looking past him, she saw one of the Mirages pull up alongside, about thirty meters from their right wingtip. The pilot looked over, oxygen mask and goggles covering most of his face, and tapped his helmet. Willy had seen him, too. "What does he want?"

"He wants to talk to us," she said. The Blitz was starting to tremble now. Jo kept the nose down and started to look ahead for something to land on. A field, maybe a road.

"He's signaling again," Willy said. "One finger, three fingers—"

"That's a radio frequency," she said. "Wave your open hand over your ear. That'll tell him the radio's out."

"It worked," Willy said. "He's nodding. Now his wings are waggling."

"He wants us to follow him," she said. "Either back to his base or to Rawson, I'm sure."

"Are we going to do it?"

"Not on your life," she said, and she put the plane into a steep dive. "Hang on!"

The altimeter began to spin crazily. They'd been intercepted at twenty thousand feet, were down to fifteen thousand after the shells struck the airframe, and now they were under ten, nine...Jo waggled her wings erratically, not enough to lose control, hopefully enough to fool the pilots into thinking they were in serious distress.

The ground seemed to be coming up fast now. Fortunately, the land appeared to be sparsely populated. Jo finally found what she was looking for, a road cutting east-west through the fields. Was it paved? Couldn't tell. Not much traffic, and it looked fairly level. Was it wide enough? Had to be. Better than chancing an open field. Five thousand feet, now four...She started to level off, pulling back on the stick, using all her strength as the combination of speed, inertia and failing hydraulics fought back. The nose started coming up, but they were still losing altitude.

Two thousand feet, one thousand...

"Gear down," she said, pushing the red button. Nothing happened, and another warning light came on. "Grab that crank, there on your left," she told Willy with more calm than she felt. "Turn it counter-clockwise."

The crank stuck at first, but Willy put everything he had into it, and with an audible crack it started to move. After several turns, he said, "It won't move anymore."

"I think they're down," she said. Five hundred feet, four, three...

They soared over a small rise and startled a man driving a tractor with a large trailer behind it. The road ahead was clear, and Jo prayed for one last bit of luck. Throttling back the engine almost to stall speed, she floated the Blitz toward the waiting earth. The rear wheels touched with a loud thump, and the jet bounced back upward, but Jo cut the speed even more, and the wheels came back down and stayed down, then the nose wheel. The road was bumpy and the aircraft immediately began to shake violently. Jo stood on the brakes and cut the engine completely. She forced everything else out of her mind, vaguely hearing Willy yelling beside her. The nose wheel hit a pothole and the strut collapsed, spearing the nose of the jet downward. Jo and Willy were thrown hard forward, but their harnesses held. There was terrifying crunch as metal and dirt collided and the nose buckled, and then the jet shuddered one last time.

"Are you all right?" Jo asked.

"Yes," Willy gasped. "And you? You were shouting as you brought us in."

"I was?" She hadn't even realized it. Panting hard, she shut down the rest of the jet's systems, not wanting to risk a fire. Her chest and shoulders hurt where the harness had dug into them. "All right, let's get out of here," she said. She helped Willy out of his harness and pulled him from the co-pilot's seat. "Can you walk?"

"Barely," he grunted.

They made it to the cabin door, which she undogged and pushed open. "We'll try to find a vehicle or someplace to hide," she said. "The fighters have radioed our position, you can bet there'll be soldiers on the way."

"You go," he panted. "Leave me here."

"What?" She looked up at him. Sweat drenched his face and hair, but his eyes were shining. "I can't leave you behind."

"Yes, you can," he said. "You must. Without me, you have a chance to stay alive long enough to find your people." He pulled himself away from her and collapsed into a seat. "Leave a rifle with me," he said. "I will hold off the soldiers. That will buy you some time."

Her heart told her not to leave him here, but her brain yelled at her to get going. "The dogs are on the trail", Den Mother had said. That meant British commandos were coming ashore, maybe there already. If she could get to the coast, she could use one of her captured radios and the SBS combat frequency Ian had given her. What if it was him? What if it was his own unit?

"Go now," Willy said. "You don't have much time."

Without a word, she found the two assault rifles and gave both of them to Willy. "One of these will only slow me down. Plus it'll look pretty suspicious," she said. "Give me your Luger." She took the pistol from him and removed the clip, stuffing it in her pants pocket, and clipped a radio to her belt. Her own Luger went into the waistband at the small of her back. She went back to the cockpit for the map. Willy looked even weaker when she got back to him.

"I guess this is goodbye, then," Willy said.

Her heart was beating fast, and not just from the excitement of the landing and the danger of the approaching troops. In another time, another place, maybe she and this man...She forced the thought aside. "You're a brave man, Willy," she said. She bent down and kissed him. He was smiling when their lips parted.

"You're a remarkable woman, Major Jo Ann Geary. The White Vixen, eh? Someday you will tell me how they came up with...that..." He was fading; he might not even make it until the soldiers arrived.

"God be with you," Jo said, and she leaped out the door to the ground.

He drifted back and forth to the edge of consciousness. There was no more feeling in his wounded leg. So this was what it was like to die. The rifle was a dead weight on his lap. He doubted he would have the strength to lift it, much less aim and fire.

Birds were chirping outside. Other noises, too. Trucks? Sirens? He couldn't be sure. It was such a beautiful day.

He thought of Heinz, lying on the floor back there. He turned his head to look back down the cabin. Yes, still there. Can't help me now, Heinz, my friend, *mein Brüder*. So many good times we've had, eh? Remember that time in Rio, the women on the beach? That was a good time. When was it?

He struggled to recall the date, couldn't, gave up. Ah, well, we'll be together again, now, won't we, in the real Valhalla?

Giselle. He saw her face, her open arms, her beautiful body on the soft green grass. He started to cry. Oh, *meine Liebchen*, so much I should have given you, my name, my home, my children. Always later, it was going to be later. After CAPRICORN...The anger roused him. Bormann, God damn him, he had taken it all from him, tricked him into thinking it was for Argentina. How he must have laughed at Dieter Baumann's idiot son, doing what he was told, never suspecting...The laugh's on you now, though, eh? Lying stone cold back on your library floor. Killed by a woman! Far away, Willy heard himself laughing. The great Taurus, der Stier, who'd used so many women, done in by one. Justice, at last.

Voices outside now, shouting in, what, Spanish? German? He couldn't tell. Get ready. He brought the rifle up, aimed at the open door. Wasn't so heavy after all. He flipped the safety. On or off? A face appeared and he fired. Off. The face disappeared. Did he hit it? There was a lot of red, maybe the man's blood, maybe his own. No, he didn't have that much left. He laughed again.

More faces, further off, and he fired again, kept firing, and things were stinging him, there was lots of noise, but he didn't feel anything. God, please let the American get away. Couldn't remember her name anymore. Vic—vixen? Oh, so beautiful, so deadly. Can she stop the bomb?

Darkness was closing in on the edges of his vision. The gun stopped chattering, and he dropped it, reaching blindly for the other one. Where was it? His arms wouldn't move anymore. Another face appeared, this one above him. His mother. *Mutti!* She beamed on him kindly. The tears were flowing now. Anna Baumann was calling him. Something appeared in the doorway, something flying in, clattering to the floor and bouncing up against the seat next to him. What was it? He didn't care. His mutti was calling him. I'm here, Mutti. He felt so warm now, so safe, as she took him. By the time the grenade went off, he no longer cared.

CHAPTER FORTY-ONE

Chubut province, Argentina

Monday, April 26th, 1982

The glow in the distance had to be their target. Ian checked his wristwatch, and the illuminated hands told him it was nearing 10:30 local. They were really cutting this one close.

The mission had nearly bollixed up right at the beginning. Bentley brought *Reliant* to within twenty miles of the shore, came to periscope depth, and took his time allowing the radar officer to complete his work. No contacts, a major worry avoided. The casing diver was out the hatch first, a sailor specially trained in prepping the vessel's exterior skin and the SBS equipment for the team's exit. The diver took an extra ten minutes before he used a hammer to tap an "all clear" on the hull. The extra time, which Ian knew had to be deemed necessary by the diver, nevertheless made him edgy. They didn't have much time to spare.

Ian and four other commandos went into the hatch next. Each man wore a dry suit over his regular camo uniform, with his weapons and ruck strapped on outside. Mask and fins, plus a RABA, the rechargeable air-breathing apparatus that would give each trooper ten minutes of air. While in the hatch, they breathed ship's air through umbilical cords.

This was Ian's fifth E&RE, but the feeling of claustrophobia was just as strong this time as the first time he'd done it in a Scottish harbor. The water rushed in from near their feet and rose to within four inches of the ceiling hatch. Resisting the urge to keep their faces in the air, the men stayed hunched down until the casing diver undogged the hatch. Switching to his RABA, Ian kicked his way out and into the black water of the South Atlantic. Keeping to his training, Ian picked his way back aft toward the sail, guided by the casing diver. In less than a minute he reached the lurking area, where the team was to gather and wait until all were assembled. Ian plugged his RABA into one of the external oxygen tanks and waited, trying to be patient.

One by one the four remaining troopers from the first batch joined him. Despite the darkness, Ian thought he could barely see the outline of the nearest one, which should've been Colour Sergeant Powers. The casing diver finally gave Ian the tap signal that told him all five men were outside the sub. Time for the second batch.

The last man out, Lance Corporal Philip Kent, inadvertently caused the problem. The sub was making only about three knots, barely enough to maintain steerage, but the current here was erratic. Kent came up from the hatch right on schedule, but he lost his grip on the sub's external hand-holds when a sudden gust of current caught him in the side. Only the quick action of the casing diver kept Kent from being swept away in the dark water. Then when he arrived at the lurking area, his RABA malfunctioned. Even the most experienced diver feels a moment of panic when his oxygen supply suddenly stops, and Kent was no exception. He began fumbling with his equipment, desperately searching for the umbilical that would connect his RABA to the sub's external tanks. The casing diver realized the problem immediately and tried to help, but Kent felt the diver's grasping hand and nearly lost control, thinking the diver was trying to keep the umbilical away from him.

The next man in line, Corporal Garrett, sensed the commotion and turned to help. He could barely make out Kent thrashing with the diver, but saw just enough to be able to grab Kent by the head and mash him down on the hull, using enough force to pin him there but not enough to cause injury or damage to the man's equipment. The diver recovered quickly, found Kent's umbilical and made the connection to the tank. They had to wait another thirty seconds while Kent got fresh air and recovered his senses.

Finally, the diver made his way back up the line of men and double-tapped Ian on the shoulder. Ian unplugged his umbilical, switched back to his RABA and followed the diver as they used hand-holds to make their way to the sail, then up its side to the periscope. Ian released his grip and kicked his way to the surface.

The seven other men bobbed up in good order, and their training held as they swam to the floating case containing the Zodiac boat, which had been released from the outer hull by the casing diver. Flipping open the case, Ian activated the gas canister that quickly inflated the boat and then climbed aboard. Hodge was next and unlimbered the waterproof outboard motor as the rest of the men were pulled in, and they were off for the Argentine coast. Ian checked his watch when they got underway. They were nearly a half-hour behind schedule.

The recon photos they'd obtained from American satellites hadn't been able to tell them much about the lay of the land. The air base, headquarters of the Argentines' Ninth Brigade, was about ten kilometers north of the town of Comodoro Rivadavia. The plan was to come ashore north of the base, well away from the town, but as they got closer to shore Ian could see they were about five miles south of the base, some ten miles south of where they'd wanted to be. Another navigational screw-up, but nothing could be done about it now. Turning north wasn't an option; the longer the boat stayed at sea, the greater the chance of discovery by the enemy. Ian passed the word that they would come straight in.

The beach, if he'd wanted to call it that, was filled with driftwood and craggy trees thrusting out from the ground at odd angles. Rocks were everywhere, creating even more of a hazard. There was a half-moon, giving them some illumination, and Hodge managed to steer the boat ashore without running into obstacles. Powers was the first man out, splashing into the surf five yards out from shore, followed quickly by Garrett and another lance corporal, Denny Henderson. The first British warriors to set foot in enemy territory during the war quickly fanned out and formed a perimeter. Sergeant Jerry Bickerstaff was next. The hulking Londoner, who had nearly made the '76 Olympic team as a weightlifter, easily pulled the boat onto the gravelly beach.

Almost without a word, the commandos stowed their dry suits and diving gear in the boat and concealed it as best they could with brush, some of it hacked out by Bickerstaff with his Nepalese kukhari knife, its two-foot-long curved blade more than a match for any Argentine flora. Then the men set off to the north, gaining some higher ground and gratefully discovering the area was bare of any signs of habitation.

The absence of a nearby road, while good for security, made for tough going overland. They were used to a rough yomp, as they called a long trek carrying a heavy ruck, but Ian had to make sure they had adequate rest. By the time he'd done his 2230 time check, the troopers were starting to feel it, although none would admit to being tired. Even so, Ian ordered a halt to the march and the men gratefully sat down as comfortably as they could and broke out canteens and rations. Hodge detailed two men, Lance Corporal Charles Wayne and the luckless Kent, to take perimeter security about twenty meters away, one on either side of the line of march.

Even though the unit was observing radio silence, Ian kept his transceiver turned on and tuned to the SBS combat frequency. The radio had a range of about thirty miles, enough for an emergency message to reach them from the sub off-shore. He'd forgotten all about it and was chewing on a candy bar when he heard a tinny whisper. He unclipped the radio from his web belt and held it to his ear as he slightly increased the volume.

"Hello, any squaddies out there, this is White Vixen. Do you copy? Over."

He almost dropped the radio in surprise. Next to him, Powers looked over with eyes that seemed to shine from the midst of his dark, camouflage-painted face. Ian glanced back at him and then fingered the send button. "White Vixen, this is a Poole squaddy," he said cautiously, wondering if it could possibly be true. "Squaddy" was Royal Marine slang for a fellow trooper. "We copy your transmission, Vixen. Tell me where you've been."

"Fonglan Island. I say again, Fonglan Island."

Good God, it was her! Ian keyed the mike. "Not a good place for swimming."

"Urgent we meet, squaddy. I am at a farmhouse, one klick north of Highway 25 and Highway 153 intersection, then due east two klicks."

Powers handed Ian a map and a red-lensed pencil-thin flashlight. He quickly found her. Only about three klicks away. "Vixen, I have your location. See you soon. Poole squaddy out." Just in case this was an Argentine trick, he deliberately neglected telling Jo exactly where they were.

"Pass the word to the lads, Sergeant," Ian said. "Time to go."

"I think I recognized the voice, sir," Powers said. "Would that be the bird from Hong Kong?"

"I certainly hope so," Ian said. "We move out in two minutes."

***

Jo squatted at the base of a tree, one of the few that dotted the landscape of the Patagonian plateau, and peered through the night at the farmhouse a hundred meters away. That she had made it this far was nothing short of a miracle. She was nearly exhausted. Hunger gnawed at her, and there was only a swig or two of tepid water left in the bottle she carried in the shapeless, stolen peasant's bag. She wiped the sleeve of the cotton shirt across her grimy forehead. One light was still on in the farmhouse. Sheep bleated from the small barn behind it and the pens flanking the buildings. An old pickup truck was parked in the yard.

Her escape from the Blitz had come none too soon. Within five minutes of her leap to the ground, she heard sirens. She scurried well off the road into the pasture, hunkering down as the first vehicles screamed past her: a police car and an Army truck, heading west, back toward the jet. She could still see it, gleaming white in the middle of the rode, nose down, nearly a kilometer behind her. She knew there'd be helicopters soon, so she did the best she could to stick to cover, using the few trees, making a zigzag course eastward. She figured she had maybe a half-hour before the soldiers discovered she wasn't in the plane and started searching.

Her first big break came a few minutes later when she topped a small rise and saw a solitary farmhouse. A woman was going inside, carrying an empty laundry basket. Clothes fluttered from a single line stretching between the house and a small barn. Jo knew she would have to do something about her own clothing, since it was likely a description of her from Bormann's servants was on the police and military airwaves right now. Popping sounds came to her over the wind from the west. They were at the plane. Willy was buying her that time.

Keeping the house in sight, she made her way toward the yard, using as much cover as possible. Were there dogs? She prayed there wouldn't be. A low stone fence divided the grass of the yard and the scrub of the field. The clothesline was only ten yards away. She waited a full five minutes behind the fence, seeing no movement in the yard, barn or house, and then picked her targets, vaulted the fence, and snatched the clothes. She got only two garments, a plain light gray peasant blouse and a black, widely-flared skirt. Leaping back beyond the fence, heart hammering, she waited another five minutes before changing her wardrobe. Her hair had been in a ponytail, but now she let it come free to her shoulders. She balled up her original clothes, along with her socks and sneakers—she doubted peasant girls would be wearing shoes like these—and stuffed the wadded garments behind a loose stone in the fence.

Transportation. She estimated she was about thirty kilometers from the coast, and getting there on foot—and barefoot, at that—wasn't an inviting prospect. She was considering what to do about that when a noise drew her attention back to the farmhouse. The back door came open and two children ran out, a boy of about eight a girl a bit younger, followed by the woman. "Carlos, Frida, wait for me!" The children laughed and ran back to her. "Come, now, if you're good on the ride to town I'll get you ice cream." The children screamed with delight.

Jo watched them walk to the barn, heard an engine starting, and then a battered old Datsun pickup pulled out onto the yard, onto what passed for a driveway and down a dirt road to the main road, then turned left and headed east. Jo checked the map. The town of Comodoro Rivadavia was about forty kilometers to the southeast, with a smaller town up the coast, and then the Ninth Brigade air base. That had to be the launch point of the attack. Another airstrip, smaller, was about ten kilometers north of the base. That's where the nuke was, had to be. Other than a small civilian airport at Comodoro Rivadavia, there was nothing else within a hundred kilometers, and she doubted they'd bring the weapon that close to a town.

Just in case someone else had stayed behind in the house, Jo hid behind the fence as she made her way to the barn. Inside she found a bench with tools, sacks of feed, a stall full of hay, and a real find: a pair of horses.

Jo's last time on a horse had come two years earlier, during a tour at a base in Texas. A man she dated for a few months owned a stable, and he taught her to ride, something she found very enjoyable. Now, she hoped she remembered enough. She chose the female, who seemed fairly docile, and in fifteen minutes had saddled the animal with what she trusted was at least minimal competence. Looking through the items on the bench, she found a leather bag which could be used as a saddlebag or carried with a shoulder strap. Into the bag went her Luger and the extra clip, plus the radio and map. A dusty hat hung on a nail driven into a post, and although it was a bit too big for her, she took it. One more quick look around brought another break. Near the side door were four sets of well-worn boots. Thank goodness this family was fastidious. The next-to-largest pair, probably the woman's, was just a bit large, but they'd do. With one last look out the barn door, she led the horse outside, mounted up, and headed east, through the fields, roughly paralleling the road.

The crackling of gunfire to the west had stopped, then came the sound of an explosion. They'd used a grenade. She looked back and saw no plume of smoke, so the plane must still have been intact. If the soldiers were even halfway efficient they'd find no woman inside and call in helicopters for an aerial search, and they wouldn't take long to spot a lone woman on horseback. She spurred the animal to greater speed.

Twice over the next hour she heard helicopters in the distance, and both times she was able to find cover, once under a tree and the next time by walking the animal through a small village. Nobody paid attention to her, and she was able to draw some water for herself and the horse from a community well. Fortunately, nary a policeman or soldier was in sight, and so she mounted up and kept going.

The angle of the sun told her it was about three p.m. when she came to another village, hardly more than a few ramshackle buildings that had seen their better days long ago. A heavy-set man sat on a bench in front of what appeared to be a tavern. He was fanning himself with a rolled-up newspaper. Jo tied her horse to a post supporting the veranda. "Excuse me, señor," she asked in Spanish, with a dazzling smile, "could you tell me how far it is to the coast from here?"

The man peered up at her, scratched a chin covered with bristly white whiskers, then looked to the east. "Oh, about fifteen kilometers, I would say."

"Thank you," she said.

"You are a stranger here," the man said. "Where are you from?"

An alarm bell started ringing for her. "I am visiting my cousin's estancia," she said, "and I thought I would go for a ride. It is such a nice day."

"Yes, it is," he said. He looked at her again. "Are you Esteban's niece, from Buenos Aires?"

She laughed. "I was told that the men in town were all handsome, but I didn't know they would be so curious, too," she said. *"Adios, amigo!"*

Jo headed down the dirt road running east out of the village, praying that nobody there had a telephone. Half an hour later, she could smell the tang of the sea and was starting to think she just might make the coast unscathed when the road turned northeasterly, and a couple miles ahead, at an intersection, she spotted a police car. Without hesitating, she turned off the road and headed across the fields to the southeast.

Another quarter-mile brought her to within sight of the main road, running southeast-northwest, which had intersected with the village road. She'd kept an eye on the police car, and now it was heading down the road toward her. Resisting the urge to go faster, she kept the horse at a canter. The squad car, an older French Citröen, speeded up. It pulled to a stop in the middle of the road, directly in front of Jo. She pulled the reins back and slowed to a walk. Two men emerged from the car. From inside, Jo could hear a radio chattering.

"Hola, mi amiga," the driver said. He was short, thin, and his brown uniform shirt had sweat stains under the armpits. The other officer seemed to be younger by about ten years, and he kept his right hand near his holstered sidearm.

"Good afternoon, officers," she said in flawless Spanish. "Isn't it a beautiful day for a ride in the country?"

"Please dismount, señorita," the driver said. "We must ask you for your identity papers."

"Oh? Is there a problem, officer?" She got off the horse with a dainty jump, her skirt billowing. She caught the younger man's eyes widening.

"Just routine, señorita. Your papers, please."

"Well, all right," she said. She rummaged in the saddlebag she'd taken from the barn. "Now, where are they? Oh, here." She pulled out the Luger and pointed it at the men. The driver, quicker and more experienced, reached for his sidearm, while the younger man froze in fear. "Don't try it," she warned. "Now, gentlemen, very carefully, I want you to take your sidearms out of your holsters and put them on the hood of the car."

The older man glared at her, but did as he was told. "You too, Junior," she said, aiming the Luger at the young cop. He was literally shaking, but he was able to retrieve his weapon and place it on the car.

So much for making it to the coast undetected. Well, it had been a long shot at best. Now, Jo's challenge was how to deal with them. She remembered the rough road she'd crossed a minute before, hardly more than a tractor-trail across the wide field, but it did pass near a copse of trees that was a good mile from the road.

Within three minutes she had tied both men's hands behind their backs with their belts and shoved them onto the floor in back, then disabled the radio. Tying the horse to a nearby tree, she drove the police car back down the road till she found the tractor path and started following it. Ten very bumpy minutes later, she parked behind the trees, then removed the engine's distributor cap. Leaving the windows slightly open, she left the men in the car and began jogging across the field, toward her horse. The policemen would eventually work their way free, but it would take them awhile. By the time they made their way back to the road and found their way to the nearest telephone, she'd be miles away.

Shooting them would buy a lot more time. The thought crossed her mind as she gave them one last look, but she quickly pushed it away. These men hadn't done anything wrong. They were just a couple of country cops, doing their duty. Besides, if she were captured, she didn't want a double-murder added to her list of charges. She left them alive, grunting and cursing in the back of the car. A few minutes later, she was on her horse and cantering toward the coast.

She'd seen this farmhouse in the distance as dusk was enveloping the land, and she decided to use it as the rendezvous point. In the darkness, something substantial would have to serve as a landmark. Ian's voice coming through the night into her radio had thrilled her, driving away the fatigue and cold, if only for a moment.

Her SIS briefing on Argentina came back to her. This part of the country had been settled by immigrants from Wales, and so some pro-British sentiment might be expected here. It was too risky to simply walk up to the door and knock, though, as hungry and thirsty as she was. She hoped the commandos would get here soon.

In the distance she heard the sounds of horses. Jo had unburdened her own horse of its saddle and set the animal free, trusting it would seek out its own kind and join them. She was thinking of the mare, and how sturdy and reliable she had been, when another sound reached her, a rustling of grass. Could've been an animal, could've been something else. She hunkered back against the tree, drawing her pistol.

There, off to her right, about forty meters. In the dim moonlight she saw a shape moving stealthily through the knee-high grass. If she hadn't heard the sound of its passage through the field, just barely above the clutter of night sounds, she would've never spotted the shape. Twenty meters further on, she saw another one, just a flicker of movement. These guys were good, all ri—

The sound was faint, but distinctive. One who has trained with knives never forgets it, and now it came suddenly from her left, and just in time she brought the Luger up and caught the blade on the short barrel of the gun, sending a chink through the night air. The moonlight glinted off a very large blade, and she grabbed for the wrist she knew had to be holding it, lifting the blade up with her gun hand while her left found the man's wrist and pulled and twisted it, but this hand was powerful and wouldn't release the knife. She pulled harder, swinging her body around, driving a right side kick into the man's armpit, a blow strong enough to dislocate the shoulder of almost any man, but not this one. All she got was a grunt, and then another hand grabbed her ankle and twisted. Jo had to roll with it or risk having the ankle break, so she released the man's wrist and went with the movement, yanking the ankle free as she fell to the ground hard, right side taking the impact, and despite the pain she continued rolling and was back on her feet. Three shapes were around her now, and she heard the clicking of firearms, saw the glint of moonlight on the knife again, and knew that if these were Argentine troops she was as good as dead.

"For God's sake, Bickerstaff," a distinctly British voice said, "put that pig-sticker away. You damn near cut her head off."

A deep voice rumbled from behind the knife, "Warn't close to that, Sarge. Only meant to get her attention." She heard the sound of a long knife going back into its sheath. "Where's the colonel?"

"Right here," a very familiar voice behind her said.

CHAPTER FORTY-TWO

Chubut province, Argentina

Monday, April 26th, 1982

Out of sight of the farmhouse, they hunkered down in the midst of a copse of scruffy trees. Jo could hardly believe it was really Ian, and even when she got a look at him in the moonlight, she would have doubted it if not for his voice. In his field uniform, face disguised with camo paint, topped with a green beret and carrying his MP-5, he looked every inch the lethal warrior he was. His men, if anything, looked even more formidable, especially that fellow Bickerstaff.

Ian was all business. When they got into the trees, he sent four men out to guard the perimeter, and then made sure Jo got some food and water. She wolfed down two energy bars and took a long swig from Ian's canteen. "Thank you," she said, handing it back to him.

"Now tell me how you got here," Ian said. She quickly sketched out the events of the past two days near Bariloche, the desperate flight east, the crash landing, and her escape on horseback to the coast. He said nothing, merely nodding now and then, but another man, one she barely recognized as Colour Sergeant Powers, uttered an appreciative oath or two.

"I had to contact you," Jo said as she finished. "That's why I made for the coast instead of Chile. The Argentines have changed their plan. They intend to launch the nuclear strike from an alternate air base, not too far from the original base."

"Damn!" Ian said. He pulled a map from a thigh pocket and a flashlight from his web belt. The red lens of the flash cast an eerie beam onto the map as he spread it out on the ground. "We should be about here," he said, pointing at a spot about two kilometers in from the coast and three south of the Ninth Brigade base. "There are no other air bases within a hundred kilometers."

"Baumann said they're using a small strip about ten klicks north of Ninth Brigade," Jo said.

In the dim red light, Ian's eyes glared at her. "Do you trust his word?"

She took a deep breath. Was it possible that Willy would have deceived her? Was it possible, even, that this was all part of Bormann's plan? She dismissed it. Something about Baumann had told her he was telling her the truth. "Yes," she said. "What he said about the alternate site made sense." She quickly described the diversionary attack.

"All right," Ian said. He looked at the man squatting next to him. "Captain Hodge. I'll take two men with me and Major Geary here to check out this alternate base. You take the rest of the men to the primary target."

"Right, sir. Who do you want?"

"Garrett's trained on the Stinger, so I'll take him, along with Bickerstaff. That leaves you with Powers and his Stinger, plus the rest of the squad." He checked his watch. "Nearly 1130 local. We'd best get moving. When you've finished your attack, get to the extraction point and get on the sub. We'll radio for pickup from our spot on the beach north of you. We won't have time to get to you on foot."

Hodge never flinched. "Aye aye, sir. Can you make this other base in time?"

Ian shook his head. "We'll have to get some transport somehow. The farm should have a lorry or a car of some sort."

"Contact with the locals, Colonel?"

"Can't be helped. If it's another thirteen klicks to this launch site, we'll never make it in time on foot, especially since we have to go around the main base. We'll have to risk it." He looked at Jo. "You need a change of clothes, I think. I have a camo undershirt you can put over that one you have on. I'll see if anyone else brought a spare pair of trousers."

A few minutes later, Jo was cinching a baggy set of trousers with a length of rope. The other marines had melted into the darkness. "Here," Ian's voice said, and in the dimness she saw him holding out a garment. She took it, and as she brought it up to her head to slip it on, the odor of his perspiration struck her, so familiar from their time in Bermuda...She flung herself into his waiting arms, and stifled a sob.

"It's all right, Jo. I'm here," he said, holding her tightly.

"My God, Ian." Everything seemed to be smashing down on her now. Her capture in Buenos Aires, the encounter with Bormann, their escape, the flight, the crash...She willed herself to move beyond it, summoning up every ounce of her ki. "I never thought I'd see you again," she murmured into his chest.

He kissed the top of her head. "Jo, we have to get moving. Time is short."

"I know," she said, pulling herself away. She slipped the shirt over her head and pulled it down. It had taken a mighty effort, but her discipline came through. "The farm likely has a dog," she said.

"We'll deal with that."

There was indeed a dog, and it started yelping when they were still fifty meters from the barn. Ian waved at Bickerstaff, who drew his long knife and vanished around the back of the barn. Sheep were bleating, but suddenly the dog was silent. Jo tried not to think about what the big sergeant had done with his knife. "Garrett, phone lines," Ian whispered. The Welsh corporal nodded and headed toward the house, hugging the shadows.

Ian and Jo made it to the pickup. No lights had come on in the house. Unlike farms Jo had seen in the States, this one didn't have a yard light, thankfully. Ian took a quick look inside the cab with his flashlight. "Caught a break," he whispered. "Keys are in it."

Bickerstaff appeared out of the darkness, then Garrett. "Lines are cut, Colonel," the corporal said.

"Right," Ian said. "Jo, get inside and take the wheel. Shift to neutral. Lads, we want to push this buggy out of the yard and down the road a bit before we start her up. Won't do to wake the house before we're off."

· Jo opened the passenger door, and the rusty hinge creaked so loudly Jo thought it would wake the dead, not just those sleeping in the house. She willed it to be quiet. Slipping inside, she climbed over into the driver's seat. The truck was a Ford, twenty years old if it was a day, with a stick shift. Jo found the emergency brake, made sure it was released, then pressed in the clutch and shifted to neutral. The truck began to move. She turned the wheel hard right and the tires began crunching over the dirt and gravel. The truck squeaked like it hadn't been moved in years. Jo risked a glance back at the farmhouse. Still dark.

Fifty meters down the long driveway, Jo heard a pair of thumps from the box behind her, and the passenger door swung open. Ian jumped inside. "Let's go," he said, panting. Jo turned the key, gave the accelerator a little push as the engine coughed and sputtered, then caught. She shifted into first gear and the truck lurched ahead and stalled.

"Sorry," she said. This time she eased the transmission into second gear smoothly. "Not a word about woman drivers," she warned Ian.

"Did I say anything?" Ian unfolded his map. The red flashlight cast an eerie glow in the cab of the truck. "It looks like Highway 25 is the best way to go north. It stays about five kilometers west of the air base."

"They might have roadblocks out. It's been awhile since my plane went down, so they know an enemy agent is in the area." She looked over at Ian in the ghostly red light. "I'm glad you're here, Ian. If it had to be anybody, I'm glad it's you."

He gave her a smile, his teeth shining in the dark of his camouflaged face. "Steve McQueen said it in a movie: 'We'll find some dumb son of a bitch to do it.' And they did. By the way, don't worry about the dog. I could tell you were upset about that. We brought along a piece of raw beef that was drugged. Just for this sort of eventuality."

She sighed with relief, pushing aside the incongruity of being concerned about a canine when she had already killed two men on this mission, with perhaps more to come. Fatigue was starting to creep back inside her. The rations and water she'd gotten from the marines had helped. She'd have to draw on what reserves she might have and hope for the best.

***

Colonel Gerhard Schmidt wasted no time as he left the provincial police station. Captain Winkler knew from his commander's demeanor inside the station that he was not pleased, but he refrained from any comments. Businesslike and professional as always, Schmidt merely asked questions. The stares he gave the police captain did little to conceal his true feelings.

The two officers climbed into the back of the Mercedes staff car. As soon as the doors slammed shut, Schmidt ordered the driver to return to the base. Winkler took a surreptitious glance at his watch. Nearly midnight, and it was at least another half-hour to the base. He waited for the colonel to start letting off the steam he knew was building. It didn't take long. Schmidt may have been promoted to full colonel after the battle on the Island of the Penguins, but his personality hadn't changed one bit.

"Incompetent imbeciles!" Schmidt exploded. "An enemy agent is loose in the area, they have two men missing for six hours before they're found, then two more hours before they think of notifying the nearest military authority. God help us."

"It was evident that they didn't believe a woman would be much of a problem," Winkler said.

Schmidt scoffed at that. "Well, they have found out, haven't they? I spoke with...some people," the Werewolves officer said carefully, knowing that Winkler wasn't privy to Bund business. "They assured me this woman is as dangerous as any man. More so, in fact. She has already been responsible for the deaths of several key people here. The two policemen should pray to their Virgin in thanks that the American spared their worthless lives."

"Could she be a threat to the base?"

"Ordinarily, I would say not. One person, lightly armed if armed at all, even one as competent as this one is, should not be a concern to us. Despite what we see in their movies, the Americans are not supermen. Or superwomen," he said, giving Winkler a glance and a sly grin. "However, we have to be prepared for any eventuality. It is possible that she has compatriots in the area."

"It is good that you called the base before we left the police station," Winkler said. "Leutnant Speth will reinforce the guards."

"I will feel better when the plane is off the ground safely. Then we can all get some sleep." Schmidt rubbed the bridge of his nose. Winkler could see his commander was very tired. Even for a man of Schmidt's iron constitution, there were limits. "Oberstleutnant Steinhorst was recalled to Buenos Aires. He has left the base, is that correct?"

"Yes, Herr Oberst, as you ordered. He departed Ninth Brigade at 1200. You are in command of the strike aircraft."

"Very good."

Winkler looked out the window at the passing lights. He wondered briefly about Steinhorst's recall, but he had been in the Army long enough to know that the generals moved in mysterious ways.

***

Ian was beginning to fear that they'd already used up their quota of luck on this mission, and they hadn't even fired a shot yet. Every marine knew that luck would carry you only so far in the field, and then it would inevitably run out. So far, things had gone well enough, but if he'd had a gauge to keep track of his luck, the needle would surely be bouncing on "E".

The seven kilometers they'd covered on Highway 25 had been harrowing. As traffic started to pick up, Jo slowed long enough for Ian to transfer to the box of the pickup, hunkering down there with Bickerstaff and Garrett. They had no cover, but Ian considered that to be a plus. This way, he could keep an eye on things and move quickly if events dictated.

Jo assured him she'd do what she could to avoid any roadblocks, and now Ian had trusted her with his life, and those of his men. He was comfortable with that. It took all his years of discipline to keep from shouting with joy when they found her near the farm. She sketched her story to him: the undercover work in Buenos Aires, the struggle with

Schröder, her capture by the Bund, the showdown with Bormann, and her flight to the coast. Martin Bormann himself! It was almost too incredible to be true, and Jo had brought him down. This was some kind of woman, all right. If they got through this, he vowed to himself, he would marry her as soon as possible. He would not let this one get away.

Bickerstaff had noticed the Argentines' lax security. No roadblocks, not even civilian police patrols. Had they really caught the enemy with his knickers down? Don't bugger it up by talking about it, Ian advised. They should count their blessings. The men kept their eyes peeled, with Garrett covering their rear, the sergeant and Ian scanning to the sides and ahead.

The lights of the Ninth Brigade base passed on their right. Vehicles were coming out the base's access road toward the highway, some with flashing blue lights. "They're spinning it up," Ian said to Bickerstaff. "Good thing we're coming through now." The big man grunted in agreement.

Ian took another glance at his men and then shifted his eyes to the road ahead, looking through the windows of the cab. Not for the first time, a random thought of imminent death flitted across his mind. He pushed it aside, but not with any sense of anger or fear. It was merely one more extraneous thought that had to be identified, dealt with and filed away. He was in enemy territory, his force had been divided, but he still had a mission to perform. SBS veterans he talked to over the years told him the fear wasn't to be feared, so to speak, but respected. "Fear will keep ye alive, laddie," an old Scot once told him once while relating hair-raising tales of jungle combat against the Japanese in Burma. "When ye dinna have nae fear in combat, that's when ye get careless."

He heard Bickerstaff and Garrett exchange one-word sentences. Months of hard training had melded his team into a single organism. The men could transition seamlessly from larger group to smaller, performing their tasks with efficiency and even a bit of élan now and then. Garrett, the young Welshman, had come along rapidly. He seemed to have a natural flair for this work. Bickerstaff, the muscular East Ender who learned to wield his wicked knife by training with Ghurkas in Nepal, had showed his courage more than a few times. Ian was glad they were with him.

Then there was Jo, in the cab, driving the old pickup, perhaps the bravest of them all. If they captured, the men would be POWs, repatriated after the war. Not her. Captured spies were still shot in many places, and something told him this was one of them.

He remembered how she'd been in Bermuda, on the beach, in their room...He had to force the memories aside. The mission, the mission, concentrate on the mission. Lives are riding on it. A great many lives...

More lights up ahead, to the right, not as many but definitely a sign of activity. Ian checked his rifle, glad to see that Garrett and Bickerstaff followed suit without being told. Ian motioned to the glow in the east. Target, he signaled, and the men nodded in understanding.

They passed a two-lane access road, empty of traffic, and Ian rapped twice on the back window of the cab. The truck slowed, and Ian swung around into the passenger seat. "Time for a yomp," he said. Jo's face was an eerie, dim green in the light from the dashboard instruments. "That's a hike, in Yank talk," he added.

"I gathered that," she said. "What about the truck? We can't just leave it along the road."

"Pull off-road and go in as far as you can. We'll get out first."

Five minutes later, Jo killed the engine and doused the headlights. They were a good half-mile from the road, and the coarse grinding sound she'd heard as the truck ran over a series of rocks told her they weren't taking it further anyway. They left the Ford sitting in the darkness, engine ticking, and Jo was strangely sad. Driving an American-made vehicle had made her think of home, and she wondered if she'd live to see it again.

CHAPTER FORTY-THREE

Chubut province, Argentina

Tuesday, April 27th, 1982

Colonel Schmidt checked his wristwatch again. Only five minutes had elapsed since his last check, five long minutes, but at least the launch time was that much closer. It was 1:15 in the morning. He had been working for twenty straight hours, since beginning his Monday by leading his men on a five-kilometer run. Fatigue was on the edge of his brain, fuzzing his thinking around the edges. He told himself that he was getting too old for this. This was a young man's game. Yes, and when they found a young man who could do it right, he would retire to his estancia. Until then, he worked.

He paced along the front of the small building that had once served as the airstrip manager's office and now was his headquarters. A phone rang inside. Seconds later, Winkler appeared from inside, putting on his cap. "Herr Oberst, that was the hangar. The ground crew is about to finish its pre-flight check. They will be ready for your inspection in five minutes."

"Very well. What is the latest from Speth?"

"His last check-in was fifteen minutes ago, Herr Oberst, as I reported to you. All is quiet on the perimeter."

Schmidt shook his head to clear the encroaching cobwebs. "Yes, you did. Forgive my forgetfulness, Klaus. It has been a very long day."

"Indeed, Herr Oberst," Winkler said, sympathizing with his commander, for he was just as tired as the older man. "But it is almost over, sir."

Schmidt took a deep breath, sucking in the chilly night air, feeding off its energy. "Yes, it is. Well, let us see what our intrepid Air Force comrades have to show us."

They strolled the hundred meters to the new hangar that was three times the size of the two old ones that still flanked the office building. It was large enough to hold three modern jet fighters, but only one was inside now, a French-made Super Etendard, the Argentine Air Force's fighter-bomber. He had to grudgingly admit that the French made a beautiful aircraft. Schmidt was not an aviator, but he had made a point of studying this aircraft's specs. Maximum speed at low altitude, 650 knots; weapons payload without external fuel tanks, 2100 kilograms; maximum combat range with this particular payload, 900 kilometers. Schmidt knew from the latest intelligence report that the English fleet was 800 kilometers away. The pilot would be cutting it close, but all he had to do was get close, after all.

Technicians in blue fatigues scurried around the hangar and fussed over the aircraft. Schmidt noticed that the Argentine roundel on the side of the jet, concentric blue and white rings with a blue dot in the middle, had been altered. Someone had painted a black German cross over the central blue dot. Schmidt had to smile at that.

A powerfully-built man in a flight suit, helmet under one arm, was circling the aircraft, pointing out things here and there, slapping some of the crewmen on the shoulder. His blonde hair was dazzling in the bright lights of the hangar, and his high cheekbones and flashing smile dominated his face. Schmidt swelled with pride at the sight of the man. "Hauptmann Ritter appears in good spirits," Winkler said.

"Indeed he does." One of the ground crew spotted the colonel and his aide and shouted for the men to come to attention. All of them stood erect, heels clicking. The officer in charge of the ground crew hustled forward and snapped off a crisp salute.

"Herr Oberst, we are ready for your inspection."

"Excellent, Leutnant Berger. The aircraft looks magnificent."

"She is a beauty, Herr Oberst, ready to strike a mighty blow for the Fatherland."

The pilot strode over to them and saluted. "Good evening, Herr Oberst," he said. "Or should I say, good morning?"

Schmidt returned the salute. "Either way will do, Hauptmann Ritter." He extended his hand. The pilot's grip was firm, and his blue eyes were dazzling. Schmidt thought it was due to the light, but the pilot's pride was clearly evident. "Are you satisfied with the aircraft?"

"Yes, Herr Oberst. I would be honored to accompany you on your inspection."

"By all means," Schmidt said. He nodded at Berger. "You may proceed."

It took fifteen minutes for the crew chief to show Schmidt every pertinent detail of the Super Etendard. Their last stop was to inspect the weapon, slung underneath the belly of the aircraft. Schmidt knew it well by now, but seeing it clamped to a jet fighter was different than seeing it sitting on the floor of an assembly room or unloaded from a crate. Now, it seemed...real. Not for the first time, Schmidt thought of how close they all were to being instantly vaporized.

"Ritter, please explain to me again how you will deliver this device," Schmidt asked.

"Of course, Herr Oberst. I will approach the English fleet from the northwest, at only 200 meters of altitude. Thirty seconds from the launch point, I arm the weapon. I then will begin a climb to the launch altitude of one thousand meters. I must maintain a proper angle of ascent. When I am within one kilometer of the target, I shall release the weapon. It will continue climbing due to momentum to an altitude of 1500 meters. At that point it will be at the zenith of its arc and begin its descent. When it reaches 400 meters of altitude, it will detonate. It will then be about a kilometer from the launch point."

"You, of course, will be much further away by then."

Ritter smiled. "After releasing the weapon I will change course and accelerate to maximum speed and climb to about two thousand meters. I must risk exposure to enemy radar because I cannot be too close to the surface of the ocean when the weapon detonates. The shock wave will be much more intense at low altitude."

"I would imagine enemy radar would be the least of your concerns at that point," Schmidt said wryly.

"That is true, Herr Oberst. I do not expect any resistance. Our diversionary attack from the southwest should draw off whatever fighters the enemy can launch from his carriers."

"Very good. Hauptmann, I need a private word with you." Schmidt steered the pilot a few paces away from the rest of the men. "In the last twenty-four hours, have you had any communication with Oberstleutnant Steinhorst?"

Ritter looked puzzled. "No, Herr Oberst. I understand that he was recalled to Buenos Aires. He was to give me one final briefing at 2200 hours. I presume there are no changes to the mission?"

"You are correct, Hauptmann," Schmidt said with steel in his voice. "The strike is to be carried out exactly as planned, do you understand?"

"Perfectly, Herr Oberst."

Schmidt allowed himself a brief sigh of relief, then looked again at the young man. "I knew your father," he said, his voice suddenly husky. "We attended *Gymnasium* together in Heidelberg. He was a brave man." Schmidt had gone into the infantry, but Hans Ritter flew for the Luftwaffe and shot down six RAF Spitfires before being downed himself and captured in Scotland. Fortunately, he had survived to immigrate to Argentina after the war and sire this fine son.

"Thank you, sir," young Ritter said. "I have always done my best to make him proud."

"You will make him proud this night," Schmidt said. If only the senior Ritter could have lived to see his son now, but cancer had claimed him ten years before. Schmidt extended his hand again. "Good luck, son."

Security at the airstrip was good, but so far anyway, Ian and his men were better. His watch glowed 01:45. Fifteen minutes till the scheduled launch. Two minutes before that and Bickerstaff would begin his diversion.

After scouting the perimeter and noting the position of the enemy sentries, Ian and his men had quickly sketched out a plan. The runway ran east-west, and with the wind blowing steadily in from the ocean, it was safe to assume the aircraft would taxi to the west end of the strip and take off to the east, into the wind. Bickerstaff set four timed charges near sentry positions around the western end of the airstrip toward the south, covering perhaps a quarter of the perimeter. Once the charges went off, the big sergeant would begin firing on the Argentines from the south, moving quickly to the west. Hopefully the enemy guards would think it was a massed assault and react accordingly.

Ian and Garrett, along with Jo, worked their way around the northern perimeter and managed to find a spot near near the eastern end of the runway, a low hill with a decent view of the airstrip. As Ian expected, Argentine troops were in evidence here, but there were too many of them to deal with directly. Bickerstaff's diversion would hopefully draw them away. If not, he and Garrett would have to do some dirty work themselves.

They'd been able to observe the hill from atop another one about fifty meters away, enough to conclude it was a good launch point for the attack on the bomber, but Ian would've preferred getting into position well in advance. Not possible this time. They'd have to hustle down the little gully that separated the hills, make the short climb, eliminate any resistance, and launch the Stinger. Garrett's look in the moonlight was as good as spoken words: Can we make this any more difficult?

Garrett had been carrying the missile launcher, already loaded with one missile, while Bickerstaff carried the backup missile, passing that on to Ian when they separated. The loaded launcher weighed thirty-five pounds, which was enough of a load by itself, but its bulkiness and five-foot length made it all the more difficult. Still, they'd trained with these weapons enough times to get somewhat comfortable with them. It wouldn't take Garrett long to unlimber the launcher, sight on the bomber and fire. All he needed was a few seconds to enable the missile's infrared sensors to lock onto the jet's exhaust. Ian estimated they would be about 200 meters from the end of the airstrip when they were in position. The plan was to fire the first missile when the jet was coming down the runway. If by chance they missed, they could load the backup and fire after the plane lifted off. The Stinger had a speed of Mach 2 and range of five miles, so Ian wasn't worried about the bomber getting away. All Garrett needed was a clear shot. The missile would do the rest.

Bickerstaff would wait till the missile launch, then break off his attack and run like hell for the beach. Ian knew they'd have no chance to make it to the original extraction point, several kilometers to the south; they would have to contact the sub by radio and hope *Reliant* could successfully pick up Hodge and his team, then steam north and send a boat ashore to get them. Ian knew the odds of pulling that off would be slim indeed. He tried not to think about that.

Downing the plane was the important thing. If they didn't, a lot of good lads would die.

They'd assumed the Ninth Brigade squadron would launch several minutes ahead of the strike aircraft, so Hodge and his men were probably in action right now. That would give them a head start to the beach and perhaps increase *Reliant*'s chances of getting north soon enough to pick up Ian's team. On the other side of the coin, news of Hodge's attack could very well be sent to this airstrip, and any security officer worth his salt would become very cautious. Ian looked at the strip through his field glasses one more time.

Jo Ann hunkered down in the chilly, damp grass next to Ian. He had a good plan, and she thought their chances of pulling it off were decent. Getting safely to the submarine was another question. One thing at a time. She had the Luger she'd brought from the plane; the Luger P08, she remembered, had an eight-round magazine and fired a 9mm bullet. She'd used two rounds on Bormann, and had Willy's full clip in her pocket. She hoped she wouldn't have to use it.

In the moonlight and the light from the strip, she could see movement on the hill they needed to use to launch the Stinger. One man at least, probably two. Jo hoped they would be looking away, toward the explosions, when the time came to take the hill. There was very little cover between the hilltops and alert guards could easily cut them down well before they got within handgun range. Ian and Garrett each had MP-5 submachine guns, but using them might alert the rest of the base.

So many things to think about, problems to deal with, options to consider. Jo marveled at Ian's calmness. Garrett appeared a bit more wired, but still in charge of himself. He'd do well. Jo had been in dicey spots before, but not with so much at stake. Fonglan Island seemed very far away right now.

Ian looked once more at his watch. "Any second now," he whispered to Jo, on his right, and he motioned to Garrett on his left. The men brought their weapons up.

There was a small flash from the southwest, and a thumping crack echoed across the flat airstrip. Then another, and another. "Go!" Ian hissed, and they were up and running down the hill.

Ritter had nearly completed his slow turn at the west end of the runway when the cockpit lit up and the aircraft shuddered. The pilot looked over his right shoulder in time to see another explosion, out in the tree line less than 200 meters from him. Enemy attack! A quick glance above revealed no sign of aircraft. Commandos, then. The SBS and their British Army cousins, SAS, were much feared among the Argentine soldiers. Ritter forced himself to concentrate on his takeoff procedure, expecting any second to feel bullets striking the canopy. The nose was properly aligned on the center line of the strip. He needed only another minute to power up his engines. If he released his brakes too soon, the Etendard would never clear the end of the runway. It was almost too short for a normal takeoff. Fortunately he'd practiced several takeoffs earlier in the day, before the weapon was loaded. He'd been able to take off easily, but now he had to allow for the extra weight of the weapon, so that meant extra time to build up thrust. Normally that wouldn't have been a problem, but under enemy fire, it was a big problem. He felt beads of sweat on his forehead. He prayed the Oberst and his men could give him another forty-five seconds.

Schmidt and Winkler were in front of the headquarters building, watching Ritter's jet in its graceful but slow turn at the far end of the runway, when the first explosion came. Instinctively, the men dove for cover behind their staff car. Schmidt drew his Luger. Winkler's radio erupted with excited voices in German and Spanish.

"Leutnant Speth reports the perimeter is under attack in the southwest!" Winkler shouted. "He is moving his men to that location."

Schmidt's mind was racing. Going for the aircraft when it was nearly stopped, on the ground, made sense. But if he were assaulting the base, he would not rely on just one attack. "Winkler!"

Two more explosions ripped through the night air, then a fourth. "Yes, Herr Oberst?"

"Order Leutnant Resch and his squad to reinforce the eastern perimeter. Immediately!"

"Jawohl, Herr Oberst." Winkler yelled instructions into the radio. Within seconds, there was movement in the old hangar to their right, which the security detail was using as its barracks. Resch and his men had come off duty a few hours before, but Schmidt had ordered them to remain awake and ready to move until the plane was safely away. Now he was gratified to see a dozen men hustling out of the barracks toward a waiting troop truck.

Gunfire erupted from the southwest. Schmidt peered over the hood of the Mercedes, expecting to see rockets screaming toward Ritter's aircraft, but he saw none. What, did the English hope to bring the jet down with small-arms fire? Ludicrous!

The fighter-bomber was moving now, much too slowly to please Schmidt. It would be another minute before Ritter could get it in the air. Schmidt had watched the practice runs earlier in the day—the previous day, now. The Super Etendard was a big, heavy aircraft, fast and graceful in the sky, its natural element, but not on the ground. They had to buy Ritter enough time.

Still no rocket fire on the jet. Schmidt thought that most odd indeed. Could the English have been stupid enough to rely only on small arms? Of course not.

Resch's truck roared past them, down the gravel road flanking the airstrip. In a few seconds they would be at the perimeter. Schmidt looked past the truck, and saw the hill on the northeast edge, overlooking the airstrip. There was movement on the hill. Schmidt leaped to his feet and yanked open the driver's door of the Mercedes. "Get in!" he screamed at Winkler. The adjutant barely had time to scramble around to the passenger side and climb in when Schmidt gunned the engine and jammed the accelerator, turning down the road toward the bouncing troop truck. The rear of the heavy car fishtailed and sprayed gravel, but Schmidt kept it under control.

Inside the command building, the young lieutenant acting as the flight controller lost his nerve. He heard the explosions and chattering machine guns, looked out the window and saw a troop truck racing past to the east, and yelled into his microphone at Ritter. "We are under attack! Take off now! Now!"

The loud voice in his helmet angered Ritter. "Calm down, you fool!" The idiot, didn't he understand, the Super Etendard was not a Porsche, you could not merely stomp on the accelerator and go. He took a few critical seconds to glare out of the cockpit toward the command center. That's when he saw the troop truck speeding away, next to the runway, followed by a staff car. That could only mean one thing: enemy troops were near the end of the runway. Ritter swallowed, forcing himself to return to the task at hand. Only a few seconds more....there. He released the brake.

Ian was leading the way up the other hill when he saw a form in the moonlight, moving past a tree, suddenly silhouetted in the light from the airstrip. A man with a gun, looking away from them, toward the airstrip and the action beyond it. In the distance Ian heard a jet engine spooling up, and another sound, a truck engine, much closer. No subtlety now. Ian raised his MP-5 and squeezed off a burst at the guard. The man's body jerked as three of the rounds found their target.

On his left, Garrett was firing as well. Jo had her Luger up and sweeping in an arc, looking for targets. None appeared, and they were at the top of the hill, moving quickly through a thin stand of trees, and suddenly the airstrip was in front of them, surrounded in blue marking lights.

At the far end she saw the jet, its running lights blinking, a fiery glow coming from its exhaust ports. It was starting to move toward them, toward the ocean and freedom.

Jo looked to her left and saw Garrett calmly unlimbering the Stinger launcher, his MP-5 on the ground beside him. There was movement in the trees beyond him. "Ian!" Jo sighted with the Luger and squeezed off three quick shots.

Ian rose to a semi-crouch and brought his MP-5 to bear, firing over Garrett's head with a three-second burst. Men screamed in the darkness.

Something whizzed past Jo's head, and an instant later she heard the crack of small arms fire from the direction of the airstrip. The troop truck was pulling to a stop not fifty meters away, and two men were already standing up in the back and firing at them. The jet was still far down the runway, too far away for a clear shot. The troops—

Ian recognized the situation instantly. "Garrett! Fire on the truck!" Without hesitating, the Welsh corporal swung the launcher toward the Argentines and pulled the trigger. The Stinger's launch rocket belched fire from the rear of the tube and the missile streaked away, almost too fast for the eye to follow. The warhead's sensors locked on the hot engine of the truck. Three seconds after Garrett squeezed the trigger the missile hit the truck and exploded.

A tremendous fireball billowed into the night sky as the truck's fuel tanks ignited, a split second after the explosion of the warhead tore through the engine and obliterated the two soldiers in the cab. Bodies flew into the air, those still alive screaming in pain. The shock wave rippled up the hill and washed over Jo and the marines, and she felt the heat on the top of her head as she hugged the earth. Red-hot pieces of metal and smoking bits of human flesh rained down on them.

Garrett yelled in pain. Jo saw him drop the launcher and bring his hands to his face. A dark liquid seeped through his fingertips, and it took Jo a moment to realize it had to be blood, Garrett's blood. He'd been hit, shrapnel for sure. "Ian, Garrett's been hit!"

The jet was halfway down the runway now and accelerating. In another few seconds, it would be past them, and in the air.

Jo was at Garrett's side, pulling his hands away. A shard of metal was barely hanging from a flap of skin on his forehead. Jo knew that forehead wounds were bleeders but rarely serious unless the skull had been pierced or cracked. She flicked the shard with a fingernail and it fell easily away. Garrett would be fine, but his eyes were awash with his own blood. He was in no shape to handle the launcher.

Ian had the launcher and was loading the second missile into the tube. More shots rang out from near the remains of the truck, and Jo saw with horror that a car had pulled to a stop and two men were advancing from it, firing as they came. Bullets snapped past them and a few struck the ground. The soldiers were fifty meters away and closing.

The jet was nearly past them now, picking up speed. Jo saw the nose begin to rise.

She heard another series of shots from the direction of the car, then a watery splat from Ian. He grunted, clutching his right side with his hand, grunted again. "I'm hit, Jo…" He collapsed onto his left side, dropping the launcher.

"I got one!" Schmidt yelled. He'd seen the English commando raise the rocket launcher and carefully sighted on him with the M16, squeezing off a four round burst. One had struck home for sure. Thank God he'd put two of the rifles in the back of the staff car, just in case. One never knew. "We'll take them alive if we can, Winkler!"

All fatigue was gone now. The years had melted away in seconds, and he was a young Heer sergeant again, laughing with his friends Rudi and Manfred at a café in Paris while the sniveling French waited on him, rolling through the forests of Poland and steppes of Russia with his comrades, routing the Bolshevik sons of bitches. He charged ahead, his rifle held high.

"Look out, Herr Oberst!" Winkler yelled at him, too late. A form near the fallen Englishmen rose up and a weapon chattered, sending death their way. Schmidt took four rounds in the chest and went down, his rifle flying away, useless. Winkler stared at his commander in disbelief, but before his emotions could turn to sorrow, a round between his eyes ended all thoughts forever.

Jo held the MP-5 another two seconds, ready to fire again if the two Argentines moved, but they lay still, some forty meters beyond the smoking barrel of the gun. The roar of the jet engine grabbed her attention. The fighter-bomber was taking off, clearing the end of the runway and the encircling low hills easily, and heading east, so very quickly.

Only moments now. Jo dropped the rifle and grabbed the launcher. If any more enemy troops showed up, she knew she was dead, but she prayed for another few seconds of life, so that she could at least try to save the lives of so many young sailors over the horizon, and so many more that would die later if the war spread north.

She sighted on the flickering orange dot of the Argentine jet's engine, shrinking ever so quickly. She held her breath and pulled the trigger. The launcher shuddered and she was nearly knocked down by the vibration and the roar of the rocket engine. The missile soared away, chasing the dwindling orange dot.

Hauptmann Hans Ritter felt a surge of elation as his aircraft cleared the end of the airstrip and the low hills just to the east. The landing gear thumped up into their wells right on command, and the trim of the aircraft instantly improved. The firefight had scared him, he could admit that now, and then there was that explosion to his left as the Super Etendard flashed down the last few meters of the runway before lifting off. But he was away now, and the English commandos had failed. Now he could just concentrate on his mission. He wished Oberstleutnant Steinhorst had been there to see him off. The wing commander had seemed on edge when they'd last talked. Was he worried about the mission? Well, no matter. Ritter was aloft, where he felt the most free.

Ritter's joy lasted only a few seconds. The threat warning alarm beeped in his headset. MISIL DE ENTRADA flashed at the top of the green radar screen. Inbound missile! There it was, coming from the west, very fast. Ritter's training kicked into overdrive. He jerked the control stick to the left and forward.

Two seconds after it cleared the launch tube, the Stinger's launch engine fell away and the main rocket flared to life, driving the missile ever faster. Four small guidance fins snapped into place. The sensors in the missile's nose, just ahead of the 2.2-pound warhead, focused on the infrared light generated by the exhaust of the fleeing Super Etendard. The Stinger's onboard computer began sending a series of instantaneous course corrections to the guidance fins, which obediently adjusted the missile's course. The target was accelerating, nearly 500 miles per hour now, but the missile was much faster. Ten seconds after launch the Stinger broke the sound barrier and began to close on the jet.

Ritter juked the aircraft again, this time to starboard, and pulled the nose up. He punched a button that ejected small bundles of aluminum chaff from the defense pods behind the cockpit, spraying the chaff into small clouds that he hoped would confuse the missile's radar. His radar screen showed the missile coming on, inhumanly fast. Ritter had no time to feel fear. He concentrated every ounce of his will on saving his aircraft and himself.

The Stinger's computer saw that the target was off-center in the image sensor. Using its pre-programmed proportional navigation software, the computer calculated the target was eight degrees off-center and ordered a course change of sixteen degrees to over-compensate, anticipating the flight path of the target. A tenth of a second later, the computer made another correction, and another, too fast for any human brain to follow. The Stinger could think much faster than a human pilot trying to evade it, and it could fly much faster than any jet aircraft in the world. The rocket pushed the missile close to Mach 2, nearly 1,500 miles per hour. The distance to the target was shrinking rapidly. The missile tore through the drifting clouds of chaff, ignoring them completely, its sensors focused relentlessly on the Super Etendard's hot exhaust, which could not be disguised.

Ritter saw the inbound missile pass through the chaff clouds on his radar screen and instantly made a decision. His aircraft was doomed. If he'd only had another minute, even a bit less, he could have outraced the missile, gotten out of its range. But he had run out of time. He leveled out the aircraft and reached for the ejection handle. Only seconds now. His gloved hand gripped the handle and began to squeeze, but one more thought made him hesitate: the bomb.

Ritter made another decision. His weapons panel included the arming switch for the bomb and the release lever. Ignoring the arming switch, Ritter reached for the release lever with his other hand and pulled. He felt the aircraft shudder and bounce upward as the 500-kilogram bomb dropped away, harmless, falling toward the sea. Then Ritter pulled on the ejection handle. The canopy blew upward and explosive charges destroyed the bolts clamping his seat to the airframe. Rocket engines ignited and propelled the seat and its occupant straight upward into the night sky, so quickly that the G-forces rendered Ritter unconscious. Three seconds later the Stinger missile streaked into the jet, colliding with the hull just to the left and forward of the port side exhaust, and the warhead exploded.

CHAPTER FORTY-FOUR

Chubut province, Argentina
Tuesday, April 27th, 1982

Jo couldn't help but watch the missile chase the Argentine jet. She didn't know the missile's range, but the jet couldn't escape, could it? The Stinger seemed to be closing the gap, but it was hard to tell in the darkness.

Beside her, Ian groaned, snapping her back to the here and now. Garrett had found a bandage in his medikit and slapped it on his forehead, but it was still bleeding a little. Jo would have to help him with that, but Ian was in serious trouble. The right side of his jacket was soaked with blood.

"Help me get to the wound!" Jo yelled at the corporal. Her training and discipline held, allowing her to stay focused. Together, they pulled Ian's jacket off and Jo pulled up his shirt. In the dim light she could see the wound, dark and ugly, blood seeping out of it. "Got another bandage?" Garrett handed her one and she put it against the wound. It was enough to cover it, and she took a roll of white tape from the corporal and began wrapping it around Ian's torso to hold the bandage in place.

"Is it bad?" Garrett asked.

"Yes," she said, lips tight. "We need to get him to a hospital."

"Fuckin' Argies'll let him bleed out," Garrett said. "There's a doc on the submarine."

Jo was about to reply when a booming sound rolled in from the east. They looked off into the night, over the ocean, in time to see the expanding fireball of what had been the Argentine jet. "You got the bastard!" Garrett yelled, pumping his fist in the air. "Bloody hell, you splashed him good, Major!"

The relief Jo should've felt was pushed rudely aside by her fear for Ian. "We might not have time to get to the sub," she said. "Maybe we should—" Her discipline nearly failed her. Surrendering to the enemy was something she never would have contemplated before, but now, things were different, weren't they? They could get Ian to a hospital, save his life. So what if she never got back home?

"Hey, look, the Argies are running like hell!"

She looked back down toward the airstrip. Past the burning wreckage of the troop truck, she saw men running crazily across the airstrip, diving into ditches. Panicky yells reached her. "They must think the bomb's going to go off," she said. "That has to be it."

Garrett looked at her, eyes wide. "It won't, will it?"

"Not unless it was armed first," she said, hoping she was right. She had an idea. "This is our chance, Garrett. Come on, give me a hand with Ian." She struggled with his weight. "For

God's sake, man, if the damn thing goes off we're all dead anyhow. We can get to the beach while the bad guys are still figuring it out!"

They had made it about a hundred meters, coming over the last hill with the ocean in front of them, when a large shape came out of the night to their right. "Ahoy there," came a whispered voice.

"Bickerstaff! Is that you?" Garrett hissed.

"Right-o, mate. What's this here now?" The huge Londoner came out of a shadow, sheathing his wicked knife.

"Ian took a round in the side," Jo said, panting from the exertion. "The Argentines thought the bomb was going to go off when the plane blew up. We don't have much time."

"I got in a radio call," Bickerstaff said. "We need to get two klicks north from here. *Reliant* picked up the other team and she's on her way."

"North?" Garrett asked.

Bickerstaff took Ian from them and hefted the wounded man over his shoulder like he was a sack of grain. "Right," he grunted. "A bit out of the way but further from the Argie base. Once the buggers are done shittin' themselves, they'll get organized and be after us for sure. Come on, then, we got a yomp ahead of us."

The beach, such that it was, offered plenty of hazards in the dim light of the moon. Jo took the lead, scouting a few meters ahead to warn of holes, tangling brush or other obstacles. Nimble as she might otherwise be, she stumbled more than once, painfully barking both shins. Bickerstaff huffed along behind her, carrying Ian, with Garrett providing cover from the rear. Jo had Ian's MP-5, with the Luger tucked into the waistband of her borrowed trousers.

"Hold up," Bickerstaff said, panting. "Gotta rest. Check the colonel."

Jo came back to him as the sergeant laid Ian gently on the gravelly sand, propping him up against a fallen log. Jo felt for a pulse, and it was still there, thank God. Ian groaned. "Jo...Jo..."

"Hush," she said, her voice quaking. "Save your strength. We're almost to the sub."

"Let's have a look at that wound," Bickerstaff said, pulling up his colonel's shirt. "Bleedin's stopped, looks like," he said.

Garrett came up from the rear. "Got movement about two klicks back," he said. "Dogs and lights."

Jo stood up and looked south, back toward the airstrip, and saw the waving flashlights in the far distance. Over the rush of the surf she could hear a faint yelping. "Infantry," she said. "Maybe they think we went south."

"If Argie has any brains at all he'll split his force and cover both directions," Bickerstaff said. "Probably call in choppers from that air base. We'll be in the soup then. No more Stingers, Garrett?"

"No, Sergeant. I took out a troop truck with me first, the major here brought down the jet with t'other."

"Right, then. Well, let's hope help arrives quick." Bickerstaff crouched down and picked up Ian again. "Major, if you please..."

Jo squeezed Ian's dangling hand, brought her MP-5 up and turned toward the north.

***

Aboard HMS Reliant, *southwest Atlantic*

Tuesday, April 27th, 1982

"How much further, Captain?"

Bentley looked sharply at the SBS officer. It was an effort to keep his voice calm. "About half a kilometer farther than we were last time you asked, Mr. Hodge."

"Sorry, sir," Hodge said. They were all under incredible strain. "Shall I ready the lads, sir?"

"That would be fine." The captain turned back to the navigational table, huddling with his officers. He checked the map, then his watch. "Hodge, we'll turn west in about ten minutes. After that, it's another ten till we surface."

"Aye aye, Captain. We'll be ready." Hodge hustled aft, where the exhausted SBS troopers waited anxiously in the mess hall. They'd been aboard only about twenty minutes, and had to wait another twenty until they could go after the colonel. It would seem like an eternity, unless he got them busy.

For a man used to traveling in helicopters and speedboats, the submarine seemed terribly slow to Hodge. Doubtless the rest of the lads felt the same way, but the skipper was being cautions. The waters where he picked them up were too shallow to allow much maneuvering, so he moved the boat a kilometer to the east before turning to the north. It all took time. Hodge was frustrated, but he knew the swabbies were doing the best they could. It wouldn't do to run on the surface and expose the boat to enemy ASW fire.

At least there was one less Argie bomber to worry about now. Hodge and his men had taken down the Super Etendard with one Stinger, saving the backup missile. There was a nasty little firefight after the missile launch, but he brought his men back to the beach and their waiting boat with only two light casualties. Besides the poor bloke in the jet, they probably took a dozen or so Argies down in the action. Not a bad night's work, but it was far from over. Thank God he'd gotten Bickerstaff's radio call just as he was boarding the sub; another minute and they probably would've missed it. He would've had to talk Bentley into staying at periscope depth to keep the radio mast up, and the sub captain wouldn't have liked that at all.

The men looked up at him expectantly as he entered the mess. "All right, lads, let's get ready. We disembark in about twenty minutes. Weapons check first."

"What's the play to be, Cap'n?" Kent asked. He'd done well ashore, gaining a measure of badly-needed confidence after his narrow escape from disaster during the E&RE.

"We'll surface and break out the extra Zodiac boat. The skipper's bringing us as close to shore as he dares, about two kilometers. I'll take the boat ashore with Henderson, Wayne and Kent. Sergeant Powers, I want you topside in the sail with the last Stinger, just in case the Argies put up a bird after us."

"Right, sir," Powers said. "Would be helpful to have another missile or two, but there's none on board. I checked."

"Well, can't blame the Navy for that. They don't design submarines to fight it out on the surface with aircraft. We'll go ashore, locate the colonel and his party and be back as quick as we can. We'll stay in radio contact so if you have to pull back and dive, we'll follow as far as we can and hope for the best." If it was absolutely necessary, they could still get back on board the submarine even if it was submerged at periscope depth, but that would be very dicey indeed, especially if there were wounded to bring aboard. Hodge tried not to think about that possibility.

***

Chubut province, Argentina

Monday, April 27th, 1982

Jo knew the yelping and flashlights had gotten a bit closer. She also thought she heard helicopters, but didn't see running lights in any direction. To the east, the sky was beginning to lighten a bit. They'd taken another brief rest stop, and Bickerstaff told her it was nearly three a.m. local time. False dawn; sunrise wouldn't be till a bit after five.

Ian was still with them, but barely. Bickerstaff was beginning to tire; the man was strong as an ox, but even an ox had its limits. Garrett's head wound had stopped bleeding and he seemed none the worse for wear, but they were all exhausted. "How much further?" Jo asked.

"I'd have to say we're pretty close," Bickerstaff said after taking a swig from his canteen. He passed it to Jo, who took a healthy drink. "Let's see if we can raise the boat." He pulled a radio transceiver out of his ruck. "Henhouse, this is Rooster Two. Do you copy? Over." Nothing but static in response. The sergeant and Jo exchanged worried looks. Behind them, facing toward the south with his rifle at the ready, Garrett had cocked an expectant ear.

"Try again," Jo said.

Bickerstaff licked his lips, then raised the radio to them. "Henhouse, this is Rooster Two. Do you copy? Over."

More static. Then, a clear British voice. *"Rooster Two, this is Henhouse. Calibrating your position now. What's your situation?"*

Bickerstaff let out a huge sigh of relief. "I have three other souls with me. One is serious and needs urgent medevac. Natives are approx two klicks to our south. Possible aircraft, approx two klicks south. North and west appear clear."

"Roger that, Rooster Two. Have your location now. Rooster One is on his way. Vectoring him to you. Watch for his signal. He'll raise you when he sees your return signal."

"Aye aye, Henhouse. Rooster Two out." Bickerstaff unclipped a flashlight from his web belt. "Major, do you know Morse code?"

"Yes," Jo said. She'd been holding Ian's hand, wiping his sweating face with her shirt. His breathing was steady, and he was in and out of consciousness. He'd recognized her, though, and smiled at her. It was all she could do to hold back her tears.

Bickerstaff handed her the flashlight. "When you see their light, they'll be flashing 'R-1'. You return with 'R-2'. Pretty clever, what?'

Jo managed a weak smile. "Right out of a James Bond movie."

"Right, then." Bickerstaff hauled himself to his feet and brought his rifle around. "I'll take perimeter watch with Garrett. I'm heading up on that bit of a rise about fifty meters that way," he said, pointing to the east. "Garrett, you get down the beach there about twenty meters and keep your eyes peeled."

"Aye aye, Sergeant." The Welshman got to his feet and hustled away.

Bickerstaff knelt and put a ham-sized hand on Ian's chest. "You sit tight, Colonel," he said with surprising tenderness. "The lads are on the way. You'll be downing a pint in the wardroom right quick."

Ian's eyes fluttered open and he looked up at the big sergeant. "Yeah," he croaked. "Leave...me..."

"No!" Jo said, nearly breaking down. "We're not leaving you!"

Was he trying to laugh? "No...leave me a weapon..." Bickerstaff grunted and handed over his sidearm, then gave his radio to Jo.

The big Londoner picked his way through the rocks and gnarled trees inland. Jo watched him as long as she could, then lost him in the shadows. Jo dropped Ian's hand and tore herself away from him, forcing herself to face toward the ocean. The surf was rolling in about thirty feet from them. She peered toward the horizon. Nothing. To the south, she heard the sounds of the pursuing Argentines, getting closer. And then she saw the helicopter's running lights, about a kilometer to their south, zigzagging over the beach, a searchlight sweeping downward. It made the helo a big target, but she supposed that was meant to flush them out into the open by drawing their fire. A gamble, but the Argentines were apparently willing to risk a helicopter.

They didn't have much time. She turned back to the east...a light! Blinking at her, yes, it was "R-1". She raised the flashlight, switched it on, and sent the recognition signal. The return signal was "R-1 OK". She flashed "R-2 OK", then paused and sent "HELO". She assumed the men in the incoming boat could see the helicopter, but she wanted to be sure. She'd also forgotten entirely about the radio.

Rifle fire erupted from Bickerstaff's hill. Jo couldn't see anything over there, too dark yet, but she flashed "R-2 ENGAGED" at the boat, then she brought her MP-5 around and crouched next to Ian. More shots from the hill, and then she heard a thumping sound heading her way. Heart racing, she trained the weapon on the source of the sound, ready to fire, but then she recognized the shape as Bickerstaff, running for all he was worth, leaping over rocks and trees.

"Squad of infantry, about 300 meters and coming in," he said, panting. "Must've spotted me in the moonlight, damn it all. Got off a couple shots my way. I think I got one of them."

"How many?"

"Hard to say. At least five or six, I'd guess."

"The boat's inbound," she said. "Any minute now. They know we've taken fire."

"All right, then," he said. "We make our stand here. The lads coming in will help even the odds." He rose and whistled toward the south. "Garrett! Fall back here!"

Jo could hear the helicopter, but was that the faint buzzing of a marine outboard? She looked out to sea, but

551

couldn't make out anything. They could be close, or they could be miles away. Jo and the marines would have to hold out.

The helicopter had spotted the exchange of fire on the hill, and was heading their way now, whining like an angry hornet. The searchlight swept up the beach. Garrett was running their way, then he abruptly stopped and crouched into a firing position, facing the helo, and squeezed off a burst. Jo thought she saw a few sparks fly off the fuselage, and the helo banked slightly to its right. Gunfire erupted from its weapons pylon, and tracers stitched their way up the beach toward Garrett, who dove behind covering rocks at the last second. He returned fire, aiming for the searchlight.

From far out on the horizon, something was coming. Jo saw a streak through the sky, ripping the very fabric of the air, heading for the helicopter, which was still firing on Garrett's position. The Welshman was cringing down behind the rocks as heavy-caliber rounds tore into the stone and the dirt around him.

Without a sound, having passed Mach 1 seconds earlier, the Stinger slammed into the Argentine helicopter. There was an enormous roar and a fireball bloomed in mid-air where the helicopter had been a moment earlier. Jo flattened herself over Ian, hearing the death throes of the chopper as it plunged into the surf, not more than a hundred meters away. A few pieces of wreckage whined over them and chunked into the ground.

Jo raised her head carefully. The remains of the helicopter churned on the water, throwing a glow over the beach. Now there was enough light, and she could see moving shapes further down the beach, heading their way, maybe half a klick away. To her right, she saw more shapes heading down the hill Bickerstaff had occupied only moments before. The sergeant was in a firing position behind a pair of downed trees, aiming his MP-5 carefully. He squeezed off three single shots and two of the shapes went down.

There was a definite buzzing to her left, and she turned in time to see a Zodiac boat appear out of the darkness, riding the light surf. She raised the flashlight and waved it at them wildly. The boat slid up onto the beach fifty feet to her north and men began leaping out and running toward her.

Things happened quickly then, but to Jo it seemed as if it was almost in slow motion. The crackling of the helicopter fire, the chattering of machine guns, the yelling of angry and wounded men, all that became just background noise. She could hear herself breathing, and she brought herself easily into a state of mushin.

She saw four men closing on Bickerstaff. He brought one down with his rifle, then he drew his long knife and it flashed in the firelight. There were screams, and Jo saw what seemed to be a head flying away, its helmet still strapped on. Bickerstaff's kukhari flashed again, bringing more screams.

The men from the boat fanned out and their rifles began chattering. One rushed toward Jo and Ian, but then went down, hit in the arm, spinning him around and to the ground. Jo saw Garrett mow down three onrushing Argentines and then fall back toward the boat, keeping to cover.

Two men got past Bickerstaff and charged Jo's position. She brought the MP-5 up and aimed carefully, taking down the first one with two rounds in the chest, but then nothing. The clip was empty. She tossed the useless rifle aside and dove to her right, rolling on the hard sand, coming up quickly. She saw the Argentine jump up onto the low rocks that had been shielding Ian. Firelight flashed off the bayonet on the end of his rifle.

Jo launched herself toward him, her flying kick knocking the weapon away and sending both of them to the ground. She was on her feet quickly but the Argentine was right with her, and she thought he yelled something in German at her. He drew a knife and swiped at her, but she aimed a side kick at his wrist and he shrieked as she connected, dropping the knife. Jo tried to follow through with a backspin kick, but the Argentine was ready for it, ducking just in time. She sensed rather than saw the haymaker coming toward her and raised her arms in a V-block, but the man was strong and the impact jolted her backward.

The Argentine came at her again with a left this time and Jo ducked under it, coming back with a quick one-two combination to the man's floating ribs. He yelled in pain, and she loosed a side kick at his exposed left knee, feeling the joint shatter with the impact, bringing another scream from the Argentine. He staggered backward, and Jo meant to follow and finish him off but she slipped on a loose rock and went down, hitting her head on the hard ground. Dazed, she saw the Argentine reach down and pick something off the ground. The knife. He staggered toward her, one leg wobbling, and Jo tried to roll away, but her fuzzy brain wouldn't send the signals quickly enough. The Argentine came down on her, propping himself on his good knee, and he swung his crippled right hand, catching her flush on the cheek, snapping her head to the side. Pain bolted through her, ripping away the fog, and as he brought the knife down with his left hand, she was able to bring her own hands up and catch him by the wrist. The tip of the knife wavered six inches above her face.

"Weibsstück! Jetzt Sie würfel!" She felt his hot breath on her bruised cheek, smelling of sausage. He was much bigger than her, and stronger, and her strength was waning. She had enough left to do something, hoping it would be enough.

She reached deep into her central being, her haragei, deeper than she ever had. A kihap roiled up from inside her and rushed through her mouth and outward, a brutal, primal scream, and as the Argentine's eyes went wide she brought her right leg up with her last ergs of strength and slammed her booted foot into the side of his head. Blood spurted from his mouth. She planted the boot on his chest and shoved as hard as she could, but she was entirely spent now, and he was heavy, and she was able to move him only about foot or so backward, and he was recovering quickly and bringing the knife down again, and she had nothing left.

Three shots rang out from behind her, and the Argentine shuddered, hit in the chest and shoulder. Jo screamed in pain as a round clipped her foot. Then another round tore into his throat. Held up by Joe's boot, he toppled slowly to his right, the knife falling away, and he slumped to the ground, blood pumping from his tattered throat. Jo struggled to a sitting position and looked behind her. Ian had crawled onto the rocks, and she saw the smoking pistol fall away from his outstretched hand.

EPILOGUE

Portreath, Cornwall, England
Friday, May 14th, 1982

Jo Ann thrashed in the bed, sweat drenching the sheets, and forced herself to wake up. "No!" She sat upright, the sheet falling away from her chest. The silk pajama top was soaked. Shaking her head to drive away the last vestiges of the nightmare, she slid her bare feet to the floor and got up.

She quickly removed the sodden pajama top, covering herself with a cotton robe, and padded to the window. The second-story view would have been charming under other circumstances. Dawn was breaking, and the Cornish coast sparkled in a new springtime morning. Fishermen were preparing to cast off their boats. Trucks—they were called lorries here, she remembered—were moving through the narrow streets of the town, delivering their goods to the stores. A few passenger cars were about.

Jo drew the robe more tightly around her and shivered. The nightmare had been so vivid, and why not? It was a virtual replay of the last hours of the mission. The desperate retreat to the beach, the firefight, her confrontation with the German-Argentine, the shots from Ian's gun that saved her life. The high-speed boat ride out to sea, holding Ian's hand as the SBS scanned the skies for pursuing enemy aircraft. The ghostly bulk of the submarine sliding up out of the ocean. The cumbersome transfer of the unconscious Ian from the Zodiac into the sub, Jo following the shouting men carrying him down the ladder, through the narrow passageway to the mess hall where the ship's surgeon had set up a crude field hospital. The last image, as she held his hand.

She gulped back a sob and looked back at the empty bed. Her foot ached where the bullet had creased it through her boot during that last fight. She hadn't wept that morning, so exhausted she was, and hadn't allowed herself to weep since then, but now she did, sliding to the floor as the tears came.

It was a beautiful service. The small country Anglican church was filled to capacity. Many in attendance were in uniform, including a well-known individual in Royal Navy dress blues, sitting in the second pew on the right side. The vicar spoke passionately about the love of Christ and the certainty of salvation. He looked at the flag-draped casket, then at the gray-faced elderly couple in the front pew. "In our grief, we must remember the words of our Lord, who said, 'Greater love hath no man than this, that a man lay down his life for his friends.'"

At the cemetery outside, the Royal Navy chaplain read from Scripture, and a Navy choir sang "Eternal Father, Strong to Save", the sailors' hymn. The special guest then rose from his chair next to his pretty young wife and walked solemnly to the grave. "Our nation owes a great debt to Ian Masters," Prince Charles said. "It is a debt, indeed, owed to him by the entire civilized world." Jo realized that he knew the real truth of what had happened so far away. The prince spoke a few more words, then was handed a small leather case. "On behalf of Her Majesty the Queen and a grateful nation, we posthumously bestow, upon Lieutenant Colonel Ian Masters of Her Majesty's Royal Marines, the Victoria Cross." He walked over to the elderly man sitting at the graveside, wearing an old World War II Army uniform, and handed him the case. The old veteran opened it up with trembling hands, rose and saluted the prince, then shook his hand. The honor guard folded the Union Jack and handed it to Mrs. Masters, who kissed it before setting it gently in her lap.

Watching from the rows of mourners, wearing a dark civilian suit, Jo wished she could be in uniform along with Ian's SBS troopers in their dress blues. The men who'd been on the mission all sported fresh new medals; Bickerstaff and Garrett had been awarded the Conspicuous Gallantry Medal. Next to Jo, Sir David Blandford provided a kind and supportive presence. His had been the difficult task of telling Jo that, for security reasons, she could not attend the service in her Air Force uniform, and could not stand with the SBS troopers. There were photographers about, and it would not do to have a U.S. Air Force officer seen in the midst of Ian's command. Too many questions would be asked. What was unsaid was that MI6 might want to utilize Jo's services again sometime, so relative anonymity had to be preserved.

A line of seven Royal Marine riflemen fired three volleys, and a trumpeter played taps. Ian's parents approached the casket one last time. Was the father's lip trembling? The mother rested a hand on the casket, then turned away as tears flowed down her face, and her husband took her by the elbow. At her other side was a young woman whom Jo knew to be Ian's sister, Yvonne.

The mourners filed back to the church and the fleet of cars waiting to take them a few miles to the Masters' home, which would host the reception. Blandford and Jo were walking silently toward his car when a young Royal Marine came up behind them. "Excuse me, Major Geary?"

"Yes?"

"Begging your pardon, ma'am, but could you accompany me back to the church for a moment?"

Sir David gave her a caring smile. "I'll be waiting at the car."

The marine led Jo back to the sacristy. "Please go inside, ma'am." She opened the door to see Prince Charles waiting, his white Navy cap under one arm. Next to him was his wife Diana, dignified but still glamorous in a navy blue jacket and skirt. Charles turned to Jo with a smile, but his eyes were sad.

"Major Geary, a pleasure." He offered a hand, and his grip was firm and warm.

"Your Highness, I—I'm not even sure if that's what I should call you," Jo said, flustered. She felt her face get hot.

"That will do," the prince said. He reached over to a table and picked up a small leather case. "I wanted to take a moment to express my personal thanks, and that of our Queen and our entire nation, for your service in this affair. Unfortunately, for diplomatic reasons, we cannot acknowledge your efforts publicly, but I would like to present you with this." He handed her the case, opening it up. A glistening medal rested inside on purple velvet. "The George Cross," he said. "It is the highest award we may present to a civilian for service."

Jo felt her eyes blink. "Thank you, Your Highness. I am honored."

"I read the transcript of your debriefing," Charles said. "A most impressive account. I commend you on your heroism. The prime minister has communicated our great regards to your president."

"I—I don't know what to say."

"We are aware of your special relationship with Colonel Masters," Diana said in her soft voice. Her eyes were glistening. "Please accept our most sincere condolences." She stepped forward, reaching out, and Jo allowed the royal embrace, welcomed it, returned it, and as she felt the pain of her loss, she felt the love of a nation.

***

Heathrow was crowded, as usual. Jo Ann stood in the VIP departure lounge, her flight having just been called, and gathered her carryon and jacket. Sir David stood by, having insisted on waiting with her.

"Well, it was a lovely service yesterday," he said.

"Yes, it was," Jo said. "Ian's parents were most gracious."

"He wrote of you frequently," the SIS man said. "In his last letter, he told them he intended to marry you after the war."

Jo managed a smile. "That would have been...it would've been just fine," she said.

Sir David extended a hand. "Major Geary...Jo Ann...it has been an honor to work with you. Your service to our country has been beyond exemplary. Without you, I daresay we would have lost this war." Word had come during the reception that the Argentines had surrendered the Falklands; the SBS troopers invited Jo to celebrate at a downtown pub, but she declined with thanks.

"Thank you, Sir David." She had to blink back a tear. "It was...a privilege for me to serve."

He placed another hand on top of hers. "I hope that someday, should the need arise again, we may call on you?" He raised an eyebrow hopefully.

She looked away, then back at him, and through her grief she managed a smile. "You know where to find me." She picked up her bag and walked to the waiting gate.

ACKNOWLEDGEMENTS

There are many people who contributed to this book, starting with my parents, who encouraged me to read and bought us a set of encyclopedia for Christmas; my teachers in elementary, middle and high school, most especially English teachers like Mrs. Millman and Mrs. Leonard in Potosi; and my instructors at the University of Wisconsin-Platteville. In recent years I have benefited greatly from the advice and tutelage of the ladies in my writers group. Donna, Marla, Marjorie and Helen, although this work was not one we reviewed together, what I have learned in our meetings has, I believe, made this book a lot better.

Most importantly, this book would never have been written without the support of my wife, Sue. There might be other husbands out there with wives as great as mine, but I doubt it.

As a youngster growing up in Wisconsin, I would sometimes go down to the basement and open my father's Army footlocker, take out his old uniforms and try them on. Dad was a bit too young for Korea but served in Germany in the mid-fifties, and spent much of his time playing baseball, he told me years later. But he and all his fellow soldiers knew that at any moment, they might go on alert and very soon thereafter they would have rifles in their hands, moving to the sound of guns.

I often wondered if I might have that courage, should my name ever be called. A high school basketball injury ended any thoughts of a military career, but as time went by I wondered about the reasons men and women have put on the uniform, in our country and others, over the decades and centuries. Some have selfish reasons, some are quite practical, but for most, I believe, there is an underlying sense that they need to prove themselves, to give something to a greater cause. In his book *The Warrior Ethos*, which I consider to be one of the finest works I've read on the subject, author Steven Pressfield says this:

"We all fight wars—in our work, within our families and abroad in the wider world. Each of us struggles every day to define and defend our sense of purpose and integrity, to justify our existence on the planet and to understand, if only within our own hearts, who we are and what we believe in."

The White Vixen is a work of fiction, but the struggles of Jo Ann Geary, Ian Masters and their compatriots to define their own sense of purpose and integrity harken back to those of ancient times, and to the work of warriors today and into the future. It is, at its core, a struggle we engage in not for wealth or power, but to define who we are and what we stand for, as individuals and as nations. Many times men and women have chosen to define themselves solely as seekers of wealth and power, determined to achieve their goals no matter the cost to their neighbors or even their own people. When that happens, warriors like Jo Ann and Ian, like my father and my Civil War veteran great-great-grandfather, have stood against them, and prevailed. In 1982, the United Kingdom chose to take a stand against aggression, a stand that exacted a high cost in blood and treasure but which, in the judgment of the British people and their leaders, had to be done. The strategic implications of Britain's decision to fight for the Falklands, and whether it was truly worth the cost, are debated to this day. But what cannot be denied is this: the British decided that at the very least, national honor demanded a response, and it was successful. A lesson, I think, that we Americans took to heart nearly twenty years later, when our own national honor was tested even more severely.

In addition to Pressfield, I am indebted to the following authors and historians for their excellent work, which provided invaluable source material and inspiration:

Max Hastings & Simon Jenkins, *The Battle for the Falklands*

Charles Whiting, *The Hunt for Martin Bormann*

William Stevenson, *The Bormann Brotherhood*

Richard Deacon, *A History of the British Secret Service*

Wayne Bernhardson, *Argentina, Uruguay and Paraguay*

Duncan Falconer, *First Into Action*

W.E.B. Griffin, the *Honor Bound* series

Richard C. Thornton, *The Falklands Sting*

Donna Barr Tabor, historian, XVIII Airborne Corps and Fort Bragg

Chuck Anesi, words and music for "Horst Wessel"

Jason Pipes, www.feldgrau.com, for details on WWII German military

The Air Force Association

John Pike, www.fas.org/irp for details on world intelligence organizations

Cover art by Damonza. Book trailer video produced by Jim Tindell.

You're invited to visit my Facebook page, www.facebook.com/DavidTindellAuthor, for updates on book signings, new novels in the works, and general ramblings about the life of an author.

THE RED WOLF

Jo Ann Geary went back to the United States and resumed her Air Force Special Operations career after the events described in this book, but she would be called into action again, sent behind the Iron Curtain to hunt down her most dangerous adversary yet, The Red Wolf.

PROLOGUE

Camp David, Maryland

January 1987

The first President of the United States that Joseph Geary had met was Harry Truman. Geary had no trouble recalling the date: the sixth of June, 1945, and the place, a reception at the State Department. Geary shook his head now as he recalled how nervous he'd been, twenty-five years of age, just a few years out of Yale and into his career at the Office of Strategic Services. On this night, the first anniversary of D-Day, Geary accompanied his department director to the reception, where everyone was surprised by Truman's arrival. Less than four months on the job after the tragic death of FDR, the former Missouri haberdasher impressed the young OSS operative with his folksy demeanor, behind which the perceptive agent sensed a stiff resolve. Geary had heard all the talk around Washington, that Truman wasn't up to the job, was a political appointee by Roosevelt who had barely been on speaking terms with his vice president, all the way back to the campaign the previous fall.

Like many others, Joe Geary wondered whether Truman had the right stuff, but after meeting him that night, he had no doubt. Over the course of the next several years, their paths would cross again. Geary also met Truman's successor, Dwight Eisenhower, and every president since then. Some he liked personally but not professionally—Kennedy, for instance, a charismatic man but whose philandering was something Geary simply could not approve of, and Carter, who was in way over his head on some things. With others, it was the other way around. Geary respected their professional expertise but could not bring himself to like the men. LBJ and Nixon came immediately to mind. But he had worked for all of them, first in OSS and then in its successor organization, the Central Intelligence Agency.

His forty-plus years in the spy business had led him to this point in time, his last stop. As Deputy Director of Operations, he had been summoned to Camp David by no less than the current resident of the Oval Office, and not through intermediaries. The call earlier that day came to Geary's own secure phone personally, with the White House operator putting the call through. Once the requisite pops and clicks had sounded to give the electronic equivalent of an All Clear, Geary heard the famous voice, chatting for a few seconds, then asking him to come up to Camp David that evening for a talk. It was not a request that Geary or anyone else would have refused.

"The president will see you now," a man said. Geary knew him as the assistant chief of staff. Donald Regan, the man's boss, didn't normally accompany the president to the Maryland retreat, named by Eisenhower in honor of his grandson. That was fine with Geary, who found Regan to be abrasive and overbearing. Ironically, both Regan and the president had served as lifeguards when they were in their younger days. The word around CIA was that while the future president had spent his time saving people from drowning, his future chief of staff had spent his time watching out for kids pissing in the pool. Geary nodded at the man and went through the opened door.

There was only one man in the room, sitting on a leather couch near the crackling fireplace. He put down the book he'd been leafing through and rose, coming forward to greet his visitor. Once again, Geary was impressed by the man's physical size, his ruddy complexion, belying his—what was it now, soon to be seventy-six years? "Joe, come in, nice to see you," Ronald Reagan said, shaking hands with a strong grip. "How was the weather on the way up?" He motioned Geary to a chair near the couch.

"Not bad, sir, thank you." Geary had met Reagan shortly after his inauguration six years ago, had briefed him on several occasions, but usually in the company of the Director of Central Intelligence. William Casey, though, was out of the country at the moment. He was due back next week, which left Geary somewhat surprised that the president had not waited. This lent a sense of urgency to the meeting, although his host didn't show it.

"Get you anything? It's after hours, so the bar's open."

"Thank you, sir. Scotch, neat."

"Good, good." The president motioned to the assistant chief, still standing in the doorway. "Bill, tell Ed, Scotch neat for our guest, please. I'll keep him company."

While the president made small talk, Geary's ever-observant eyes took the measure of the man. Wearing a denim shirt, open at the neck, with khaki pants and loafers, Reagan looked more like a successful retired executive than a man still very much active in the world's toughest job. Geary knew of his exercise habits, his regular visits to the White House gym and his horseback riding and wood-chopping on the ranch out in California. That demanded Geary's respect; since becoming DDO several years earlier, Geary had barely any time to take a walk at lunch, much less get in regular workouts. He was ten years younger than the man on the couch, but he knew he looked like he was the older man, and not just because he was bald.

Geary was well aware of the stories about Reagan, how he was detached and incurious when it came to the details of shaping policy and managing his staff. There were plenty of people in the government, including some in the White House, who spoke of the president in disparaging terms. Geary had heard the occasional comments at cocktail parties, at meetings, even in foreign capitals. He tended to take those with a grain of salt. Stories were one thing. Geary heard a lot of stories in his job, but you couldn't discount the value of personal observation. He'd met with Reagan several times, and while he'd known presidents who had a better understanding of the details of one thing or another, none were better than Reagan at seeing the big picture. Geary remembered his meetings with Reagan's predecessor; Jimmy Carter was truly one of those who not only couldn't see the forest for the trees, he couldn't see the trees for the leaves. In the end, Geary was sure, those contrasting perspectives were the reason why Reagan was here now and Carter had been sent back to his peanut farm in Georgia.

A steward came in with the drinks and served each of the men. "Thank you, Ed," the president said with a grin. The steward closed the door behind him on the way out. "Well, Joe, there's something I wanted to talk to you about, as you may have guessed."

Geary nodded. CIA had several things going on right now that Reagan might've been interested in discussing, but the DDO had tried not to anticipate the president's thoughts. That turned out to be a good thing.

"You did some good work, helping me get ready for Reykjavik last fall," Reagan said, his mood instantly more serious. "I was ready for everything they threw at me over there."

"Thank you, sir," Geary said. His office had worked hard to assist Casey in putting together a full briefing for the president in advance of his first meeting with the new General Secretary of the Communist Party of the Soviet Union, Mikhail Gorbachev. The result had been an agreement to reduce the two countries' nuclear arsenals. "It looks good for INF," he added. The Intermediate Range Nuclear Forces Treaty would hopefully be signed later this year. It was a significant breakthrough in Soviet-American relations.

"It looks good for a lot more than that," the president said. He took a sip of his drink, then gazed into the fire. His eyes turned back to Geary. "If we play our cards right, Joe, the Cold War could be over in a few years. Gorbachev wants that and so do I. He understands that the only way his country can survive is to move forward, economically and politically."

"He's got a long way to go, sir," Geary said.

"That he does," Reagan said, nodding. "I have to tell you, Joe, I was impressed with the man when we met in Iceland. He has some good ideas but he's got a tough row to hoe over there. I wished him luck."

"He'll need it."

"I intend to keep the pressure on him, Joe, and I told him that. I'm going to Berlin this summer and when I'm there I'm going right to that damn wall and I'll challenge him to tear it down. What do you think of that?"

Geary took a breath, turning it over. "That will take some guts, Mr. President," he said finally. "It's a little bit stronger than '*Ich bin ein Berliner.*'"

"Yes, well, Kennedy was there in the middle of this whole thing. We were still playing catch-up in many ways. Now, we're starting to see the light at the end of the tunnel. We can afford to be a little more aggressive, I think."

"It's not so much Gorbachev, it's the people who are running the Party," Geary said. "They're the ones who have the most to lose if democracy ever comes to Russia."

"Exactly. Gorbachev knows that. He's walking a real tightrope and we've got to keep him on it as long as we can." Reagan looked at Geary with a penetrating eye. "If he falls and the reactionaries take control, we've got some real trouble ahead. If they still had Andropov…"

"Fortunately for us, they don't," Geary said, remembering the former KGB chief who had briefly headed the Soviet government upon Brezhnev's death a few years ago, before his own untimely demise.

Did he detect a little twinkle in Reagan's eye? "Yes, isn't it?" the president said. Reagan, of course, was one of a handful of people in the world who knew what had really happened to Andropov. Geary was another. But the less said about that, the better.

"How can I help, Mr. President?"

Reagan reached for a file on a side table, leafed through it briefly, and dropped it on the coffee table in front of Geary. The file had been sealed with red tape, was bordered in red and labeled TOP SECRET. "When I came back from Iceland, I had Bill Casey look into this situation for me. He found out a couple things and brought them to my attention. I got this report the other day and Bill recommended I talk to you about it. He thinks you're the man for this job."

"What job is that, Mr. President?"

"We've been informed through some back channels that the hard-liners over there are planning to move against Gorbachev. They want to play it safe so it won't look like a full-scale coup. That would be dangerous. Who knows what would happen? They're worried that some of their satellites might react to trouble in Moscow by starting trouble of their own. Poland, especially."

Geary nodded. "Poland could go if there's turmoil in Moscow. Others might follow suit—East Germany, Czechoslovakia..."

"If their empire starts breaking up, the hard-liners won't be able to hold it together without a real risk of bloodshed. If the Poles and the East Germans and the Czechs rise up, Moscow will have to send in the tanks and if there's real resistance, they risk NATO coming over the hill like the Seventh Cavalry."

Geary had his doubts about that. He was all too familiar with America's NATO allies. "With respect, Mr. President, would you authorize that? Would you order American troops into Eastern Europe? With or without NATO support?"

Reagan looked at him with a bit of a smile, but his eyes were narrow. "Well, now, Joe, I might not. Or I just might. We didn't do anything to help the Czechs in '68, or the Hungarians in '56. Maybe this time, we just might do something. That might actually surprise some people. After all, we didn't do anything even to help our own people when they were taken hostage in Iran, and that was just a few years ago."

Geary saw the point. "Moscow wouldn't know for sure. This isn't '68 or '56."

Reagan's eyes twinkled. "That's right. They can't take that chance, so their idea was to use one man, a very dangerous man it seems, to take out Gorbachev."

Geary was surprised, but not very. "An assassination plot," he said. "A hard-liner steps in to save the country when its leader is killed."

"That's pretty much the gist of it," Reagan said. "Apparently they have someone picked out already for this job. Not even the KGB is in on it, which surprised me, but the evidence is pretty convincing." He pointed at the file on the coffee table. "One rogue agent, highly-trained, operating independently of any control. They call him the Wolf. Your job, Joe, is to find him and deal with him before he can get to Gorbachev. We need to do this because Gorbachev can't trust his own people right now. He apparently feels he can trust me." Reagan took a sip of his drink. "This Wolf fellow, he sounds like a pretty tough customer. *Spetsnaz* officer, two tours in Afghanistan. The *mujahedeen* were terrified of him. A crack shot, and he's an expert in hand-to-hand combat, some sort of martial art I've never heard of. Very tough customer indeed."

Geary looked down at the file. The enormity of the mission started to well up inside him. "Russia's a damn big country, Mr. President. To find one man, to stay a step ahead of the KGB, that's a pretty tall order."

"I know it is, Joe. But Gorbachev thinks it won't happen in Russia itself. His information is that the Wolf will try for him when he goes on a state visit to Budapest next month. Take a look at the file and tell me what you think. I told him that we'll do everything we can."

"Very well, Mr. President. Am I to report to Director Casey on this?"

"No, Joe, I want you to report directly to me on this one. Not to Don Regan, just me. We need to keep this loop very closed. Bill has signed off on this one. He trusts you, and so do I. You've done great work for your country. I know you've been thinking about retirement. I'm asking you for one last job. I know there's a lot riding on this one, but I need a top man to oversee this operation and you're the best I've got."

"Thank you, sir. I'll do the best I can."

Reagan smiled, nodding his approval. "I know you will. Now, I don't expect you to go over there yourself after this fellow. Do you have anybody in mind who can lead your team over there?"

Geary looked straight at the president of the United States, but in his mind's eye he saw the face of a young woman, someone very dear to him, but very good at what she did. "Yes, sir, I do."

16752866R00308

Made in the USA
Charleston, SC
09 January 2013